Rustler on the Rosebud

The Legend of Jack Sully

First published by Dog Ear Publishing
4011 Vincennes Rd
Indianapolis, IN 46268
www.dogearpublishing.net

ISBN: 978-1-4575-4696-9

This book is printed on acid-free paper.

Printed in the United States of America

Acknowledgements

For
Sandy and Claudine
Joana
Paul Swedlund,Esq
Tom Tobin,Esq

Ft Pierre

Westa

THE ROSEBUD

Badlands

Little White River

Rosebud
Agency

Key

South Dakota

Nebraska

Valen

Niobrara River

Missouri River

Presho

Oacoma

□ Chamberlin

White River

Bijou Hills

Sully Flats
Sully Ranch

CHARLES MIX Co.

Platte Creek

Whetstone Creeks

"Ol' Muddy"

Brandon Springs

g's Ear Lake

Pa ha

Bonesteel

White Swan

Ft Randall

"Running Water"

Springview

*"When all the land, without no fence or fuss,
belonged to God, the Government and us."
Badger Clark, poet laureate, South Dakota*

FOREWORD

My father was a personal friend of Claude, Jack Sully's youngest, and I had also met him in my youthful days in Witten, SD, having contributed indirectly to him winning $100, me being the losing jockey in a horse race, one of his lovely daughters the winner. After the race, my father related the story of Jack's betrayal by a friend; it has haunted me, encouraging this effort.

This work is historical fiction. For the readers' instruction, most of the adventures in Jack Sully's life as depicted herein are based on remembrances of his contemporaries. Those stories were gleaned from books listed in the bibliography, which contain numerous comments from contemporary ranchers, cowmen, and his acquaintances on the Rosebud. Most of the basic, brief comments found during my research lack dates and other details; thus, the fictional embellishments. Most of the people and places depicted in the novel are real, based again on the bibliography and stories from my own youthful Rosebud days.

What is mostly fictional are the details of Jack's birth and early life. At his grave site on Sully Flats in Gregory County, SD, are two headstones, each with different birth dates. The older, lists 1839, the newer, 1850. There are at least three quite different accounts of his beginning, either in Minnesota or Virginia or Ireland, but none have ever been confirmed. He was apparently, according to the newer headstone, a Private in the 1st Minnesota Infantry, presumably during the Civil War. That belies a beginning in Virginia, which Wikipedia now contends. Wiki also states that he was born an Irishman, "Arthur McDonald"; other sources say "John McCarthy", each contending that he changed his name. No source offers credible substantiation of the details of his birth, and no reason for changing his name can be found. Sully is not an Irish surname, but French. Since he very likely was in the Minnesota 1st Infantry Regiment, and himself told some of his friends that he came from Minnesota, I have fictionalized his beginning there, based on a father of French origin. This ties well into the heritage of early French settlers in the Rosebud.

Most of the facts of Jack Sully's life in South Dakota can be best be found in John Simpson's book *West River*, which includes sources from the South Dakota Historical Society.

Episodes of Jack's life on the Rosebud are found in numerous interviews and letters compiled in *Round-Up Years, Big Muddy to the Black Hills*, by Bert Hall. It remains the definitive source for first hand stories and accounts of life in Western South Dakota during the reign of the cattlemen.

On Sully Flats, Gregory County, South Dakota, May 16th, 1904

Jack stood at the stove, eased the pancake turner under a flapjack, took full measure and flipped it. Fresh batter splattered onto the stovetop and the girls laughed. "Mommy can do it better!"

"I'm sure she can, but if you want breakfast, this is what you get." He smiled. Monday morning breakfast constituted his one concession to any form of housework. Mary departed the day before to the Jandreau's for a visit and a break in her daily routine. Orange juice and milk at each plate, bacon and eggs in another big iron skillet, he had the situation in hand, if a bit awkwardly. Eva quietly surveyed her eggs, picked at them, still not with a hefty appetite, yet much improved. George came up from the barn, announced that a rider approached from the south tree line, "Its Ben Diamond, Dad."

Jack crossed to the door, invited Ben inside, "Fresh coffee, Ben, get down and sit with us." He looked to the high sky, no clouds at all, a crystalline blue May day. The sun already warmed away morning coolness. One could say with conviction, summer abided. The look on Ben's face gave away any casual intent. "Jack, we need to talk…outside." This obviously intended to rule out a social call, to exclude the family. Jack handed the spatula to George, "Turn those pancakes, hungry kids awaitin."

Ben dismounted and angled toward the barn, looking back, intending Jack to follow. "Jack, a posse is coming with John Petrie, the marshal. They intend to take you in to Mitchell, and hold you for trial. He sent me ahead, askin me ta ask you ta come with him without resistin. Marshall's givin you a chance, don't want no one to get hurt."

"Damn, Ben, I have drafted up a letter to the governor, asking fer clemency if I turn myself in. They take me in, it ends that. I ain't stickin around." He pulled the halter off Jim Longstring and slid the bridle bit into his mouth. He turned Jim toward him, buckled the neckstrap, hitched the latigo tight, and led him out.

"They're all around the west already, you can't get though the creek, they got ten men along it." The quandary for Ben shown in his eyes. Jack, his friend, had helped him more than any other neighbor, his wife Betsy, close to Mary. He wanted truly to keep Jack from harm, yet he could not draw his pistol, he could not bring himself to assert what he knew was his duty as a deputized marshal. He followed Jack out. He felt the moment pass. "Listen, they are all along the creek, take off across the flats, they ain't expectin you to ride that way."

Jack looked at the house, the girls were at the windows, curtains aside, eyes wide. There was no time, no time for goodbyes.

Jim Longstring spun in the dust, Ben reached out to hold the reins, but Jack booted the big bay, he leapt to a full gallop.

Table of Contents

PART I

EPIPHANY

EPIPHANY

Heading South, - Winter 1883

J ack stretched his aching back against the coldness of the ground, arched up out of his bedroll in the blackest darkness before dawn, groped for his saddle, his pillow for the night. His winter wool trousers, long johns, wool shirt, even with the buffalo robe coat, were inadequate defenses against a ragged night's sleep, the unskilled art of sleeping on the prairie. He checked his stockings, pulling out a sandbur and cheat grass seed before donning his winter moccasins, and scrunched his red voyageur's cap, gifted by his father, down around his ears. Without coffee or breakfast, He cinched up the buckskin, and got underway before fumbling to pull jerky from his saddlebag. He rocked lightly in the saddle to let the gait of the buckskin loosen his bones, and re-acquaint his muscles to the rhythm of the ride. In an hour came first light, then the sun escaped horizon's edge, a pale golden glow to start a clear, cold day. Within an hour he was working his way down the low bluffs of the Cheyenne River; he dismounted and shuffle-footed across solid ice, Buck picking his way, slipping straddle-legged, but sure-footed. Across the flat, treed bottomland, up the short bluffs and back onto the plain, the first chill of morning wore off; a faint warmness came over the prairie. Fifteen Dakota winters imbued Jack's bones with the import of this atmospheric change. Biting cold often changed to a beguiling and deceiving warmth before snow.

He booted the buckskin into his unique rocking chair lope. When he moved beyond a trot to his slow gallop, rocking gait, he was a silken marvel of horseflesh that rolled up the miles, and seldom broke a sweat. Jack had ridden him for a full day before trading for him. The previous owner was not wise to what the other Rosebud ranchers knew: if Jack Sully wanted to acquire a horse from you, there was sure as hell a good reason. Thick in the withers, round, full croup. Jack ate up miles with this mis-defined "work horse" like few others. His destination, the old U+ line shack in the Badlands, beckoned 30 miles away and Jack needed to reach this respite before nightfall. He had already spent two cold, nearly sleepless nights on frozen ground since leaving Deadwood, often nodding off in the saddle by day.

And he needed hot coffee and the mental rejuvenation gained of being alone in the quiet dugout after the physical and moral deprivation he had brought on himself in Deadwood. As was his wont, he drank too much the first day there, and did not let up until he rode out of town two days later. The riding out part he barely remembered; the whore less beautiful than through the whisky filter of the night before. He had avoided a fight, which meant that he had avoided the occasional licking he took when inebriated. Only drink made him cantankerous and mean; at least that's what his friends told. He could not have explained it, the time between the first few drinks, and loss of awareness. Euphoria would come over him, sublimate his angst, transport him onto his own new planet, where the ranch prospered in spite of the burning sun and the dust, the snow and the frost of the seasons. Hangovers were bad enough without aching ribs or a broken nose as well. Now, two days later, he blanched at the thought of whiskey, at what a fool he had made of himself, how spiteful he was of himself. "What am I doing to myself?" he asked the horse. He pushed back on the saddle horn, arched his back against the cantle, adjusting to the weariness. He had been asking that question for the past two days, but heard no words of solace in the wind, except when Buck farted as he broke into a gallop.

Mid-morning, the sky turned gauzy white, the horizon faded into the sky beyond the buckskin's ears, the sun a paler, burnished gold disk, offering a mesmerizing, translucent light as the wind slacked into stillness over the unbending prairie grass. The white fog wrapped a cocoon around Buck and him. He slowed the big horse to a walk, to take in the entrancing moment. There was no wind, no flutter of a breeze. Snowflakes the size of silver dollars soon began to sashay from the misty veil, waltzing gaily unto the grass, and the saddle, and the horse, melting quickly away. They fell slower than wild rose petals. This other-world isolation transported Jack to a winter garden of soft white snow-butterflies dancing for his childish amusement, a private pleasure. He smiled. A snowflake, large as a Christmas tree ornament landed on the horn of the saddle, so delicate, so pristine, then gone. He smiled at the pure, fragile beauty of it.

Within the hour, a northwest breeze cleared the isolating fog, slanted snowflakes into the winter grass, turning the prairie floor into a giant antelope hide of tan hills and white gullies and draws. Between the Cheyenne River and the Badlands scarp no landmarks graced the softly undulating waves of brown hills. He booted the buckskin back into his rocking gait. Dakota experience kicked in, reminding him that the transcendent moment had passed and what now lay before him could be fateful. Wind picked up, drove the snowflakes into his buffalo coat, into Buck's rump and tail, freezing into a white, crusty topping. Colder northwest wind stung his eyes as he looked back into his tracks, fast closing behind him. Realism replaced his euphoria; enchantment would be fire not ice. He must reach the Badlands Wall before early winter darkness.

Blowing snow nearly obscured gray forms ahead, buffeted ships on a wintery ocean. Cattle, drifting south too, heads down, tails flowing along their flanks, some nearly all white now as the wind drove snow even harder into their hides. With some cows were young calves, spring roundup two months away. There were mostly longhorns in one bunch, and a few white faced Herefords, neither by nature inclined to forage through the snow for food.

Yesterday he would have pushed these steers south but preservation for himself and Buck now paramount, he reined past them. The snow that the earlier warmness had foretold was not to be denied.

He could with some difficulty keep the cold from his feet and hands; he dropped the reins on Buck's neck, pulled off the leather gloves, and warmed his hands within his coat, in his armpits. He pulled the red wool voyageur's cap down, nearly across his face, and tightened the neck scarf under his coat collar. His real fear now became the vulnerability of his feet. His winter moccasins in the stirrups were exposed fully to the wind. He first pulled his right leg up to the saddle pommel and massaged the foot, then the other. He walked Buck for several miles, conserving his warmth and strength. He knew that overworking his mount would only increase his susceptibility to weariness and loss of strength. He had ridden horses to exhaustion. He knew that feel under him. He could walk with Buck and gauge from his gait, the height of his head, the weight of each hoof on impact the measure of his weariness; there was no more gallop in Buck.

At length, he dismounted, walking in the snow, moving his toes, stimulating circulation. The snow was six inches, a foot in places. The wind now blew fresh open patches and drifted snow into banks in the draws and coulees. He was so tired, worn from the lack of sleep, and dulling cold. Should he burrow into a snow bank in a draw and hunker in for the night? A Dakota blizzard could last for days, what then? The lure of the fire drove him on toward the dugout.

As the late afternoon darkness began to enclose the two wanderers, the opaque morning had turned to the blizzard's whiteout, and now evening approaching, a darkening gray...five yards visibility at best. Jack slogged through the snow, head down, leading the tired horse. Then Buck snorted and squealed, jumped right, jerking the reins from Jack's numb hand. Jack turned to face him, saw his nostrils flared, startled eyes fixed ahead. He looked into the gloom, saw the dark-ringed yellow eyes of a wolf, crossing their path, stopped to face them, tail low, not in the least frightened, surveying their intrusion upon the tangential path to his den. Jack stood rooted in place; his pistol bundled under the heavy coat, fearful of losing his horse. They exchanged stares. The wolf seeing no threat or promise, then turned, trotted slowly out of sight, unconcerned, uninterested, seeking his own home burrow, just as they sought theirs. Jack turned, but Buck was gone. The wind blew away his call to Buck. He walked back ten steps, but could see nothing, the snow blinding his vision and stinging his face. He turned again, walking slowly toward where he had last stood calling out for Buck, "Here boy, come on Buck, lets go home, here Buck." The horse would continue toward home, Jack knew. He must overtake him. He broke into a shuffling run; nothing could diminish his fear of being without horse on this unforgiving prairie.

Adrenalin rushed through him, invigorating the cold-dulled brain; his feet recovered feeling; his cold-stiffened hands splayed into the snow as he fell. Yes, as he rose, he glimpsed a faint trail, fast filling. He ran on. Then, ahead, a nostril blow from Buck, out of the gloom, head bobbing, turned aside to avoid the loose reins, he appeared, and stopped, taking in Jack with big, warm brown eyes under the ice crust, seeing his lost companion. "Here Buck, here boy, don't you want some company?" The fear of losing his horse, sure death, adrenalin pumping through him, plumbed his resolve as he mounted, picked up the wind, and set onto a line to drift with it. If only they could travel as fast as it did.

He was still hours away from the wall, cold still curled down his back like an ice snake. Cold again began to dull conscientiousness; he could not tighten the scarf or raise the collar enough to control the shaking. Yet, the real danger was frostbite in his feet. Desperation stopped him, he was still thinking, now beyond convention. He slid awkwardly from his mount, loosened the cinch, pulled the damp blanket from under the saddle and cut it into covers for his feet, tying off the stiff, damp wrappings with leather strings from the saddle conches. He pulled the remainder of the saddle blanket around his back, wrapped his lariat three times around, and in desperation, pushed Buck back into the lope.

Without landmarks, he must ride with the wind, southeast its destination and his. He could hardly see Buck's ears now. The force of the wind was as strong as he had ever known, blew the horse forward. On the lee side of the draws, little mounds covering the yucca and cactus outgrowths disappeared in the depths of accumulation. Snow circled into his face, his eyelids frosted nearly shut. His breath froze in the scarf across his face. As the afternoon sky continued to darken, stories of people lost in blizzards flashed in his mind. The situation now fully engulfed him; he drifted in a full blizzard, the worst he had known in all his Dakota prairie winters, an apocalypse horseman of winter's deaths.

He would not reach the wall before dark.

Over the Badlands Wall

Unaware, a rider approaching from the north could plunge into the void, so sharp is the break from the rolling, grass covered plains into the moonscape that characterizes the Dakota Badlands. Not as deep as the Grand Canyon, but the effect is similar. The North Wall runs east-west for 25 miles, from 50 to 100 feet high, cliffs sharply demarcating hundreds of miles of prairie grasses northward from the pink, green and tan pastels of shale, clay and sandstone pinnacled canyon below. The White Earth River carved its serpentine path beyond the wall as nature's divide, where the gumbo earth of the north plains transmogrified into the Sand Hills of western Nebraska, its alluvial waste, carried into the Missouri would add its creamy-mud contribution, fostering its nickname of "Big Muddy".

This land, bereft of all but the most tenacious plant and animal life, was *Mauvaises terres* to the French trappers, *Mako Sica*, bad lands, to the Indians.

Years wintering in Dakota made the weathering of it second nature to a native such as Jack, but this was not an ordinary blizzard. He struggled for coherence, for a solution for this dilemma. He knew that a time could come when fear, the cold and the unrelenting wind could incite hasty decisions with fatal consequences. Dislocation, traveling in dazed circles had doomed many blizzard victims. Seeking imagined shelter. Hoping falsely. Wishing the way forward. Persisting in their own failed certainties; he had seen horses and cattle frozen into fallen statues, half-covered by drifting snow. He determined to keep his head, keep the wind directly at his back, to not press the horse too hard, to take time out to walk and move his feet and to keep his hands close to his body. Indians and some old cowboys and trappers had even killed their horses, gutted them and curled into the cavern. There were cattle moving south with him if such a drastic solution was required. Yet, he also knew of plainsmen who perished in Dakota blizzards, only their bones and those of their horses, found with a rotting saddle during the spring roundups. This

Dakota blizzard could blow for three or four days before the wind died away, even then followed by Arctic cold, crusted snow, and a prairie turned to barren white desert. In the dark now, time was unmarked in his mind. Had he ridden an hour, a few minutes; had he slept in the saddle, were his feet beginning to frostbite?

A fragment of a magazine article congealed in his sluggish mind: one Mark Twain and party set out in a Nevada blizzard for a stage way station, found themselves traveling in circles and realized they could not find it in the dark. While grouped closely to fend off the wind in a vain attempt to start a fire, their horses wandered away. Devastated, sure of death, they huddled together determined to meet death at peace with themselves. Somehow surviving the long, cold night in which they had given up to sleep's balm, they saw at first light the way station 50 yards ahead, and their horses stamping in the lean-to. How did they feel? Stupid and lucky. For Jack, he took two lessons from the little saga. Don't give up and go to sleep; let the horse take you home. He walked again, still wriggling his toes, still able to move them, though walking could not diminish the ache of the coldness, the stiffness in his bones. He could only press on.

Buck had been kept at the dugout for the past wintering. During a warm spell in late February Jack had taken a chance, and ridden home for two days. Coming back, he had ridden his big, half-thoroughbred bay mare, west from his ranch on the Whetstone, and left her at the corral, taking the fresher Buck along with the Flying V string to Ed Lemmon's ranch on the Moreau River. The dugout lean-to, with sufficient hay and oats laagered there, was home to Buck.

He talked aloud to his only friend, reminding him that it was up to him to get them home now. Only the horse's instincts could be trusted. He knew he must give way on his own judgment. Buck must know where home is, where the path descended to his corral, to the hay. Jack knew as many stories of horses taking their riders home as he knew of bleached bones and rotting saddles on the spring prairie. Crippled cowboys, gunshot soldiers and dying Dakotas had trusted and been rewarded for relying on a good horse. Two winters ago, up on the Moreau, one of Narcelle's cowboys was lost in a storm, but his horse arrived home with an empty saddle. That spring they found his bones, scattered by wolves and coyotes. Buck remained his sole hope now. The northwest wind that he had relied upon til now, swirled and whipped about him, his kerchief frosted over, his eye brows sagging with ice, black mustache turned white, his senses dulled.

Darkness quickly and totally enveloped the drifting voyagers. Jack nodded off in the saddle, the plodding rhythm of the buckskin rocking him into a dreamy unconsciousness. Fully aware of the danger in letting this false euphoria grip him, he fought it, but failed. Hope of surviving left him, bit by bit, as the wind continued unrelenting, he gave in to the rhythm of hoof steps rocking him to a false euphoria. He slept over the saddle horn.

The face of the wolf emerged out of the white, on Buck's right, the silver face, glowering dark-ringed eyes, the black forehead, the black nose, then he leapt, snarling. Jack threw up his arms to fend off the beast. He lurched at the saddle horn as Buck jerked to a stop... He had slept again, he had dreamt. Awakened in midst of a dream, his mind reeled; was he even awake now? The cold flushed him, the wind bit. He scraped the ice from his eye brows and mustache. Fear of the dream-wolf faded, replaced by the truth of his current real danger. His feet were beyond feeling, a new ache, coldness crept up the legs. Panic washed over him; he struggled to think, wrenched from the bad dream to a bad reality, he had to have a fire, he had to get out of this darkness, he felt the cold clot of doom in his belly. He booted Buck forward, surely they must be close now. Buck threw up his head, stomped his hooves in place, pounding the snow. He booted him again but the animal's instinct for knowing where he stood, his danger held him still. Jack's dream-kludged mind began to clear to a different fear, at the cliff's ledge of his sanity, he grasped for reality, could Buck have taken him to the edge of the wall? He might have urged his savior over it in his stupor. He leaned forward, trying to edge his right leg out of the stirrup, leveraging his aching leg across Buck's icy haunch, lowering his tree-stump legs onto the frozen prairie. He lifted the reins over Buck's head, and inched forward in the snow. In the pitch blackness his right foot seemed to find the edge, snow crumbling downward, but there was little feeling in the foot. He led Buck back from where they had stopped, and walked to his left, eastward, and stomped lightly, regaining some feeling in his feet. He could not know if he was paralleling the wall, or would plunge over one of the crevasses jutting out from it.

Still, fighting fear, he could not find the descent. He could hardly feel his toes. He worked them against the icy, brittle grass, and hoped that the pain meant they had not frozen. His body shook uncontrollably. Desperation near, wind unrelenting, he dropped to his knees, rubbed, worked his toes. He struggled back into the saddle without finding the stirrups. He reined Buck to the east, hopefully parallel to the wall, dropped the reins free on his neck, took the saddle horn in both hands, leaned into his ear and whispered "go home Buck, go home."

Buck plowed on through knee deep snow, head down; finally, the cantle rose up pressing his spine, Buck's forelegs stiffened and jolted with each step, seeming to descend... now surely so, Jack was thrown forward in the saddle. Then Buck's stride leveled off, he turned right, moving a couple of hundred yards, head down, into a less fearsome wind. The snow was deeper here, drifting in where the wind slacked below the scarp. He must to be under the Wall! His mind cleared; yes, he was beneath the Wall, the knot in his belly ebbed away. Finally stopping under the dim outline of the small pole lean-to next to the dugout, Jack arched forward, nearly falling out of the saddle, his right foot caught in the saddlebags, kept him from falling full force on the ground. The jolt brought back more awareness. Grasping the saddle horn, he arched his leg over the cantle, dropped painfully to the ground, and braced against the horse. Buck swung his head toward the lean to, knocking him aside, consciousness spread back over him. He struggled with the cinch, finally with both hands, slipping it lose. He rubbed his hands in the bare, warm dampness where the saddle had been, stamped his feet, pain jolted up his legs. Throwing the saddle against the log wall, he lurched toward the dugout door, the sense of relief, salvation, plausible; the realization of how close death pursued him; he had nearly let himself succumb to fear. Pain shot through his leg as he kicked the snow banked against the dugout door, he kneeled, scraped it away, stumbled in.   Uncontrollably shaking, he fumbled to break open a .44 caliber cartridge, poured the powder on cow chips, dried bark and box elder twigs to start the fire, tugged off his moccasins, and gently rubbed his toes. Wrapping himself in his blankets, feet toward the fire, he tried to sleep, nodding off, but always waking, cold and shaking still.   He slept in fits and starts. He warmed a bucket of snow water, soaked his feet, and massaged them slowly.

Renewal

During the next two days, the wind, unabated, blew snow through the cracks in the caulking of the rough hewn logs, at the roofline, under the door, miniature snow drifts across the room. Outside, snow had banked as high as the roof and formed a kind of igloo, which eventually stopped the influx. The stove warmed no more than three feet beyond its steaming sides. He stayed in bed mostly, fitfully massaged his stinging, burning feet when he woke, intermittent with bouts of intense shaking. Blisters formed, and he excised them with his hunting knife, unsure if he should. In the early morning darkness he shivered not from cold, but from fear; he could lose his feet. He would be bound to a chair evermore, life as he knew it ended. How could he ride a horse with no feet? How could he run his ranch? He closed his eyes, forced himself to think of home, of Mary, little Louisa, anything but his feet. He turned face to the wall, curled his feet to his hands, massaged the pain, the throbbing in his toes, the soft, mushy soles and ankles. Why had he not come directly back, why did he detour to Deadwood? Weakness, foolishness ripped craters in the core fortress of his self-esteem. Slumbering in fits, awakening again near dawn the second day, he forced the fear of losing his feet out of his mind, turning to the depressing thought that his own stock back in the Rosebud exposed to this blizzard, probably drifting south, dying, suffocating in snow banks, freezing in mounds of snow, only stiff upturned legs visible. The other families back east, what of those who might have been caught in the storm? Any who wandered even 20 feet from the house, would have no chance of finding their way back in the blinding whiteness. What of Mary, of his neighbors the Dions, of Olaf Finstad, of the Drapeaus? Had they made cover before this great storm? He saw himself losing the house, all of his homestead and holdings. The hunger ache in his side came more often, resurrecting the memory of working on the river again, backbreaking wood chopping, stacking cords, loading wagons, cold every day in the winter, or sweat dripping in the stifling summers, shimmering heat waves blurring the line of the horizon. His depression lingered, the vague sense of despair coming back over him with a shiver when he thought of his years building the ranch on the Whetstone, now to what avail? No longer a young man; hope was not as easily resurrected. He curled back into the blankets, trying to drive away the angst with sleep.

The blizzard finally exhausted itself during the third night. The next morning, after tending to his feet, gnawing the remaining jerky strip, staring into the half cup of tepid chicory coffee, he tried to repress the ache of impending loss welling in his gut. Action was always his way. He might not know just what to do, but he would "do something, even if it's wrong", an old saw his father used when he was young. A saying he could never accept until, older and wiser, he knew his father had trusted him to always try to do the right thing, if only he would just get started. His moccasins bound loosely, he pushed hard against the snow-banked door, squeezed through and made his way into the wholly new terrain of snow drifts piled like white desert sands, dwindling in soft curves away southward from the cabin and the Wall and the Badland castles and spires. Brilliant sunlight reflected off the snow, the sky devoid of clouds. Sparkling ice crystals glinted in the scrub pines and tiny icicles decorated the layers of sandstone pinnacles. The violent wind had died its slow death, leaving a deceiving stillness below the rim of the Wall.

He had worked hard, avoided legal trouble, foreswore rustling as the easy, but dangerous way to start his ranch, relying instead on his knowledge and love of horses, corralling mustangs, breaking the good ones for riding, wagon or buckboard. Yet, after fifteen years of hard prairie life he found himself fired from a $40 a month job as a cowhand, now sure that his ranch stock had drifted, many frozen, and he, stranded 150 miles from salvaging anything, even if he could withstand the dangers of a ride home. He stared at the pristine snow, blank as his soul. What, he asked himself, had he done to deserve god's reward thusly. Righteous? Merciful? Just? Would a just god punish him for shooting a rancher's horse to save a man? He would not lie down and die. He would persevere. Stop feeling sorry for yourself, man, get on with it; do the next thing, work the next opportunity, whatever it took, do it. The world can go to hell. If it's not already there, ice replacing fire.

Buck and his own bay mare, to which he had afforded the lean-to, arched their necks toward him, "Oats!" they would have said. Taking an old saddle blanket, he scraped away snow and ice from their backs as best he could. He stumbled to the buried woodpile, scraping through snow to find dry cottonwood logs. He went back, pitched some hay to the horses, then walked on out into the landscape.

The dark days in the cabin focused his thoughts to an epiphany. There was in any case no real law here in this god forsaken corner of the Rosebud. He saw no future in eking out an existence any longer, buying and selling a few head of cattle each year, with horse-trading providing scarcely enough cash. Three dismal nights of fear and loathing had finally conquered his principles. Here were cattle that could have been, should have been and might still become dead rotting beef before warmth graced the grasses.

Back in the cabin, he stared at the red-hot ring of the stove, massaged his feet. They had turned to a mushy white, yet his worst fears were unrealized. The burning and tingling in his feet promised recovery from frostbite. He gazed, lost, into the weak light from the stove flickering in the dark corners of the room. He envisioned the drifting and dead cattle, the bare, starved prairie, his own horses feeding on bark and plum thickets. He needed quick money. His experiences in the Lamont organization came to mind. They schemed, had big ideas, now he must also.

In the days ahead Jack moved out into the cold, white, deserted land, venturing along the base of the Badlands Wall, at first searching for jackrabbits, prairie chickens, or other game, then coming upon mounds of dead, frozen cattle. He counted over a hundred the first day, and estimated a thousand head further west in the next two days. He would not soon lack for food. He scraped away the snow on several hides finding mostly U+, E Bar markings, not unusual as the ranches were not far north of the rim, but there were also brands for ranches as far as 200 miles away, Sword and Dagger, VVV, the Matador. Ironically the Flying V cattle that he had herded onto the Reservation found shelter beneath the White River bluffs and the Badland plateaus, avoiding the full force of the killing blizzard winds. The drifting had gone on for three days, cattle driven by the cold and wind to keep plodding on. These tough old longhorns, had learned to forage to survive, raised in Texas, but had never seen snow and winds of such magnitude. Wolves had already found the easy pickings, coyotes hovering to clean up. His rifle back at the dugout, He fired his pistol, uselessly, for they would return soon enough. He wondered how cattle had fared above, on the prairie. He saddled Buck and they picked their way back to the top of the rim. Here a light breeze wafted and ground winds snaked the snow into new drifts tailing away to the south. Cattle huddled for protection in gullies and cut banks across the white waste. Horses too, pawing for the dry grass in wind swept patches, as were some longhorns. There were still white mounds among them, cattle dead, frozen to the land. Fortunes lay in waste, here and over the rim.

Jack knew the cowmen, the ranchers large and small, would soon venture out onto the waste land to assess the losses, and to move what cattle they could to coulees and draws for wind breaks, to work horses into the mix to scrape away grass patches, break ice in the wallows and creeks for water, to try to salvage what could be. They would hunt the draws and creek lines for cattle still alive, trapped by snow drifts. They would shoot threatening coyotes and wolves. Cowhands would work to exhaustion to save any stock, regardless of brand.

He circled wide north, finding snow-encrusted cows bowed up against the wind. Steadily he pushed small lots of cattle and a few horses toward the descent trail. By nightfall he had finally included three horses, and about 12 shorthorns into a herd of 55 longhorns he trailed into the Badlands, behind the spires and domes of sandstone south of the line shack. Ground drifting on the prairie above covered the tracks soon enough. The following morning early, he pushed the herd over the frozen White River, and a good five miles south into the reservation, toward the Sand Hills, picking up other stock along the way, leaving the herd behind the north wall of a small ravine where the horses soon pawed the snow to the grass below. They would be unobserved and would not likely drift far for a few days. Action relieved his depression. The White River became his Rubicon.

His father, an introspective, quiet, but stern man, had from an early age instilled a sense of right and wrong; his school days in the convent school in St Louis, limited though they were, taught him the value of property, rights of ownership, the virtue of work, and the right to the fruits of hard labor. Yet, greed had a firm claim on the character of the most daring men in this rough, feral land. Desperation in the face of the hard, unforgiving life on the frontier either whittled away the souls of learned, moral men and women, or lacquered them to hardwood bitterness.

Back to Life

After warming again overnight, checking and settling down the accumulated herd, needing a warm meal, Jack rode Buck hard into Rapid City. He warmed up in Jack Clower's "notoriously rowdy and intemperate" Saloon and adjoining restaurant, where Corb Morris later happened in for supper. Jack crossed through the double doors and pulled the boss cowman aside. "Corb, you got a thousand head of beeves at the bottom of the Badlands Wall, frozen stiff as boards, I seen em, an tallied at least that many in about a 7-8 mile stretch comin' west. Could be more on east." Corb raised his eyebrows quizzically at him, shook his head, and said famously, "Well ya know, easy come, easy go." Jack pondered that, a fortune lost in a day, without anger or regret; finally opining to himself that Corb had probably started his herd the same way Jack planned to start his.

"You gonna skin out the hides, Corb, bring em back for sale?"

"Jack, would you go out there and skin frozen beeves in this weather? How much would I have to pay a man to do that? Ain't no cowboy gonna do it, and the buffalo hunters and skinners are long gone." He turned back to a free table, sat down and ordered supper, beefsteak, as if he hadn't a worry.

Jack knew who would willingly skin frozen beeves. He lingered over his beef stew with three cups of black, strong coffee, stayed far from the din of the bar, and slept until just before sunrise. He rode back east, only cutting south as the western edge of the Badlands Wall rose out of the distance haze. He plowed Buck through stirrup-high drifts southeast, over the White, and nearly into Nebraska before he found Red Shirt's cabin.

Red Shirt was a friend, having worked with Jack when he had teamstered Government Issue to the agencies. Red Shirt had wrangled reservation herds on the reservations for the Sicangu at Rosebud and for Oglalla Lakotas near Pine Ridge. Red Shirt replaced the brave's culture in his psyche for the excitement of the cowboy's life, learned to drive cattle, and took to white men's ways faster than most Indians, even the Indian

Policemen ("Jack, I don lock those guys, they killed Sitting Bull. I don forget that, Jack.").

Red Shirt's countenance suggested genetic influence from some white forbearer, yet culturally his Lakota upbringing dominated. Like Crazy Horse, according to an Oglalla custom, he took his father's name as a young man. His light complexion, his height, his hair not completely black, a tint of dark brown, his straight nose, round eyes. Dressed in cowboy gear he could easily pass for a white man. Yet, he wore his hair long, parted in the middle and braided in bright wrappings near his waist, but like most Indians, he could grow no facial hair. He had been raised in a teepee, and however beneficial acting white might have been, he did not forsake that upbringing.

After spending two years at Carlisle Institute in Pennsylvania he had come back to Dakota to work with the Agency. After a stint with the Indian Police, he turned to being an Indian cowboy, herding issue beeves on the reservation after delivery by the big ranchers, working roundups for spreads needing a good roper, and had, before the Wounded Knee Massacre, scouted for the Army.

His working outfit consisted of moccasins, wool trousers, a buckskin shirt under a floppy brimmed cowboy hat adorned with a single feather in a beaded hatband crafted by his wife. His leggings were obviously cut from US issue black cavalry boots, a fact that Jack noticed shortly into the acquaintance, but not one he questioned; having been an Indian Policeman. He had helped Jack haul supplies to the Lakota at the headwaters of the White River from the Whetstone Creek station on the Missouri until it closed, then had worked the ranches from time to time, mostly for the spring and fall roundups, but never wintered over with a ranch, even as a line rider. Cowboys would tolerate any good horseman and cowhand, as Red Shirt was, but not to the point of sharing a small, claustrophobic shack in a cold winter with "a inyun". Red Shirt would not himself have wintered as a cowhand. After Carlisle, he was better educated than most cowboys.

He was highly skilled with a lariat, noted for roping head or "tailin" hind legs on first try nearly every time. Foremen competed for his skill at roundups and the money he made went a long way with the agency store, compared to what the other braves had. His Carlisle training gave him an accomplished command of English though he usually slipped back to the Lakota's broken English depending on the company. While he seldom squatted in the circles of cowhands palavering at mealtime or during a break in branding, with friends such as Jack, he loosened up, spoke of what he had learned at school or on the prairie.

Speaking his broken Lakota among the cluster of dugouts, teepees and Army-issue tents, Jack sought out Red Shirt's small cabin, low roofed, but warm and smoky. A strong smelling beef and elk stew simmered over the fireplace; his squaw stirring the big iron kettle, nodded at Jack's entry, but said nothing.

Red Shirt offered Bull Durham in silence. "Red Shirt, there's a lot of dead, frozen beef at the bottom of the Wall, waitin' for someone to skin it out and make use of it.

Red Shirt smiled. "I seen some raggedy old cows drift in from the west with the storm. I think they are all gone down some gullets by now."

Red Shirt remained silent. A Lakota brave seldom skinned animals, and he was in part a cowboy; he wasn't about to hack away at frozen hides, but there were Lakota squaws who would do that work.

"I need you for something else, anyway. I got a small herd south of the White, which I rounded up just after the storm, and I need to move it to Nebraska. I'll pay wages, give ya a cut if it works out."

He lingered over his cigarette, then said, "I know what you are talking about, Jack. I never don that before. Butchered a few cows, you know. It's not safe for no Inyun. By the way, thanks for the help up there north. I wouldna made it."

"It ain't safe for no white man either, Red Shirt, but I've started it and I aim to carry it out. I know a man in Nebraska. He wanted some beeves a couple of years ago when I sold him some horses. The herd will stay put for another day or two, then start wanderin'. You know where the line shack is over on the east end of the Wall? I'll be there another day before I start out. I think there will be more drifters to pick up along the way.

We can get em across the reservation easy, then there ain't many ranches on into Nebraska. I know the Colombe ranch over east on the Rosebud, we can head that way, and we won't have no trouble. We don't take no Colombe or Lamoreaux cattle, just drifters from up north, an' move fast all the way."

"Huh…" Which Jack took to be approval.

Jack crunched across the ice hardened snow banks back to his saddlebags and pulled out a bag of Bull Durham, back at the cabin door he flipped it to Red Shirt. "See ya."

"Ah see you soon."

'Soon' meant the end of the next day, as the brilliant sun reflecting off the snow faded to the silver blue of a new Colt pistol. Red Shirt walked into the dugout without knocking, ate some beef which Jack fried up, rolled and smoked a cigarette while Jack cleared the second bed of his paraphernalia and the dirt clumps which had spattered from the sod roof through the ceiling logs.

"Jack, you never took no cattle before. Lots of cowhands did, still do, an butchering white mans' cows ain't legal, even if it's right when we have great hunger. I just never thought that you would do that."

Jack stared at the pot-belly stove, red around its middle as the cottonwood snapped and crackled within.

"I never wanted to take no chances before. I branded mavericks, but that ain't outright stealin'." As if his comment would explain away his lingering moral dilemma. He said no more, and Red Shirt silently drew on his cigarette.

Shipping to Chicago, How It All Began - 1882

After the second of two devastating dry summers in western Dakota, John Clay, Ed Lemmon, and James Craig organized among the ranchers of western Dakota, one of the first large, coordinated roundups, solely to collect up survivors and move them to market before winter resurged, for whatever price could be recovered. North range cattle were destined for the Evarts railhead. The southern roundup was attended well; large and small ranchers equally interested in salvaging anything from the devastation. Combined teams of chuck wagons, local reps, cowhands and bosses assembled in a large open area northwest of Presho, for trailing into Oacoma, then across the Missouri to the railhead at Chamberlain. Weakened cattle died along the trail or were left behind, standing heads down, their hide-covered bones unresponsive to the snap of lariat whips. The distressing heat of the devastating summer lingered into early fall. Cows bawled for lost calves and heads bowed, tongues hanging slack, lowed for water. With little grazing available, no time was allotted to brand mavericks or complete verified tallies on each brand. Each rancher provided the tally representative with his list of brands, copies of bills of sale for the final count at the sale point, the Union Stockyards in Chicago. All agreed to share the sale of mavericks according to the ratio of their branded herds.

Olaf Finsted, Jack's neighbor rancher, shrugged, "We have little choice, the grass is gone, Jack. Our cattle are in pretty good shape now, compared to the other ranches, but they ain't gonna hold up over the winter with no grass."

"We need the money too, Jack." Mary had a household to maintain, a task she continually worried Jack with, to the point of irritation.

"Mary, I know, I know. Olaf has hit upon it. No grass, no gain. Its just that tyin in with the likes of the assholes runnin this show leaves me wonderin what protection we got. Loses will happen along the way, as usual. I need to go to Chicago with em, or we ain't gonna insure our numbers and brands, much less get any money from mavs. Now ain't a good time for that, but I just don't trust the syndicates."

"Jack, we have a new baby, I can't manage the horses alone, Olaf has his own homestead now to keep up."

Jack leaned back in his chair, silently acceding to Mary's logic.

"We'll detail all our beeves, update our brand books for every cow. Ed Lemmon is no crook, so we just gotta trust him."

Olaf and Jack's cattle had fared better than most during the drought, largely because they could water from the Missouri and graze on the richer patches of grass along the bottom land after the plains had scorched away. He added to his herd each time a honyocker gave up the dream, sold his few cows or traded them for horses to make their way back to Iowa, Illinois or wherever families would take them in. Jack held bills of sale on several brands, rebranding often. By his own tally he counted over three hundred critters into the roundup area.

It was not Ed Lemmon who managed the full operation. Instead, John Clay administered the Chicago end of the operation, Ed the Dakota roundup. Clay took two reps with him for tally purposes, and arranged the bargaining and sale of the herd. As the cattle detrained, the reps kept a hard tally, marking a strike in the tally book according to brand. The cattle looked rough, and even on a relatively fast trip, had lost on average 75 pounds per head. The bargaining went hard, even the tough Scots negotiation skills of John Clay could not negotiate fat onto these longhorns. The preliminary price at $19 per head dwindled to $15 after the buyers saw the herd. "Quite fortunate to get that," thought John Clay.

Jack set out against a cold northwest wind in late November for Bill Bordeaux's Trading Post. He represented the small ranchers from his area, agreeing to bring home their shares. Upon Clay's return to Cheyenne, Ed Lemmon had agreed to bring the money to Rosebud Agency where the results of the sale would be presented and paid out.

Jack took a wad of bills from Ed Lemmon, counting slowly, at end, three thousand, eight hundred and fifteen dollars. "Ed, this ain't near enough. I expected over $5000 what with mavericks. Where's my tally?"

"Jack, here's the list I got from John Clay. Got you for 259 head, and the price was $15 a head. You work that out, and its right."

"Goddamit Ed, it ain't right. I counted over 300 head a my own brands into the herd at Presho. Where's the tally books? And I thought the price was $19 a head?"

An edge crept into Ed's voice; he reared his back, stood straight, hands at his side. "Listen here. John Clay handled all that and I had nothing to do with it. I set up the roundup, me and Harry. John went to Chicago, with the reps. You gotta talk to them. He told me the buyers would not go higher on stringy, half dead longhorns. They had lost weight on the trip, its natural. Some died in the cars."

"Hell, I had better cattle than any of the Texans, mine had water, more feed. I bin hornswaggled, and I am supposing that my neighbors bin done wrong too. Let me have a full copy of all the other Rosebud ranchers. I ain't goin back to have em shoot me for stealin."

Looking at the tally sheets, he said, "Yep, for sure Olaf had more than a hunert head, and Joe Blackbird too. I ain't pickin up for Colombe or Lamoreaux, ther coming to Rapid City themselves. This ain't gonna set well with Chris, and you might see some fireworks when he finds Clay. Lemme see the tallys on those big shots, they dint miss any I'll bet."

"I am not at liberty to share any of that information. It ain't your business."

"You won't share, but it is my business," he said with a snarl.

Ed tried to mollify him, Jack's vehemence failed to ebb. For Ed Lemmon his only obligation was to protect John Clay and the brand reps. "Jack, I'm sorry for any losses you may have but you gotta talk to John Clay about that. I can't believe he would outright cheat you."

"Yeah, not outright, but cheatin is cheatin."

"…and you might wanna have some proof before you go after him, Jack, he's not a man to fool with."

"I ain't either…I'm goin to Rapid to talk to him. I got to. I gotta answer to my friends." He stared at Ed.

Ed pulled out the straight back chair at the table, and sat down. He rearranged the tally sheets before him and pushed his hat off his forehead, seeking to lower the tension. There was no restitution coming at this table. Ed could, in his heart, sympathize with Jack. Better beeves going for lowered prices was not uncommon in Chicago, nor was it uncommon for that burden to fall heavier on the smaller ranchers. They tended their herds well. Yet in his years of experience Ed knew that the Reps had made mistakes. With thousands of cattle moving down the chutes, checking brands and marking strikes, as skilled and basically honest as they might be, errors in favor of the bigger ranchers would accumulate. Conversely, Ed also knew that marketing under the current circumstances, small ranchers had the advantage of low shipping costs afforded by railroads discounting volume to the large ranchers. He shifted his tone and the subject; further discussion on the issue was pointless.

He looked up, with a slight, comforting smile, "Jack, the Shieldley outfit moved operations and headquarters up on the Moreau. Come early December, we got another train coming into Pierre with 10,000 Texans. I could use some hands with your experience. I pay top dollar, and a string of good hosses. You could bring up some of your good ponies, I might be in the market by then. I'm aiming to put most of the herd on our southern range, so you could look after them, and winter in at the cabin over in the Badlands. Let me know."

Jack's trip to Rapid City turned to naught. He composed a pained letter to John Clay, "Gone to Cheyenne," the clerk in Harney Hotel said, and left it there. He stated his claim and asked for audience, but Mr. Clay declined to reply.

Working for Ed Lemmon

Olaf and Jack found Ed Lemmon at the Prairie Rattler Saloon in Ft Pierre. He had a herd 30 miles north, at the mouth of the Cheyenne, preparing to move on from the Evarts rail head, and needing hands for the drive, and for winter line riding, took them all on, sending them out the next dawn. Jack had done the bargaining, getting them $35 a month, with a two-dollar raise in three months if they did well. Ed advanced $10 each for new ropes and other gear, and covered their supper at the hotel. Ed Lemmon did not shortchange his men, whether newly hired or not. His reputation as a boss cowman was well earned, from years of dealing with every kind of cowhand. He abided no foolishness, no drinking or gambling on his ranges or in his bunkhouses. In town, when they could get there, the men were on their own, and yet could count on Ed to bail them out or pay off a debt with advance pay, as long as it happened seldom, and to a good hand. Men worked for him because he was fair, if gruff and tough. He was the epitome of the company man; cows were money and he guarded the company wealth assiduously. He saw that every animal unclaimed gained a Flying V brand. He kept the toughest, savvy hand as tally rep, and kept him on the move to the various meet-up points during roundups. His men returned every stray to its rightful home range, and expected the same honesty from other ranchers. If he did not get it, the transgressor gained an enemy with a long memory. He was personally at every important event on the ranch, on the ranges, or association meetings in Rapid City. He fought the reservation tally fees, the association membership levies (based on herd size), or any other hindrance to furtherance of Shiedley Cattle Co fortunes. He employed more hands than most ranches, but moved the cattle charged to him to the best corners of the range, brought them in fatter, and suffered fewer losses than the less astute boss cowman.

The early fall rain had greened the sun-tanned prairie in small patches leaving morning dew on the salt grass. Clump grass reddened to its winter hue. Along the Bad River, cottonwoods floated their leaves along the wind, into the patches of water, shading the river flats in yellow-brown. Turkeys and cottontails scattered dry leaves, sprinting ahead of them in the underbrush. A few late summer wild roses were still dropping their pale pinkness, their subtle fragrance waft on the breeze. They rode slowly, expecting to spend a night bedded on the Moreau River before making the trail site. Sated from steaks, potatoes, cigars and whiskey the night before, they would eat rough tonight, and take in the noon meal next day. They scraped out cockleburs and sandburs from the river bottom sand, built a large fire and slept till after sun up. They walked the horses most of the morning, arriving in camp, as planned, just as the cookie rang his bell.

Olaf and Jack cowboyed together until late December when Olaf decided to go back home for the winter.

"Ed asked us to stay, Jack, but I done wintering too often to want at be away from my wife anymore."

"I am considering it, cause I ain't got the cash to last the winter. The family takes more now. If I can strike a deal with Ed, I'll stay on." The contradiction weighed on him, and he continued to study the mud on the bunkhouse floor, toeing away a small clod toward the door. At least, Mary was not pregnant. It would be a long two day's ride, but he could get back to the Whetstone over the winter. "I will count on ya to look in on her regular, Olaf. John Jerkins might help too. I don't mean no burden."

"Think naught a that, Jack. A course I will."

Ed Lemmon was in the process of thinning out his team of hands for the winter. It was a time when some hands had saved up over the working summer, looking to spend the winter in different social company of a nearby town. They intended to lay up till spring, parsing out their cash. Still others considered a warm bunkhouse the counterbalance to an occasional saunter into the wild, cold winter. Ed asked for a volunteer to winter in the south, lay over and tend to cattle near the reservation. Needing the money, Jack raised his hand first. The job would be a lonely one, but paid an extra ten dollars a month. He could weather three more months.

Jack bargained for a one month advance on his pay, and leave to proceed to his Whetstone home before moving on the Badlands.

Mary listened to the plan silently stirring her stew. It did not set well with her, but having no cash was a fact she also had to deal with.

"You come home once every month. Tend to your children and your livestock." Her voice was stern, even unfriendly. Parting impended, and she offered no solace.

"I have made a deal with the boss cowman ta do that. John Jergins will also stop by to help out."

He packed winter gear, including his big buffalo coat, gloves, mufflers, his winter moccasins, and the old red voyageur's cap. Riding Buck, his big buckskin gelding, and leading his bay pack mare, he rode back to the Flying V, got his orders from Ed, picked up food supplies, adding three remuda horses, swung south, over the Cheyenne to the old U+ line shack under the Badlands Wall.

Freed by the northern climes of losses in the hundreds of better stock to tick fever, "Texas fever", in the south ranges, the cattle companies now chanced against the cold and blizzards borne by Arctic winds across the treeless ranges west of the Missouri, wolves, Indians, and rustlers. They were to learn hard lessons. How to winter herds on the open range when overgrazed prairie would not sustain them? Already cattle little accustomed to foraging were bowed up against the early winter winds, rib bones latticing their bodies. Ed Lemmon solved his problem by sending Jack to move Flying V herds onto the rich reservation grass.

From this order a significant event, not unusual on the open prairie, presaged Jack's fateful trip back north to the Flying V headquarters.

Butcherer

The gray wolf skimmed across the prairie just below a low ridge line, his head down, nose forward, his tail flat out behind, a rudder steering a straight, determined course across the swells of this ocean of grass. It was early February, cold, but a spell of weather lulled by gray overcast into a nondescript blandness. Wind hardly stirred. Jack was riding line north of the Badlands for the Flying V, the Sheidley outfit, with the task of moving cattle south onto the Reservation. He spun in the saddle to locate the "sput, sput, sput" of distant rifle shots, and saw a lone rider spur his horse into a lope and cross the ridge behind. Reining his red-roan gelding to the near ridgeline, he saw the rider stop and pull his rifle. The wolf kicked up, recognizing the sound of rifle shots, turning sharply north, sprinting away from sure trouble. Two riders about 500 yards away on the next hill line with Winchester rifles drawn, 50 yards apart sprayed rounds into the draw below. He urged his mount forward to the crest of the hill, unnoticed by the busy shooters. In the draw a critter lay half butchered, a figure hunkered behind it, protected for the time being from the shots. Surely a Lakota.

Butchering beef on the open prairie was sure sign of a thief, and chances were good that the beef belonged to the Flying V, since he had himself herded a large bunch toward this area only a day before. The two shooters, he could see, were cowhands, and they were doing what cowhands should, interrupting a rustling. Jack dismounted, drawing his Henry carbine with him and rested it across his saddle. As he took in the butchering scene, a piebald Cayuse, dragging a rope and moving slowly away from the beef distracted him. It was an unsaddled Indian pony.

Just then the two riders spurred to a gallop, low over their saddles, shooting as they came, to soon extract their brand of justice for the butchered cow. Shooting an Indian, given the chance such as this, could be likened in those days to shooting the wolf that had just escaped over the hill. Both predators killed to live but were fair game to be killed in turn.

On the other hand, Jack was not an Indian killer. He sought to stop what the cowboys meant to be a quick ending with no burial. He pulled down on the martingale across the chest of the nearest horse, the rider within a hundred yards of the Indian and still shooting. He chose between the Indian's life and that of a good cow pony in only a fraction of a second and pulled the trigger. The horse's front legs buckled, he pitched forward throwing the cowboy clear. The shooter rolled as he fell, tried to rise, stumbled and lurched toward his dying horse. Jack shot again, killing the squealing gelding. The other rider slid his horse to a stop, saw what could have been an armed Indian on the next hill and started back over the rise. The first cowboy yelled, and the mounted hand turned to see his mate stumbling toward him. Unhorsed, against a sharpshooter, the odds were suddenly against them. He reined in, leaned low over his saddle, and came back for his partner, swung him up behind him. Jack fired again, over their heads to encourage their departure as they vamoosed over the rise at a fast clip.

Jack propped his rifle butt on the saddle fender, walked his horse slowly down the hill, not to prompt any untoward action on the part of what appeared to be a frightened Lakota. Jack did not see a weapon, but stayed plenty alert. A man that he knew, Red Shirt, *Ogle Luta,* in Lakota, rose and waited for Jack, hands at his side.

"What the hell you doin' killing this heifer, right out open on the prairie?"

"This is the reservation, this an Inyun cow now."

"Well, you won't convince Ed Lemmon of that, and you know it. Those boys woulda killed ya, and not thought about it atall… Are you outa issue meat back home?"

"We suppose to have a herd come in a week ago, no sign ovem, not enough food for all the people. It is always this way, late, excuses, then they want to kill us for butcherin' a beef that's on our land. I know this is not right."

"Ya, well then again, getting' killed doin' it ain't right neither." Jack flapped the hide back over the half butchered cow. "Yep, its Flying V, I just drove it down here yesterday. Know where the resta the bunch is?"

"I headed em on south, drove this heifer out first. She's still got some fat on 'er. Didn't think no cowboys would see me."

"Where's your saddle? I never seen you ride bareback much."

"My ridin' horse is back over the hill in the plum bushes, you passed him coming up. That's my pack pony there. Those cowboys will not know me, think I'm just a reservation Inyun. I shot the heifer, then rode away for a while, tied up my horse, and rode the pony over. I got a surprise when they come. You think they gonna know us?"

"Well, I'm riding a Flying V horse, so being the only red-roan I saw in Ed Lemmon's remuda, they mighta recognized him, yeh. They gonna come back for that saddle and the cowboy's gear. Let's cut off a shank or two and get outta here. I don't know any Flying V cowhands were down here but me, anyway, they might recognize me later."

They hacked off the two rear haunches, slung them across the pack pony, and rode together for a mile or two, before Red Shirt turned south, and Jack east.

Open and wild as the Dakota plains were, Jack knew that there would be consequences. Eventually the episode with the cowhands and the butchered critter would get back to the boss cowman, Ed Lemmon. There was a better than even chance that the waddies were from the Flying V. Ed would not abide his actions; not only because of the loss of a cow or horse, but because he was duty bound to protect every head of livestock on the range, on principal. There was no misdemeanor for rustlin' or butchering beeves, it was a hanging crime; or at least a crime requiring prison time now that law of a sort was beginning to impose itself on the frontier ethic. Proof of rustling need only be circumstantial for a tough old Boss Cowman like Ed Lemmon to exact justice. Next day at the line shack, Jack tied off the Flying V string of horses to Buck's saddle and headed north.

Below the Moreau River, at the ranch, Ed met him at the bunkhouse door.

"You shot one of my horses, you sonofabitch!" As much question as statement.

"What are you haranguing' about?" Jack's directness slowed Ed up, but he cocked his head, squinted at Jack.

Jack, well aware that his time as a hand had been forfeit, tossed caution aside. "I'm not a man to stand by and see somebody killed over a beef, and one on the reservation at that. It was a Flying V heifer... you had me drive em down there yerself, so get off your high horse." Ed was unaccustomed to hearing his cowboys talking to him so brazenly.

"It was nothing but a dirty Inyun, and he was thieving! And, goldarnit, shooting that horse is the same as rustling. You should be hung."

"Shootin a horse, to stop a man-killin, ain't nearly wrong, and it damned sure ain't rustlin. Besides, that Indian has more schooling than you do, and you'd likely find a cavalry troop at your door if I reported it."

A lanky hand, with high crowned Texas hat and plain leather batwing chaps sauntered over to Jack's string, pointedly surveyed the big roan he had been riding during the incident. Not looking at Jack, he went to Ed, talked low in his ear.

Ed turned back toward him. Killing an Indian was never a good thing, and Ed wanted to let that issue drop, especially since it would have happened on the reservation. He straightened his back, hooked his thumbs over his trouser pockets, took a different tack. "Jack, the Shiedley outfit has some new rules, among other things, decided not to hire hands that own their own spread. Too many maverickin' beeves their own way."

"Ed, you know damned well I ain't never stole a critter from Flying V or anyone else."

"I ain't sayin' ya did, I'm just tellin' ya the new policy. You got cattle down near the Missouri, and that ain't gonna cut it no more. Even if you got a bill of sale on 'em, you cain't ride for this outfit no more. Drop the lead string and get the hell outa here."

Jack stared him down. He could abide leaving because of new policies, not for being labeled a rustler at this juncture. He turned away and said, "I'll pick up my back pay and move on, Ed."

"Movin on you will do, but back pay accounts for the horse, or I'll take this to the marshal in Deadwood. If you can't watch over Flying V cattle, you ain't no good, and if I see you rustlin' or helping rustlers I'll have ya …. Well, I'll have ya run down and run in." He started for the ranch house.

Jack knew what he really meant, but had not quite said. Ed might not do it himself, but he had the Stock Growers detectives, other Association cattlemen, and more than 20 hands at his call.

Jack followed and stopped him at the porch. Out of earshot of the other hands, "Ed, that horse weren't worth four months back pay. I don't think its right, but I'll settle for three months and let this issue drop. Otherwise, I'll give the Agency less to wonder about when they see so many Flying V cows on reservation land."

"I could have those boys hang your thievin' carcass right now."

"Ed, you and I been friends and I been a good hand for you. I won't make trouble, this thing's settled when I ride away. Otherwise, make your move."

Ed Lemmon had no fear, but he also had no desire for trouble. His job as Boss included not involving the syndicate in any lawsuits or other trouble. Stringing up Jack Sully, a well-known and well-liked Rosebud rancher at the Flying V ranch house, with opportunity open to take him instead to jail and court, fell well within the "other trouble" category. Jack had faced up to the situation, had ridden right up to the ranch to turn in his string and face his Boss. There could be no hanging. Jack had friends in the Flying V bunkhouse; more men than him might die here. He turned, went up the two steps to the porch and into the house, not looking back. Jack waited for his money, 'No wonder Red Shirt calls him 'Crooked Ass'', he thought. Still in the saddle, Jack accepted the silver pieces, spun Buck around, galloped west. Deadwood presented a far destination before dark.

Heading East – Spring 1883

Leaving Oelrichs next morning, Jack stayed south of the White River. All the fury of the late winter blizzard had changed to water and ice, rivulets expanding creeks to feed the torrents of the ice-choked, raging White River. A gray wolf glided along the opposite bank of the White; it's coat just darker than the water itself. Great ice chunks toppled upon each other, tipping on edge, gouging banks; tumbling dead trees, and black, bloated carcasses floating in the flood plain. There would be heavy flooding all along its tributaries and mother Missouri, nature's force relieving itself.

He daydreamed of Mary, rocking in the saddle, through the scrub brush, cottonwoods, greening buds, just peeping out of gray spackled, white branches. His mind leapt to conjure up a plan for next month when few big ranch cowhands would be crossing up river, and cattle to the south would go unattended before roundup in May, after the river had expended its fury. He had time to make another run with a herd to Nebraska. He also needed a better method of selling the cattle. His first trip required four days finding an "entrepreneur" willing to risk buying.

On the route east, as the first serrated peaks under the Badlands Wall appeared to his left, the cool morning air rebalanced his equilibrium. Late April was transforming the prairie, snow finishing it's slow ran-off, frost giving up its hold, moisture turning the grass back to green from the brown and tan of winter. Greenish shit-slurry, product of the soft spring salt grass, plastered the rears of the feeding cattle, soggy tails slinging spray across their backs as they swatted black swarms of flies. Spring calves kicked their heels, stutter-jumping, running in short circles around their mothers, suckling, head-butting into drained utters. Cattle were strewn across the grassland, deployed in platoons on line, faces to the breeze, grazing as far as the eye could see.

Cows stamped away flies, buffalo wallows turned muddy black as cows waded in to escape the heel flies. Grouse and prairie chickens flushed from new nests as Jack passed. By mid-afternoon, the heat brought out the dung beetles. Where were they going, rolling shit backwards with their hind legs? A pair of meadowlarks relayed in front of him, leading him away from their nests; clouds of migrating redwing blackbirds slanted across the grass top at bullet trajectories of red flashes. The greening land gaining strength to defy the wrathful singeing from southern summer winds which would soon threaten the exuberance of new grass.

Brands were becoming more distinguishable as cattle shed winter's growth, and Jack saw mostly Flying V and L7, E Bar and U+ cattle. Cows were suckling new calves, some heifers were still to calve. Round-up would be underway in little over a month. Cows and calves scattered themselves across the rolling hills into bunches of 10 and 20, sometimes as many of 50, heads down, snuffling and jerking upward as they snatched the grass away. But look at these cattle, lean from the hard winter, feeding without pause except to head to the water holes and creeks which by summer would dry and turn to caked mud. The walk to water would line cow paths through ravaged, dry grass prairie. The cows would roam ever wider, inconsiderate of ranges not theirs by rank of brand. Stealing grass. That's what it is, he thought. Stealing cows that steal grass can't be much of a crime.

He was no transcendental thinker; what the big ranches did characterized a form of thievery and he had agreement with every other small rancher. As he headed onto the Lamoreaux spread near Curly Huggins' ranch, he thought of what a real cowman could do. Chris Colombe and Bill Lamoreaux stocked the range with what it could handle. Their spreads were large, took in half the county, but they were not overgrazed. Not until the northern big ranches let their cattle, even pushed their herds, to graze on reservation ranges that were not legally or morally theirs, like Chris and Bill's. New companies were starting up out of Sioux City and Sioux Falls, a rendition of local absentee owners. Becker and Deegan mortgaged 2000 head to Olaf Finstad and Harry Ham, Jack's neighbors, and they were the most miserable cows he had yet seen. Some would not even survive the summer, let alone a winter in Dakota.

He thought of the big Swede, Bergstrom, as he remembered, who set his mind to a homestead north of the Flats. Came back from Fairfax to find his sod house caved in on one side. He fixed it, only half suspecting the work of vigilantes. Two months later, ten riders, kerchiefs across their faces, stampeded cattle through his homestead at midnight, marched the family outside and pulled down the walls and roof with ropes. They were warned to leave, and this time they did. The cattle herd of over twenty-five head that he had accumulated must have been stolen, because they were never found, even though all were branded. No room for hard workin' small guys on this range. It was hard to tell whether the ranchers hated the honyockers more for plowing or for suspected rustlin, but they never left them alone. "I'm lucky" Jack thought, "I been here since before them. I worked as a cowhand for years. I got my horses. And I got some rancher friends. Scotty Philip don't like me much, but Bill and Chris have stood by me.

A rusty-tailed chicken hawk circled, and a goshawk beat his wings to hover in the sky, surveying the ground below, predator to the moles and prairie mice darting from grass clump to hole in the early morning light. He walked his bay mare, rocking in the saddle, contemplating the unsuccessful rustling events of which he had cognizance. Rustlers were normally caught with a small herd on the open range by cowboys riding line for the large ranchers, vigilantes trailing missing stock, or at the point of exchange, when faulty bills of sale alerted authorities, strangers with money splurging in local bars gained attention of local ranchers, or other unusual transfers were suspected. He needed an effective cover plan while on the ranges, a warning mechanism, and he needed a safe exchange method. The cover plan would require more hands, trusted drovers, who would not sell out, another frequent cause for failure.

Of his Whetstone neighbors he first thought of Olaf Finstad and Harry Ham, two who had rustling experience, if of a less formal nature. Frank Waugh, his son-in-law, needed the money badly enough to chance an adventure. He had asked Red Shirt to come, and if he did, three hands besides himself and Frank Waugh would be enough. He needed at least two hands to stay on the ridges and signal trouble, while he rode point, and two or three hands moved the cattle advantageously through cover of draws, cut banks, and the Running Water bottom land of cedar pines and cottonwoods and plum thickets. Most movement would be at night, full moon lending a hand.

Jack passed the scrub pine, gnarled against the cut banks east of the Badlands, threw open his coat, midday heat of another warm day relieving all that winter cold, early spring chill, and the winter's bleakness. Prickly pear cactus and yucca grew in clumps here. The first of a string of low-lying buttes loomed to his southeast. Following the flattops would take him on a line to the Chris Colombe ranch, then bearing straight east he would traverse the softly rolling hills until they dip into the Missouri breaks and the north fork of Whetstone Creek, home. He skirted a prairie dog town, chirping dogs bobbing in and out of holes, the signal of his approach echoing across the village; a prairie owl half out of a dog hole, cocked his head curiously. Twenty antelope rose out of their beds sprinting to skirt the prairie dog town away from him. Buck kicked his heels, irritated with the pack, and loped nearly along side the mare. Coming over a low rise he could see for miles, nothing but cattle.

PART II

COMING TO
WEST RIVER

COMING TO WEST RIVER
Father

I n 1861, the Great Sioux Uprising frightened away many settlers from southern Minnesota. Promise dampened by threatening problems with the Sioux hardened his resolve to leave, to take his son to safety. His trap lines were robbed and sometimes ruined, he carried a musket to his fields to plow. For two years and more, danger lay in the tree lines, the creeks and rivers where he worked his trade. Claude Sully lost patience with the Minnesota end of the trapping industry, running trap lines, constant skinning and stretching hides, in summer the hard work of farming; the quicker way to wealth lay in the cities. The ember that glowed in his breast, the dream of building an American chateaux, slowly lost its heat, doused to a cinder by his wife's passing. The safety of a city beckoned.

Upon arrival in Minneapolis, his father enrolled him in a Catholic school, run by priests and nuns of Irish extraction.

During the summers, Jack accompanied his father into the lumber camps of Minnesota, working out of Minneapolis and the lakes north. Beside evening fires, as they rested of the evenings, John learned all he would ever know of his mother, and his father's past life. In melancholy tone, his watery stare into space the few times he spoke of her sufficed to render her a warm, loving person to Jack's willing imagination. "Big brown eyes, *beaucoup* black hair, high on her head. She worked hard, but the winters got her. Cold took her smile away, drove her to melancholia. She died slowly, in the winter. No doctor could help her. She coughed until she could no more, without strength, she passed." He stared across the fire, into the dark.

In lonely winter logging cabins, Jack learned more of his father's early childhood. He warmed to his son, sensing his obligation as a father, to impart some history of his family background, As the second born son of a French land owner who had served in the French cavalry, of noble birth, and a position in the local government, Jack's grandfather presided over the Sully chateaux in Normandy. As his second son, Claude, though of noble birth, had no claim on the ancestral holdings. Thus, he ultimately gained of lesser attention from his father, and eventually, because his mating prospects were only so good as an arranged marriage would bring, he found himself in trouble with a local village girl. The wrath of his grandfather was uncontained when he surmised the situation, not less because of the price to pay off the girl's peasant father. Claude stole away one night within a month of learning of the girl's delicate condition. He shipped out to England by way of L'Orient, then to Canada with the Hudson Bay Company. He married in Quebec. Learning that Minnesota had opened to ever more settlers, tiring of the endless canoeing, skinning, and portaging, he joined the American Fur Co, for the purpose of crossing over the Saint Marie du Sault portage to Ft William. After his bound year, with his young pregnant wife, settled on the west bank of the Mississippi as a farmer and trapper.

Jack had no recollection of his mother, nor gained much knowledge of her later in his life; his father was a quiet man, seldom talking of himself. She had "passed on" he later told him, Jack still a baby.

Jack matured quickly during his three school years. The nuns were mostly tough old birds, strict, lacking in humor, vengeful toward any threat to their strict authority. The slightest infringement of cloister regimen brought physical punishment, either isolation in closets, corners, or confinement to bed; failure to do well in class brought yardsticks across the hands or back. Jack suffered his math exercises at the blackboard, each figure slapped out of him by a sister's two-foot ruler. On the one hand, he was disabused of any lingering French vocabulary and accent, and gained the fundamentals of mathematics; his fervor was books, which he collected and read at every opportunity. On the other, he forsook religion, disdaining the nuns' continual threats of god's Old Testament vengefulness, when they might have won him over with Jesus' more compassionate teachings.

His father continued to ply the lumber trade until Jack's third year at the school. With little explanation to Jack, he left on a log raft down the

Mississippi, not to return. Older than most of the students, the desire to leave overcame his fear of the unknown outside the sheltering school.

Jack found work in the lumber mills of the city, still seeking word of his father among his old acquaintances, to no avail.

Enlistment

The tavern light dimmed with the setting sun, and beer loosened talk among the lumberjacks and mill workers.

"I'm jainin the Army, Jack. The war's getting bigger, the Union needs soldiers and the pay ain't bad. You could get a paid enlistment even. I talked to an officer from the Minnesota Infantry, lookin fer men. I caint see waitin out another winter like the last one. No work, hardly a place to bed down. You seen it."

" I don't know nothing about the infantry, or much about shootin. My Father let me shoot, but not real huntin even. You go into the infantry, you gotta shoot people, right?"

"There is regular food and a place to bunk. You got friends all round. I ran through a nine month enlistment at Fort Snelling two years back. We marched and paraded a lot, but otherwise, twerent bad. Now the Cause is great. We need to keep the Union together."

"Well, I don't see the Union breaking up, Mac, why would anyone want that?

"Jack, its mostly broke now. I was born in Kentucky, and there are folks with slaves that will fight ta keep em. I seen it. My daddy had none, and so we moved out west, but others got money in slaves, and work ta be done. Come along to the court house with me in the mornin, ya got nothing to lose talking ta the Captain."

At $13 per month, food and board provided, Jack took the oath, gathered his meager belongings in a knapsack and trudged to Ft Snelling. There he was outfitted with blue uniform, kepi, and brogans. And the marching began. First, on the Parade Field; left face, right face, to the rear, march; left turn, right turn, forward march. Then do it again.

Soon enough, burdened with full pack, and a nine pound Springfield musket loader, the company marched the roads and trails of central Minnesota. In spring, once the ice broke, they marched headlong through the ice clogged Minnesota River: "Because in a battle, you might need to do it," the Sergeant kindly explained.

The closest to real soldiering came during guard duty at the fort. Dakota families were impounded to punish and forestall support to warriors still eluding the forces sent to quell the Dakota uprising of 1862. There were nightly fights in the camp, disease broke out, and hunger prevailed. Attempts to escape were discouraged after several deadly failures.

Watching the suffering of the Dakotas while on guard duty, having long ago tired of marching and bivouacking, when a notice of recruitment for cavalry soldiers was tacked to the Adjutant's posting board, Jack was among the first to apply. Soon assigned to the US Cavalry, he and twenty other soldiers were sent to Davenport, Iowa. There the soldiers were offered a choice, either go east with the regular cavalry, or chose to change enlistment to the newly forming Iowa Seventh Cavalry for duty on the western frontier, controlling the Indian situation. Jack and nine others, chose Iowa Cavalry.

Coming off the steamer late in the evening, the troops were sent directly to a row of Sibley tents with makeshift bunks. Tired, most went to bed early. Jack lay awake long into the night remembering the stories told in the barracks and canteen of the bravery of the 1st Minnesota Infantry Regiment at Gettysburg, of the gallant charge, the marksmanship from the log barriers, the rock solid defense paid with the blood, the gore, the limbs lost; he could even imagine the screams in the dark of the tent. None of the men had talked of this now, many destined for replacement in the Regiment. But, Jack had selected the cavalry, going out west. He had seen the Indians in the stockade at Snelling, and they could not be as fearsome as a screaming reb with a bayonet. If nothing changed, if at the last moment pulled from the line, sent east, to die in a trench? Finally, came sleep, troubled.

Lined up at dawn, Sergeant Mahoney paced in front of the formation. "You, Laddie, what's your name?", pointing at Jack.

"Jack, sir!"

Jack? That's all…Jack Mule, eh?…Well I'll not have you near the jenny mules then….heh, heh. "

"And you next, your name?

"John Kinkaid, Sergeant."

"Jack Mule, you ever hernassed a team?"

"I have, sir, loggin horses."

"Well then you laddies, see them four dapple greys, they be yours Jack Mule, and the four mules be yours John Kinkaid. Now hernass up and hitch ta the wagons, and we'll be off for the territory."

And with angst abating by the moment the two set about their task, fear of death in the east relieved.

Cavalry on the Frontier

J ack lay in the tall grass along Horse Creek. Whooping and shouting, keening women's voices rose from the camp site only a hundred yards back upstream. Screams of pain interlaced the war whoops. The gray morning sky began a slow drizzle. No sun pierced the heavy clouds. Jack looked into the spitting rain, wondering how he had succeeded in avoiding the war in the east, only to arrive so close to a painful and ignominious death at the hand of savages he had so recently guarded.

During the crossing over Iowa and Dakota, he and the young Irish lad, John Kinkaid, remained as teamsters, charged with care for the draft animals. The fighting troop was assigned two horses each. At bivouac the two attended to the mounts and teams, feeding, watering, checking hooves and shanks, general caring.

The assignment continued after arrival at Ft Laramie. Jack and John grew to appreciate this duty. After a day in the field, when other troopers headed to a meal and a drink, or off to a rendezvous with a Dakota maiden, they talked, took casual but good care of the teams, wandered to the mess for their meals, then back to their quarters near the corrals. The only drawback being that they were not yet fully accepted troopers.

The year since arriving at duty in Ft Laramie had passed uneventfully in patrolling the plains, on lookout for renegade Sioux bands, but primarily bringing scattered groups to the growing encampment of Dakota and Lakota at the fort. By June, the government planned a move of the aggregate of 1500 to Julesburg. Wagons with 70,000 rations were assigned and under the command of Captain Fouts set upon its journey. The situation is best described in the official report of the Iowa Seventh Cavalry:

"The Indians were all well armed with bows and arrows and most of them with firearms, also. They were ostensibly quite friendly, and expressed themselves as being pleased with their removal. Nothing of interest transpired during the first three days of the march, except signal smokes by Indians north of the Platte by day, and reputed conferences by night between them and the Indians in charge of Captain Fouts. On the evening of the 13h Captain Fouts and command encamped for the night on the east bank of Horse Creek, and the Indians pitched their teepees on the west. Late in the evening the Indians had a dog feast, and three hundred and eighty-two warriors sat in secret council on the morning of the 14th, reveille was sounded at three o'clock A.M. and the order of march announced to be at five....

Captain Fouts crossed the creek to ascertain the cause of a commotion among the Indians, and was cut down by fire. Firing continued and a hundred braves charged across Horse Creek. Without cartridges, Fouts men fled as they could, four more cavalrymen cut down in crossing. Jack and John, fortunately near the corrals on the creek line, were first away, seeking the only cover available.

He did not move nor speak. John uttered something, Jack shushed him, squeezed his arm. Silence was imperative. After the initial attack broke off, braves would scour the area for more soldiers, horses, weapons, any treasure.

Just to their right, a small cutbank along the creek offered better cover. Jack inched toward it, slowly dropping down. John moved, not so slowly and joined him just as two young braves whooped and charged down the creek bed, lance forward, aimed directly at Jack. John stood, shouldered his carbine. The first brave hesitated, not knowing that John had no bullets. John swung, knocking him into the shallow water. Jack's knife struck at the beaded chest plate, again he plunged the big blade and the young Lakota lay draining red into Horse Creek. As the second brave fled, Jack grabbed at John, guided him, running, further down stream, stealth of no concern now, around a bend into the scrub cottonwoods on the nether bank. Their only chance to escape the screams dying away back in the camp. This then was the only outcome of advantage to not having been issued bullets, the silent killing saved the two cavalrymen.

Within the half hour, Captain O'Brien, commanding Company F, returned from the advanced guard, charged at the remaining braves on Horse Creek, killing several, and engaged the trail party of the retreating warriors near the Platte. Greatly outnumbered, they recovered the mutilated remains of Capt Fouts and his four men and crossed back to the east bank of Horse Creek.

Still stranded on the east bank each with blankets wrapped with rations were three Sioux squaws. Surrounded, at the mercy of CPT O'Brien, they stood stoically.

"Kill and scalp em, now!"

With their mutilated comrades lying before them, three soldiers obeyed without hesitation.

"Sergeant, take the reins of the horses of these two men. They will not ride for me again. There will be no cowards in my troop. They are yours to reassign." He wheeled his horse and paraded his troop out of the camp.

Sergeant Mahoney looked to Jack and John, motioned them to him. "I saw the two of ya, at the creek line. Go back and take the scalp off that brave. Take these horses, they are your mounts. You are troopers now."

Jack would never forget rolling the young Lakota to his back, pulling on the long, greasy black hair as he slid his knife across the forehead. It did not set well with him, but now he and his friend were troopers.

Jack and John joined the other surviving cavalrymen and with the advanced party, proceeded on to Julesburg. The captain reported:

> "I demanded of Lieutenant Haywood why he did not stand and fight the Indians. He replied that his men had no cartridges, and that his Captain (Fouts) had refused to issue them. Stating that they would not be needed…It was very evident that Captain Fouts was the victim of misplaced confidence in the good faith of the Indians in his charge, and that his death was the first result of their treachery."

This skirmish marked the beginning of general hostilities by the Sioux across the western plains of Dakota Territory, Nebraska and Montana. Bands raided ranches and farms, besieged the forts, harassed wagon trains moving along the Platte and further west.

The continuing hostilities prompted the Dept of the Northwest to station detachments of the 6th and 7th Iowa Cavalry throughout the plains, assigned to protect and defend the growing number of pioneers and miners venturing west. For Jack and John, their troop travelled to Fort Randall on the Missouri River, and began patrolling assignments west and south in Nebraska and Dakota Territory. The two had bonded as only soldiers who have faced death closely can understand. They had, under fire, graduated from horse wrangling duty to full cavalrymen.

Leaving the Fort - Spring 1867

The old brown mare showed little more than a toss of the head, jangling the bridle, as Jack booted her down the post road away from Fort Randall. Her hooves splayed, needing trimming, a split in the left front hoof subjected her to little more than fast walk or trot. She was all he could afford, no prancing cavalry horses could he obtain with his mustering out pay, just this USIC branded horse, inspected, condemned. Though, he thought, she might be serviceable with a little feed grain and horseshoes. He took the road northwest past the small cemetery, pausing only to remove his sweat-stained cavalry hat to honor the worn crosses, etched with names of men he might have known, had he lingered to read. Pneumonia got some the past winter. The log barracks shrunken caulking allowed piercing winds to sift snow freely through the cracks. The Colonel promised renovations, but money for the Western Department ranked low as the Army extracted itself from the Civil War.

His dissatisfaction with Army life and drunken reaction to it, left the Colonel little intention to expend more than perfunctory effort at re-enlisting him. Two years in uniform, long days scouring the plains for elusive Indians, little fighting, he relieved his boredom with drink, suffered the consequences of sobering up in the post stockade, and now left the service as a Private, as he had entered. The Colonel did feel obliged, his duty almost, to recommend him to a Union Army associate, E. W. "Bill" Whitcomb, who had given up his commission to establish a ranch in Indian territory, in this case, along the North Platte River. Promising to hook up again, somewhere, he left John to complete his enlistment, and set out for the only piece of civilization he knew in direction of the Platte Rivers. Cavalry patrols had often stopped at Bill Bordeaux's trading post near what would become the site of the Rosebud Agency. It was a forlorn place, wanting in civilized fare in all ways, but a refuge for the weary, store for staples, and on occasion a bottle of whiskey. Old Bill spoke French and Jack had resurrected some phrases and sentences from his boyhood to enliven their conversation.

The loose fitting wool shirt, a worn, patched, buckskin jacket, shed of the blue cavalry garb except for the trousers, suited his feeling of newly found freedom. At the crest of the hill, he reined in the mare, she dropped her head, already winded, and always hungry, she chomped at the sweet salt grass. He pushed his slouch hat back from his forehead, His face tanned from patrolling the these ranges, his black hair nearly to his shoulders, and the lean, high cheekbones caused more than one, on first meeting, to think him Indian, yet he stroked at the beginnings of what would become a drooping black mustache, and he looked more Métis.

Away from the bosom of the U. S. Army, determined to live by his own wit and energy, the prairie's vast emptiness took on new, more forbidding meaning, lacking the comfort of company with a cavalry troop now. Venturing out of the Missouri breaks he contemplated the light south wind stirring the grass before him, his gaze venturing to the horizon. How far must that horizon be? There were no mountains to define it, only low rising hills, no dark forest line or even cut banks to interrupt what rolled forever westward. A gopher scampered through the grass unseen by a prairie hawk, which caught a slight updraft, tilting its gliding wings; a golden-breasted meadowlark trilled, flitted away, and trilled again. Then silence, only a whiff of wind to suggest that the planet cared enough to move. Three crows drifted overhead, circling ahead of him, craned their necks, beady eyes seeking food, then, out of rhythm, cawed, flapped, floated on, winging north hoping for a more fruitful plain.

A sea of grass, a lolling, nearly calm, sea of soft, greenish-brown swells. How could one newly free from civilization's constrictions see purchase of a future from this? Vast, pseudo sea. There might be buffalo out there, but they were mostly gone, into hats and great coats and coach seats. Indians, mostly herded into pauper's villages near agency sites around the Whetstone, the mouth of the White River, and farther west. Not even cattle; the Texans had yet to survey this vast emptiness for the richness that grew higher than the old mare's fetlocks. He could hardly conjure onto this semi-desert the neat farms of Minnesota. So little rain, so few trees here. No easy comfort awaited him out there. He leaned back, checked the bindings on his bed roll, tugged at his war bag. Secure. Just at the next rise, a brownish-tan shape slipped through the grass, pausing stock-still to stare for a full minute at the strange intruder silhouetted against the southern sky. A prairie wolf, prairie scavenger, he turned and disappeared off the plain, into the draw. It was the direction toward the trading post, and Jack prodded the mare, now chomping her grass, tonguing it around the bit, he reined her on, booting her three times to get a response. Head bobbing, she sauntered along, jerking the reins as she stretched down for bites of the prairie grass. She moved on now, more slaps of the reins across the rump and she broke into a trot.

Old Bordeaux's Trading Post

J ack wandered around the rolling hills of prairie landscape that had yet to become Rosebud town, for half a day, seeking the lone cabin, the last "civilized" abode west of Ft Randall. At least for the entire distance from Ft Randall to Cheyenne. Old Bill Bordeaux was already a second-generation trader. His own father, John, had trapped the Missouri, the White and the Running Water, until the furs ran out. He settled in with a Sioux squaw early, and young Bill came of age at just the time to take over the trading post his father had started. To Jack, even young Bill seemed old. He shaved weekly, and bathed every second shaving. He seldom drank his own trade, but to be sociable with Jack, a rare white man not a soldier, and because his wife and young son were away to her village, he relented.

The first day Jack rested, ate his fill, and shaved in the blue-gray soapy murk of Bill's leftover bath water. He took trimmers and file to the mare's hooves, and treated her with oats. Next day James offered a sociable toast, which lasted well into the night. The third day, Jack could hardly remember, but the fourth, in mid-afternoon, Bill relieved him of enough mustering out pay to stock his gunny sack and his war bag, then bade him goodbye, pointing him due south.

The north Sandhills offered unlimited grasslands, innumerable spring-fed watering holes, some lake-sized, meandering streams grateful for the name of river, and most interesting for Jack, bands of wild horses, mostly mustangs, but several with the long legs and trunks of thoroughbreds. Running in these variegated troops were even a few stocky, big barreled work horses, once foals of spavined, overworked stock left by '49ers and wagon trains following the Platte to Oregon. As he rode, he conjured plans for returning to capture these wild beauties when he was better mounted.

Each day the wind persisted, twenty miles an hour, hot, desiccating, sucking water from the bodies of horse and rider. Water holes sporadically spaced across the grassy Sandhills plain, seeping up through the sandy soil from the great Ogallala aquifer. Clear cool water, as long as it went unused, clean and undisturbed by horses or cattle or buffalo, as it did the first two days of Jack's journey. He slept under a cut bank the first night, shielded against the wind, but woke to brush the sand layer from his clothes, shake out his gritty blanket. Next night, he bedded in a line of trees he found in a shallow draw, draped his slicker to fend off the wind. Still, sand and sweat and wind combined to limit his comfort and his sleep. He tossed about, frustrated and tired, and at first light, unhobbled the mare, and faced into the searing wind and unrelenting sun of western Nebraska.

After four days astride the slogging mare, his provisions low, hope rose with the appearance of Longhorns across the clump grass covered hills, and though he could not identify the brand, he anticipated that the Whitcomb ranch lay close. The mare ducked her head against the continuous furnace blast of the south wind, plodded faithfully forth. She labored up the knobby knolls of the south Sandhills, unrelenting up and down, the soft sand slipping beneath her. Jack squinted, then closed his eyes against the wind, sporadically sleeping in the saddle. The water holes ran out. The wind burned his cheeks and nose a painful red, the heat loosed sweat streams that soaked his shirt, ran into his trousers. Mirages of water holes beckoned, than disappointed as they faded into the heat waves shimmering across the horizon of this unchanging landscape. The last of his food consumed two days before, little water, the effects of mild delirium set in. He lost track of time and of when he slept.

The mare jolted to a stop, jerked her head up, then turned to look toward the fading western light. Silhouetted, two horsemen trotted toward the somber horse and rider. In this great expanse of seeming nothingness but grass, dried up water holes, rolling hills, occasional buffalo, antelope, deer, the inexperienced interloper might suspect little, yet dangers lurked. Rattlesnakes, alkaline water, rogue buffalo and longhorn bulls, unseen cut banks and badger holes, occasionally hostile humans: Indians exacting vengeance for their eternal grudge, outlaw wanderers of the plains preying on the defenseless. With the cavalry troop Jack had ridden the open spaces of western Dakota, nothing but buffalo and antelope. A band of Indians might appear, but the sight of cavalry, well mounted, and well armed, sent them into the draws and gullies and buttes to slither away under cover. The troop's policing had once come upon a dried body, obviously scalped, clothes and boots gone, no doubt the result of too little caution by a wandering soul. As likely as not the man was a fugitive, for there were as yet few ranches in Dakota's west river; nevertheless, no one deserved to die as this man had. The lieutenant ordered a grave dug, and said a few words over the unmarked wooden cross. This image foraged in his mind for meaning. Now, in his gloomy, fuzzy minded state, fear's adrenalin struck and he sat upright in the saddle. The dark outlines on the horizon had sunk below the knobs of the next hill, but the imminent threat remained. Jack slapped the mare, spurred her down the draw to the southeast. Her best pace confirmed what he knew, she could not elude these intruders on his course.

Chances were better than even that greed or vengeance or fear lay in the hearts of those venturing across this vacant landscape. These silhouettes seemed intent on intercepting him. He could not flee, the mare had no reserves of endurance, to say nothing of speed. He tried hard to focus, to anticipate. He loosed his Navy Colt, checked the cylinders, added the sixth load to the empty chamber where the hammer had rested, but reholstered it, resistance his last resort. There were in this day, men who would kill for his saddle, his tired old horse and his outfit, regardless of the paucity of recompense, for there was otherwise little constraint of law.

Too late to elude them, Jack waited. He looked down at the pistol, loosened it again in the holster. He had carried it through the last days with the cavalry, and on surveillance forays in Dakota. After a skirmish north of Ft Robinson he had found it on a slain Lakota. It had belonged to a trooper, and should be with one now.

As they topped the last rise, he made out wide-brimmed hats; not likely to be Indians. This eased his mind considerably. Maybe waddies, but maybe fugitives. He dismounted, stood near the mare. She might be worth something yet if bullets flew. Now he saw batwing chaps, red neckerchiefs, muslin shirts, long mustaches, ropes curled at the pommels. Jack would come to recognize the Texan look, but for now gained hope for the good company of cowhands, and directions to the Whitcomb spread.

The two cowboys were, themselves, a bit suspicious of a loner in their line riding assignment. They saw no beef haunch on the saddle, allaying a natural concern of the working hand.

"You look lost, boy, where you headed?" The older cowboy asked.

"I'm not lost, I'm on my way to the ranch of E. W. Whitcomb."

"No, you ain't lost, but yer a tad west of a direct line to Ol Paps operation."

Jack lacked a retort.

"See that low rise to the southeast, just over there?" Pointing, "over that's the spread, in about a day you'll see it as you mount the top. I suppose yer looking for work. Not sure on that count, Pap's stocked with hands, working a roundup right now. We got 50 head a steers held at the creek back yonder."

"I ain't got money at the moment, but would be beholden to ya if ya had some jerky to spare."

"Well, we'd be more hospitable than that, jain us fer suppa. Got some coffee, a few biscuits left. Just back there," pointing southwest. The Texian drawl of the older man raised more concern, a Confederate veteran, come from Texas. The old fires burned in many of the defeated; and Jack, wearing blue cavalry trousers, even with the yellow stripe sliced away, determined to watch himself.

They turned back to the southwest and the mare needed little urging to follow her kind, though shortly fell behind the pace of good cow ponies. The younger man turned and spoke to his partner, too far away for Jack to hear. Half hour later, he spotted their slickers tied to plum branches and bedrolls laid beneath.

Finally, the older puncher squatted at the burnt-out fire, then asked Jack to gather some dead branches, and a small fire soon crackled. The younger opened a can of tomatoes, skinned some boiled potatoes from his gunny sack, and combined the two in the coffee pot. Jack found a clear pool of water in the mostly dry creek bed, rinsed his canteen and drank voraciously. 'Clean my insides out,' he thought. He removed his shirt, rinsed away the sweat stains in the streamlet, letting it dry in the unrelenting wind. He caught a glimpse of the cattle down stream about a quarter mile, and figured the hands for what they appeared.

Now, his wits regained, he asked, "You work for Whitcomb yourselves?"

"Yep, at it for nearly a year, both of us. Come up from Texas with a small herd Pap bought back there. Like I said, not sure he needs another hand, but if so, you won't work for a better boss. Emmit here ran out a horse on the drive up and Pap saw that lathered-up horse and fired him right then. Weren't Emmit's fault, really, he was recoverin some runaways, and tried too hard. Pap, anyway, took him back when we got to Burlin'-ton and I could explain what had went on. Point is, you work hard and work right an you'll do OK."

"I could ride on in with you if you don't mind."

"Well, lookin at your mount, that ain't likely, but you'll find the ranch."

Young Cowboy With E. W. Whitcomb

Tired, hungry, and the worse for wear, Jack arrived mid-afternoon at the low slung cabin that served as headquarters of E. W. Whitcomb's Bar T ranch on the North Platte. Jack had pushed the mare until she reached the extent of her strength. Still, he trailed his new found friends by an hour. As he alighted from his noble steed, a man of commanding presence strode to him. The cowman wore batwing chaps, blue wool shirt and a mouse-gray hat, large brim drooping front and back, that Jack recognized as a cavalry officer's well-worn headgear. Clean shaven, hair short cropped, he might have passed for a businessman in faux cowboy attire. He spoke clearly, if a bit of Texas twang did intersperse itself among his words.

"So you have a recommendation from a Major John Randolph. I have served with a John M. Randolph, and value his opinion of any man. I am not short a hand right now, but I have a wrangler that's itchin' to punch cows, not horses. You willin' to take on that task?

"Yes, sir, I'll start at what you say," and with as much false confidence as he could muster, said "I've had some experience with horses."

"Well, first thing, throw that McClellan saddle in the tack house. You'll find a good working saddle there. I'll take the price of it from your monthly pay til you own it. Rope, you can have gratis. Work with Bob Hamel a couple of days to get the lay a the land with the remuda, and round out a string. Now that mare has seen better days. Turn her loose, maybe get a colt outa her eventually. I got about ten horses new, need breakin' and you got that as well as a separate task. These cow horses ain't like cavalry horses, so look to how you handle em. Bunkhouse's right there, supper at dark, you'll hear the bell."

His first year served well as preparation for prairie life; becoming a good cowhand, he learned all the necessary skills, roping, wrangling, sorting cattle, moving a herd, identifying brands, tallying, line riding, ...anything the foreman needed, Jack set out to do it with dispatch and pride in his work. Searching for strays, bringing horses or cattle from a neighboring ranch, tracking down wolves, anything that left Jack alone on the prairie, overnight on a patch of buffalo grass, free, free to wander but end with a task completed, lifted his spirits. There were hard days and cold nights, but in all, he responded to the challenges and savored the freedom. Jack watched, listened, spoke seldom. He took some ribbing from the old hands, smiled, and let go of some of the stinging comments about his blue trousers until he could afford new ones in Ogallala. He learned to drink with the old hands and this talent would in the end not serve him well, if it did lend him more immediate acceptance by the crew.

Working first as a wrangler, the normal assignment for young, newly imagined cowboys, he learned to buck out any bronc, but his experience with horses at Ft Randall, and an innate sense of the nature of horses taught him to train them with more patience then most, patience and caring made a better cow pony. Old Bill let him use his methods when time permitted, but on a busy ranch, expediency sometimes required bucking out a horse. He took his lumps, bruises and a broken arm, but never shirked his bronc breaking duties. He grew to appreciate the strength of larger horses, especially those with thoroughbred blood. He picked out this type for his own string, as much because a horse wrangler always needed a horse with the speed and endurance to outrun other horses. The natural work for a wrangler quickly made him an expert horseman and expert rider. The ranch hands scrutinized his method of working new horses with little comment for they had seen him stick to broncs as few of them could have when occasion arose. From old E. W., he gained respect as a hard working and enthusiastic hand.

By the end of winter the following year, his assimilation into the life seemed complete. He had discarded his cavalry boots and blue Army trousers for high heeled riding boots and sail cloth trousers. For work he settled on a new pair of fringed leggings; (he was no Texian, and batwings seemed pretentious) new wool shirt, and two pair of gloves, the second pair hand fitted in Ogallala, and saved for Sundays, so to speak.

E. W. "Bill" Whitcomb set a fine example of what hard work, and a hard head could make of life. Though he mustered out of the Union

Army as the Civil War ended he held no truck with revenge, and hired good cowhands regardless of wartime allegiance. While he might be a "blue-belly" in the bunkhouse, where mostly Texans reigned, the epithet never passed its walls. He first cowboyed in Texas, then came north to Ogallala, Nebraska with a herd and stayed to start his own ranch. He married a young beauty from Red Cloud's tribe, gaining first of all, rights to grazing land, and as life will sometimes bestow its favors, three lovely daughters.

By mid-summer of Jack's second year on the Bar T, the Platte had drained itself into the sand, dried to shallow wallows stirred to mud by foraging longhorns. Bill Whitcomb looked across the weathered brown prairie and pondered not long when he heard in Ogallala that the government needed beef up north. He had word of two contracts for beef upon delivery at the Yankton Sioux agency near Ft Randall in Dakota Territory. His team from Horseshoe Bend would be bringing in his stock from the west in a day, at most two. He called in Jake Harmon and sent him with three drovers five miles east to round-up anything in the near vicinity. He saw no choice but to set out with what he had, salvage what he could. He was not new to cattle driving, having come up from the south with some of the first herds to Kansas after the war, bringing longhorns to markets from parched and overgrazed breeding grounds of Texas. He had seen this before, knew he had little choice. He would lose some, but not all if he managed the drive well. Even these tough old longhorns needed grass and water. North again. Seemed salvation was always north. The drive held the prospect of over 300 miles, three river crossings, which with luck would be shallow now. He turned back to the cookie, languishing near the chuck wagon. "Tie down your shit, Cookie, we're going north a bit further."

E. W. knew that Jack had lived at Ft Randall, knew some people there maybe, and knew the land, the trail they would take.

Bob Saunders with three hands, including Jack, brought in 800 of what remained of his once fine TOT branded herd. The beeves and cows were separated, and tallied, added to Ol' Pap's two thousand head of Bar

T's, and the herd began to trail north. Of the cowhands, only Jack had ridden the entire route from the Running Water to the North Platte, and then only once. Still, that experience counted for more than any other's.

"Jack, you will ride point and scout with me. We need to seek out water, move the herd slowly, we have time now, late summer, to get to Ft Randall before first frost. You've told me of oceans of grass up north, water aplenty. Now, I'm stakin my ranch on your powers of observation. If you are right I can bring in a good quality beef herd to sell to the Agency. I stand to forfeit a thousand dollars good-faith money if I don't. This herd ain't there yet, but if there's grass tween here and there, we could profit."

"Mr Whitcomb, I did not come on a bee line from Ft Randall, I came by way of the Rosebud trading post. Its most due north. It will take a week longer to go north, then east, but with the herd needin water that's the way I know."

"Time is on my side. Its water I'm needin. You said you seen water all along your trailin, so that's where we take our chances. Other thing, I may have estrays to include in the herd if we move direct north. The cattle have sought out water, and have ambled toward it as is their nature. First, we must trail several days with little water… lets get 'em rollin."

As Jack had noted in passing through, the southern Sandhills evidenced less water than up north, save from the Platte itself. They pushed the herd to its limits, cows slogging forward, heads drooping, huffing forward, calves bawling, their mournful, scratchy rasp. Ol' Pap called out the ropes, something he would not otherwise have allowed, but now need for movement overrode his ranch rules. Cowboys snapped at cattle, flickin the rumps of the dawdling, thirsty, reluctant cows.

Into the third day, the lead cattle sniffed water and began a near stampede to a wallow, still muddy from the buffalo that had beaten them there. The water soon gone, moving the herd away north again forced more hard riding, hard pushing. Cowboys wore out their string of trail horses in the half-day forcing the herd off the water hole. Already short, only three saddle horses in a string, the pace slowed to a tired walk for horse and cow. Limited to two barrels of fresh water on the chuck wagon, canteens were running low for the hands themselves.

Ol Pap removed his hat, looping it across his saddle horn, turned to Jack, his dark tan face crowned white above the hat line. Jack could not remember seeing him unhatted. Below the crown, worry studded his face. "Its time to strike out ahead, find a water hole or river. If we have to turn the herd we will. I gotta know what aim ta take. You said there is water, and now you find it, or this herd ain't gonna make it worth the while to go on. Get on, boy, come back with water." Canteens bouncing empty from his saddle, Jack rode north at a pace near his mare's limit. Not only water, he should scout for the dangers of mustang stallions that could disrupt a remuda, buffalo that drained water holes, and not least, marauding Indians always ready to cause trouble and run off a few head, if not stampeding the entire herd as a course of action.

Jack rightly sensed the concern in Ol Pap's tone, questioning Jack's word indirectly. He had trailed longhorns across a barren Texas panhandle, and knew the cost. What had Jack really experienced, those months before? He had dozed in the saddle, parched, not clear in his thinking. He could not remember how many days he had wandered without water. Had he moved as fast as the herd moved now, slower? His own doubts grew. He had taken the most sensible mare out of his string for this ride. She would know before him, and her head sagged as she plodded on. Surely he had not exceeded five days without water on the trip south. He spurred her on. He knew the saving water lay up ahead just uncertain how far. At the end of the second day, he located a small water hole where he and the mare drank deeply. He scouted east along a drainage line and a mile further found a small lake. Spring fed, large enough to sustain the herd for days. He scouted on east, then back west, where he scattered a buffalo herd heading toward the lake. Hazing them north, his horse tired, had done her day's work. Jack rolled early into his bedroll, and broke out before dawn back to the herd.

The herd rested, grazed on blue stem and clump grass around the lake; Pap let them wander and feed, close herding enough to maintain control. Though the herd was mostly steer beeves, there were cows enough included to keep a naturally stable herd. The drovers rested as well, feasted on buffalo calf that Jack brought back. Water barrels full, cows and cowboys refreshed, the herd continued its push north to a new hole a day's trailing that Jack had located. Four days of water and grass resuscitated the herd, and with it, Ol' Paps confidence in Jack's savvy.

Following this pattern, E. W. Whitcomb moved his herd north at a very leisurely pace. He stopped for days at a time as they found more grass, better buffalo grass and blue stem. Finally, over the Running Water, they strolled the herd through salt grass fetlock high broken only by great beds of buffalo grass.

At Bordeaux's Trading Post, Ol Pap bought out most of the supplies on hand, including a small stash of whiskey. With pistols secured in the chuck wagon, night riders assigned, Pap passed the bottle, the hands talked and voices raised into the night. Not Pap's custom, but the trailing had been hard and the hands equal to the task, little complaining through the troubles.

Jack's home territory in front of them, Pap guided the herd along the Keya Paha River, following it at the same leisurely pace, until late September. Gaunt steers had responded to Ol Pap's wise approach, filling out, covering stark ribs with fat. Due west of Ft Randall, he turned the herd into the Missouri River breaks and halloed the Agency buyer.

Jack and Bill Whitcomb now fully recognized the potential of the Rosebud prairies. Jack had gained a wealth of cattleman's wisdom on the trail, the kind that could make him a cowman, not just a cowhand. Two years on the Platte with the wise and wizened Ol' Pap and the energetic Bob Saunders had quickly taught Jack the necessary skills. Now, the true value of water and grass proven to him, they had seen none better on the trip north then that of the Rosebud.

Uncounted days on the hot and dusty trail north to Dakota built a thirst in all the hands, who, with the herd safely deposited on the Yankton Reservation, made fast for Whetstone Agency, where a sutler's store carried whiskey and beer.

"I'm stickin out the winter here, Bill, I know some folks east over the river. You won't need me for line riding now."

"Enjoy yourself young man. Your word was true, the water and grass saved my investments. I would like to make you a gift of a horse out of your string. You have your yearling paint colt and I'd recommend the mare you are on, you surely earned her."

Jack reached across the mane of the chestnut mare and grasped Bill's outstretched hand. "Hope ta see ya down south again."

"I want ta scout out the territory on the way back, see how far west this salt grass extends, and where the water is. This is cow country. I can make beeves outa skeletons on this land….Adios".

His quest would take him to the southern Black Hills, in the time before Custer discovered gold on French Creek setting Indians and whites on the warpath again.

Back at Whetstone

He elected to stay at Whetstone Agency, wandering east over the Missouri when need accrued for more civilization; when his waddie pay ran out, soon enough in the White Swan road ranch, he took ax and crosscut to the bountiful timber on the Missouri River islands. The work was hard and the paddle wheelers up the river were intermittent, but the wood was free but for labor. For added cash, he turned to teamstering Agency freight from Whetstone Landing to the reservations west. The US Cavalry's job mainly consisted of buffering a growing number of east river homesteaders from the numerous small bands of Teton Sioux, encouraging them to settle into reservations. This they did with varying levels of success. Red Cloud and Spotted Tail worked at populating the reservations, whereas Crazy Horse, Sitting Bull, Gall, and others still harkened to the old ways and found willing followers among the young braves disenchanted with teepee life around the forts. After winning the Battle of the Little Bighorn, they would lose the war to civilization's advance. Until then, the rogue bands among this contingent would keep Dakota in turmoil for another ten years.

The Rosebud

*T*he Sea of Middle America, many millennia old, began to drain into the Gulf of Mexico as the earth's tectonic plates shifted to raise the Rocky Mountains. The old sea bed, collected sediment of ages, gave way first to a vast rain forest, home for an assortment of dinosaurs, flying reptiles, mastodons, and a tangled, labyrinthine maze of plant life. Over more millennia, with the vast bog waters receding as rainfall lessened, the jungle sank into the seabed, creating today's Great Plains, becoming a metaphorical sea, a grassy sea of gently rolling hills with intervening flatlands, home to prehistoric horses, rhinoceros, tapirs, llamas, camels, deer and elk, mostly grazers and their predators. The receding waters cut the Missouri and Mississippi Rivers into the veldt. Viewed from above, each appeared veined like leaves, with ribs of tributaries, creeks and rivers molding the land, softening the contours of hills at the breaks, carrying the residue gumbo, sands, shale and clay of western Dakota into the Missouri, making it the Big Muddy, spewing brown fluvial into the Mississippi at its juncture where now stands St. Louis.

For several miles west from the Missouri trees crept back up from the creek beds to the flats where the wind and dry prairie defeated further progress. The scattered lone tree randomly taking root over the top took the shape of the wind, branches spraying north, distorted by unrelenting summer currents. The soft, molded, grass covered hills of the breaks, indented by creeks and gullies crowded with cedars, bur oaks, green elms, box elders, and scrub pine entangled with plum thickets, wild grape vines, and chokecherry bushes; home to cottontails, badgers, raccoons, deer; nests of eagles, owls, crows, hawks, and any number of small bird species. Up from the river breaks the land immediately turns to the great salt grass prairie which, three hundred miles out, envelopes the Black Hills, then extends on to the Rockies. On this great veldt the antelope roam, the prairie dogs dwell with their burrowing owl neighbors and their eagle, black footed ferret, rattlesnake enemies; the grouse and prairie chickens squawk at evening, yellow breasted meadowlarks trill their inimitable stanzas, redwing blackbirds flit red-dashed streaks across the meadows; and where once the buffalo covered whole ranges in a rambling, flowing brown carpet.

As little rain as this land is afforded, as accustomed as it is to aridness, yet rivers and streams define it. Natives call this land the Rosebud. Along this creek and others, scattered wild roses entwine the plum trees and grape vines, delicate, bell-shaped flowers drop pink and white petals aflutter, wafting a subtle but unforgettable perfume into late summer breezes. As the petals drop away in autumn, leaving a bright red bud, capable of healing powers claimed the Lakota, a fine base for herb tea before white men brought coffee, and Lakota winyun crushed the buds into a thick soup. Perhaps this subtle beauty and appreciation of its utilitarian worth inspired an Indian name, translated to French, then English, but no one seems certain.

As early as 1856 the US Army established a cavalry and dragoons post at Fort Randall, on the west bank of the Missouri. The mouth of Whetstone Creek, a few miles north, provided the best site for paddleboat moorings, soon sprouting a landing village housing laborers and teamsters. The Indian Bureau established Whetstone Indian Agency in 1868. It became for a while the last outpost west until Ft Laramie. Spotted Tail soon became exasperated by the deterioration of his tribe, being too close to the frontier elements of white civilization, the whiskey, fighting, fornication and shady dealings which he could forestall with neither cajoling or threatens.

As chief of the Brule Sioux, he exerted his political acumen to successfully sway the Indian Bureau to close the reservation headquarters there. After relocating several times within the next two years, he and his band settled permanently on Rosebud Creek, establishing the Rosebud Indian Agency (a town of sorts springs up later), just southeast of the Badlands and nearly two hundred miles from the evils of Ol' Muddy.

Rosebud became the name for Old Spot's reservation lands which at investiture stretched across nearly a quarter of Dakota territory. "The Rosebud" came to encompass land lying between the White and Niobrara rivers, bounding north and south respectively, and west from the Missouri River, "Ol' Muddy", to the Badlands scarp. Thus, within this realm, the open, undulating flatlands of salt and buffalo grass of the middle prairie, are bordered on three sides by the lush growth in the creeks and valleys of the Missouri, White, and Niobrara breaks, until in the west they end at the desolation of the clay and shale fortresses and sandstone spires of the Badlands. In this land, the creeks: Cottonwood, Dog Ear, Oak, White Thunder, Old Lodge, No Moccasin, and Bull, run north to the White River, which curls east, flowing into the Missouri, angling in its course southward. When blessed with water, this maze of nature's giant drain whirls clockwise to the ocean. As the melting snows of winter find paths to the creeks, the rivers, and the mighty Mo, water, ice, gumbo mud, slick shale slime defines the landscape. Hooves and boots slide in the muck and accrete the gumbo earth, when traversing this expanse. Earth soaked until satiated, pours its overflow downstream. River flood plains lake up in spring, then recede to become repository for bones and carcasses, trees and limbs and effluvial of king winter's wrath; of the year's share of Badlands shale and sandstone and clays; of the last vestiges of the year's lost hopes, a homesteader's cabinet, a wagon box, stirrup from a rotted saddle, a flopping grey Stetson, a beaded moccasin. All who lived through the winter will have lost some measure; of friend or enemy or family; spirit, energy, largesse, chattel. But winter will admit defeat to spring, rebirth of hope, regaining energy from new buds, uncurling leaves, blossoming 'prairie smoke' flowers, green shoots bursting through the brown grasses of the past dead season.

In its turn, spring will not long prevail; spring will arbitrate but lose its fair share of the year's seasonal allotment of bounty to the desiccating sun of summer. Grass will succor the life cycle of the prairie, as rain the grass. The worms, the beetles, the ants; the moles, mice and prairie dogs; the weasels, ferrets and badgers; the wolves and coyotes and eagles and hawks; and not least, man, through his cattle and horses will, most of all, rely upon the grasses to reap his sustenance, his nourishment, his ability to prevail, and with luck, his wealth. As summer rays wear away at the land, it survives when nature blesses the grasses with rain. The cycle endures; water its god. In this land, the horizon fades far distant, no hills or mountains before the Black Hills foreshorten it.

Whiskey

Whiskey being available in quantity in bars along the Missouri was solely through the providence of river boat captains who augmented their sporadic deliveries of flour and meal, clothing, blankets, and other items for the reservation Sioux. The whiskey was totally off-limits, legally, for the Indians, but much found its way to the reservations, a source of money for sutlers, boss farmers, and other members of a bureaucracy intended for government support of the Indians, as designed by General Sherman's department.

In late fall during Jack's first year of the Whetstone Agency, Narcisse Drapeau, who, with J. T. Smith owned the freighting consignment at the Agency, hired him to join the crew taking several wagon loads of supplies to the Pine Ridge location of the Red Cloud agency. The steamer *Chippewa* had docked the day before, and an Army squad guarded the boat and around the dock. Loose security was not being tolerated at present, as the investigations gained more interest back in Washington, several of them so spurious in method and findings as to be ludicrous even to the Indian Bureau. Rumor from the crew spread that several cases of whiskey were on board, for the bars at Ft Sully and Ft Pierre, further up river. Intercepting a couple of bottles quickly became a mission for Jack and his old friend John Kinkaid, recently discharged. Jack approached their old friend Sergeant Mahoney leading the security detail, and with a promise of sharing the wealth, they planned a stealth visit to the steamer after third watch.

At ten past midnight, as arranged, the sentry at the gangplank strolled to the stern and relieved himself on the paddle wheel. Jack and John slipped aboard, past a sleeping civilian boatman, to the storage room door. It was louvered, no light within. In the hold, they found four cases of whiskey stacked neatly in a corner.

"John, this ain't all right," Jack whispered. "I heard there was a whole load a whiskey comin' in on this boat for bootleggin' at Pine Ridge. Only four cases, ain't hardly anuf for the bars up river. What happened to the rest of the stuff?"

"Well, I wouldn't know about that, I'm just a thirsty ex-soldier."

Jack surveyed the cargo; corn meal sacks stacked ceiling high, blankets in roped bundles, barrels of salt pork against a bulkhead. He moved aside the top two boxes, slide out three bottles of real Kentucky whiskey for each of two blankets yanked from a bundle, and restacked the whisky crates. He and John slung the blankets over their shoulders and crept off the gangplank.

Next morning early, Jack helped pile high two wagons with corn meal and salt pork, sideboards added, which set out for Pine Ridge before noon. John Bergen took the lead wagon, and a young ex-soldier unknown to Jack followed closely in a second wagon. These were four-horse teams, two geldings and two mares with each team, broken to harness by Jack for the Agency. By evening the other two wagons were loaded with blankets and clothing bundles.

Meeting Red Shirt

C ool fall mornings turned to hot breezy mid-days, meadowlarks and red wing blackbirds flitted across the land, giving up their nests for a turn south. Ducks and geese rose in gusts off the Missouri, drafted their respective V's, jetted southward. Deer finishing their night feeding pranced into the ravines and brush of the breaks. Like Jack, they would winter in Dakota, brave out the winds and snow. With cash in hand he might have ventured south with the geese, avoid the aimless boredom of his room at Harney City. He and John would timber out some of the island wood, teamster to Pine Ridge when afforded the opportunity, spend some time across the river in White Swan, with some luck win a few poker hands in the raggedy slop house of the settlement. The bountiful grass-lands of the Rosebud Reservation over the river remained out of bounds for settlers and ranchers, only legal for the Lakota. Even now, Jack saw the land opening someday. He determined to weather out the winters, and save to start that ranch of his daydreams.

Out early on this day, he hitched his team to the *Drapeau & Smith* wagon loaded with blankets and clothing for Pine Ridge. A light frost still lined the north side of the corral poles, the sun warming frost to dew on the grass. Already clouds maneuvered into place on the west horizon, high, lofty cumulus, foretelling an early fall rain.

As Jack steered his team into line behind the lead wagon, a rather tall, young Indian emerged from the loafer pack near the store, sauntering pigeon-toed in moccasins, wool trousers tucked into black leggings, and buckskin shirt, climbed aboard the seat of the lead wagon.

In near perfect English, he announced, "I am your guide, Red Shirt... Oglalla. Don't worry, these loafer inyuns won't bother us. Farther west we cannot be sure, but its safe most of the time. No one has been done-in for years." He pushed his slouch hat down on his head, "Let's go," he yelled at the lead pair, slapped the double reins hard. And they were off, first over the muddy wagon ruts, out onto the grass, wheel streaked, then five miles out, hardly sign of a trail. This man possessed the countenance of a white man in the clothes of a loafer, if, indeed, cleaner and more neatly set. Surveying him further, Jack saw his hat band unstained and his leggings were burnished black tops of cavalry boots. His belt held his tucked shirt snugly.

Red Shirt set out in the lead wagon, Jack kicked the brake handle lose, slapped the reins, "hiya, hiya" guided his wagon closely behind. They carried Army-issued Spencer rifles under the seats, and wore their own pistols, not because they expected trouble, but out of habit…one never knew. If it came, they suspected it would be from agency thugs, whites, living off the Indian Agency graft. The wagons of bulk clothing, being lighter than those of John Bergen which had gone the day before, were drawn by single teams. Their path would lead directly west, in a day picking up the old Lakota travois road along the Keya Paha, staying on the flat expanse above the Running Water, skirting the Badlands to the south, finally catching the Agency before the head waters of the White River farther west.

Around the campfire the first evening, Red Shirt summed up the Indian situation west of the Missouri. "These young braves drink too much, and don't like the life around the agency. They only become warriors with scalps and horses. They break off the reservation for horse stealing raids on the Crow villages farther west and Ponca villages to the south, some spend the summer in Montana with Crazy Horse's band and Hump's band, which did not settle on reservations with Red Cloud's Oglallas, and Spotted Tail's Brules. These braves don't wanna work no farms. They goin' to Powder River to become a true brave, get that squaw they want, steal the horses of the Crow and Bloods and Arapahoe to bargain for her with the old man, brag at the campfires and the Sun dances?"

The day began overcast, a morning coolness suggesting the approaching autumn, the grayness breaking up mid-morning. By noon, puffy gray lined cotton-ball clouds rolled eastward, the remainder of summer heat accumulating in the grass, now sending heat shimmers along the rolling horizon of the south hills. Approaching Dog's Ear Lake, Red Shirt wrinkled his brow, squinted into the western light. The two wagons far in the distance should not have been there. They should have been nearer the water and trees, where John Bergen might have chosen to camp. A broken wheel or axle? Crows circled, dark specks, three redheaded turkey vultures, big as eagles, sailed languidly in descending circles, and there another joined from the west. Red Shirt raised his arm, reining back, letting Jack pull along side.

"No horses there, Jack. Somethin wrong." They reined their teams forward. As they approached they saw flour sacks blowing against the soap weed, yellow-spackled white mounds of half-ground corn flour slowly sifting into the grass, several broken salt pork barrels. Not until they had closed in on the scene did they see the bodies lashed, spread-eagle to the wheels of the wagons. A hundred knife slashes each, their privates in their mouths, gutted, flies swarmed over red patches on each scalped head, arrows had been ripped from their flesh, some broken shafts still protruded.

Jack picked up an empty bottle, and saw another nearby. "The whiskey was in the corn meal sacks."

"This was the young bucks, coming back from the mountains. They don't like the corn meal, it's for 'round-the-forts'. They threw it out, cut open sacks and found the whiskey. Whiskey made 'em kill these men." Red Shirt walked the trail of unshod pony tracks leading south. His stomach roiling from the smell of the bodies, Jack began digging a double sized grave. Red Shirt returned with two broken arrow shafts. "Arrows from Sioux or Cheyenne. Not Ponca. These bucks going to the Runnin' Water, follow in the river breaks and go west. We go north, around the buttes, and then west. I think there are only six or seven braves. No blood here but from John and the boy. They did not fight."

"The Sioux have not done this for some time, Red Shirt, why now?"

"Like I said last night, more soldiers now, want the Powder River Indians to come in. More talk in the lodges, more young braves against the new ways. Where are the buffalo now? We don't see many and we travel now in buffalo country. No wild horses here. Now too much whiskey. Me, I like the coffee with sugar, whiskey makes me sick."

"Well, I could use some right now. This makes me sick...This job is not as much fun as I expected."

They camped a quarter mile on, to avoid the stench of death. No fire, though chance of the braves returning was unlikely. Early fall rains had raised the mid-summer pond from mud flat to fresh water lake. Next morning, prairie chickens flocked around the corn meal, attacked by crows and magpies. Drooling, lustful coyotes slunk from the bloody site. A pack had cleaned out the broken salt pork barrels and scratched at the others. Jack determined to come back with horses to retrieve the remaining pork barrels and wagons.

The whiskey delivery weighed on him. He talked to Red Shirt about it at the next night's camp. Aside from the money earned from selling whiskey, others saw value in keeping the Sioux dysfunctional. The boss farmers worked to make productive citizens of the Indian men, to plow, to raise grains, and to ranch. The reservation agents used some braves to herd the reservation cattle. The big stockmen, afraid of the consequences to the range, staved off the better effects as they could. There were plenty feeding at the government trough through misuse of the "open ranges" willing to prolong the swilling, making the condition of the reservation Indians deplorable. This episode set up a contradiction in Jack the he never could resolve. He drank whiskey, and thought it a right, not a privilege. Yet, for Indians, he believed it totally wrong, providing an excuse for whites blaming Indians for their lassitude, for their original sin, for their laziness, for their viciousness. Some part of that was true, as he had just witnessed, but most blame he placed on the white man's ways, his government. He had not forgotten the conditions he had witnessed on guard duty at Fort Snelling.

"Jack, this trail we on, old trail, some from my tribe came over this trail from Laramie to Yankton many years ago. Soldiers make Lakota move back to Ol' Muddy. The braves fight each other, all the time, no one want to go. Food not good. Soldiers sell whiskey, sell blankets, steal from Lakota, try ta take their squaws. No one was happy. One small band, 20-25 Sicangu, go away from the trail, stop here and made a village, in this area, near the Dog's Ear Lake. This is old Sicangu hunting land. Soldiers come back, track them and kill everyone, women, children. All dead." He looked down, scratched the ground with his knife blade. "Nobody know about this band 'til later. Lone Bear and Whirlwind Soldier work for soldiers, scouts. When they go to big New Year's dance in Ft Randall, one, two years later, they hear the Major, drunk, talk about killing all those "stinking Inyuns". Stabbed babies. Raped women. Shoot all, left them on the ground.

"Lone Bear and other Sicangu find all these soldiers, 11, including major. Kill them all. Took two years to find and kill them all. Lone Bear in Canada now. Whirlwind Soldier also a bad Inyun. Still at Rosebud, still makes problems. John Bergen, he was a soldier, maybe he rode with these bad soldiers?"

"That I do not know. I was at Ft Randall when that Major was killed, four or five with him, when he was heading to Rosebud. This is a bloody trail, but I never knew of the Indians killed here. Curly Huggins has this land now, small spread, but water here at the lake, and most of the time the Keya Paha has water. He ain't had no trouble that I know of"

When they arrived at the Agency site, it was clear some of the whiskey had already found its way before them. That evening braves passed bottles in groups, some lay out drunk already between the teepees. They saw two knife fights, and pushed braves looking for more drink away from their own agency wagons. Soldiers were on guard around the agency buildings, expecting trouble. They unloaded the blankets, cared for the horses, and threw their bedrolls in a bunkhouse. Red Shirt rode on northeast to his own cabin. Jack reported to the lead agent, and the Major of Cavalry in charge. He told of the grisly deaths, and the loss of the corn meal.

"Why the hell wasn't there a guard detail on those wagons?" The lead agent's face reddened. Short and stocky, shirt once white, maybe once an honest man, but as an agency man, little chance of that now. "Lost men, the pork and corn meal gone, what the hell?"

"We had no warning, and nothing like this has happened in more than two years. Ft Randall can't spare the soldiers anyway. They're closin' down, some soldiers goin' to Laramie. I got two more loads of corn meal and pork to move here. I need a detail to go back with me, like you said. I expect the Major will want to confiscate whatever's in the last load of meal."

"Bring the damned corn meal out here, and we'll take care of it here."

"Or, Ft Randall can send up a detail to the Whetstone and get the whiskey."

"Like you said, they're short handed, just bring it back here."

Sarcasm unhidden, Jack said, "So you and the Major intend to spend the winter drunk, eh?" He turned sharply, strode away, wandered to the Indian pony herd a mile out. He found four of the draft horses, as he expected. He confronted no complainants when he roped them, led them away, who dared claim them? Red Shirt returned the third day, then they set out back to the Whetstone.

Jack went directly to Major Reading at Ft Randall, who curtly over-rode objections of Lieutenant Conart, in charge of the Pine Ridge detail, to confiscate the whiskey. This all soon guaranteed the end of Jack's employment as a Whetstone teamster.

Cutting Timber, Jail, Cowboying

Jack's misfortune, loss of the Agency teamster position, now left him with few prospects beyond more timbering along the Missouri breaks and islands. Jack spurred the big blue roan gelding eastward. The early autumn morning started cool, but the sun promised warmth by noon; trees, changing colors, swirling winds spread yellow and brown leaves out of the creek line, onto the bowing prairie grass, lifting his spirits as he set out for Whetstone Island, which lay just east of the headwaters of the selfsame Creek. Next morning, he pulled on low heeled timber boots and a heavy wool shirt. Best to work in the early mornings, leave the hot autumn midday for rest. He and John Kinkaid bucked cedars and cottonwoods in the morning, trimmed back the fallen trees, skidded trunks to the river bank, and across to the east side in the afternoon. Smaller trees they stacked in cords for the paddle wheelers coming up river. Timber was always in demand, the supply being low in this land, and the money worthwhile, thus the territorial politicians soon made the practice of taking timber on open land illegal. Logging without a license became a practice not tolerated within the growing east river establishment.

One morning, after a month of working the Blackbird Island timber, Jack heard the splashing of oars, and the grunts of men hauling a boat onto the island sand. He grabbed his double barreled shotgun and slipped through the trees to the rivers edge. He leveled the shotgun, and calmly asked what they wanted. They looked up, surprised and concerned. When they had calmed themselves, the larger one, wearing a badge said, "Now, you don't need that, we come to tell you logging here is illegal, wer sposed to take you back to talk to Marshall Petrie."

"Boys, I ain't goin'. Undo those pistol belts and let em drop, and git back in yer boat. That's right. Now, listen up. My partner's got a rifle on ya from back in the trees."

Two days later a small man with a silver-gray, straight brimmed hat, black vest over a white shirt rowed out into the current, working hard to steer onto the island. Close in he threw a rope line to Jack. Jack pulled the boat onto the sand, and leveled the shotgun at him. "Marshall John Petrie, what brings you here?" The little Marshall calmly reached behind his seat and brought forth an old Sharps breechloader, which he aimed directly at Jack's chest. Jack slowly tilted the shotgun, broke the barrels, and raised his hands.

"Marshall, it ain't loaded. I wouldn't shoot nobody," he smiled.

"Well, you ain't gonna point a gun at my deputies without consequences, young man. Turn around." He began to rope Jack, when John walked out of the trees, rifle in hand. The Marshall looked at him, not so sure of his advantage now, his rifle leaning on the bow of the boat. Jack sensed John near, and lowered the tension more than a little with, "Let John go back on home, Marshall, he was only working for me, he didn't do nothing wrong."

Jack spent a week in jail and paid a $50 fine for logging on government land without a permit. John, in the meantime, sold the wood, leaving them with a few dollars for their trouble. Jack did spend his time well in getting to know the Marshall. John Petrie came from a family of lawmen in Missouri, south of Kansas City. He was not himself the physically imposing man has father had been, but respect for the law, and a quiet resolve forged a character often only understood after more than one meeting, but one few took for granted because of his small stature, fine small hands, or slim, chiseled face. He continuously wore a straight brimmed Stetson set square on his head, except at his wife's table, hiding a thinning pate that made him look an even more innocuous example for a lawman. A pocketknife with a thin, razor edged blade proved best for apple peeling, and the Marshall spent the quiet times of the day attentively applying whetstone and leather strop to his blade. As implored by the Marshall the day he left, Jack would not cut government timber without a license. It was not the Marshall who Jack resented; it was this new authority invading his domain.

"Marshall, it takes time to get a permit, and usually dealin' with someone I don't wanna know. Also, its damned hard work. I think I can live without it for a while. Take care. And don't bet any money on yer checker playin. I'd say not on your card playin either, since I own all your matchsticks."

"Jack, you go on ahead, cut some more timber, and I'll have company for a month next time. Don't mind havin you, but the county don't appreciate payin for your food. Territorial govt don't reimburse for months."

"I'll go on over to White Swan, or maybe back to the Platte, catch up with the fall roundup wagons. Hold me til winter." They shook hands and parted.

John Kincaid - Off to Texas

Jack and John Kincaid reunited, after John's discharge from the Army at Ft Randall, bonding again with timbering and shared drinking bouts. John was a handsome, free spirited youngster, with a disposition unfitted for the discipline required of a long enlistment. His pale green eyes reminded Jack, if his sparkling demeanor and rambunctious ways had not already done so, of his brash Irishness. He was forever on the move, always ready for a new idea, and quick in his decisions, though he never tarried long in thought or contemplation enough to qualify them right or wrong, good or bad. After mustering out of the of his cavalry troop at Ft Randall, he worked as a teamster with Jack until Spotted Tail's persistence got the Agency moved to Rosebud Creek, near the headwaters of the White River, and suppliers began to use the new rail terminals in Nebraska. The Whetstone Agency closed and rotted away.

John took off north to Ft Sully, working first for the agency there, then on to Ft Pierre working some time as a cowhand. He proved a tough hand, good with a gun and a rope. "He could shoot the head off a chicken with his six shooter", a high form of praise from Jack to friends after his death. As good looking as he was good shot, he attracted women, and one should surely say women fascinated him. This young cow puncher's eye fell on Mary Gullette, a half breed Sicangu and Cheyenne beauty from Ft Pierre. Her father was a stern man who trapped the Bad and Cheyenne Rivers before they were depleted of fur bearers. He managed his family strictly, and had no use for the rambling nature of young cowhands interested in his daughter. John Kincaid, being of the most rambunctious type, soon soured the familial oversight even more by being seen drinking in bars, horse racing in the street, and in an occasional fight. John did not lose interest, but his fortunes regarding the lovely Mary were at a low ebb by the time Jack gave up farm labor in Charles Mix county and found John at Ft Pierre in early fall.

"John, I see no future in choppin wood, nor working for the Agency, and I see more cattle coming into the area. I'm heading for Texas, looking to hook up with a drive north. We could look up Ol' Pap on the Platte for a while, then move on. Pay is better, and it's not as cold down there in the winter. I need some company, and you could do for a change yourself. I can share my packhorse if need be."

"I got my own, Jack, won her off a dumb ass thought he had a faster horse than my Billy Boy. On the other hand, I ain't so sure I need to go south."

"I talked to some punchers from down there. Indians are quiet, ain't much law. Said its damned hot, but there's work, and big herds trailin' north, for contracts with the Agency at Pine Ridge. We could learn something, and see some country. Its fall now, we ain't got a lotta time to clear out before the snows. It's the "dammed hot" part I like right now."

"Well, the other thing is, I got no money, and no traveling outfit. In fact, I hocked my saddle coupla days ago. Don't say nothin'; I know what yer thinkin' about a man with no saddle, but I can get it back if I can work up a horse race. Billy ain't been beat yet, and there is a gent from across in Pierre that's got a fast horse, been talkin' but I ain't got a lotta cash to put up at this point."

"John, listen. Sell your pack animal and share mine, you ain't got nuf plunder ta matter none."

"No, cain't do that. Like I said he's more than a packhorse. We will need more than three horses anyway."

"So, I guess we will need to sell somebody else's horse, right?"

"Gotta plan?"

"Where is the racehorse stabled that the dude from Pierre owns?"

John turned to look Jack square on. He had not witnessed this facet of law-breaking; illegal timbering constituted a level he could accept, a misdemeanor of sorts, but horse thieves were hung at apprehension, nearest tree and no trial, as both well knew.

"Whoa, Jack, runnin all the way to Texas wasn't in my plans…"

"Well, if these horses yer talkin' about's fast, they won't catch us. Tomorrow, you take this gold piece and get your saddle and some plunder. Take the packhorses, and light out right away for the Little White, and stay at Bill Bordeaux's place til I get there. We used to stop there on our way to Pine Ridge, you know it?"

"Rightly so, I know it. The gent's name is Gentry. Wears suits, and habitate's the saloons on Main St, gambles some. It's a bright red sorrel horse, cropped mane. He's bigger than Billy Boy."

"Look here. You won't be involved in the run from Pierre. I can out-leg anybody on my mare, and the race stud won't hold me up none. Once onta the reservation, law ain't gonna go there, and most others won't have time for trailin me. Just get on out to Bordeaux's and wait for me."

The Big Muddy being lowest in the fall, Jack crossed with no problem as the sun set next day. He rode through the open stable door and dismounted, looking for the sorrel. In an end stall, eating oats, a sure sign that the gent knew the worth of his horse, Jack found him. He kept his back to the stable keep, a hired lad, busy mucking out stalls. The back stable door led to a corral where Jack left his bay mare.

The evening chilled quickly. After a full supper, by way of disguise, Jack slipped on a wool cap and a mackinaw he found hanging in the hall entrance at "Mrs. Greavy's Boarding House", better known as the Miz Gravy's. The full moon still touched the east horizon when Jack returned to the stable, brought the bay inside and saddled her. He moved to the sorrel and ran his hands down to the fetlocks, and examined the setting of each shoe. Solid, and of a peculiar design, treads all around the edge. Made for traction. Easy to track, even within the mess of horseshoe prints packed on the street and at the river crossing. He cut the stable rope, and strung out his lariat, tying onto the sorrel's halter. He mounted the bay and walked the two horses out the front door. Avoiding Main Street, he made for the river crossing. He let out the lariat lead on the sorrel, and waded his mount knee deep before turning south, keeping in the river stream. Nearly a half mile later at a fast walk, the brush and dead branches along the near bank forced the horses out of the river, still on the east side. At the top of the riverbank he spurred the horses into a fast lope for five miles before slowing. He rode on until nearly dawn, then, went into the river, back upstream for a mile, exiting on the west bank.

In the cover of plum and grape thickets he dropped the wool cap and mackinaw, unrolled his own coat and hat, and pressed southwest. South, in the White River bottom land he rested the horses, sleeping three hours himself. The sorrel had proven a runner, on a longer lead he often forged ahead of the bay during the run up. This was a horse that Jack could love. He saddled him, and made excellent time over the undulating waves of prairie hills. Arriving at the Little White before dark, Jack sought out a creek mouth and rode back into the cedars and box elder. He slept again, waking well into the darkness. The moon had again slipped under the horizon. He judged the time after midnight before he set out, finding Bill Bordeaux's trading post within the hour. John Kincaid's horses were not in the corral. Jack tapped on the glass window near the door until Bill cracked the door and stuck a gun near Jack's ribs.

"Speak up."

"Bill is that you? What's the gun for? It's Jack."

"What the hell, why didn't you get here for supper? Anyway, one never knows these days what a man might find at his door."

Inside, Jack asked about John Kincaid. "Ain't seen him. He comin' here?"

"I'm to meet him, we are headed to Texas."

"You and John goin' to Texas, what the hell for? I cain't see John leavin' his girls here."

"Old man Gullette does not take to John's ways, and others are courting her. The old man has not takin to John in any case."

John showed up by early morning next day.

"You spent an evening with a lady, I'm bettin'. Dangerous thing to do, me known to be a friend of yours. Pull that shit again and you can find another partner."

"I needed to see her, Jack, I don't want her to think I ran out on her."

"There will be those who may think you took that red horse, John, and that was not the plan."

John looked away, knowing he had set himself up for a hanging that Jack had tried to forestall. He considered not to fail Jack again.

They crossed the Niobrara and spent the warm fall days moving ever southward, over the Sandhills, to country John had not seen, sandy cut banks, knobby hills covered with red clump grass, clear ponds in the draws. They made steady, if not fast time, stopping at Ogallala on the Platte for whiskey and fresh food, a night with Bob Saunders, where they learned that Bill Whitcomb was already in Texas seeking two year old longhorns to restock. There were no trail herds now in Ogallala, which suited them fine, they wanted to get on farther south, new territory. Already many folks in Ogallala spoke a distinctively Texian drawl. Moving south into Kansas, along the Republican River they saw new homesteads spring up, sod houses, fenced quarter sections in clusters of five and six, trails already packed on the section lines. All-in-one Post Offices, usually with a general-purpose store, and nearly always a saloon nearby, seemed randomly strewn, rising up out of the horizon from miles away.

Nearly a month from Dakota, near the Arkansas River, they came weary and thirsty into a little town festooned with saloons, called Newton. South and west of the city, the prairie, with grass trampled to ruin, held vast herds of longhorns, bawling calves, riders circling at intervals around the milling beasts. Near each herd, a chuck wagon, and white tents dimming to gray with dust. Here were the cattle herds they had come for. News that the Santa Fe railroad would be in Newton soon, extending the route to Kansas City sale yards, and still south of the quarantine line, encouraged the big herds to pause here.

They stopped at the first saloon on the main street, a large, crowded building, "Tuttle's Dance Hall" sign, cheap paint already scaling away, hanging across the boardwalk in front, filled with loud cowboys, fresh off the trail, many already drunk at noon. Their trail's end money was flowing, and the laughing, boasting, raucous cowboys would know only one limit: the end of the dough.

The Dakota cowboys propped their elbows on the bar, heads down, just letting the whiskey take away the trail fatigue. Second drink into the afternoon, a large, rawboned cowman and a small, wiry, well-dressed dude popped thru the swinging doors. The small man, in black suit, white shirt and ribbon tie, his Stetson propped at a slant over a high-cheek-boned face took a seat near the door, surveyed the room, then turned, and looked over the shoulder of a nearby poker player. The big man, sporting a wide brimmed Texas hat, deerskin shirt and dark leather batwing chaps, pushed his way to the bar and elbowed in. Other cowboys said not a word, and gave him plenty of room.

Jack and John, never ones to be easily offended and certainly not looking for trouble, seeing the look in his eye, moved away quickly. The man drank a shot, and as he pointed at the glass for another, the swinging doors slammed open with a bang. The din of gambling and laughter stilled instantly. Seeming to know the sound of trouble, the big man whirled, just in time to take two slugs into the chest and two or three more in the stomach. He had not hit the floor when the small dude near the door began firing, first the gun in his left, then his right. The first shooter fell, the second shots blasted his partner back out the door. Two Texans followed swiftly in over the bodies, both meeting two slugs each in the chest. A man came forward from the bar and was sent rolling with a shoulder bleeding. The poker player grabbed for the little shooter, and tried to spin him around, but the dude shoved his gun under the man's left arm and pulled the trigger, never looking around, taking the Texan through the chest. Jack and John stood, still with glasses in hand, too stunned and too frightened to move. Wiser men at the bar hit the floor, some headed for the stairway, others the back door.

The little cowboy stood silently in the gore for a long moment survey-ing the crowd and the human wreckage, then walked calmly out the door.

"That'll be Jim Riley, GTT, said the bartender.

"Means Gone to Texas, John, lets go too. Man could get killed just drinkin a shot."

They left the saloon, and wandered toward the livery corral. From the stable barn, the little cowboy led a big black gelding, which drew Jack's attention. He raised his hands slowly, and smiled,

"Nice looking horse. Doesn't seem like a time you would be selling him, I guess."

"Not likely, mister."

"You heading south? We need some company, and some directions toward Texas if you're onto that way."

"Don't need no company, but since you aren't wearing guns, tag along til I get to my outfit."

Jack and John went along, warily, as cautious as the cowboy. "They said you was Jim Riley, I'm Jack Sully, and this is John Kincaid. We came south to find work as hands, and stay in Texas for the winter.

"My name is James M. Riley. The man those sonsabitches killed was my friend and employer for the past year, Mike McCluskey. He had a runnin feud with Anderson, first one a those I shot." He said this as casually as if it happened every day. "I know the foreman at my old outfit and he was takin on hands, but if you think Texas is all that warm in winter, you need to think again. Winter in Texas seldom means much work either. Need to wait til herds start north in the spring. We'll talk to the trail boss, whoever that will be now." He touched spurs to his horse, and edged him up the main street.

Jack and John were taken on at low winter wages to help move the herd west into better sustaining grassland, for the new trail boss had received orders not to wait to entrain his herd, but to hold it for moving north in spring. Being familiar with the area north, Jack and John offered fair value. The herd was moved thirty miles west of Newton, where grass was available, if not plentiful. They herded during the winter, a milder one for them, compared to the windy Dakota blasts they had known.

John had ridden the sorrel thoroughbred well in the weekly races in Newton and had gone to Dodge City twice, winning again. It was all out stakes for John, who won four saddles, seven sets of spurs, random ropes, bridles, and a wad of cash. Jack won some moderate bets, without taking the risks John did. Jim Riley not only became a good friend of Jack and John, but also had a personality much the same as John's. They were of the same physique, small, wiry, dark brown hair and clear, cool green eyes, quick on their feet, and with their hands. Riley and Jack were of one mind about horses. They both loved them, respected them, and had particularly good sense in judging the strengths, weaknesses and eccentricities and personality of each animal. They tended to train a horse in the same quiet manner, if Riley was at times more likely to buck out a surly horse, or a stubborn one, or a canny one.

The three passed time practicing shooting a day or two every week. They took breaks traveling west and as far south to see the open plains of Oklahoma. Riley could draw and shoot a pistol faster than anyone they had ever seen. Jack and John on the other hand, were better rifle shots. They had trained in the Army, and actually had never needed a fast draw in their previous lines of work. Even now, they saw little use for fast draw shooting, but the competition among themselves relieved the boredom of herding. Stories from Riley convinced them further that thirsty cowboys in wild cow towns and saloons made a fiery combination. Later, Dakota would only have its Deadwood to compare, and that far west of the Rosebud.

With all this low key time of gentle herding, John's desire for Mary Gullette not only would not subside, but his concupiscence blossomed and the distance apart festered within him. He grew a sustained case of nervousness and anxiety, interspersed with fits of melancholy. He sat for long periods looking over the empty horizon, slept late, then again became hyperactive, off to Dodge and a horse race. Jack read the signs of a mopping man, pining for his old sweetheart, and allowed as how they needed some adventure, some travel. They wanted to go to Texas, and now seemed the time. Go down, hook up with a herd. Riding south, John only continued his sour demeanor and anxious ways until Jack turned them back after reaching the dry, cracked ground and unfaltering horizon of the Texas Panhandle. They were back at Jim Riley's herd by early spring, where they learned that the trail boss had gotten orders from the East to take half the herd to Wyoming, and the remainder to Dakota, to hold for reservation sales. John saw this good fortune as a sign to have another go at Mary Gullette.

"I'm goin back, Jack. I gotta admit, I wanna to see Mary again. I can convince her, I know it. What I really want is a little spread, her, and some horses. I ain't afraid a work. I got some money, and I can sell the saddles, get some store suits. Maybe a team and buckboard."

"Well, I think you're about to break up this team anyway, so I'll go south with Jim, see more of Texas."

"That makes sense Jack, but I just can't go. My heart ain't in it no more." John stared north again, as if to confirm his resolve.

Jack wandered over to Jim's tent where he told him the news concerning John.

"Well, I ain't so sure Texas is a good place for me right now. The gunsels from the old Anderson crew are still waitin for me, especially in the part of Texas where my kin come from. They think I'm GTT, and I'm thinkin' John's idea might be better. In fact, this tussle ain't the first I've had. Texas, at least parts of it, ain't all that friendly ta me."

They finished spring branding, roping calves and doggin the bigger ones, tailing some big steers. They helped cut out the butcher cows and steers for Dakota, and cows with calves for Wyoming.

The work revived some wild oats in John. The foreman tasked him and Jack to castrate a big, brindle-tan and white longhorn bull that was particularly mean, often a nuisance around the chuck wagon and the remuda. They loosened out their lariats, and cut the bull out from the herd, without riling him up a bunch. John finally roped his long twisted horns, but the old bull was too wise to let even a good roper like Jack get a loop under his hind legs. Finally, Jack rode up to him and grabbed his tail, jumped from his horse and tried to tail him down. The bull swung his butt left and right, flinging Jack like a chicken on a twine. Jack hung on and the bull tried a different tactic. He snorted, and took two lunging steps toward John's horse, gained slack in the rope, and whirled around to get at Jack. He hung tight, dug his heels up to the spurs in the ground and pulled him straight, just as the bull spurted a long green shit stream. Most of it hit Jack, who let go the tail and groped for his horse. Cowboys had gathered to watch the fun, and laughed til two fell off their horses. That day was done, but the task was not complete. For the next two days they tried to rope that old bull, but he would have nothing to do with ropes on his legs. Jack took more care with the tailing business, but he could not get the bull on the ground before he was completely worn out. The fourth day, from the other side of the herd, when the bull saw Jack and John ride toward him he lit out for the west at a high gallop stopping nearly a half mile away to snort and paw the ground. The trail boss loped out to stop the chase, and allowed as how that bull had earned his balls, and could keep them. "He'll be back. We'll move him in with the cows; he might be a good leader if he settles into the drive."

"He would make a big hunk of beef for the Indians, Boss."

"Likely kill half a dozen steers afore ya got him there."

The Dakota herd streamed out straight north, seldom resting to graze the steers. The Republican River was nearly at its banks when they arrived. Dead tree branches and random logs swirled with the turbulence. The foreman directed the herd west to parallel the surging river until they found a wider, shallower ford and the storm water receded. Jim Riley brought the remuda along with few incidents. Wrangling fit him, racing after quitters, spurting to turn a wanderer back into the herd, bucking out a bronc, these were the challenges he sought.

For Jack, it would be the last time he was so far from the Rosebud.

The great drive crossed the Platte Rivers, South and North near Ogallala, stopping only to let the cattle forage, pushing into the northern Sand Hills over the next two weeks. Jim spotted two bands of wild horses that had grown plentiful in the western Sand Hills. He planned to leave the drive near its end, and go into Chadron, the nearest town. A day after bedding in the herd, John led the big sorrel to Jack. "Take good care of this boy, he's worth money. I'm headin back to the Whetstone area, or Ft Randall after I see what's up in Ft Pierre. Cain't hardly keep this horse."

"John, you need to make a deal with Jim, cause I ain't staying away from the Rosebud long myself. This horse will attract too much attention. Jim will take care of him, and may even make a sawbuck racing him."

Jim gladly took the horse, promising in return one of the horses that he expected to tame at some unknown future time. "Treat him right,

Jim." From there Jim Riley began the horse wrangling business for himself, rounding up wild ones, breaking them, and selling where he could.

With Jim gone, John continued only two more days as wrangler with the outfit. Jack took lead on the drive that in a few days he led through the Dakota country he knew well, into the Yankton Agency.

Sheriff Jack Stops a Rustling - 1873

J ack laid up for the winter of 1871 in Bijou Hills. He made the rounds of the road ranches of Charles Mix County, using up his horse racing winnings. He gathered, trained, bought and traded horses, cut wood, provided beef and horses to the Agency, trucked supplies. He found work with several local farmers, long days at harvest and haying, work which offended his sense of independence, and certainly not contributory to his dream of owning his own ranch, putting his cowboy skills to his advantage. Through his rambling and random work as hired hand, he had made friends with all the people of the county, not so difficult, considering there were barely a hundred souls living there at the time. He had established a reputation for fairness, an open, receptive demeanor, and undisguised toughness, all in all, a well-rounded resume to promote a spot on the county elections ballot. The quasi-political Lamont organization had set in motion plans to control the politics of Charles Mix county, among others, and thus to arrange collusion with an adequate number of spokesmen in the Territorial legislature to forge power in eastern Dakota. Their setup would bring in tax revenues, which they could, through subterfuge and politics, divert to their advantage. They did little to hide their intensions, or methods, to secure the votes needed.

The organization saw Jack as a malleable candidate for sheriff and advanced him $400 to win the election, after which he was promised a monthly stipend and advised to run the business of law enforcement within the county very quietly. As if there was no crime here. Nourish a civilized territory. Sustain order and prosperity; make Charles Mix county a credible seat in the legislature for the Lamonts. Jack visited nearly every man in the county over the next six weeks, and at $3-5 a head, pretty much insured that sufficient votes would obtain. That left over $100 for himself, and knowing his electorate, he bought a new gun and holster, plenty of ammunition, and put on a shooting exhibition wherever he could gain interested folk. That easily done, the implication was plain.

He was competent, and "worthy" of their support. Only one miserable county resident failed to vote for him, that idiot at the hog ranch who dained to oppose him on the ballot, Will Hollbraugh. From the 52 registered voters in the county, Jack gained 61 votes. Surely, this statement of support confirmed his qualifications as sheriff.

After winning, Jack made the rounds of Charles Mix County, stopping to join in the fun and gaming at each road ranch, farmstead and ranch. Though not a naturally boisterous man, he could get rowdy under the influence of ample draughts of whiskey, even though most of it was watered. He became an excellent card player who only lost when he drank too much. Jack kept the peace in a quiet but firm method applied through the road ranches where the type of troublemakers Jack wanted out of the county always frequented. Soon known as a tough, fearless man, fast with a gun, he quieted more than one troublesome situation with a lingering look. He had a sparkle in his eyes which flashed to a penetrating wolf's stare when agitated. Half drunk, he was a fearsome fellow. Encountering wanderers, he urged them to continue on; he kept the unmoneyed opportunity seekers looking over their shoulders. Nearly all were short of cash. They seldom worked unless it staved off starvation, so their eyes drifted to the easy hit, the touch that gained quick reward with little work. Overall, his performance was exemplary. He kept the east river county relatively safe and unmolested by such opportunists.

His charge from the Lamont cabal required him to investigate incidents, keep trouble out of the newspapers and forestall the inevitable gossiping. Keep vigilantes from forming to arouse the ire of Charles Mix county residents and quietude of Yankton pols. Keep the bureaucracy of governing, such as it was, intact for the regular peel off, and gain the legislature's official recognition of the county, thus gaining a state senator and representative at the capitol, from whence came the best workable money decisions. The Lamont organization was close to gaining that little pearl.

The undefined boundary of Charles Mix County, and thus the sheriff's jurisdiction, extended nearly fifty miles west of the Missouri at the time, and the Lamonts looked at this area for expansion. Only the most adventurous ranchers crossed the Big Muddy to establish outfits. Chris Colombe and the Lamoureauxs launched the first large spreads legally, being either part Indian, or married to Lakotas. While the Nelson brothers did not bother with the legal formality of marriage, with little to no bothersome law on the reservation, they busied themselves stocking their growing herd with mavericks from north of the White River or outright rustling east river stock. They could not, on the other hand, abide the same tactics from enterprising wanderers passing through the Rosebud.

Bijou Hills grouped together shoddily constructed buildings of rough pine, a store doubling as post office, a livery stable doubling as saloon, called itself a town, if barely qualifying. The livery offered whiffs of sweaty saddle blankets, oats chaff, horse dung and stale beer improved only by the perfumed mixture of new hay, new pine boards and new leather.

The relentless 100 degree wind rising across the south flats convinced Harper Stoddard he had already gone to hell; he stopped caring, and drank half his product every month, spitting chewing tobacco in large slugs between exaggerations and lies which sufficed for the only entertainment within fifty miles. Gumbo dust worn by wagons and horses the wind whipped away, pelleted the white washed slats, sifted dust over the product and produce through the open door and window in the general store, until the parched-earth main street turned rock solid. Jack edged up the center aisle of the store, stopped at the counter, and waited. After a minute, he found the small bell, and rang. A few minutes lapsed, and Winthrop Tarkington turned the corner from the back room, in a full apron, once white, hair pomaded smooth, forced smile. "Well, it's the Sheriff, Mr. Sully. After more taxes are you?" A mild, yet clearly English flavored accent. Jack stared, not answering, not smiling. He despised the tax collecting aspect of this job.

"You have come about the complaint, I presume?" He hardly hid his sarcasm, and it then occurred to Jack that all the stores and businesses seemed to be run by Englishmen, most with an air of superiority. False front stores and saloons carried English names, almost inevitably in eastern Dakota of the day. 'Too good to get their hands dirty and calloused,' he harrumphed to himself.

"I have ridden here to hear the complaints, as I understand you are aware of some cattle thieves working this area."

"I was told by August Nelson to pass along to you, that he knows of ten cows taken within the past week, and from John Jergins, another 7-8, from his herd. Both trailed their animals, and suspect they now have come east over the River. They left the brands with me. Here on this slip of paper."

Jack looked, recognized the Nelson's and Jergin's marks, and two others from north of the White River, the Flying V and U5. He pocketed the paper, and sauntered out, without farewell. Tarkington mumbled something that Jack preferred not to acknowledge.

Jack surmised that his investigation would take him south toward Pratt Creek searching for sign along the way, look for a tell-tale river crossing. First, a visit with old Harper Stoddard at the stable.

"Harry Ham came through about a day ago, on his way to Ole Finstad's with a big herd a cattle. Looked tired, only had one drink, not like him." Jack slugged another drink, changing plans, working out where Harry might now be. Were the cattle for Ole? Not likely. Ole was a straight shooter, stayed out of trouble, unlike his rambunctious brother, Olaf. "How many head, Harp?"

"Don't know. Never saw em. He came in from the north, tired, horse worn to a frazzle. Not a bad horse. That's him after the oats trough again. I exchanged him for a brown and white spot and five dollars. He'll be all right, rested up. ... Don't have change, have another slug, and we'll call her a dollar even"...Jack obliged.

The three-mile ride to Ole Finstad's farm failed to sober him, and after abiding his incoherent mumbling and refusing him more whiskey, Ole aimed him at the hay in the overhead mow, where he slept soundly.

Jack arose bewildered, head pounding, already sweating, before dawn, pulled hay stalks from his socks, and drifted toward the coffee fragrance signaling Ole's start on a new day. Light-headed, blinking to focus, he mused on such a life, riding around the country, drinking and getting paid $50 a month. Such decrepitude could not last. 'I'll start west river, near the Drapeau's...soon.'

"Mornin' Ole, I smell the coffee's real stuff." Hot, it burnt his mouth, woke him to the new day.

"Ole, you seen Harry Ham lately?" Jack started off the conversation directly on point, respecting Ole's natural honesty.

"He come by yesterday, sold me five head of two year olds. Good stock. $20 a head, a good price, and he had a bill a sale."

"He give you one too?"

"Yep."

"Who'd he buy these critters from?"

"Nelson boys, least wise it its their AN and ON, marked."

Jack rolled his head against the chair back, stared for a moment at the rafters, then closed his eyes. The coffee was taking slow effect. "Well, those two complained to the Lamonts, and I gotta find the cows, and hang Harry."

"Hang 'im? I though you was sheriff, not a judge yet."

He sat forward, drained the cup. "Just jokin, Ole, but I need to set this right. Where's he goin', any idea?"

"Just headin' south from what I could tell. He stayed fer supper, such as it was, then lit out. Said he had to get to his brother, down at White Swan, I think he lives. Harry's onto bad times, Jack, the weather ain't been kind to him... nor anybody for that matter."

"Rather drive at night I guess, cooler, but could be he also needs to stay outta sight."

"You think these cows was rustled? Think Harry would do that? I cain't see his brother acceptin' that. He's got a hard set of his own rules, John Ham. Law abidin'. Even ornery sometimes."

"Well, in the first place, Harry ain't no loafer passing through taking a few head a someone else's cows. He's local. 'Less he plans on going way south, he could be in a peck a trouble...trouble I cain't likely stop."

Ole and Jack traded news, had he seen brother Olaf? Was John Jergins, another Norski doing OK? Any dances planned, when would the county get official, heard anything about taxes, anything new in the Bijou Hills store, and of course the weather? His wheat had been flattened by wind two days before, but the hail that would have ruined his harvest year missed by a quarter mile.

Jack found traces of the herd's trail, though the wind had rearranged the grass to its natural northward tilt over night. The hard ground beneath bore enough hoof scrapings to ascertain a destination straight south.

Harry laid up at sunrise, watering and resting the 11 cows in the tree line of Pratt Creek near the Missouri. Jack reached the creek in late afternoon, having loped against the unrelenting south wind. He easily spotted the hoof marks headed down stream, tied his mare at the tree line, and with his Spencer, started through the burr oaks and honey locusts, careful to skirt the crunching sound of rocks in the creek bed, stalking through the plum and box elder, toward the river. A small spring seeped out of the far hillside, draining into the creek bed. A pothole, a small dam farther down, that's where Harry would be, near water, and able to easily contain the cows. The sides of the creek bed became higher and steeper. As he rounded a small cut bank, his foot caught the tangle of a wild grape vine and he stumbled forward, nearly falling on a heifer still bedded down. She startled up, plunging into the thick bushes. Jack scrambled to his feet just as a rifle shot exploded and echoed past, too close. He had lost the surprise he had wanted to keep Harry from using a gun.

"Harry!" He yelled. "Harry, its me, Jack. Hold off!" He lifted his rifle over his head, hands high.

Harry's rifle held at the shoulder, he rose up from another cut bank, eyes wide, "What do you want? What are you doing here? Who's with you?"

As neighbors, they had socialized, but Harry's reticence, under hooded eyes, and his brooding nature precluded real friendship. Harry seldom drank with pleasure, whiskey deepened his funk, darkened his personality. Yet, out here, a neighbor stood for something, and each of value. Many drifted through this harsh land, but those who stayed needed each other, respected mutual travails, kept their sanity by intense, if infrequent socializing.

Recognizing Jack, and seeing him alone, he dropped his rifle to belt level. "Thought you mighta been a rustler. Sorry. Want some coffee?"

"Harry, I thought you might be a rustler too. Still do. Lets talk." Harry turned back, saw Jack had not raised his rifle, but stood looking intently at him. "I came by Ole's, he said you sold him five head a cows. Nelson cows. My badge is in my saddlebag, but I'm here on sheriff's business. I think we can fix things without no trouble."

"So you think I stole these cows? Here's the bill a sale."

"Harry, the Nelson boys all been schooled. They don't use their initials to sign anything like a bill a sale. It ain't like they got these cows rightly themselves, but that ain't the question. I got a complaint from them, come through the Lamonts. I ain't ignorin' it, but I don't have to hang ya on the spot."

"Ya ain't gonna hang me long as I got my rifle here in my hand, Jack, and I ain't one to joke about those things, like you are. Bein sheriff ain't cause for gettin' smart with me. You know me long anuf ta know I ain't a jokin' man. I don't take no crap from you, or even my own family." Harry had squatted at the small fire, pouring coffee into a tin cup, the rifle across his lap pointed conveniently at Jack, still standing close enough to take a round without aim.

"The Lamonts know what I'm doing, and Ole and Tarkington know that I am on your trail. Shootin' me won't solve no problems. You and me just need to discuss what we can do in this sorta awkward situation. For you that is. I can get shot right here for doin' my duty, but the Lamonts will hang you for upsettin' their plans... or we can fix it..." Jack settled onto a large rock near the fire, took the coffee cup, sipped at the obsidian colored gritty liquid, and said, "Here's what I propose. You let me take the cows ya got here back to the Nelsons, give me the hunert and fifty dollars you got fer the ones sold to Ole, and we let him keep those cows. And by the way, five or six a those cows belong to John Jergins. You take to rustlin', don't do it from your neighbors."

"I dint get but a hunert dollars, you know that. I ain't got no money er I sure as hell wouldn't take no chances with these cows. I owe my brother, and I intend to pay him back."

"You might owe, but this ain't gonna be the time. You shoulda knowd the Nelsons don't take rustlin' kindly from their side. Only works one way with Gus Nelson. Lamonts ain't gonna let you do it. Lemme see the money."

"Its all here. Take it. But I ain't got no more."

"You got that paint, worth maybe 40 bucks.

"Hell, ya cain't take my horse out from under me, I got him legal anyway. I cain't walk outta here, dammit."

"Here's the thing. You mount up, we cross the cows back over the river. Its real low now, won't be no problem. I leave you near your cabin, and take the herd back. What I promise is that I won't tell Gus Nelson all about this, just that I run off the rustlers and brought his cows back. Ole won't say nothing, less Nelsons want more money, since twenty dollars ain't but half what the cows would bring, but the horse will even it up with em if I talk right."

Harry stood, rifle butt on the ground, head hung, staring at the fire. He pulled his hat up off his back, clamped it down on his head, and kicked out the fire.

The herd crossed easily. Jack accompanied Harry back over the river, dropped his bridle and saddle at his cabin, and pressed northward with the cattle. A day of idle time in the saddle will cause a man to ponder, even plot. It was easy enough to pick up two cows with the Nelson brand on the way, making the $100 a fair price for "three" cows that had been sold to Ole. Gus did not complain, and smiled as Jack commented that he had roped this fine paint before the rustlers could get him off picket when they escaped into the river bottom. "Reckon its fair pay for four hard days in the saddle."

Gus's persistent frown bent at the corners raising a sardonic smile, acknowledging the overly simple rationale; but then, he had gotten his cows back, and some cash.

Will Hollbraugh's Hog Ranch

J ack walked his black mare slowly over the ridge, and up to the door of the Hollbraugh Hog Ranch, as much not to cause suspicion as to case the joint. Only two other horses at the hitching rail, so maybe there would be some quiet time to talk out their problem. Will approached every conversation in a confrontational, in- your-face manner, regardless of subject, so Jack reminded himself to restrain his disdain for this man, as he dismounted. The ranch house door resembled the gate at Ft Randall guardhouse; two iron bars used to fortify the place hung slack, big locks at end of each, closed up only on those nights when it did not stay occupied until dawn. The low slung cabin was larger than the normal settler's abode, accommodating 10-15 people at the wood plank bar and makeshift pine plank tables. The heavy door swung open to a gumbo encrusted, board floor, smell of rancid whiskey and over-ripe wild game. Two cowboys, hats on, sat at a back table. Jack assumed that the heavy set, unsmiling woman in a blue headscarf was Mrs. Hollbraugh, whom he had never met.

Busty, in a plain coarse brown dress of gabardine, she eyed Jack with restrained suspicion, a necessity in her line of work. Will came out of the back lean-to, and in his usual loud, bull-buffalo voice, "Well, Sheriff Sully, come to call. Wearing your badge I see, not drinkin today then. One shot won't hurt ya... here," he snarled, as he slammed down a small shot glass.

"One will do, just to be sociable," Jack smiled.

"What ya doin here, come to rub it in?" as he slopped the whisky into the glass.

Will's terrible showing in the election for Charles Mix county Sheriff, run against Jack and the Lamont organization, would have rankled any man, but more so Will Hollbraugh, who could find perturbation in any resistance to his own outpourings.

"Seems like I'm the only one to vote for ya Will, since you only got one vote."

"I would think that your own damned outfit could have counted mine and my hired man's vote, since you won 61 to one."

"Think it woulda turned the election, Will?"

Hollbraugh wore farmer style bibbed overalls, dark gray, besotted with stains from whiskey, meat juices, butcher's blood. His shirt was woolen, dark green, sleeves pushed over his heavy arms to the elbow. Three days growth of beard, pink, bloody hands indicated the butcher's work, a calf or deer in the back room, no doubt. Interrupted from his labors by Sully's voice, he wore his mood on his sleeve. "I asked what the hell you want. State your business and move on. Protect the good honyockers of the county, cause you sure as hell can't catch any real outlaws. You come to tell me you found the thieves that took my horses?"

Jack sauntered to the bar, and lowered his voice, keeping the cowboys out of hearing. "I came to say that I ain't found em, and if you want someone to track em, if any tracks still exist, you will need to pay a month's wages to have me deputize someone. I know a good Inyun tracker, comes cheap."

"Bullshit, I ain't payin. It's the county's duty, and you ain't doin it cause you ain't good enough yerself. And you don't give a plug nickel about me, except when you want some good whiskey. I want someone to get after that gang of rustlers, cause I know they's still in the area. Raymonds lost some horses too. I aim to get the cavalry after these outlaws if you don't get movin."

"I heard you already went to Ft Randall in that regard, Will."

"Who told ya that?"

"Not important, but I'm warning you, it ain't their job, ain't in their jurisdiction. This is county business, no way is it the Army's."

"Its in their goddam jurisdiction, its in the Rosebud, that's their area."

"I know your hired man has gotta idea who these horse thieves might be, and you need to tell me what he's got. If I need to run em in, I will. The Colonel at Randall already reminded me who's job this is, so I don't need you talking to him any more, and I need the names of the rustlers you think did this."

"You go find em yourself. I'm thinkin you know allov em, that's why you ain't doin your dammed job. Ifn I was sheriff, I woulda had em already. You can't do your job, and want me to do it for ya. Go to hell."

Jack slugged back the shot of whiskey. "I'll pass on the second glass, thanks anyway."

Which Will Hollbraugh had not offered, nor had intended to offer.

Jack spurred the mare away toward the Bijou hills, knowing that he would not be chasing shadows of horse thieves when the chances of finding them were nil, and while he had his own business and sheriff's business to care for. The Raymonds, who ran the largest horse ranch in the Rosebud, would not charge this duty to the sheriff, but would pursue rustlers themselves. Will had called him a rustler, or in cahoots with the band. This troubled Jack, because if he would make that accusation to his face, he was telling anyone else who would listen. Jack's intentions for talking to Will included the possibility that rustler bands would take unkindly to having the Army come after them. Few of the rustlers realized the jurisdictional difficulties in that regard, but feared the Army's power if it should be called against them. And Will's hired hand was rumored to have ridden with a band for a couple of years. Will's open threats indicated to the rustlers that a snitch was at work. They found strength in numbers and armament, and were a force of their own.

In the days that followed, Will Hollbraugh traveled again to Ft Randall, then on to Yankton, where he proselytized several assemblymen to goad lawmen or the cavalry to go after the horse thieves. Still, the capitol listened intently, but refrained from pressing any territorial law enforcement to mount a search or trailing party. Had Hollbraugh convinced him at Ft Randall that the rustlers were Indians, Ponca or Sioux, the Colonel would have reacted, but keeping the civil law on the plains was not his mission. Hollbraugh went, loudly protesting, back to his Hog Ranch. Will hated Jack Sully for being sheriff; aiding him in finding the rustlers he could not abide even at the prospect of getting the horses returned. He stomped back to his bar, and slammed his fist down. "Gimme some whiskey," he snarled at his wife. Obvious that things had not gone well at Ft Randall. He turned to the three cowboys drinking at a back table. "I went to the goddam cavalry, and by god, they will do somethin' or I'll go to Yankton again. I know those cocksuckers er still thievin' around here." The cowboys stayed quiet, looked away, and adjusted themselves uneasily in their chairs. Presently, as Will turned back to the bar, the tallest of the three, a holster at his hip, rose and casually commented "all the ranches lose some animals, it's not the end of ranchin'. I'd guess those rustlers are long out in the Rosebud, ther Will." Will Hollbraugh turned slowly, anger welled up in him. His face showing red through the scraggly beard. "I don't think ther out of the county, and I don't think ther gonna get out. Ther gonna claim six feet of dirt next. I got ther names."

He had names, but he could not himself have readily placed the names to faces.

Three days later, he and his hired hand left early in the morning, fog still in the air, to bring in the remaining ten head of horses. They might have returned mid-morning, but other ranch chores apparently delayed them. Yet, when they missed supper, Mrs. Hollbraugh saddled her mare and sought their whereabouts. Nearing the Missouri, she saw her fears extant. Two dark lines extended from a big cottonwood on a ridge near the breaks; she galloped up, seeing the bulging eyes of Will, his stained work pants, the boy's mouth agape with the scream still bursting silently from his soul. She cut Will down, shook him, screamed at him, but he would not wake. "Jack Sully done this, killed my man. Revenge; he took revenge and I will too."

She told anyone who would listen and many who did not want to think about the possibility that Jack Sully, their own county Sheriff, in league with a band of horse thieves, might have orchestrated the foul deed. With her own hateful solution so clear to her, she never pieced together the fact that the three strangers in her bar were never seen again. More quietly, others in Charles Mix and Gregory counties allowed as how a horse thief already met his just reward. Will had few friends; this, the final example of his braggadocio overwhelming good sense. Neither opposing opinion died quickly, as hog ranch gossip prevailed for years. Jack's own defense remained the simple truth; he had nothing to do with the hanging.

Robbing Stagecoaches

With money from his stint as sheriff and taking time between odd tasks tendered by the Lamonts, Jack crossed the Missouri and began building a two-room log and sod cabin on land that would bear his name, Sully Flats. The Flats lie at the top of the Missouri breaks, the first large expanse of level land, the beginning of the western Dakota prairie, bordered on the south and west by the headwaters of the two forks of Whetstone Creek. The creeks gorge in spring as the winter snows run off, flow clear blue-green in summer, and even the hottest months, before fall rains, maintain a freshet from a natural spring at the north fork, near Jack's ranch house. From Whetstone Creek, the Flats stretch miles to the northeast where they again confront the White River breaks, then westward, until they meld into the great west river prairie. Since he numbered among the first small handful of white folk to come across the Big Muddy as settlers, he found no opposition in his choice on the Flats, which provided him its prize of grass and game, and the sweet water spring.

His modest cabin suited him, enough to get started on the ranch of his dream and plans. John Jergins, the Dions, and Drapeaus his only neighbors, pitched in as neighbors did in those hard days, notching heavy cottonwoods, using his team to drag logs to the site, ramp them up the walls. He first fashioned a makeshift roof of his tent over a part of the cabin, until John could finish his own summer work, to help with a presentable wooden roof.

Thus partially settled, Jack bought five horses, unbroken, from two cowboys passing through. Being on the west bank, trailing unbranded horses, asking price more than reasonable, Jack strongly suspected that they were procured by nefarious means. Well, he thought, I ain't Sheriff now, not my problem. The waddies told him they had acquired the horses from a rancher north, near Ft Pierre, and had expected to sell them sooner. The Bull Creek Lakota had little interest in buying them, and they found the range without settlers until they arrived at Jack's cabin. He exacted a bill of sale, let drop the comment that he had been sheriff of the county. At that, one cowboy signed with an X; and Jack continued to watch them progress up the other side of the Whetstone creek line onto the south flats. He hobbled the horses near the cabin, and slept fitfully with his rifle, half expecting them to return for another try for the horses, but they did not. Days passed, uneventfully now, as he spent time breaking the horses and working hackamores, braiding bridles, tended to soaping, cleaning, and oiling his newly acquired but used saddle. By late summer the horses responded well to his instructions, he had even trained them to respond with knee pressure turns, the 'ksk, ksk', tongue-to-teeth signal to speed up, leaning forward to gallop. One mare, for sure, he could sell as a lady's mount. He roped the big black stallion, and with two mares, led him south to John Jergins ranch for safekeeping. The other two, including the little ladie's mare, he roped into a long lead line, and set out for the east river settlements.

Summer had been kind to the East River homesteaders, wheat coming in at 30-40 bushels per acre, corn tall and promising for the fall huskers. He sold the horses readily, traveling into White Swan, and around to the new homesteads of the Swedes, Norwegians, and Bohemians. His reputation as sheriff boosted his credibility, and the well-trained, well-kept horses nearly sold themselves.

At the Svenson homestead, the eye of a tall, blond, svelte beauty distracted his attention to business as he discussed the mare with her father. The old man called her to him, asked her opinion of the color, and lapsing into English, "Inge, pud die mare trew her paaces." Jack cinched up the side saddle from the old man's tack room, and boosted her foot into the stirrup. She rode well, the horse responded as trained, and Jack's heart could not resist the girl, anymore than she could resist purchase of the mare. Father smiled, and after the obligatory bargaining session, paid $30 in silver coin.

Flush with cash, light of heart, Jack spurred off to the closest road ranch north of White Swan, Pap Ducharme's on the Yankton-Chamberlain trail. The first whiskey burned, but felt good, the second went down easier, and even as Ol' Pap watered down the subsequent shots, Jack's caution mellowed, and he sat into the ongoing poker game. Sober, he might have discerned the ploys of the card sharps preceding his downfall, but not this night. Pairs were beaten by higher pairs, a full house by a larger full house, and finally, too drunk to remember, he slapped down his last dollars on three treys, saw it whisked away by a straight, a very unlikely hand in five card stud. Yet, he found himself fortunate the next morning not having bet away his horse and saddle, to have only a pounding headache and empty wallet. He awoke with his arm under his head on the poker table. He stumbled to the bar, Eliza Ducharme back by 11:00 o'clock and sympathetic to Jack's condition, offered a free beer. Jack nursed it, his mouth dry, his brain desperate for serenity. Jack sat, disheveled, distraught and despairing into the late afternoon. He checked his gelding, still at the hitching post, walked him to water and unsaddled him. He drank a couple of gallons himself, dunked his head, brushed back his hair. He could not meet head-on the task of riding out today, feeling as he did.

He sat staring at the table, recovering slowly from the effects of mediocre whiskey if not downright rotgut. A man ought not have to pay for such crap twice he thought. Three men entered as the last light faded. One, stared at Jack, came over and sat down.

"Jack, its me, Joe."

Jack coughed, cleared his throat, "Joe Somers, what brings you here?"

"Ya look the worse fer wear… things ain't going so good as bein' sheriff, eh?"

"They was goin' fine until I ran into a whiskey jug and deck a cards last night."

"You seen Art or Possum lately?"

"Neh, just recovering from a bad night, sold a horse down in White Swan, need to get my head back and get on home."

"Lookee here, we need some help. There's a stage coming up from Yankton, through White Swan, and we know there's a couple of dudes on it likely got some cash. Watches, stick pins, who knows."

"Joe, I ain't in ridin' condition right now, money or not."

"Its tomorrow morning, give ya time to rest up. We figure its leaving White Swan at near sunup. We plan on going down the river a ways, pick it up as it crosses Pratt Creek, when it slows down."

The conversation continued, two others entered the bar and brought glasses to the table. "This is JT, JT Newell, and Art Maupin. Joe brought the talk to subdued whispers, and proposed that they could all benefit from some expropriation of private property. They agreed on even shares for the cash, and to decide later how to divide the jewelry.

The stage had been robbed twice during Jack's tenure as sheriff, so he was well aware of the difficulty in finding, much less prosecuting, the perpetrators. Knowing better, but totally broke, he bought in. With bandanas across their faces, Joe and JT dashed into Pratt Creek as the stage descended the far bank. Jack came up from the rear as the driver pulled up the team and looked to retreat, and waved his rifle. Soon, Art Maupin, a mean spirited man at any time, took pleasure in dragging the two men and one lady from the stage-coach, slamming them against the stage door. He jammed his pistol into the asses of the men and threatened to shoot their balls off before relieving them of their wallets, watches, purse, and in one man's case, cash from his boot tops. They stood very still. He ran his hands along the woman's body, and across her breasts, before yanking a necklace from her. His pleasure obvious, he pulled down his bandanna and snarled a smile at the lady. "I'm Art Maupin, a lovable bandit, my sweet, and for a favor I could return the necklace." She did not return the smile.

"Let's get outta here, Art, cut the bullshit," Joe summoned.

From the robbery, the spoils included cash, and some jewelry, from which Jack chose a gold pocket watch and chain. He had never owned a timepiece, but admired those who had. Yet, he sensed the quality in this piece. Later, though he realized that he could be linked to stage robbery through this watch, he could not bring himself to throw it into the river. After another robbery, one more distasteful for him, he decided he had enough money. Art made it known that, in any case, Jack was unnecessary to the band's endeavors.

Building a Home

Jack took his leave of Charles Mix county proper, seeking the relative legal safety West River and averting the temptations of further dangerous stage robberies. He surveyed the flats at the head of Whetstone Creek, he had positioned his cabin well, out of plain sight just before the incline into the thickets and brush of the riparian creek line.

He and John finished the roof of his two-roomed log house over the summer, whitewashed the inner walls, added shelving, and shaped tight-fitting doors hinged with rawhide.

First, just under the spring at the head of the Whetstone, Jack fashioned a small rock dam deep enough to dip his wooden bucket. From White Swan be purchased a 30 gallon wood barrel, filled it to age the barrel staves, and drug it with a stone boat near the house. Within days he had a continual water supply close at hand. He fashioned a wide bunk in the second room, stuffed prairie grass into gunny sacks making a mattress, laid out his ample supply of Army blankets, anticipating that with some luck he might obtain a bunkmate in the near future.

To great disappointment and embarrassment, Inge Svenson, left him after a week in which she had worn out his patience and he had resorted to force in his effort to convince her of the natural duties of a wife. She sobbed into a fine white handkerchief, returning to a mother and father too stoic and taciturn to have instructed their daughter about the rudiments of life itself; at least about procreation. Jack, courting in the manner of the day, would know very little of Inge before their marriage. Old Knute Svenson, devote Lutheran, expected the mature Jack, to educate where his own reserve had failed. Jack's patience wore very thin by the third night, words were exchanged, contact was made but consummation was not. Inge spent an evening fixing her damaged skirt, and sat quietly in the buckboard during the long ride back to White Swan. Jack slapped the reins on the rump of his black matched pair as she turned back to her father's house, and left the explaining to her.

The cabin lay within walking distance of the spring at the headwaters of Whetstone Creek. The creek offered cover of trees, plum thickets, and brush. When he first moved onto the Flats, his only neighbors were John Jergins, the Oliver Dions, Narcisse Drapeau's and, Lakota of the Spotted Tail and Corn Brule scattered in small bands, mostly around Bull Creek, west and northward toward the White River. As the renegade bands were forced onto the agencies, other enterprising families settled permanently in the area, primarily by marrying Indian women. The Drapeau brothers, John and Narcisse, who had lost extended freighting contracts following the agency move when Spotted Tail worked his own deal to get resupplied through Ft Laramie, soon followed, settling on land to the south. As "squaw men" gained access to reservation lands, more settled in the area, but until the Homestead Act opened the Rosebud to farmers, large cattle ranches, interspersed with a few smaller cattle and horse ranches, dominated the general populace. Cattle and horses ran free; fences would come only after the homesteaders forced their claims.

The first settling ranchers saw grassland stretching for hundreds of miles, so plentiful no man could predict that greed could overwhelm its abundance. Yet, in 10 years, the absentee cattle barons would wear their good fortune so thin that not even their vast bank accounts would suffice. Nature's balance began to tilt; the buffalo hunters first pressed their thumbs to the scale. By early 1880's they had depleted the plains of the great woolly beasts. Indians were by then roistered into unnatural settlements, roaming and hunting allowed no more. Gray wolves began to filter onto the prairie from the Montana and Wyoming mountains. Grouse and prairie chickens, once so plentiful and unafraid that they were often caught by hand, filled homesteader stew pots nearly to extinction. Bears, mountain sheep, cougars, bobcats, and finally wolves, were hunted to extinction in the Badlands, Black Hills, and western Dakota. Beaver and other fur bearers had long ago been trapped out of the rivers and creeks by the French, sent off for hats and coats carriage seats in the East and in Europe.

Now those Frenchmen, fur trading spent, married and settled among the Lakota, to become, with their children, the first settlers, ranchers and businessmen, starting ranches, establishing trading posts, later working for the Indian Bureau. Among many other Frenchies, Bordeaux, Colombe, Charbonneau, Counoyer, Ducheneau, DuPuy, Drapeau, Dion, Dupree, Lamoreaux, Landreau, LaPlante, LaBeau, Narcelle, Scissons, Sully, …families first sunk their roots into the Rosebud and on both sides of the Missouri. Army posts established at Ft Randall, Ft Pierre, Ft Sully (named after the General, no relation to Jack), Ft Lookout, and other permanent stations along the Missouri patrolled westward, secure the land for the English, Germans, Irish, and Scandinavians that followed, some after a stint at the Army posts, but later in covered wagons, carts, and buggies they came as pioneers.

Second Marriage

The humiliation Jack suffered from the failure of his first marital encounter did not defer him; in fact, he realized very soon after, that his mistake was marrying "out of his kind". True, she was a perfect beauty, but of strange ways and religious, pampered, and unaccustomed to the vicissitudes of frontier life. He must stay closer to home, to his own.

Actually, he had known her since he freighted for Narcisse Drapeau and J T Smith out of the Whetstone Agency. Too young of course at that time to be more than a pesky kid, he had little inclination for a serious acquaintance. He teased her and her brothers equally when he stopped for freighting assignments at the Drapeau house in Harney City, but developed no interest of a serious nature. Just a skinny, playful kid. When the Agency closed, Narcisse built a homestead northwest of the dying Harney City, near the south fork of the Whetstone.

Narcisse played a mean fiddle, and at the first barn dance, to which Jack was naturally invited, he met the maturing Louisa. Still barely a young woman, she immediately attracted Jack's attention, and he hers. Black hair to her shoulders, light olive complexion, supple and vivacious; she danced with the grace of a deer, stepping lively to her father's music.

For Jack and Louisa, the courting naturally progressed, at a near feverish turn; importantly, the family wholeheartedly approved of Jack. They had known him for a pleasant and upright man, stagecoach poaching aside, of which they knew nothing. For all her youthful beauty, her sexuality did not intimidate Jack as had that perfect figurine, Inge Svenson. Long walks along the Whetstone, love in the lush underbrush, and the inevitable soon obtained. Jack and Louisa married in Charles Mix county before fall.

Catch Them If You Can

Freezing cold; it sucked the warmth from every living thing. Tree trunks cracked like rifle shots, cattle bedded down and froze overnight. The sky stayed silver-gray, a dull sun cast its weak light through crystallized air, rising late, hovering low, fading to black in late afternoon. Wolves and coyotes curled into dens, dark hawk silhouettes graced leafless branches. Unbathed bodies huddled around stoves, the human reek attenuated only on the occasion of an untrimmed damper puffing cedar smoke into a room or cabin doors opened only for fetching more wood. In bunkhouses and line shacks, cowboys stoked fires, played cards, checkers, and bantered and taunted. Attempts to overcome boredom, wandering outside, each time they sought to confront it, the shear weight of the cold pressed them back to warmth. A month of Arctic winter dropped like a curtain across the range; the world foreshortened, distances traveled measured by the time it took to freeze a warm-blooded being. The Whetstone spring froze shut; Jack and Louise wrestled the barrel from the stone boat into the house and chipped ice to melt on the stove. Neighbors and towns were out of reach. For two weeks, wind forsook the ranges out of pity, for the cold could punish sufficiently to chastise its strongest and weakest, the faint and the courageous, the wily and the foolish inhabitants. Into February a wind resumed its trek as a mild Chinook, it brought warmth of a fashion, raising the temperature noticeably, and if yet cold, unthreatening to life. Animals resumed their natural order of hunting and scavenging, and men began to move out of doors.

A light snow whisked from the gray overcast, catching on cactus and yucca and the remaining thin grasses, into the lower gullies and creek lines. Cattle and horses stiff-legged it from clump to grass clump.

Jack ventured onto the plain between the north and south branches of the Whetstone, seeking his horses, to account for his provenance, expecting that the cold would have been hard on his twenty head, but that these tough rangers would have survived. He had left Louisa close to the fire, as she was with child. She seemed little burdened by the pregnancy, no problems, and Ben Diamond's wife would be called when the time came.

After counting 14 horses, in relative good condition, he spent the reminder of daylight searching for the remaining six. He followed the south fork to the Missouri bottomlands, finding no trail, no hoof prints or disturbed grass or snow patches. Retracing his route to the Flats on the other side of the creek, at the top of the south fork of the Whetstone, he found his piebald mare standing over her colt. The mare tossed her head, snorted, nuzzled the lifeless body. She had a rope around her neck, trailing onto the grass. Jack roped her, released the lariat. A small blood spot marked the forehead of the colt. It had clearly been shot. Jack grasped the general situation quickly. Horses thieves had chosen the mare with four other horses, expecting to take the unbranded colt as a special prize. As a mare with her foal will do, she had attempted to break away when the thieves herded the horses away from their familiar habitat. She had caused trouble; forcing one rider to give chase, keep her in check, moving with the other band of four. It slowed the getaway, so they shot the colt. Her strong motherly instinct prevailed; she struggled to return for her colt, and caused more trouble. They roped her, attempting to drag her with them, but she had broken the rope, or they had cut her loose. Getting away from the area would have consumed their interest for she had slowed them more than prudence allowed. They had $150 worth of good horseflesh; chancing discovery to save another $40 they found unappealing. They would go south or east, Jack thought, for otherwise the reservation offered little opportunity for a meaningful sale, and they could lose the horses to a Lakota hunting party or roving band. Jack lost the trail of the bandits at the top of the rise, snow had blown away traces of hoof prints, and the grass whipped bare of trail on the frozen land. In fact, these thieves would want to cross the Missouri ice as soon as possible, get onto the roads and wagon trails east to lose anyone trailing them. The cold, the dead of winter, the unlikelihood of cowboys on the range would make them more confident of alluding followers.

Jack pulled off his left glove, felt under the body of the colt, and found warmth. They had taken advantage of the cold, but the break in the cold spell had gone contrary to their plans. Yet, they had proceeded, very early this morning, most likely. If they were smart, they would travel fast, get well east over the river. If not, he had a chance at catching them.

Jack roped his big red sorrel gelding out of the herd on the way back to the house, switched his saddle to him. At the wood pile he picked up an armful of logs, kicked some splinters back near the wood pile. "What is it Jack, what's happened?" Louisa sensed him pondering, rolling a situation in his mind. "They've stolen four of our horses...and in this cold."

"Jack, you can't ride out in this weather."

He stood over the stove, lifted the iron lids and dropped the two logs into the flames as he warmed in the house. "Louisa, I can't let this happen, I can't let them just ride in here and take my hosses. They shot the spotted colt as well. I don't like it, but I gotta go after em." He laid his mittens on top of the bun warmer, went to the bedroom, worked at his bedroll and war bag for the chase. He changed his boots for winter moccasins, rolled extra mittens, socks, long underwear all into his buffalo robe.

"I'll call at Ben Diamond's, ask Betsy to come by tomorrow."

Louisa smiled, "I'll be fine, Jack, the baby has been quiet in there, just a little kicking. We have plenty of wood and water. But, hurry back...please...and take care, it's not worth freezing for four horses. They will have guns."

Jack bent to kiss her forehead, stoking her long black unfettered hair. He felt her stomach, smiled and turned to go. He thought of the cold facing him; he turned back, kissed Louisa full on the lips, lingering over her lower lip. She smiled, and he pulled the door snuggly behind himself.

Jack respected the cold, but did not fear it. These horse thieves were an affront to him personally, they belittled him, tarnished his self-image. He felt degraded, no better than a honyocker if he suffered thieves for lack of courage. Common sense dictated that he stay home, let this go, but he was not the man to give advantage to such as these brazen men. Everyone in the Rosebud knew that only fools stole from Jack Sully. And he accounted these rustlers for fools.

Outfitted with his warmest get up, he rode hard for the river bottom which the cottonwoods and hills sheltered from the wind. He picked up the trail where they crossed the tight-frozen Missouri, and up the breaks on the other side, with little effort. Knowing the prey's destination is half the expertise of the seasoned tracker. These Jack knew would not stray far from a warm fire. Jack knew Charles Mix County; it had been his back yard when he was sheriff. 'What the hell did these crooks think, stealing from me,' Jack thought. Would they turn north or south after crossing? Straight east lay the shortest route to a town or settlement and warmth. He followed tracks up the short eastern breaks, and after circling twice found the trail northward. These men had come from the north, and were headed back that way. Maybe they had a deal waiting in Chamberlain, Brule City, Bijou Hills. The wind had died down again, but the cold intensified. Alaska settled back into Dakota.

The little village of Platte boasted only a few scattered houses, and a post office in the only store. No one stirred, the store door locked. He looked around the two barns, and near the houses, all shuttered against the fierce cold. He swung west, again eventually found the trail indicating that they had skirted the town, much as he had expected. Wisely for them, they hoped to avoid notice, and hoped for the cold to deter followers. He calculated that they had not rested for two days, were cold, hungry and looking to lay up. He spurred for Bijou Hills, where they now must seek respite, heat, food, and water. He stopped for only a half hour at Ole Finstad's place, warmed himself, watered the sorrel and bummed a half-bucket of oats. Ole had not seen the thieves. They would have circled any ranches in daylight.

He avoided the little town itself, doubting that these men would expose themselves during the day, at least not leading four stolen horses. The Hills rise up out of the prairie with no reason or excuse. Rocky top-soil laced with gravelly cut banks, scrub pine, outcroppings of rock, and pure water springs seep out of the hillsides to form small frozen waterfalls.

The lingering gray overcast hid the tops of the hills, ice crystals hanging in the air, evening fast approaching. He came in from the east, slowly scouting across each change in the lay of the land, each gully and draw. Midway through the hills he found the four horses tethered in a copse of wind-twisted cedars along a draw half way from the hilltop. No men were in sight. He ventured that they had gone back to the village, any warm spot, any food. Would they return here this evening or settle into the town? He found remnants of a fire beside a boulder at the head of the draw. They might not feel safe in town, on the chance that they were followed. He could hardly endure the cold much longer himself, but if he rode into town, those who knew him, that is nearly everyone in town, would know something was awry with two strangers already there. He wanted the horses returned without great fuss, and the perpetrators jailed with the evidence in hand.

Darkness would be complete in an hour, maybe less. He sought out a boulder just higher on the ridge, pulled his buffalo robe close, and waited. Shortly, three men approached the campsite. Two pulled sawn logs from their saddlebags and began to relight the fire. The larger man brought the horses into the gathering fire light, where a man wearing a mackinaw and a bowler hat over his head scarf ran his hands down to the fetlocks of each horse, examined for saddle marks and brands. He found a small S brand on the right cheek of a bay mare, and said, "This was one of Jack Sully's hosses, you got a bill a sale?" The bigger man said "Yes, I do", and reached inside his jacket.

Jack stepped from behind the boulder with the Spencer leveled at the big man. "No you don't, not signed by me you don't". The big man flashed forth with a pistol, swung around and fired before Jack could clearly see his intention. Jack had leveled the cocked rifle at his hip; only ten yards separated them. The pistol shot snapped chips off the boulder; Jack reacted, pulled the trigger. The big man went down like a sack of rocks, like the piebald colt must have. Jack pulled the Navy Colt from his waistband as the other man went for a saddle gun. Jack intended no further mistakes like that last one, and shot him in the back, dead center, as he pulled the rifle from its scabbard.

In the confusion, the smaller man disappeared. Jack dropped back behind the boulder, avoiding the fire light, and averted his eyes from the fire's glare, sought a shadow or movement. The horses settled down, and shortly Jack could hear rocks sliding, sensed movement to his left. He eased forward, saw a weaving shadow. "Mister, yer in my sights, the fire casts its light on yeh just right. Put your hands where I can see em, and come out very slowly." There was a moment when this young man thought he might escape in the dark, but fear welled in his heart, denied him the chance. He slowly moved into the light. "I ain't armed, don't shoot...I'll go ta jail, whatever you say."

"Yer a horse thief, and you'll hang, jail or not."

A small figure, more boy than man, edged into the light. "Mister, I ain't never done this before and I didn't wanna do it now but I ain't gotta red cent. I can't eat. We begged food down below... I won't never do this again."

In the light Jack could see a young man, poorly dressed, trousers worn and torn, long johns exposed, tucked into unpolished cavalry boots that looked too large. His mackinaw ragged at the sleeves, showing years of wear. He had a pair of good leather mittens, likely stolen. Jack marveled that he had ridden in this cold for at least three days without freezing; maybe he was frostbitten now. He had not run, and maybe couldn't. He went immediately to the fire, sat with his boots nearly in the fire, dropped his mittens and rubbed his hands over the warmth.

"Where you from, boy?"

"I come up from Missoura, worked a boat up ta Chamberlain. My god, I think my feet are frozen. I hired on ta help Ben Trabert. They call him 'Duck'... but I didn't intend to steal no hosses, I just couldna hepped it, but couldnt get away neither. I cain't live in this cold without him helpin' me. We was going back to Chamberlain, I was gonna leave him. He's a mean sonofabitch anyway. ...Is he bad hurt?"

"He looks dead to me. Ain't moved since he went down that I can see."

"Please Mister, I'm tellin' the truth, I ain't no thief."

"Well, maybe you ain't by choice, but ya are a hoss thief." He looked at the kid. He could not bring himself to shoot him in cold blood, the easy thing, with two dead already, and if he took him to Bijou Hills or Brule City, the law would likely hang him or send him to Sioux Falls pen for years. He saw a bit of himself, not so many years before, uncertain, easily in trouble at some hog ranch. Jack saw in his face the despair of knowing that he had done wrong but not knowing just how or when he had lost his footing on the slippery slope of legal doings, seeming to have had little other choice, and now the realization of his peril, the anguish of having been caught. He could be lying, but Jack considered him too naïve to lie so well. Yet still, he was old enough to know better.

"Boy, put your hands on the boulder, and spread yer legs." Jack, came up behind him as he leaned forward, slipped his knife from its sheath, drew off the boy's scarf, pulled on the lobe and sliced away half of his ear. The boy screamed and grabbed at it, turned, blood seeping through his fingers. Jack stepped back, stared at his terrified countenance. He thought he would be tortured more. He crouched, prepared to run or strike back, but he knew not which. Blood ran down his neck.

Jack raised his pistol, threatened him back against the boulder. "Now you been marked as a hoss thief in this country. You best get away from here, and know that if you come back, anyone losin' a horse that you might be near, might be workin' a spread, ther gonna come fer you....Get your horse an bring it here. You got a rifle?"

"I ain't."

The boy led his horse to Jack, covered his ear with his kerchief and wrapped his scarf under his chin.

"Where'd ya get this horse, ain't yours likely?"

"Duck gave it to me, that's all I know. 'Cause I was ridin' fer him,' he said."

"Its got a brand, but I can't make it out. You get caught with this horse by the wrong people, yer still in trouble. Reckon you better sell him and get back on a boat come spring. I see you again in Dakota Territory, I'll shoot ya."

"Mister, I'll go easy, I ain't about ta cause no trouble."

Jack saw tears. He was pathetic, silently pleading. Jack saw in him the animal will to endure, but to persevere? He doubted. Yet, he wavered, help a hoss thief or send him to a frozen tundra, likely to freeze to death? Jack's own experiences with cold Dakota winters crossed his mind. It was no way to die. He could no more throw him to the elements than he could shoot him. The ride to Chamberlain would surely kill him, or he would lose his feet, his hands; shooting him now would almost be humane. "Boy!...come here." He searched him for a pistol or knife, his body odor wafted pungent as he opened his coat, but found no weapon. "Get some wood outa those saddle bags, build up the fire. Warm yourself."

Jack went through the bowler man's pockets and war bag. Inside was $150, a faded daguerreotype: a whiskered man in a dark suit, boiled collar, sitting, a women standing behind; stern faces, his parents, most likely. He regretted shooting this one, he was local, a horse trader most likely, but after the narrow escape with the big guy, the reflexes Jim Riley had trained into him as they had practiced so often in Texas took over. He thought of John Kincaid and Jim. They would not have hesitated; Jim would have shot them both from behind the boulder, took no chances. Jack laid out the bodies, legs straight, arms folded across their chests. They would be frozen by morning, but ready for the coffin. The big man's pockets were empty save a Barlow knife.

Jack tucked the money into his shirt pocket and moved close to the resurging fire. "Why'd you leave Missoura, Boy?"

"I hate mules....followed those big asses in a furrow for so many years, I wanted outa Misoury. My Pa was a son of a bitch. Mean as a snake....Ma, she was alright; never whipped me, even when I was a youngun."

They sat near the fire, warming themselves, silent, gazing into the flame, knowing it would barely last the night. Jack could let him go, and if he sought no revenge for the ear mark, he would go on to another territory. If he were really thinking of ways to bushwhack Jack, letting him go would cause no end of trouble. On the other hand, he did not sense real danger in this boy.

As black night turned to gray dawning, Jack said, "Listen here....I'll tell ya what to do. I don't want those horses you rode in on. Take the best one fer yourself, and later, sell the other, get some money for food. I'll make out a bill a sale, might get ya through to some other place. You go straight east toward the sun in the mornin, don't chance Chamberlain with that hoss. I'll tell the deputy sheriff that you and I jumped these hoss thieves, had a fight an ya lost yer ear. They's no doubt about them bein' hoss thieves, deputy will see that. Then ya get goin' east. Can ya do that?" In fact, Jack had no intention of involving the law in this fracas.

"Mister, I am grateful, I am. I can do that."

"Get outa Dakota. I'll kill ya if I see ya again." Jack almost meant it.

The boy believed him with all his might. He struggled into the saddle and pulled the horse around, lifted the reins of the trail horse. Jack took up the lead rope of his horses, and they headed down the hill.

Back at his cabin, Jack saw Betsy Diamond's buckboard at the front door, horse standing, head down in the wind and spitting snow. Inside, Louisa lay asleep, did not wake when he entered. Betsy rushed to Jack held him from waking her. It could not be...yet it was. Louisa, the baby.

"Jack, I was too late, I didn't know she was in trouble. I came this morning, I left home at daylight. Still, it was too late. She is hurt. She fell on the ice, near the wood pile, and her leg is badly hurt. She has had stomach pains. I don't know what to do."

"Betsy, is her leg broken?"

"No, but her knee is swollen and she cannot walk."

Aside from the wind, the house was cold as the outdoors, the fire Betsy had rekindled just beginning to warm the room.

He went to her, but her sleep interrupted by babbling, stirring, restless but not awake. Betsy pulled Jack away from the bed. "Jack, she must rest now, but the baby could be in trouble... she must go to a doctor. You must get her to Chamberlain."

Jack sat on the foot of the bed, with his head in his hands, still, tears welling. He watched the snow begin to slowly drip from his moccasins. He had seen death and the dead; the fear of losing his child consumed him, his whole being overwhelmed with the weight of his failing. He should never have left her. He had ridden the reservation lands on patrol, his squadron had chased renegades and reservation leavers but he had never knowingly shot an Indian. There was only that young buck down at Julesburg. Betsy's concern showed in her face, obvious from her tone, her demeanor. He had gone through all that war and raiding and pursuing, surviving, avoiding more killing. Now two deaths dealt. A death at his door in return; punishment so soon.

"My god, how will I tell Papa Drapeau?" He said aloud.

Betsy put her arm around his drooping shoulders. "I'll help as I can, Jack. I will stop at the Drapeau home and ask them to come here quickly, but you must tell them of the worst. I fear for the little one."

Jack helped her to the wagon, wrapped her in her blankets and sent her off. He sat still, head down, waiting, hardly moving until Louise awoke, her eyes avoided his. "I stooped for another log, and my leg slipped on the ice, I must have hit my head too." She took his hand. He turned to her, held her close. Uncertainty and fear he could not hide. He spooned Betsy's soup for her. It was all he could do. She slept again and Jack waited.

In the coming week the weather broke. Jack bundled Louise into Narcisse Drapeau's buckboard and set out for Chamberlain, and Dr Harringdon. His news gave little comfort, though he confirmed a faint heart beat in the belly. Louise wanted to stay East River, with her family, south of Chamberlain. It made sense to Jack, though he would be away from her tending to his stock, she and the family would not have to confront the vagaries of the Missouri River should she need the Dr. During Jack's visits, Louise found her voice, and regained much of her vivacious spirit, but surely not all. She pressed her stomach, feeling for life, wishing and hoping to herself. She saw the sadness in Jack's countenance. He tried to perk her up, joked as they had before, and she tried to laugh with the vigor of before. Yet, she broke off her laugh too soon, looked away too soon.

For three months she lingered, slowly succumbing to the burden of the child, the uncertainty. She could hardly confirm a kicking, live baby. Jack remained constantly at her side, but she could not regain her strength or her vivaciousness; she pined away at Jack's ever guilty countenance, pleaded that he not blame himself, but his nature would prevail, guilt not assuaged. By end of May the lack of pulse made an inducement imperative. She was too weak by then to survive. In the end, the family returned her body to the little church and cemetery over the river where they had married, to bury her beside her kin.

Mary

She had survived three husbands, she reflected, and had not deserved to lose any of them.

Each of them a good man in his own right, different as chickens and turkeys and eagles, but deserving of the love she felt for them, that also being different in each case. Yes, she had loved each to full capacity of her place and occasion, as she could feel it in her being, as it grew and matured until being with Jack was all of her. She committed to each in their time, completely, and could not imagine living without them when she lived with them. Her grief, so intense at each death, taught her love, intensifying in each case, until Jack's leaving exhausted her soul of any possibility to accept, live with, or love another man.

Henry Brindell loved Mary, in a stolid, reserved way. He directed his limited intensity more to his work as storekeeper at the Whetstone Agency than to intimacy. He was an attractive man, possibly more lonely than in love when they married. This Mary surmised years after his death of pneumonia ended the only year of their marriage. Her father had approved of him, and he was a solid, grounded man. She had been comfortable with him, his simple shyness, his daily small kindnesses. His pleasure in seeing her happy. He was well aware of her difficult childhood, her father away for long periods, her mother working odd jobs, cleaning, washing, ironing to see their way, a day at a time. But she grew into a great beauty, dark brown hair, fair of skin, straight of posture. Her dark eyes warmed the recipients of her gaze, her smile seldom long from her countenance. He brought her dresses from the store that showed her figure to best advantage, though surely not ostentatiously; a blue calico, a light pink cotton for summer; fine wool, loden green, with waist jacket for winter. She wore them well, they suited her well. Before becoming ill, he had even promised her a piano.

He lay sick for six weeks, and as he seemed to get better, one day tried to walk in the back yard, among spring flowers, only to return to bed and die within hours. Mary mourned truly, missing his calmness, his presence, and then she mourned for her loss and what he had meant for her own future. The store was in debt, and she had no means of payment. The bank sold it soon enough when she deeded it back to them.

Only days passed before John Kincaid returned to the Whetstone and began anew to court the grieving widow. He had lost out to the more stable and less rambunctious Henry the previous year, but now her bad fortune was his good fortune; with himself in position to fulfill his south Kansas dreams. John made her happy, he laughed and joked, showed off on his horses, took her on picnics, but he drank, and remained away from the Agency for unexplained reasons during the year he first pursued her. Her mother had found him beguiling, but she worried too much for her daughter to approve his courtship.

Now those barriers did not fully obtain. That he had money upon his return was plain. He seldom drank now, and worked closely with Jack Sully, his old acquaintance, who had returned with him from Texas and places south. She laughed again at his new and wilder stories. She watched him win the Sunday horse races, seeming never to have a hard race against the local challengers. She found his remonstrations irresistible, his persistence always cheerful, though nearly daily, never failed to enchant nor were ever boring. She removed the black arm band before her year of widowing ended, marrying John a week later on an island in the middle of the Missouri, close to the Charles Mix County side where the license was issued.

Quickly came three children, first Amy, then John's pride, William, young Billy, named after his favorite and most lucrative racehorse, and last, Estelle. John the strutting peacock had won his prize, and settled in, as few who knew him would have imagined, to care for Mary and their family. Jack could not suffer living in the cabin in which he had lost so much, his first family, and built another cabin farther up the hill, on the edge of the Flats. John often worked with Jack, within the year becoming his foreman, overseeing a herd of over 200 cattle, and working Jack's horses. Jack helped John move into his vacated cabin in the creek line. John began again to take unexplained trips; he said only that he was chasing mustangs in the Sand Hills with Jack, and the growing size of Jack's horse herd left no suspicion otherwise. She would understand later that Jack's cattle holdings were also increasing. For the family, life was as good as it got on the Dakota prairie, not to worry about food, just enough hard cash, prospects for building a ranch, trips to Oacoma and Chamberlain twice a year. They would travel for as long as two days to attend a dance at a lone ranch house. They helped the honyockers shuck corn two or three times, taking home several bushels for the milk cow's wintering. They bought a used buckboard, John repaired and repainted it; they loaded the youngsters and a picnic basket on warm Sundays and went to the river to pole fish, swim, and lay out a trot line for catfish and bullheads; in the fall to bring back wagons of fire wood. In season, they spent days picking berries and fruit from the creeks feeding the Missouri. Mary learned canning from the honyockers and put up plums, buffalo berries, and tomatoes from her small garden; and, when she could muster enough sugar, also grape and chokecherry jams and crab apple butter. She especially looked for chokecherries, which she pounded into jerky for the pemmican John and Jack always carried. The joy in the girls' eyes when Jack brought them a brown and white spotted pony on Amy's birthday, making them promise to share. She could still see them, riding double on that little pony, Scout, their hair long and free in the wind.

John's Passing

And John's death. She could hardly bare the image, even these long years later, of his emaciated face, his sad, watery eyes sunk into his skull, his voice fallen to a rasping, hoarse whisper. So distraught, the smile gone forever, the pain doubling him into a cramped fetus, groaning and moaning, even as he bit his fist attempting to stifle his embarrassment in front of the children. The laudanum from the doctor in Chamberlain ("tumor in the belly", he said, "can't cut it out, and no cure is known to exist") was never enough, he ran out after three months, no shipment expected for months. She bathed him in warm Epson salts soaked scarves and handkerchiefs. The medicinal smell lingered in the cabin, a tortured reminder for a year.

He could not lie on his back to sleep, the tumor pressured the nerves of his internal organs. He sat, day and night, slumped in the one cushioned chair they owned. He could not control his moaning. He gasped, short rasping breathes, holding back the sounds of pain, releasing the pent-up agony with a groan, then a long despairing moan. She could not for years, remembering John later, ever forget the rhythm of agony and despair, his staring, ocean green eyes never meeting hers, always looking past her shoulder, as if ashamed of himself.

He begged for death. He whispered as she held him, "Take me to the river, let me sink in, let me float away, let it end." He asked her to shoot him. She could not, she was Catholic. Mary hid his pistol and rifle. He knew but said nothing, having accepted that she feared more for his eternal life than for the corporal pain. She truly feared that such a sin assured eternal damnation. Not so for John, but he could not press his own trigger in the cabin where the family would have to live with the image forever. He pushed up from his throne of pain, yet could not stand; Mary rushed to his side, lifted and eased him back, unable to move beyond the chair without her aid.

Jack came nearly every day near the end. He sat with John, quietly reminiscing their partnership, Texas and Kansas, the Sandhills, horse races, horses they had known. The big red sorrel that had won them so much independence, had won him Mary Gullette. He rolled the cylinder on his revolver, no bullets, aimed at a knot in the wall, clicked the trigger. Jack felt the question rising, avoided it. Later, when Mary had hidden the pistol, John asked Jack to see his. "Take out the bullets if you care to." But, Jack suspected somewhere in the cabin a bullet lay stashed. Jack told him what he had seen out on the Rosebud, new families coming in, honyockers, hardly building a home before plowing up the prairie. Did the rain follow the plow? Then maybe they would get some soon. The past summer had been dryer than usual, this new one tending to follow suit.

They discussed the increasing danger presented by the Sioux in western Dakota. Raids on outlying ranches for cattle and horses had increased. The bucks were leaving the reservations, meeting up with Sitting Bull and Crazy Horse in Montana. Generals Crook and Terry had left Ft Abraham Lincoln in Bismarck moving west at their chosen speed, which was slowly. They could not leave John nor could he survive a trip to the safety of east river settlements.

And in the end, Jack took John by buckboard to the river breaks. He was gone a long time, appearing again, like a ghost in the low lantern light of the cabin, to whisper that "He is at rest. No more pain."

She poured him lukewarm coffee, and thanked him softly. "He loved you too, Jack. You were his best friend, nearly his only true friend."

"He asked me to care for you and the children. I promised. I will....I have marked his grave, and propose a stone marker later." He stared into the fire for many minutes, then, rose, pushed his hat down firmly, and left into a pitch-black prairie night. All the implications, unsaid, seemed untoward at this moment.

Rising Fear

J ack honored the grieving ritual for Mary. She owned no black mourning dress, instead wore her plain gray wool work habit with a black band at the arm. She did not smile, and rarely spoke, and then only with the children in a soft, patronizing way. He allowed her the time he felt she must need, providing deer and some grouse for the larder, a trip to Oacoma for flour and condiments to sustain her. He suppressed his urge to comfort her, knowing she must in the end find that within herself. At month's end, John Jergins rode at a gallop up to Jack's cabin, with news from Ft Randall. Custer had been killed in Montana, mutilated, him and all his soldiers and his kin. Inflamed by boldness, bands of Sioux were raiding throughout Dakota and Montana. The fort crowded with anxious settlers, demanding safety, they had left their belongings, their hopes and their optimism out on the prairie replaced by the contagious fear that burned, gutted houses, stolen livestock would foment. The Major commanding, at Ft Randall, struggled to accommodate the influx, and to prevent the steady flow of young bucks from around the fort into the raiding bands. He filled the fort area with the families from nearby encampments. Bravado had rekindled the ember of the warrior spirit never quite suppressed by reservation life. Yellow Hair defeated, his scalp on a Sioux coup stick. Stories of the triumph ran rampant through the lodges. From the west came the call to rise, and the bucks responded. Fear amplified from stories of burnt homesteads, black smoke on the horizon, scalped and mutilated bodies wagoned into the fort. Tales of butchered cattle and stolen horses fed the frenzy.

In fact, little evidence of actual destruction and killing in east river Dakota obtained. Braves continued to leave for the western lands of the Black Hills and Montana, to join the victorious Sitting Bull, Gall and Crazy Horse, intent on victory now in a war they had been losing for 15 years. Ranches were raided as bands worked westward, a few actual deaths were recorded, but the myth and panic exceeded the actuality.

John Jergins brought more immediate disheartening news. Red Shirt was among those jailed at the fort. He had not resisted, expecting that an explanation of his history working with Whetstone Agency and the contingent at the fort would result in his quick release. His case went unheeded. He was Indian, the major told John, and would be treated like any other. With the major's permission, John spoke with Red Shirt for but a few minutes. He sought Jack's help.

Jack immediately understood the feverish spirit of roaming Sioux bands, and the real danger they presented. Whether or not there were raiding parties in the Missouri River area, safeguards must prevail. From his experience, Jack could not underestimate the renowned skills of Sioux raiding parties. His thoughts turned immediately to Mary and her children.

"John, I will need your help. Mary Kinkaid and her young are recently alone and now in danger. You have a covered wagon still. I need to use it to move her and her things east...are you moving yourself?"

"Red Shirt says the danger is not as feared. He sees the action more out west, Sittin Bull's gettin' chased ta Canada. Our friendlies won't be moving, from what he says. I would have more fear of horse rustlin' from wanderin' trash then redmen. I'm gonna stick it out, and watch my stock. Only reason to go east is if my stock is run off. I'd rather not let that happen."

"Understand. But for Mary Kinkaid, I need to take precautions."

"I'll bring the wagon up in the mornin', have em ready and we can load out. The fort ain't the place to go. Little food, too many people. I would take em straight east, cross the river and head for the settlement along Platte Creek. Spite a what Red Shirt says, some young bucks parta the Bull Creek Sioux might get excited, I would avoid a trip through their territory to Chamberlain."

Mary looked back into the cabin as Jack explained the plan, fear for her young obvious, knowing that having Indian blood would have little bearing on the intentions of raiding hot-bloods. Jack's own serious countenance overcame any possible reluctance to leave her home unsecured.

She folded quilts, blankets and clothes, stuffing all into flour and gunny sacks. Canned stock and flour she secured into two lidded boxes. Jack stood quietly, gazing at the sacks and boxes. Mary turned away; how little of John Kinkaid's life and work remained for this surviving family. John's wagon could float the river, but aside from that its bulk was of little use for Mary's sparse possessions. She would be gone, and he would miss her. She remained so calm, repressing open anxiety for the children's sake.

Jack snaked out the rope length to two lariats, slipped one end to the wagon tailgate, the other to his saddle horn, using Buck's size and strength to help maneuver the wagon across the river at the point where the team had to swim and the wagon wheels lost traction. The big team struggled, but the wagon stayed course with Jack's help. Billy waved as he loosed the rope from the tailgate, and Jack pulled in the slack. John waved, Jack coiled up and set out for Fort Randall.

The Major cared little at first for Jack's request to release Red Shirt. "I have my orders, Mr Sully, and will not make exceptions for every whiner that petitions my office. He's Sioux, he stays."

"Red Shirt has ridden as a scout when I soldiered out of this very Fort, and he worked as a teamster at Whetstone Agency with me as well. He is more white than Indian in his heart."

"He was in the lodge of Lone Wolf when we rounded up the bucks, and that makes him Indian. Look what he wears. Braid, buckskins, moccasins, leggin's."

A useful lie had slipped Jack's lips before, and he found no compunction to do so now. "As I said, I have long known him, and his father, ole Bill Bourdeax out at Rosebud. He is a Métis with few ties to Lone Wolf's band. Ain't like he don't smoke a pipe with him, but he'd be far more loyal to workin' with you than those loose, rampagin' bucks."

Jack had sown some doubt. "I'll allow as how he is light enough and looks like a breed."

"And its one less mouth to feed what little rations you got here. I'll take him to my cabin, he will work with me and be my responsibility until this Sioux fracas is done."

"You take him, and you will pay for any damage arising from his actions. I don't need to hold a half breed that knows his station." He called his adjutant and passed the order for release.

Red Shirt's compassion for the sorry situation of the locked braves showed in his face. He had not eaten since his confinement, his face was drawn, and the inner pain of disloyally leaving the suffering innocents behind was clear to Jack. Yet, they both knew that no good purpose could be achieved by his continued sequestration. He walked beside Buck through the double doors and up the hill past the cemetery before Jack persuaded him to swing up behind for the ride home. Too much pride in this guy, sometimes, he thought.

Bringing Mary Back

Jack paid more than usual attention to the news of the Sioux Uprising that he could obtain in Chamberlain and Ft Randall. In the months following the Battle of the Little Bighorn, after raids subsided, more of Crook's and Terry's troops lumbered into eastern Montana, and Sitting Bull finally headed over the border to Canada, pursued aggressively by the adventurous Colonel Miles. Life in western Dakota eased back to normality. Homesteads reclaimed, stock rounded up, burned ranch houses, rebuilt. Cowhands traveled in threes, herds were more closely herded. Some beeves were lost in Dakota, but the turmoil swirled in Montana.

With the river at a seasonal high, Jack brought Mary and the children back to their cabin by way of the Chamberlain pontoon bridge. The Van Patten family that had been quick to offer hearth and home in the face of Indian raids, could not be expected to suffer the inconvenience of an overlong stay. Mary gracefully thanked those kind Dutch folk and packed her meager belongings, in hopeful anticipation of the independence the old cabin afforded. She would miss the afternoon teas served in Delft blue, the calmness of the house, when the men were away, the Dutch plat mixed with broken English. Couldn't she build such civility into her own west river life some day? Or couldn't she find a home of her own back in the civilized east river?

John weathered the trip anxiously anticipating Mary's every word for acceptance. With John alive, their discussions were amicable, friendly and cheerful. Now, his longing drove out the casual approach. He took care to speak of the weather, the possibility of Sioux raids, how the Bull Creek Sioux were reacting, the state of the Kinkaid cabin (in which John had dusted down and set a fire in the fireplace). Finally home, Jack offered his hand to the weary Mary, helped her from the wagon to the cabin. The children dropped off the end gate, stretched and ran around the cabin, to the empty corral. Jack assured them that their ponies were safe and cared for at his place. Mary squeezed his hand and thanked him with a smile

Jack would never forget, for it promised the encouragement he sought, longed for during her absence, so close now. That she had come back offered promise.

A few days later, as had been his custom, morning light just creeping over the Flats, Jack knocked at the Kinkaid cabin door, and entered, as if John were there. He walked to the stove, lifted the black-bottomed coffee pot. The room just overcoming the morning coolness, quiet, with three children still abed, and Mary at the table staring at the cup in her hands. His intention had been to frequent the house only when entirely necessary, staying away as long as he could responsibly, deferring to the widow's customary grief year. Knowing she would need his help, he remained true to his vow to John.

With pot in hand, he turned, speaking clearly, a bit awkwardly, in his best diction, "Good morning, Mary. May I have some coffee?" Had John been there, he would need not have asked. Now her presence dominated the warming cabin air. She turned to a pan on the table and quietly began snipping the ends off green beans from her garden. Her new accessibility Jack felt imposing, it shortened his breath, constricted his chest. He could not find the words to speak of the obvious bond between them. Taking her silence for consent, he stood sipping at the tin cup, delaying what he hoped to say.

"Of course, Jack, you are welcome now as always." She smiled, a slight turn of the mouth, cocking her head, curious at this unusually formal tone, a small sign intimating at inner tension from the stress during John's dying, the suffocating gloom of this house of pain and suffering.

He began in a blurt, "I have attempted to keep my promise to John. I have thought of it, I have puzzled a bit over how to do that and not cause you trouble, ...gossip. Coming here so often. I don't know how to say it, but I have feelings for you, and I think marrying you would be the best thing for us both....and, ...and it would be the best for relations with our neighbors."

"Your sentiments echo Marshall John Petrie, strangely enough. Do you love me, Jack?"

It was not a question that he expected. He fumbled for words, for a dignified response, but failed. "I think I do, I…, I don't know how to say it."

Jack could hardly find the words for what he felt. No small tincture of guilt for the way he had looked at Mary while John lived. At her body, and how he had stifled a young man's longing, telling himself 'not her, but someone like her'. And for her sweetness, and kindness toward him. Their exchange of glances. He felt she wanted him, he daydreamed that she wanted him, there was a warmth, something intense. He found relief with women in Oacoma and Chamberlain, sometimes Ft Pierre, but the gentle longing returned to his soul when he rode back onto the Flats. Each return visit only heightened the longing.

Did he love her? Such a hard question he thought. Or did he just desire her? That, of course, but surely more. She was a fine women, a hard working and compassionate wife to John. He respected her, surely. Yes, with all, he told himself, he did love her.

And, however true that may have been then, throughout the remainder of his life, that love grew to the grandest proportions possible within him.

"You must know, Jack, you must do more than 'think it.'" Her demeanor changed, her smile disappeared as she turned to Jack. "But, another issue has arisen, and I am unsure as to how to handle it. Marshall Petrie visited me in Platte, and asked about John. I told him that John had died of the cancer, and that you had buried him. He asked about the official death certification, and I could not answer. He may ask us again. He did not seem satisfied with my answer, seemed concerned that I was coming back to the Whetstone."

He sipped his coffee, tested its temperature, gulped it down. He walked to the table, placed the cup down. "I will come back soon, Mary". He avoided her eyes, but she sought his. At the door, he paused, glanced to see her smile, her moist brown eyes, and closed it softly.

In the week's absence he felt obligated to observe, Jack rode to Mitchell to find Marshall John Petrie. John's death and burial must be explained.

Mary returning to Whetstone, his own desire to have her, determination to have her, all amounted to basis for rumor, for trouble, possibly legal if anyone suspected how John had actually expired. He rolled the possibilities around his head for most of the trip, and confounded by his own culpability, they did not stick until he remembered the doctor in Chamberlain and the laudanum prescription. The doctor knew that John was a goner. He had taken the essential step of easing John's pain because he knew the inevitable end. Jack need not go further than to describe the death, the burial and to offer the Marshall the opportunity to examine the body. That would be a bluff that he hoped would play out.

"Marshall, you've heard the explanation from both Mary and me. John Riley died of cancer, a miserable dying it was, and I buried him among the trees along the Whetstone, up the ridge above the Missouri. You left Mary with concern because she felt you were unsure of her explanation. I wish to ease your concern with my own explanation, and to offer that you contact Doctor Harringdon in Chamberlain, who attended John on more than one occasion, pronounced his condition as incurable, and provided laudanum to ease his pain."

"Its not that I don't believe either you or Mary, but as Marshall, its my duty to administer the details of a death, and with the coroner, record such officially." The Marshall saw Jack's countenance change, his teeth clench. He did not care to question his word, the doctor's confirmation would make an end to it. As Sheriff, Jack had occasion to perform the same administrative tasks, he was aware. "I will complete the certificate, and ask that you present it to the Charles Mix county coroner upon your return home. Please put Mrs Riley's concerns at ease, Jack. She is a fine woman of good upbringing, and I am pained to have cast any shadow on her integrity."

Jack crossed the room, grasped the Marshall's hand. "This will put an end to it, John. Mary has borne this sorrowful period as well as could be expected. She has lost her second husband, and has three children to care for. I intend to keep the promise asked of me by John to care for her. I have lost my best friend, a man I cowboyed with up from Texas, through

Kansas. We hunted horses in the Sandhills, we drank from the same coffee pot in the middle of the prairie. We raced and won with the best of horses." Jack could have gone on, but the effect was clear in John Petrie's gaze. He sat, and motioned that Jack take the adjoining chair, offered coffee.

The discussion turned to the Indian rising, the fears among the populace, even in the towns of the east river; to the weather; to the continuing lawlessness in the west river reservation lands. Jack sat quietly, passively, as the marshal recounted examining the bodies of two men found on the north slope of Bijou Hills, apparently one horse thief shot in the back and the local horse trader from the Hills Livery stable done as well. "I know the killer went east, took the horses, whatever these two had. No money on the bodies, but guns and a saddle left behind. Still frozen stiff as boards when I got there." Jack just shook his head, pursed his lips, implying a "what next" attitude. The Marshall went on to chat about a local bank robbery in Mitchell, brazen, broad daylight, "scared the dickens out of the lady customers, only got a hundred dollars or so." Coffee gone, Jack scraped back his chair and rose to leave. "Mary Riley deserves the care that you promised her dying husband, Jack. I expect that you will meet that promise with the same good intentions I have always seen in you." He intended no sarcasm and showed none. Life and the vagaries of survival on the frontier were not strangers to John Petrie. Jack correctly understood that he approved what the natural outcome of caring for Mary meant in real terms.

Jack prepared his words on the long ride home. He knew then, and should have spoken plainly. John was gone. He needed to throw off his guilt for his current wanton desire for her, there was no further need of caution. Next day he dressed in his black suit, a clean white shirt and his best boots. He wore no spurs, but uncovered his best pearl gray hat, brim stiff and clean. As he rode to the cabin, his mind played again at what he might say, but nothing seemed right. He breathed deeply, trying to calm himself, not able to think at all. He tied his horse, loosened the cinch. Rising to full height, he pulled his suit coat straight, tugged at the shirt sleeves, stepped to the door, scrapped his already clean boots, and knocked. She had dressed in a fine gingham full length dress that day, light blue, snug at the waist with swooping neck line, hinting at the soft flesh beneath. As though she had anticipated exactly his day of return.

"I wish to speak plainly and fervently with you Mary. Would you step outside, away from the children?"

She dropped her apron across the nearest chair, took his arm, closed the door and they walked quietly across the dusty prairie yard toward the pole barn. Inside, she stopped at the manger, half full of hay and looked up at him, beguiling smile, knowing eyes, asking without words.

He looked down at his hat brim, rolled in his nervous hands. "Mary, I love you,... I am so very sure ...will you marry me?"

She kissed him fully, a kiss of consent, of promise. She turned her back, reached behind to grasp the long skirt at knee level and pulled it above her unfettered waist. She bent forward, grasped the manger log, shadowy light through the uncaulked poles revealed the round, white, smooth, firmness, as perfect as Jack's dreams. He entered her quickly. The heat of her, his own eagerness overwhelmed, his anticipation of this dream turned to reality so unexpectedly, precluded a sustained sexual encounter, but it was one totally satisfying to both and held promise of a great future. She had offered with no condition but love, and he had taken likewise. Mary fluffed her skirt and turned to Jack, placed her hand along his cheek and kissed him softly, fully, her lips moist and fervent. A future without this woman now became unimaginable.

Mary had answered his question with action, as he could so well appreciate. There was a marriage, and a wedding dance for all the neighbors, none of whom were surprised that Mary and Jack had soon married. Maybe Jack was the most surprised.

Beyond simple pride in his handsome offspring, he strove to envelop the Kincaid children into his realm as if they were his own blood. She would understand later: his own childhood family disrupted brutally, his father's long absences, and final departure, must have steeled him to provide well for his own family, what he had not experienced in his youth, what he must have longed for, seeking warmth and love. She saw him at the door, hands on his hips, staring as the girls urged Scout across the yard, at Billy working a mare in the corral. He threw back his shoulders, breathed deeply, exhaled a long, relaxing breath. She turned back to the stove, stirred a simmering pot of beans.

Building a Ranch

T hough eager to forsake the old log cabin, he put first things first, and built a new, larger pole barn, the timber cut from the breaks and tree stands of the Missouri islands, Dakota timber laws notwithstanding. Off to the west edge of the barn, his round pole corral easily restrained 20 horses. Before winter, he had freighted two wagons of cut timber beams, shingles, and clapboard to build a house. Neighbors pitched in, quickly raised the roof beam, and had the shingles on before the first snow. The family luxuriated in the expanse, the high ceilings, the second floor bedrooms. Soon enough it would become crowded, but for now, it brightened prospects for everyone. They slept in cold bedrooms, crowding around the pot bellied stove early every morning, rekindling life, preparing for a day of striving for wood and water, after all, surviving until spring.

Late evening in early June, Billy brought two large catfish and bad news up from the Missouri. Along the bottoms and into the breaks north of where the Whetstone meets Ol' Muddy, were 50 to 100 strange cattle, maybe more; Billy did not track north more than a mile. Next morning, he, Billy and Mary rode to the river, found over a hundred head of mixed brand steers and cows from the northern and western ranges. The Rosebud being open only to Indian cattle, Jack could legally move the cattle back northwest. In two days, he had the herd near the Nelson boys spread south of the White River. He sent Mary and Billy home, and rode to Olof Nelson's ranch to inform him. Nelsons had also rounded up over a hundred head, and promised to move Jack's herd with theirs to the White River crossing.

In similar fashion, Jack, Billy, his neighbors, Olaf, John Jergins, and sometimes Mary and the older girls spent days in the saddle, cleansing the Rosebud ranges of the creeping pestilence of longhorns from the big ranches, like giant locusts, scourges of the land.

Butterflies and a Milk Cow

J ack broke out of the White River bottoms two miles west of its mouth
on the Missouri and stopped at the crest of the bluffs. He slowed his
mare in a patch of buffalo grass, lush, curly leaves soft as a shag carpet.
Two white butterflies caught his eye, twirling, pirouetting, twisting in a
dance or a fight, he could not discern. He chewed at a bittersweet stem of
salt grass and laid down on the buffalo grass, basked in the warming sun.
Like Mary and him, he thought, were the butterflies fighting or a dancing?
Of course, he and Mary rarely argued, but the sparring between them had
grown over the years. She had cast a mystical spell over him when he first
saw her, light of step, slim of waist, slight knowing smile as she glanced
back at him from her doorway. She was Jim's and he made no overtures,
yet his heart raced in her presence.

The tragic circumstances of their joining overcome, how close they
had become now; at first a mating frenzy, drawn to each other, the sex so
intense, like those white flitting butterflies, fast and furious. Time mellowed that, children always nearby, but the caring and love did not diminish as it changed. She tolerated his long absences, knew there were parts
of him she could never tame; attempting to do so would damage the relationship beyond repair. He thought of himself as never having betrayed
her. 'I came close, I guess. That time in Deadwood; but he did not
remember any sex, he hardly remembered going to the hotel room, and
woke beside the woman, head throbbing, recalling nothing of the rest of
the evening. As much as he had consumed, it was unlikely that anything
happened. Nor in Valentine, at the Purty Ranch, or was it Pretty Ranch?
Same thing…and he had his long johns on when he woke. 'I wouldna
done either time if I wasn't drunk.' The butterflies rose into the air but
dropped back to the bed of grass to rest, their wings still slowly waving.

By mid-afternoon he was within a few miles of his home on the flats.
He saw a lone figure standing on the next hill, so turned into a draw and
skirted back into the Missouri ravines, coming up the next tree-lined draw

to get a closer look. A boy, now striding south, bib overalls, and no shirt. He approached out of the box elders at a walk. The boy stopped and stared at him. "What er ya doin' out here alone? You lost? Runnin' away from home?"

"Nope. I'm lookin' for our milk cow. I came out this mornin' and she was gone. She's bullin' I guess, looking for some company up here where the other cattle are. But I caint find her."

"Come here, ride with me a while an we'll look." He pulled the boy up behind him and set off. "What's your name, son?"

"George McDonald. They call me Shorty, cause I ain't growed much yet. I live over on Phelps Island with the Miz Matson. The cow went across cause the river is so low now. She's a reddish shorthorn cow, you seen her?"

"I came from the north, and did not see such an animal. She a real milk cow?"

"Yep, big bag, gives near a gallon right now. Her calf died or was stolen, and like I said, she's bullin. They get sorta squirrelly then. We need that cow, ain't got much to eat right now, its good that she's still wet."

Jack now understood. The boy was still living with the widow Matson, whose husband was shot in the back by Phelps or one of his henchmen. They had used the island as a holding area for rustled stock, but after convicted of the murder, Phelps was held in jail, where he died, whether from the poison of evil, or the poison of revenge only the deputy sheriff knows. Now the Nelsons used the island for the same purpose. Jack had not been on the island since Phelps shot Matson.

"What's Miz Matson doing there now? She makin a go of it?"

"Well, hardly doin so. She has her own horse and some cows, but she is moving soon, she says. The corn was washed out with the rains in early summer."

They continued to search for the cow in the draws and gullies as they moved south, but to no purchase.

"Stay the night with me, son, and I'll take you home in the mornin. Its late, and my wife will fix supper soon. I've a house full of kids, myself."

The boy was silent. He had seldom been in company of those his own age. Orphaned before he knew his mother or father, he survived solely by the good graces of Ms Matson, she herself, now left with no family but Shorty.

The Sully family children nearly overwhelmed the naturally reticent Shorty. They showed him their hand-carved toys and dolls, shared a long session of wonderment at each new page of a Sears and Roebuck catalog, all self-consciously speeding past the ladies garment pages, as their Mother had taught them. He ate voraciously, constraining his gulping mouthfuls as best he could. After supper, he played with the wooden horses and cows Jack had whittled and carved over the past long winter, but blanched at even touching the toy pistols and rifles. Jack conjured the vision of a ten year old, seeing his step father shot in the back at the supper table, having to scramble out the door to avoid the same consequences himself, and running ten miles barefoot to retrieve medical assistance for Matt Matson, who died in the meantime. The boy testified at the murder trial, sending a murderer to jail, with vile looks and threats as reward.

Next morning, Jack called the boy aside and asked if he could "put a rope halter on that red milk cow in the small pasture over there?"

"Yes, sir, I could, if I can get close nuff to rope er."

"Well, she's plumb tame, so just walk up to her." Jack saddled his mare and pulled the boy up behind him, and with rope tethered to the milk cow, rode off to his island home. "Use her as long as her milk holds up, Mrs Matson." She could hardly speak, seeing the boy and this stranger come into the yard, then turn away quickly. The boy ran after Jack, "Thanks, Mr. Sully, thanks a lot." Jack smiled and loped away...

The Root Cause - Great Dakota Boom 1879 -1884

*E*ntrepreneurs, aspiring landowners, naïve city slickers, riff-raff, even a few lone, hardy women, responded to the Homestead Act, heading for the lands of opportunity freed up by Congress and the end of the Indian Wars, during the good, wet years. In their multitudes they came to escape the feudal nightmares of old Europe, the slums of New York, or even the growing populations of the good, green lands of Ohio, Illinois, Iowa; to dream new dreams, to rekindle their old ones, to reach for freedom from civilization's constraints. The grasslands greened early, prairie grasses grew knee high with the June rains, browned slowly, naturally, in the August heat. The gumbo-loam earth beneath, plowed and planted, spewed forth its bounty, 40- and 50-bushel per acre wheat. Letters east gushed with hope and promise. Free land. No taxes. No trees or rocks to clear. Varieties of wild game plentiful. A stage for the American dream, wealth for the fearless, the man or woman with backbone. Train lines extended to the Missouri's east bank carrying farmers near the promise of the nether bank. As the East River lands teemed with homesteads, small ranchers began to cross the River into the Rosebud, and they prospered as well, herds of a hundred cattle, a few horses, thriving on the rich grass, ample water, open spaces. The Dakota Boom which filled the eastern half of the state compelled hard pressed late arrivals to expand west and began to compromise the small ranchers. The old Texans, coming north through Oklahoma, Kansas, had seen all this before. They were pushed west and north off the best grasslands of the southern plains, slowly choked out of free, open range by homesteaders. Western Dakota was the last great grassland frontier. They responded by filling that range to its bursting. Their ranches, often little more than a dugout on the open prairie surrounded by ten thousand head of cattle, thrived too. There existed a period of calm in the social strata. The land provided for all. Its great breadth satisfied all. Yet, while the vast ranges, north and west of the Rosebud were still open, the threat of encroaching homesteaders, the possibility of losing the open ranges vital to their welfare, quickly began to register with the cattle syndicates. Their concern would prove premature, for nature would intervene and they would put their early fears on hold.

Feast in the Rosebud 1880-1884

*T*he first most venturesome pioneers in the Rosebud spread out from the railheads on the Missouri River's east bank onto the fertile prairie in the early 1880's to find a rich loam based soil, adequate rainfall, an environment where hard work could make real a farmer's dreams. They came in all manner of prospector, some with just a plow and a scythe, their family in a wagon, tent tarp as wagon cover, their home on wheels. They were escapists: from corruption, from family problems, from the claustrophobia of civilization, from the lack of fair prospects, from poverty, from the law. Each crossing their own new, personal border, a promise of new prospects. Within them, of uncommon measure, was a grit and determination beyond that characteristic of the motley crowds from which they had escaped.

Rain makes grain. The rains in May and June sustained the wheat and rye and oats, as much as 40-50 bushels to the acre, helped sprout corn that reached "knee high by the Fourth of July". Game, deer, antelope, prairie chickens, brought variety, vegetable gardens spiced up their corn meal based cuisine. A man could easily forecast prosperity in light of these prospects. Desolate though it now looked, venturesome newcomers saw towns and cities blossoming on this great grassy expanse. Visions of wealth from its soil sprung forth in promises as profuse as any land in America might provide. Land free of trees and rocks, no need for backbreaking land clearing. Lucky had been the adventurous. Surely, as the railroads and land speculators prophesized, rain follows the plow. Those who had disdained this land for that further west over the Rockies missed their great good chance; here, in the great disregarded middle of America, once on maps described as "the Great American Desert", lay America's last frontier.

The government's grand plan, as witnessed in new homesteader laws and policies, though not a transparent campaign, was to squeeze the Indians onto the reservations, free up the farming lands, attract settlers, and encourage the railroads to help populate this promising kingdom.

German, Scandinavian, Bohemian, Russian family farmers settled in, built their sod houses, planted their fields and for the lucky ones, realized five years of plenty in spite of backbreaking work, hard winters, and little hard cash.

Prospects

Jack learned from a cowboy in Oacoma that 'Ole Pap', E. W. Whitcomb, had pulled out of Wyoming, headed east to the southern Black Hills area where pure grass ranges, clear of rock and sagebrush and yucca, were plentiful and land still free and open. He had established a ranch there on Hat Creek and rapidly improved the homestead and the size of his herd. Looking for opportunity, for good advise, Jack sought his wisdom. A naturally fair man, and an enduring relationship of mutual respect, he might well be in a position to help expand Jack's own ranching situation. For Jack, his burgeoning daily workload, and natural ambition demanded action, change, vision and hope. Billy still too young for heavy ranch work, John gone, Olaf settled in as his foreman and steady hand. Horse trading provided a strong base operation, but in the larger view was limited by demand. There was a market for maybe fifty horses, whereas the Eastern market for cattle, tallow and hides, numbered in the thousands each year. He needed to expand his enterprise. He had proven himself a good cowhand, an excellent horseman, and would find no satisfaction in any prospects less than building his own expansive range operation.

Jack's awareness of 'Ole Pap's' talent at mounting capital for large operations piqued his desire to learn. With his backing, Jack saw an opportunity. Bill Whitcomb had seen the eastern Rosebud grasslands, he would know instinctively how substantial were the prospects. Great herds of Texas beeves continued to spread across the landscape. A timely investment could cement his position, set him on the path to enterprise.

Fall horse sales ended well. He took a mixed herd of draft and buggy teams and some saddle horses east over the river to good effect. Only some light herding remained before settling in for the winter. The price of a long ride seemed worthwhile and the time most opportune. Late fall weather had held, each day starting cool but warming by noon, each day sunny, clear skied.

After a short night in the Lamoreaux spread's bunkhouse, he made for Bill Bordeaux's Trading Post for layover on the second day. He and Bill bantered a while, sipped some whiskey, ate flat bread and stew before retiring early. He aimed to stay the next night at Pine Ridge rather than push his horse hard to make Pap's ranch. He had no specific directions on getting there in any case, so he ruled out a search after dark.

Pap welcomed Jack warmly. He was a man who valued a good cowhand, which Jack had proven to be.

"Son, you look right well appointed, some nice tack you got."

Jack swung easily out of the saddle, shook his hand, and tipped back his hat. "Well, I seen how you worked at settin up a ranch, and decided to do the same. What I come for is ta say hello again, and ta also get some advise. I gotta bottle from Bordeaux's ifn ya got a mind to sip a bit."

"Whiskey never hurt a man with a head ta know nuff ta stop. Bring it in. Two oldest gals off to school, young Liddy still here. You come courting Jack? I seen ya eyein my girls on the Platte."

"Pap, they are an eyeful, but I have settled with a fine woman from Ft Pierre. She is the widow of my friend, your old cowhand, John Kinkaid. I am sorry to say that he has passed. He left Mary and three children, and I have taken them under wing. John died hard, and too young. I have lost a true friend."

"By gun you mean?"

Jack could not answer directly. Neither Pap nor anyone else could have accepted the truth. "He had bad stomach cancer....his pain was great, just agony. Nothing to do for him but wait....its been some four years, Pap, an I ain't over the agony of it, really."

Pap glanced at Jack, saw his dark stare, and changed tone. "Let's go on in now, no sense ta relive that. So you want advice about marryin this woman or some other social grace you ain't yet learned?" he joked.

Jack took advantage of the change. "I come for the one thing ya know something about Bill, cows an ranchin. You know anything else in this life?"

"I do, Jack, but it don't matter much more than ranchin, least ways fer me anymore."

Jack spelled out his plan, his need for capital, money to buy large, maybe move a herd up from Texas himself. That was an undertaking of considerable magnitude for a man in Jack's position, and he knew it. Yet, he also knew that he could do it. His confidence was evident to Bill Whitcomb, but he also knew how difficult it would be to convince banks and investors of this venture. Jack had little if any collateral, was unknown but to few other than Bill of his character and capacity to succeed on a larger scale. Bill, already in debt for his new operation, could not offer financial help.

"Jack, I will talk to a man, the man, who might be able to help. I don't know anyone other than John Clay with connections back ta the East. Let me get ta Cheyenne and set up a meetin. It won't be of no good fer ya to go alone, that I assure ya."

"Bill, I am near Oacoma, leave a letter at the post office there, or with Bill Bordeaux at his tradin post. I get out that far on occasion."

They drank enough to feel warm, to recount old times on the North Platte, recall old friends and their fortunes. Bill spoke of Cheyenne with some optimism. Cattle had been trailed into the Wyoming ranges by thousands, just the reason he had moved east. Ahead of what he saw coming to Dakota. Jack's case for a large ranch in the east Rosebud made sense to him.

Bill slapped Jack's mare on the rump as Jack turned back east, and assured him that he would look into his idea. Yet, in Dakota of those days, the seasons passed, relentlessly devouring the best of intentions. Bill Whitcomb was not a man to forsake his word, but there would pass two iterations of roundups squeezed between frigid winters and stultifying summers before Ol Pap could well and faithfully respond to his promise.

Death of a Friend

Jack rode back east aiming for Bordeaux's before late evening the second day. He pushed his horse at a slow lope, and pulled up to the hitching rail just as darkness foreclosed on a brilliant western sun.

Bill did not greet him at the door, though it was unlatched. A candle stub flickered an unrevealing light across the worn and cluttered table top. Bill slumped on it, head on his arm. He looked up slowly at Jack. The effects of too much drink shown dully in his eyes. "I lost my son, Jack, my only son. Shot dead a day ago. John's dead."

"Bill, whatta yeh mean,... what happened? He wouldn't hurt nobody himself.

"He was at the Casterline road ranch. Some deserters from the fort came in, started shootin, and John was hit. Red Shirt was through here at noon, on the trail a the bastards. They shot a Army Lieutenant, Lt Cherry too. Army came out from Ft Niobrara, after em.

"What the hell started this thing?"

Bill sat quietly, staring at the dying candle. "John was the new foreman fer the Agency. He and soma his boys went to get some strays down easta the fort. Went inta the saloon ta get warm, I guess. Three deserter soldiers came in after Ol' Casterline's cash and he took his sawed-off to em. Wounded two of em, but there was lots of shots fired. Red Shirt was there, with John. He said he threw up a table, hid behind it, but John couldn't get back fast enough. They shot and ran out. One a Red Shirt's Inyun Police saw em going north, followed fer a while but lost em in the dark."

"Red Shirt is not a Inyun police no more. He quit when they killed Crazy Horse."

"Well, what happened was, then the Lieutenant signed him up to help chase these bastards, do the trailin. Then, before they could light out, another drunk soldier shot the Lt. Red Shirt brung back his braves and took over the chase, came by here on his way north, going to Westover. Said he figured they was headed that way, and he'd get em."

"He's the closest I ever had to a brother, Bill. Those times huntin out here, riding out horses, halter breakin. Remember that little spot he first broke, just a young kid then. I helped him up slow, the colt never bucked, just took to John, trusted him. I'll catch up with Red Shirt. If I was ever gonna kill a man, it'll be the onet shot John."

"Well, Jack, you ain't gonna catch Red Shirt an his boys. They got more'n a days start on yeh. They hit Westover and they could go west to Deadwood, or east to Chamberlain, Ft Pierre, who knows. I need some help here, if yeh don't mind. My boy is still at the fort, and I need someone to bring him to the cemetery at St Charles. The wife still don't know, and I am gonna have to go to Rosebud to give her some awful bad news."

Jack took Bill's light wagon to Ft Niobrara, which lay thirty miles south. Even the wind at his back on the way down was raw, and facing it coming back burned his face, numbed his hands on the reins. The cemetery was near St Francis, on the reservation, near the Nebraska border. Light dry snow wisped through the short grass, so he walked beside the wagon part way, exercising for warmth. Jack helped with the funeral arrangements and stayed for the church service. Nothing the priest said made sense to Jack. He didn't know John, who probably never set foot in a church, and the words rang hollow. Jack looked past the priest at the door, refused his hand as graciously as he could on the way out. He stood stamping his feet in the cold, watched the coffin lowered, seeing part of himself and Ol Bill go underground. Just when he had made somethin of himself, Jack thought, a real foreman, getting ahead. There weren't no reason for it, just none.

The gloom at the trading post, Bill staring at the fireplace, his wife silently weeping, arousing the stew pot, stabbing at the log fire, trying to busy herself. Jack begged leave, and set out on a cold ride to the Whetstone early next morning.

Two weeks later, Red Shirt rode onto the Flats, trailing a horse with rider tied to the saddle. "There was three of em, Jack. I knew they was set fer Westover; it's a badman's town anyway, and they was gonna need food and supplies. They was there, and I followed the river west, and then east, finally saw where they came out, moren two miles down river. River was open some, but I saw the broken ice. Tracks headed up north, all the way to the Bad River, then east, so I knew they would hit Ft Pierre. I found em in the Rattler Bar, already drinkin too much. I put my braids up under my hat, looked like a white man. Swift Bird and Oliver Dion and me come up behind em and tried to take their guns. I got this one's gun outta his holster, but the other two jumped over the bar and ran. We all shot, and the one soldier was killed, Johnson it was found to be. Dick Burr got away, and I had my gun in the back a this one all the time. Oliver said for me to take him to Yankton, and I'm doing it."

"I don't want this sonofabitch in my house, around my wife and kids. Take him to the barn. I'll be down to help." Jack stepped back into his house, directed Mary to keep the kids away from the barn.

Red Shirt had tied the man's feet to the stirrups, and his hands behind his back. It made for hard riding, but insured his security. Jack was unacquainted with the man, "Tedde Redd," he answered through cracked lips, head hanging, when asked his name. Jack tied him to a pole, hands behind him, legs and neck fast to the center pole. "Ya can't leave me here in the cold, I'll freeze to death!"

"Well, I'll warm yeh up. And he hit him hard in the stomach, then a right and a left to his head. The man had no chance to avoid the blows, and he got more before Red Shirt stopped Jack. "You killed a good man, a good friend. You go ta court and some goddam lawyer is gonna get you off, but I will have my satisfaction." He hit him again.

"Jack, that's enough! I gotta take im to Yankton, I'm trusted with him. He don't get there an the Major at the Fort will know I done something to him. I got $40 coming when I get him to Yankton."

They left the man sagging in the ropes, went to the house and ate supper. Three hours later, the cold sharpening, they tied him in the manger, wrapped him in two saddle blankets and covered him with hay. The next day they rode out with a weak and defenseless prisoner who Jack tended to with his fists each evening on the way to the Territorial capitol.

The Missouri had not broken up, the air holes plainly in view, even with the light covering of snow. "We could drop the sonofabitch through a ice hole, Red Shirt, take him in dead, drownded, nobody would complain much." The man groaned, looked up, surveyed the river, his eyes glazed, said unheeded, "I never shot that cowboy." "Might not get my money, Jack." Two weeks later, the Territorial Court pronounced his guilt and hung him the next day.

Bull Creek, Summer - 1883

The new day sloughed its nightshirt just as Jack did, morning light spreading over dewless prairie grasses still curled overnight from the burning June days. The top of the sun's orange disk peaked over the river hills, rose to a formless, burning yellow brilliance within the hour.

Jack pulled a white shirt from the clothing cupboard, a clean, pressed pair of black trousers. He stepped into his dress boots and took his good white Stetson from its hook. He needed a quick run to the store for Mary.

Jack laid a loose toss of his lariat over a nearly white, gray-spackled mare that stood at 16 hands. Already at a sweat, he saddled her slowly, and looking out over the cloudless sky, took a chance and hung his slicker on a nail. Sauntering back toward the house, he skirted the sad looking flower bed, and stopped as Mary came out the door, letting the screen door bounce behind her. She handed him a list of groceries and a gunny-sack to tie to the saddle, asked quietly and calmly for his swift return. "Please, no whiskey." He smiled, "Not this time, lady, only business." He pulled Mary close before mounting and pointing the gray mare north to Oacoma. At the corner of the house, he paused. "Maybe a little water for that petunia, looks mighty dry." He had his little joke and lightened the departure. The spring was dry, and he had gone south along the Whet-stone two miles before divining another worthy location, hollowing out a small dam, lining it with rocks as it slowly drained away muddy residue. They had rationed water, sacrificing Mary's marigold and hollyhock gar-den to the unrelenting sun, until she insisted upon water to save just one plant. "Seeds, Jack, for next year. Please, I'll bring the water from the new seep." His silent smile signaled his acquiescence.

The prairie wind, unceasing, in a word. A still day being as infre-quent as rain in the desert. In the winter, from the northwest, winds bringing biting cold Alaskan temperatures across the northern Rockies, revving up across Canadian plains, blasting the Dakotas, Nebraska, even as far as Texas and Oklahoma before expending themselves. Bringing wisps of snow, lightly sprinkling the dry grasses or blizzards dumping oceans of snow, changing the leather tan prairie to a desert of white shifting snow. Ground winds shifting white snow snakes along the ground, or hardening crusts on man-tall snow banks. Bending trees into bizarre shapes. In spring, mixing a cold norther one day with a warming southern the next transforms the frozen gumbo to slogging mud. Boots packed with gumbo mud one day, slipping on frozen ice patches the next. The southern winds of summer bring the heat of Texas and Oklahoma and Kansas, shimmering heat waves along the horizon, a steady 25 miles per hour until it blows into the brain, a maddening, unrelenting pressure that drove the toughest homesteaders crazy. The homesteader women nearly always posed, hand to head, holding flying hair in place while her apron and full skirt flared north by the droning, snaking wind. It bleached the grasses to browns and tans and beiges, stunted the cottonwoods, desiccated the plums and grapes and buffalo berries, dried the White River and its sister Missouri tributaries to ankle deep, slothful flows, pools with shimmering minnows drying up until the silver flapped in mud, dying .

Cattle turned white faces to the summer wind, keeping flies from their eyes. Tails constantly switching, heads slinging saliva as they swung across the mats of flies on their backs, finding relief from the heel flies by standing in the wallows and sloughs and the river. Finding shade in the plum thicketed draws with wild grape vines and wild rose bushes, rubbing on the rough bark, throwing heads across their backs to scatter flys before they settled back in black clouds to feed again, to bury larvae in the hides, grubs welting their backs.

The wind weathered the faces of Indians and cowboys alike into browned husks, lines as records of years spent turning into it, bracing against its brutishness, yielding to its relentlessness.

The searing, dry days of summer, southern wind unabated until eventually in rolled great cumulus clouds, white fluffs with graying linings darkening into black with evening light. Gray thunderheads rolled up as day progressed, blackened bases, trailed blue-gray skirts of rainstorms onto the horizon, moving in from the west by sundown, bringing a cool stillness minutes before high winds lashed rain and hail swathes into the grass, and every living thing ducked its shoulders and sought shelter. Lightning blitzed the sky, cracking thunder, low rumbles trailing away into another onslaught of flash and crack. Leaving struck trees, dead cows, and occasionally an unprotected cowboy, vulnerable when his body heat and that of his horse made him a lightning rod.

Jack angled westerly off the Flats, to ride through the Bull Creek Brule settlement, take a look at the cattle in the area. It was still his task to clear strays from the Indian range. He supplemented his income as a reservation ranger, but normally the day-to-day operations of this enterprise, Olaf attended to. The area had been set aside by Treaty for Indians not wanting to relocate to the reservation proper near Rosebud agency, but who stayed on so called 'non-reservation trust' land. They had been granted herd cattle, oxen, plows, yokes and chains, and most importantly to them, land of their own. The government's treaty had allowed appointment of boss farmers, along with a doctor, carpenter, miller, blacksmith, and engineer. Government also saw fit to provide a gristmill, sawmill, and school. While noble in principle, the nature of men who would move to a village in a nowhere land, without, for the most part, the company of women, at least a day's journey from a proper town, often lacked the motivational characteristics envisioned by the more liberal and enlightened treaty progenitors and signers. In fact, aside from the boss farmer, usually appointed from the Dakota east river area, those other essential skills as intended by Congress generally remained lacking. The lonely boss farmer was on his own.

Jack had faithfully policed these reservation tract lands, both at Bull Creek and Milk Camp, and gained respect for these people, most of whom were of an enterprising nature. They had seen the worst of agency loafers, around-the-fort Indians, who retained the old ways, the old macho spirit of the hunter-warrior Sioux, too proud to plow...which they maintained was work for squaws. Coming across the rangelands south of Medicine Bull's cabin, Jack saw only a forlorn and quizzical yearling heifer, and an old horse, head down, unshod, spavined, asleep on its feet. Where a herd of two or three hundred cattle should have grazed, only a hot wind moved the long-suffering, random tufts of salt grass.

Jack approached the first cabin south, no horses, children, dogs or sign of movement. He saw no clothing or provisions in the cabin, the door swinging open, the squeak and banging of the front shutter the only sound. He set out immediately to the northeast, toward Medicine Bull's small settlement. Small, yet within the Sioux mentality, the center for their own brand of organization. The Sioux are a private people. The family adheres to its piece of land, its teepee, its cabin, but to live in clusters like the whites-built towns belied their solitary, often inward-directed nature. In Medicine Bull's cluster the boss farmer lived, in this case with a young half-breed wife happy in pride of place.

From across the gully before Medicine Bull's house Jack saw no movement except for a yellow-dun spotted dog, tail half curled over its back, which rose up to bark two or three times upon noticing the incoming stranger. He slunk back, around the corner of the cabin as Jack continued his approach, then snarled a low growl, but declined engagement.

Jack dismounted and wrapped a single rein around the porch post of the cabin. Braves, now farmers, revered their intelligent and experienced leader; they had quietly built him a porch, and purchased at relatively considerable expense in Oacoma, a rocking chair. Jack knocked, though he expected no answer, and stepped back, startled, when a voice inside, said, "*How kola,* friend." A small figure rose, raised his hand. Slight of stature, his physiognomy was distinctly Lakota. His graying hair long, tied with red leather strips in two braided strands reaching nearly to his belt. In contrast to the wool suit with vest that he wore even in the stifling heat, his moccasins sported a finely beaded set of six-pointed stars.

Jack entered, his eyes adjusted to the darkness, he saw old Medicine Bull, a cup in his hand, his elbows planted on the table in the room center. "Do you find any cows south of our lands, Ranger?"

"One lonesome heifer, *Tatanka Wakan.* An old horse that you do not want... Where are your people, where are your horses, where are your cattle?"

"Soldiers came, at the last moon, order us out. This land is not for us, they said. The captain, he was polite. He said we are to move, and he brought wagons, soldiers to help, and food for us. He said there is a treaty that says we must go to the reservation. He said that this is no land for farming. He said the land must be open. I have signed the treaty, and I have understood the treaty. I have spoken for my people, for my band. I have eaten the sour words of Spotted Tail, of Red Cloud. I have become a farmer. I have promised peace and food to my people. I have explained the ways for peace, for our own lands, for no one to interfere with us. Now, they take us to Rosebud Agency. They say these lands are not good for us. But they are good, because they are for us, we have our peace. We learn to farm. Our cattle are not many, not so many as you have, or the big ranchers, but we have our peace. My people do not drink, they do not fight, we want to become as the white man who lives in Oacoma, in Chamberlain. Our clothes are as your clothes. We have wagons. Our children are in the schools. Now, they say we must move to Rosebud."

He paused, walked from around the table, dropped his head. "We will die there." He paused, looked out the open door. The prairie slanted away from the porch, the old horse plodded a lonely trek, head down, following the trail of Jack's mare toward the cabin. "Also, two Santee snakes came here, cousins of Lone Wolf's woman, who is part Santee, until a sheriff from south came to take them. I did not know. The Santee are not welcome here, but they have harmed us now by hiding among us." He stopped, looked out the open door. He surveyed his domain. The desiccated, curled, brown grass matched the feeling in his heart.

"You see what is correct, my friend, but this land has not helped you, it has dried to nothing. Your corn never grew, your wheat is only this high," as he spread a single hand across Medicine Bull's vision. "All the white men are also poor. The land is dry for them too. The farmers are leaving White Swan, are leaving the Niobrara, are leaving the flats. This is land for buffalo and cows and horses, not for farming."

Medicine Bull ranked amongst the most learned and intelligent of his race. He had visited the "great white father", and had believed what he heard. He spoke American English, understood it well. He bought into the same future of prosperity that President Grant and his deputies envisioned and truly wished for, but could not deliver, nor could foresee as the consequences resulting from actions carried out by the unprincipled, greed-lust of his minions out west.

"Why are you alone here, my friend? Why have you not gone with your people?"

"I have come for my dog. He does not love me, he loves this place more. I have sent my people with Milk. He takes them to Oacoma, then to Rosebud. I cannot look in the eyes of the women. I do not know myself. I have been weak. They know that, more than the men. My woman left the dog here. She spites me. The Captain told me to return, to see that my people are all moving, that the cattle are moving. That no horses are lost. But our houses are here. Our cabins are here. We cannot take them with us. Now we have no crops, no grain, but we Brules can live here, we can live from the land if they let us."

Jack saw the outcome of all this, the Indian cattle moved, and within a week cattle from the U+ and Scotty Philip ranch, north range herds, would be moving in. Some things never change, he thought.

"Some young bucks are staying in Oacoma, Jack. You see them there. Maybe tell them to come to Rosebud. Me, I don't know."

"You are *Tatanka Wakan*, the leader of your people. You are the only one who can fight the agency on this. It is still your land, by treaty." Medicine Bull hung his head. He had already fought, and lost. His people were moving. He rose slowly, his short, bowed legs strode a jerky walk to his spotted pony back of the cabin. Even at his age, he swung effortlessly aboard and trotted west. "I go now." He did not look back.

Jack nudged the yellow dog in the ribs and then booted his ass; he laid his ears back, Jack threatened again. Retreating sideways, he glanced back, twice, saw Jack swing his leg, then loped after the pony.

Bitterness within him rose up again. Jack had just lost a paying job; who would now clear the Brule lands on Bull Creek of the constant drifting from north and west ranges?

PART III

JUST GET STARTED

JUST GET STARTED

The Plan

J ack rode hard back east after surviving the 1883 winter storm and began in earnest the occupation of professional procurer of other men's chattel. It was not long before his activity drew notice from not only his neighbors, from whom he never stole, but from the larger cattle operators. After three near misses in the court at Presho, he knew it was only a matter of time before someone gave him up. Staying on the reservation usually kept him safe from East River law, but from the rancor on the opposite side of the courtroom he sensed it would be time to lay low, take a vacation. His network of local supporters held up, but one of the accusations came very close to the truth, and the rancher, Scotty Philip, held especial grudges against cow thieves, if few other miscreants. Fortunately, two other accusers set up a time frame which would have caused him to be in three places at once, neither of them would back off their stories, so a sympathetic jury did what it had destined anyway, and threw out all three cases. In the late spring days that followed, Scotty Philip's cowboys roamed south onto the Rosebud, watching over their brands, and as Jack knew, him as well. They would need little excuse to rid themselves of a pestilence in their business. Small time mavericking held no purchase now. Rustling close to home but not from one's neighbors became too selective and thus too dangerous. Opportunity waned.

Mary, again in the early stages of pregnancy, asked him to stay, to work close to home, but because of Jack's sense of survival, his knowledge of occasions where quick ropes without courts solved too many of the syndicate's problems, prompted his resolve to take full precaution. And already bored with the tranquility of home life. Well he knew, a week or so out and he would wish he were home. A warm, bright summer morning put him in the rambling mood; leading a pack horse, he headed to Bordeaux's.

He revisited in his mind the past three years at some length on the long, slow ride. His bank account, in tin tobacco cans under a tree on the Whetstone, grew with each venture into the reiver's art, but he knew that he must find a better way to sell his catches. It was in the illegal sale, the moment when the money changed hands with the false paper accompanying it that presented the real danger. The option of taking cattle west and south to the growing ranches of Nebraska seemed worthy of exploration. He would avoid selling to the syndicates moving more cattle into Dakota, they already held strong suspicions that the small ranchers were cutting into their profits. Its how the west was won, it was how the cattle business worked for striving ranchers. He provided bills of sale, worthless, but off-putting to other ranchers who replicated the practice anyway. Brands were being published more often in local papers, but for the nonce, until the practice grew into brand books and stock growers associations became more powerful, only marginalized the work of the smart rustler. Yet, this kind of operation netted sub-optimal payoff unbalanced against a high level of risk.

Jack contemplated the other alternative, moving cattle south in larger herds. He would not have to traverse the more congested lands near the two Reservation Agencies, where he could be interrupted by Indian cowboys or the wilder braves looking for game or other action. The Sandhill's rolling terrain, ample water holes, fewer, larger ranches presented a good avenue, though the lack of ranches in northern Nebraska presented a problem. Who could he sell to? Omaha's large packing plants were a far reach, but because of their constant need for critters, and the sure fire quick disposal of evidence, they were a good option. He needed a connection to the meat plants, a relay ranch in the eastern Sandhills. A possibility. Maybe he'd ride on into Valentine, fast becoming a prospering end station for the westward creeping railroads.

Now, prospects for a bottle at Bordeaux's kept him pointed west, a lay up, some palaver with Ol' Bill, and a run over to Rosebud to see Red Shirt.

Jack, cranked his aching back out of the saddle, dropped Buck's reins, and eased the cinch. He checked the packhorse, keeping the diamond hitch tight for now. Bill eventually stood in the doorway, smiled, and waved Jack into the cabin. "The wife ain't home Jack, down to Rosebud to see her folks. Still got some stew, some fried bread. Hunker in."

Having eaten only pemmican for two days, Jack lit into the warm stew, and half stale bread, willingly even. "Bill, ya old coot, how's days? Getting' rich? They catch you selling whiskey to the Indians yet?" So the talk went, weather, how they survived the winter, who had been by the trading post, and what new ranches had sprung up. Bill mentioned the T Bar, E. W. Whitcomb, owner and boss cowman, one of the largest spreads, out west of Pine Ridge, south of the Hills. "You talked to Ol' Bill yourself?"

"He wandered in, late spring, looking for drifters, I guess. Didn't know the Post was here. Small fella, older looking? Rode a real nice roan gelding."

"The same. I worked for him down south, heard he came north, and talked to him a couple years back over on Hat Creek. Hell, that gelding must be moren ten years old. Bill ain't as old as he looks, but he is as wise as he looks. Knows his cattle. Ran a good outfit on the Platte. I came north with a herd of his, taking it to Ft Randall for the Yankton Sioux. Stayed on there, as ya know. Yeah, I need to see Ol' Bill again. His men call him Mr Whitcomb, but among themselves he's Ol Pap, er Ol Pappy. After I ramroded the herd north, he told me to call him Bill. I'll head out that way from here, catch ya on the way back."

Jack's visit coincided with Bill Whitcomb's thoughts on how to enlarge his own operations in Dakota. He saw prospects for bigger herds north on the Cheyenne River and on up to the Moreau and the Bell Fourche arteries. The lush prairie easily sustained the scattered small herds, the range was legally open to all, and the Indian problems of 1876 had subsided. There were no reservations between the Pine Ridge on up to the Standing Rock. He foresaw the larger influx of cattle that Eastern and English money conveyed.

For now, Jack listened, held his thoughts on illicit trading in western Dakota. Bill simply would not tolerate rustling. He might suspect Jack, many small ranchers worked the edges of the game, but he knew nothing of Jack's delicate encounters with the Presho courts. Jack gazed into the fire, putting aside plans for large scale rustling. It was but one way, a dangerous way... better to remain on the level if he could.

Bill Whitcomb had arranged the meeting, respecting the hard work and skills of Jack from his days cowboying for him on the North Platte. They proceeded to Cheyenne, Bill advising Jack on the proper suit and hat for the occasion, black gabardine would do, and a regular Stetson, no short-brimmed bankers style. Boots, dark brown and plain, well polished. Bill fashioned a black ribbon tie to Jack's top buttoned white shirt, held in place by a cheap glass stick pin. He looked like a "dressed up cowboy", but was the image Bill thought would sell. "I look like a dude, Bill."

"And right dapper you are, young man.."

The Cheyenne Club (John Clay)

J ack stood before the long mirror in the parlor of the Cheyenne Club
for a moment, reflecting on what he saw. New black suit coat and
trousers, boots shined, white starched shirt. He removed his hat,
smoothed the pomaded hair, and backed away a step. Though under six
feet even in high heeled boots, his lean frame rendered the notion of a
taller man. His angular, muscled arms strained against his new coat.
Straight black hair to his collar and a drooping mustache over a dour countenance left a lingering impression of strength and intelligence not to gain-
say. He sought no trouble but stood granite-like in its face, confident that
at the table this evening, he would find no dissenting diner.

There was champagne before dinner. Two glasses. Weak stuff to
him. The chicken, so tender that it fell off the bone, came in a white, creamy
sauce (coq au vin); some boiled vegetables: white cloudy shaped things (cau-
liflower), round green balls (Brussels sprouts), long green snaky things
(asparagus), thin sliced potatoes (au gratin), and small carrots, the only two
vegetable he recognized. All in a cream sauce. Jack went for the chicken,
watched as the others ate their heavily sauced vegetables before he picked at
them and found them delicious. In all, very fine fare. He finished his meal,
and still not sated, waited to see who might order seconds, but none did. A
mellow rose wine came with the dinner, followed thereafter by a tumbler of
Scottish malt whisky Clay had shipped all the way from Edinburgh. Jack
played follower during the meal, using the same silverware as John Clay, as he
seemed to dominate the table. He put the diners at ease, chatty stories of his
time on the range, true enough, they seemed. Dressed like an easterner, but
he surely knew cattle and horses, knew the plains and mountains of
Wyoming. Yet he talked often of Scotland, his friends there, the syndicates
and banks he worked with. Strange man. He came across as 'Ol' Pap' said,
self-possessed, confident, the most powerful man in the cattle business.

John Clay had earned that distinction, whatever men may have
thought of him as a miserly, hard driving protector of his sponsor's money.

Clay was, in the old Scottish sense, *factor* for large ranching interests for his Scots bankers. Guarantor on the ranges for the herds which they had bet would repay them ten fold. He wasted little of their capital on offices, expensive foremen, over-priced bulls, fancy horses or carriages (though often as not he traversed the range in a handmade, sturdy buckboard). He took particularly good care of his working cowpunchers, and never fired anyone that had cared well for his cattle. He stopped the practice of "tailin" and rope whipping by the Texans who called that sport, as too abusive of the animals. He sought quality bulls, valued weight in his herd above shear numbers. He prohibited drinking and gambling at any time on ranch property. In town, he bailed out the drunks and misdemeanor offenders, but low the rustler or robber that crossed his path.

Bill Whitcomb had moved operations east from Wyoming to run the largest ranch in southwest Dakota, putting him closer to the beef market the Reservations provided. The prospects for moving more cattle into the territory interested Clay considerably. Bill owed him money now, but with more cattle, another year or two, and he expected to be fully out from under his obligation. The northern prairie lay in waiting for large herds. Bill had taken John Clay aside before dinner, and made the case for the Rosebud. On east, with only one or two large ranches, it also had the water and tall grass to sustain larger herds. Bill touted Jack as foreman for a large holding on those Indian lands. He knew the Indians, the territory, and had friends. He had been sheriff in the area. He knew him to be smart, ambitious, and capable of running a great spread, given the opportunity.

Jack sat upright, uneasily in his chair, eyes averted to the floor during the discussion among the cowmen, as the distinction in name and interests became quite clear. The cowman was first a businessman, protective of his herd, which was his equity, essence of his being. Jack listened intently over his whiskey to the expressions of evil against the thieving homesteaders, small ranchers, Indians, wolves. He stilled his tongue, looked into the whiskey glass, taking in the one-sided argument: where was the concern for all the legitimately acquired cattle belonging to small ranchers that the big boys rounded up and sold each fall? When did they ever pay for fields trampled, gardens ruined by foraging range cattle, and even cattle purposely driven through homesteads; where was payment to the Indian tribes for the thousands of illicit syndicate cattle grazing the reservation ranges; or what consideration for fellow ranchers contributed unceasingly to massive overgrazing on the open ranges. If the ranges were open, were they not open to all? John Clay was an outspoken, articulate and emotional proponent of the noble cowboy, discoursing on the purity of range capitalism, on the dignity of the cowpunchers work, the value of dividends to the syndicates, their risk and rewards for this noble god's work. To the depredations of thieves and rustlers he not only allotted a special place in the cowman's hell, but seemed bent on assisting their early consignment thereto. He was a friend and doubtless, but unproven, employer of Tom Horn, a man committed to summary dispatch of known, if legally unproven, rustlers. The fine whiskey and receptive company brought out the cheerfully garrulous nature of John Clay, as he recited from memory, poems of his school and university days. Cigars were brought out, and they wandered toward the veranda that encircled the great house.

Jack could find no words to counter such beliefs, no eloquence to match this well-educated Scotsman. The frustration in him swelled, an urge to lash out only overcome by his own good sense, understanding innately the futility of such an action. This was not the place, he was a guest; it was not his nature. He did not speak now, but the financial machinations of John Clay and his cohorts, specifically James Craig in Dakota, would inevitably arouse in Jack a strain of righteous indignation sufficient to provoke significant action against them, and more particularly their greater, general interests, the cattle syndicates; and not just a cow here and there. What would Clay have thought had he known the true nature of the well-appointed cowboy drinking his best whiskey, with a deceptive smile taking in his arrogant implications of superiority?

Jack felt himself begin to slide on the slippery slope of too much whiskey. He turned and headed toward the door.

"That's a chesty bastard," Jack blurted, stumbled against a porch chair, and leaned against Ol' Pap Whitcomb. The whiskey curled his toes, smoother but alcoholically stronger than the hog ranch stuff. It had raised his testy side, but Pap eased him toward the steps before the cowboy nature came out. They stood on the veranda of the Cheyenne Club, Jack weaving in place, Pap with a hand under his elbow. John Clay, a sinister smile passing his Scots countenance, standing inside the door, had heard, and as always, noted, not to be forgotten. He had not succeeded in life by harboring snakes at his bosom, and this cowboy would never be close again.

"What the hell was he talkin' about in there? The 'noble cowherd'! Fer chrissakes, he says he rode the ranges himself, then he oughta know better. I ain't no cowherd, and if I'm 'noble' as he says, I'll damned well shoot his balls off and see if he accounts that as noble. He meant to make a fool a me."

"As I have on many the occasion heard Mr. Clay expound on old Scots ballads, I can say he suggested no insult by his use of the word, its from an old pastoral poem. He don't mean nothing by all that, he sees cowboys as the knights of the range, loyal, true to women and horses alike. Hard riders and hard livers, but capable of great feats. He gives lectures, and some a that carries into the Club. He talks like a foreigner cause he is one, but he knows the money business together with the cow business, and out here that makes him a damn important fella. He rode for me two years, I hardly knew he was nothing but a cow hand. Worked hard, never drank or played cards. He left for a year and come back in city clothes, loaned me money to move to Dakota. I'm beholden to him, but with more cows, I can damned sure right that.... You can forget about workin' as foreman for him, Jack, you can't call that man a " silver tongued city slicker" in the Club, in front of all those real city slickers, even if you thought you were jokin'. Damn. I think you had a chance for a while. He listened real well."

Jack had no answer now, turned to face the night breeze. "That's some good whiskey, Bill, no bite, but its strong. I could feel it coming on me fast...He don't carry no pocket pistol does he?" Jack joked again.

"Let's go, we ain't gonna find out." He grasped Jack's arm and conducted him down the steps. He looked back at the domed Club, saw the lights in every room, heard the music from the parlor, and wondered when he dared return. Not like the regulars there did not get wired up, but anyone hoping to continue partaking of the Club's fancy food, refined whiskey, and fortunate business connections kept his feelings and thoughts constrained around the likes of John Clay.

E. W. Whitcomb found himself on both sides of this schism on the ranges. He was both owner and foreman, close to his men but protective and caring of his cattle. He looked old when he was 25, a wizened face, lines forming prematurely; his sage comments came in short bursts, but impressive for all that. He had weathered the Civil War, the open range, Indian wars, and would figure in the range wars to come. Jack never heard him yell at man or horse, maybe some dumb cows or a stubborn mule, but an even temper and countenance prevailed in his life. Old Pap walked the high wire between both sides, lived on both sides, and respected the positions of both sides. Jack's respect for him kept him from walking back into the Club and buying another whiskey, even if it meant slugging John Clay in the mouth. Hell, there must be another saloon in this town, he thought. They wandered down the street and found it.

Jack wandered the streets of Cheyenne the next day. He did not feel like riding out, civilization here was at its highest in the old west. The everyday ordinariness of surveying the goods in mercantile stores, buying a new shirt, new underclothes, something he surely needed, and a dress for Mary, some small things for the girls. Late afternoon found him at the end of the boardwalk, where he sauntered into a hardware and gun store. Lying in the glass gun case right of the counter, Jack spied a pearl handled revolver. He enquired, and the owner smiled, commenting on how fine a piece it was, one that he had only acquired the past day from a man down on his luck and heading East.

Jack noted with interest that it fired 44.40 caliber rounds, exactly what his Winchester 73 used. He switched it from hand to hand, spun the cylinder and pushed the ejection rod. Well oiled, its functionality and feel were perfect. On the other hand, this gun was designed to kill people, something Jack had foresworn. His rifle's practicability sufficed for range work, this he knew, but to walk down the street with this special piece could serve the useful purpose of silently stating "leave me alone". From the case the clerk pulled a finely tooled leather holster. "This was made to order for that fine revolver, and I would recommend it highly. Fits the barrel size, and rides snuggly on your hip." Jack began the haggling, but the clerk relented little; he could read that look in Jack's eyes. He laid down the cash, took also a box of shells, and hitched holster and gun to his belt. He sloughed his jacket over it, felt its presence with a new sense of confidence.

"Jack, it's a fine piece of work. I might have purchased it myself, had I seen it first." He hefted it, aimed it out the window, ran his fingers along the pearl handle. "In fact, I don't need it, an neither do you. Don't get ta thinkin you have to use it for its intended purpose. Its made for the cavalry, for the Army, to kill people."

Jack took the piece from Ol' Bill, nodded, and holstered it. He bought it for show; having it was deterrent enough. He had no intention of drawing it in anger.

Olaf Finstad

I have known Jack ever since I come across the river to live.

'Yah, I talked like an old Norwegian, but I came to America and wanted to become American. I'm like Ole in that regard. He never cared to stay with the old Norwegians, he felt at home in America right away. Hell, I din't even want to stay around Ole that much. We was educated in Norway, eight years. Our father made us go ta school, and then wanted us both to be fishermen. When I read books in school about other lands, I knew I would never stay there and smell them damned fish all my life. I don't even fish in the Missouri, when it's got big catfish, and bullheads galore. Ole does. Comes over, spends a day or two fishin, goes home and fries em up. Miz Sully made some catfish steaks one time, and I ate em, but could just as soon had beef. So, when I got to America, I spoke English all I could, and began to read newspapers, books when I could find em. I stopped talking "sing songy" as Jack would call my talk, right after callin me a dumb Swede. Took me a while to understand what he was talking about, but when I went to White Swan and heard all those Swedes talking, I knew. Ther worse then us Norwegians, but Ole does it still, I notice when I go see him. Jack and I go in the fall and buy a pig from Ole, butcher it right there. It's nice to have something besides cow on occasion. Once in a while we get a deer, or turkeys, when we hunt in the trees and along the bottom. In the fall there's plenty of prairie chickens. Antelope is good if you know how to fix it, but damned hard to shoot one a those running devils. Harry could do it, and brought em back after wolfing trips. The elk are all gone west, never had many here anyways. I'd sooner eat a gopher as a fish.'

Olaf ventured to America from Norway a year after his brother Ole, who had come to get rich, but soon settled on being a farmer. Olaf came because he hated fish, and Trondheim meant fish. Hauling stinking nets, throwing tuna and bluefish and halibut into buckets and carts, kicking fish heads as you walked home, rotten fish in summer, frozen fish in winter, and on top of that, nothing to eat but fish and bread. Two letters from Ole fueled his long held desire to be anywhere but Trondheim, and in spite of his father's ranting, then his pleading, he shipped down to Oslo, and took a boat to the US. He set out for Minnesota, searching for Ole, arriving at his homestead to find him loading a small two-wheeled, box wagon to go west. Indians were still troubling farmers in Minnesota, and too many people for Ole. Land he heard was free in Dakota, so he lit out, one horse, wagon full, though Olaf's one shoulder bag easily fit in. They went first to Beresford, but, again, the best land was taken, and Ole said he didn't want to be around all those Norwegians for long, he wanted to learn more English, and he wanted fewer neighbors. Olaf had little objection to that logic, and they continued on to the Missouri, then northward. Bijou Hills' three-building main street suggested just the right amount of civilization, so after a long walk, with open, unclaimed land stretched in all directions, Ole found his ideal place in the rich gumbo south of town.

For Ole's ultimate dream was to build a set piece farm like those Swedes had done in Minnesota, one he could write to father bragging on his ambition and foresight, urging other Tronheimers to come to the land of plenty. Contrarily, in Olaf's case, a father's approval rated near last as inspiration.

'Being the youngest, I guess I had an independent streak which prevailed after a year. I helped Ole harvest a good crop of wheat, laid a board floor in the cabin, and bought a horse with my remaining money. Ft Pierre and the ranches west, the life of the open prairie, pure freedom, beckoned me. On the way north, riding barebacked with a hackamore, I laid over in Chamberlain near the Missouri, and was persuaded to sell my old horse, buy saddle and tack, and hire on with August Nelson and his brothers as a cowboy. They were Swedes, but the old world animosity toward Norwegians never surfaced in any of them. They also spoke clear, nearly unaccented English. They took me in, provided a string of five cow ponies, taught me the rudiments of handling cattle, and made me a cowboy. It suited me fine to spend 12 hours in the saddle and sleep on the ground, maybe cause I won't never forgot the lunging and plunging of a Norwegian fishing trawler in a cold, wind whipped sea.

'The Nelsons ran cattle along both sides of the White River, 75 miles on west. They sold to the Brule agency while 'Ol Spot', Spotted Tail's band was there, and with little opposition, ran herds on reservation lands until the Agency and lawyers limited that. The way I am today is because of those good Nelsons. My spread on Bull Creek ain't far from Jack. They had their own ways, and sometimes seemed cool and unfriendly to them that didn't know em, but they treated me right. I still wear the Stetson Gus bought for me, just makin me feel like I belonged, at the first Christmas I spent on their spread. Fer dumb Swedes, as Jack always called em, they did pretty damned good. They had Olof in Presho and later in Bonesteel to keep an eye on the judges and lawyers, and the brothers on the cowboy side did the cattle movin. They never lost a case of rustlin' against em, and they built up their own ranches in the Rosebud. Respected citizens. Along with a few others I could name who got started the same way.

'Jack and I was only neighbors when we started. I think John Jergins, another Norsky mighta been first on the Flats, but I ain't sure. I came up on the flats one day and found Jack there. Cabin already built. He had John Kincaid workin as a hand, and then John, too, built his own cabin and settled in and had one of the first families here on the Whetstone. Well, Drapeaus came right soon after. Had a big breed family. All them mighta been the first ones in the whole Rosebud, least wise along the river. Not countin, Ft Randall. We worked together so much, our cows and horses all runnin together, rustling wernt even a second thought to us. We branded mavericks fast as we could, but never stole a branded animal. Jack worked his horses more than me, cause I din't mind bucking em out. Faster, and if ya just kept riding em, they would get over the morning buck. Horse that ain't got the energy to buck probly ain't all that gooda horse. Jack don't believe that, but bout every other cowboy does. Other thing is, Jack don't care that much for cow horses for himself. I know when he learned that the hard way, and we barely escaped a buncha Scotty Philip's boys up on the White, cause he was on a cow horse, not his big running horses. He and John used to race on Sundays of a month, whenever they could get up a bet. They both loved their gambling, and I think he lost some money too, I know John did playing stud. Jack said he always won, but that ain't poker as I know it, you gonna lose parta the time, no matter what.'

Earth, Wind and Water

Jack leaned over the withers of the white mare, at full speed, sound of her hoof beats thundering in his ears, the mane whipping his face. Clods of grass and gumbo spun into his body from the hooves of the big bay in front, but Olaf soon lengthened the distance between them. He turned in the saddle and pointed east toward the river, but Jack waved him on south. The breaks near the river now were too sparse in trees and growth, averting a deceptive getaway. Glancing back at the top of the ridge, he counted five or maybe six riders, still pursuing at a high gallop. He turned back, into the wind, hat gone, and smacked the reins across the mare's rump again; she gave her best but it would not suffice. A great cow horse, quick to turn a heifer back to the herd, slice between a cow and calf, set her legs rigid against the roped calf, but now only speed counted. Jack fired his pistol high over Olaf's head, pointed left when he turned, and spurred the mare toward the river.

Olaf reined the big bay hard left, and scrambled down the hill. He took up a cow path, leading to the bottomlands, through the low-lying bush, headed for the cottonwoods along the river line. The mare's nostrils flared, she dropped her head, winded, lather blew onto Jack's trouser leg, and he knew the consequences of a winded horse. At the edge of the trees, the cow path split in a Y. He yelled at Olaf, made a running dismount, pulling his skinning knife. He cut the latigo on his saddle, carried it into the brush, and slipped the bridle from the mare. He headed her up the south branch of the trail, and smacked her hard on the rump with the bridle reins. In the gathering evening light, just maybe the trailing cowboys would take white-mare bait, expecting Jack to go south.

Jack and Olaf had taken the south road out of Oacoma mid-afternoon after delivering four draft horses to a trader from Chamberlain. They had eaten at the restaurant, taking a beer with their steaks and eggs. At a table to the rear, six cowboys finished their meals and lazily sauntered out of the room, two eying Jack and Olaf, and muttering to each other. They crossed main street to the bar. Jack spun two silver dollars to the waiter, ambled out the door. He had not recognized any of the cowboys, their horses bore several brands, none from the Rosebud.

Jack and Olaf crossed the White River, headed west, and picked up the trail of a large herd of cows and calves just over the fording point. They trailed them south another three miles, encountering a herd of over a hundred head, starting to spread out, heads bobbing as they chomped the salt grass. So, those cowboys had crossed these cows from the north onto the sweet grass Rosebud. Jack and Olaf picked out thirty or so cows, with calves, and pressed them hard to the south. Several miles later, Jack's natural caution, sprinkled lightly with paranoia, turned him in the saddle to peer at the last ridge line just as six silhouettes began a dash into the draw, headed directly toward him. He spurred the mare past the cattle, yelled at Olaf.

Now, the white mare heading north as a decoy, Jack riding double on Olaf's big bay, they stayed the south path, hugging the tree line along the bottom land until the river veered sharply to the right, cutting into a long sloping hill that ran to the waters edge. Here was decision time. Traveling faster across the flats above, if the cowhands were persistent, Jack and Olaf would expose themselves crossing that ridge. Here they could take to the water or try to hide in the trees, but there was still more than an hour to darkness, and the pursuers, after discovering the ruse, would surely come down to the river before turning back north. The river swirled and eddied, carrying tree branches and sticks, already encroaching onto the flats from fall rains to the north. He had fought this river and endured its unrelenting, unforgiving, sometimes lethal flow. It had taken two friends, in spring flooding, and a neighbor, his horse and hay wagon had crashed through the ice, he lost a horse once, and suspected that several of his cows perished in their carelessness. First seeing the river as obstacle, he now realized it could be an outlet from nature's *cul de sac*. "Olaf, back this way, lets see what we can find. Olaf reined the horse into the trees, and Jack slid off the rump, crashing through the bushes on the tree line until he found among the dreck and effluvia of the spring flooding, an old half-hollow cottonwood log. Tearing the brush away, he told Olaf to unsaddle the bay, and hide the saddle. Olaf slapped the big bay hard across the haunches sending him south.

"Help me here, roll it into the river."

"Jack, I ain't fer this, hell I can't swim. I know what yer thinking, but that water's cold, we'll freeze to death."

"Hey, you dumb Swede, we'll live a little longer floating on a tree than hanging on one. Let's go."

They struggled with each end of the tree, alternately walking it by ends to the water's edge. The river here was deep and fast at the bend. Jack edged the log forward, the current took it, and Olaf loped along side, finally dropping into the forbidding blue-gray cold of the "Big Muddy".

"Olaf, work around to the off side, take off your hat, they could come on down to the riverside."

"Damned cold, Jack! How far da ya think we need to float?"

"Whetstone Landing, maybe one a the islands. Its this or walk. I don't see goin 10 miles in wet boots and clothes." As evening descended, Jack could make out dark shapes along the bank leading the white mare, turned back north.

They struggled to steer the log unto the shallower river edging the bottomland at the Landing. Once there, Jack worked an hour, but finally started a fire Indian style, and they huddled around it until nearly dawn, half drying their clothes and socks. They had lost two good horses, but their neck size remained the same and they had had a half-assed bath. Now an aching five-mile walk lay ahead.

"Ya know, Jack, this business is not all its cracked up to be. Ruinin my boots, lost our horses, and not a damned thing for it. ....It was quite an adventure though, wasn't it, and he chuckled."

"Olaf, those heifers will be there tomorrow ifn we got the nerve to go get em. Maybe later."

"Dammit, I ain't even dry yet. I can't think about such foolishness as riding back into a posse."

"Well, I learned something agin I already knew, and it won't happen agin. I ain't never gonna use a cow horse for driving cattle. We coulda outrun those bastards if I had a big racer like your bay gelding."

Olaf Signs On

Jack considered his plan a good one, thought out, workable, and had not been done before. He designed it to use for a lengthy time, safety being very important, because he intended to stay in the Rosebud, not drift to new territory like so many rustlers, nor to be limited in scale like so many of the small ranchers. As with any secret, the fewer who knew, the better. He had Red Shirt and Billy for sure, and Frank Waugh, his son-in-law. Oliver Dion would surely join in, he loved adventure, good natured but a bit of a daredevil. He could trust them explicitly. Still, to work his plan he needed two more good riders, men that knew cattle, but who were not overly concerned about the illegal nature of what they were doing. Being neighbors also was important, they could help with alibis, provide refuge, were close enough to cut down on communications time. Two neighbors fit that bill, Olaf Finstad and Harry Ham. Both he knew to have rustled cattle before. They would not blanch from the proposition, and would not run to the law. He wanted Olaf on board first, and expected that he would be easiest to convince.

Dating from his work for the Nelson brothers, Olaf Finstad had evolved into the archetypal cowboy. His wide-brimmed hat seldom ever left his head, except in the presence of a woman. When he uncovered, the line separating his brown leathered face from his forehead and shock of light brown hair explicitly attested to his days on the range. Over his perennial white shirt he wore a dark brown, well worn leather vest complete with cigarette makins and a lone silver dollar, just in case it might be needed. For several years it had not. He had a year or so ago changed his wool trousers for blue canvas Levi's as he called them. Working horses or cattle, he sported leather chaps, darkened and worn across the thighs. His boots betrayed how little walking he did, yet were worn on the sides, emphasizing his bowed legs. His only show of ostentation appeared as a red bandanna at his throat.

Jack came up to the cabin from a day west looking for strays, both horses and cattle, to find Olaf's big bay mare at the hitching post. Save me a trip, he thought. He and Mary were in conversation comparing log cabins and houses, both his wife and Mary respectively having been promised new homes "soon". Jack determined to have a house bigger than his neighbor's.

Mary brought out two coffee cups and the pot to the center table, lifted Jack's hat, with a slip of a smile, and left the men to talk. She little knew of Jack's plan, he intended for her to be out of the loop, for her own safety. What she did not know, she could not be inveigled to tell. Of course he trusted her completely, but if the children were threatened, would she talk to save them? He held the details of the business closely.

Olaf liked his coffee hot, and slurped a mouthful that Jack would have gagged on. "Jack, the news outa Yankton ain't good. I read in the Chamberlain paper that there's new laws brought out. They changed the estray law, and all strays gotta be auctioned, and the money goes to the Stock Growers, to be divided up. Not only that, but the herd law now says small ranchers and honyockers gotta fence with good fences or they cain't claim against the cattle that run through their fields and pastures. Stock Growers got power in the legislature now, the money from the range cattle is gettin inta the west towns. They ran this crappy law through those goddam politicians like shit through a goose. No more two wire fences. Gotta be good nuf to keep out range runnin longhorns, and you know that's gonna cost. Jus an excuse so's they don't hafta pay no more, got the run of the grass now."

"Damn, Olaf, that's just a loada bullshit. Don't those sonsabitches know its against what the homesteaders want, and there's lotsa homesteaders."

"Well, it ain't no problem easta the river. No big ranges and herds there, so the law is gonna be against only those west river. Now, that's all big operators. Big money."

"Its that god dammed John Clay and Jim Craig. So what happens with the maverickin?"

"Jack, it means that brandin only can be done at the roundups. No more brandin loose strays...oh, and not only that, they made runnin irons illegal. They can throw ya in jail just fer ownin' or carryin' one."

"It gives the hangin cocksuckers more right to loop a rope over a cottonwood, that's what it does....goddammit." Jack leaned back in his chair. He looked at the ceiling, felt the heat of the room, warm body odor musk in his nose. Mary, poked at the fireplace and shook the skillet on the cook stove. Its not what he wanted. Mary pregnant with their third child. 'No, he did not need the Cheyenne Club, the big town houses, but he worked a helluva lot harder than them English, cold blooded store keepers.'

Jack hunched over his cup, warmed his hands around it. "Olaf, we ain't gonna build new houses for our women without more money than wer taking in now. I been working this spread for nearly ten years. I got some horses, and they make the most money per head, but cattle is where the real dough is and a herd's hard to build up. Its gonna take ten more years to afford a real house at this rate." He slurped his hot coffee, blew into the cup.

"This new law is the last straw. Maverickin' has made the difference fer me. My herd, yours too, has been built that way. It ain't stealin', its survivin', and if ya ain't growing out here yer dyin'. Wer losing cows in winter, mostly, but there's disease, some wolves, couple a steers every year from cutting infections, other stuff." He pondered in silence, looked out the west window. "There's more cattle now than the land can hold. Look on west, its just more an more beeves. Water holes fulla cows and mud. Can't find clean water out there anymore. Course I don't care about the fences, but can't carry a brandin iron? That's too much. Olaf, its too slow this way."

Jack mused more to himself than Olaf. Olaf looked up, waited.

"I got a plan in my head to make money faster, and its not new."

"Well, Jack, I bin resisting the urge to take up old ways, especially since there is some danger involved in such practices."

Jack smiled as he looked up; Olaf seldom missed a beat. "Yeah, but the old ways won't work for us. We can do it better, faster, get in and out."

"We?"

Jack recited his plan. Olaf listened, saying nothing. He let Jack get into the details, still quiet when Jack looked up, expecting him to respond. He did not. Jack continued. "The most important part is the sale of a herd. Its where the waddies go wrong. I made an arrangement that cuts the danger of getting caught. I sell to Nebraska handlers who take the cattle way south, out of our ranges, deep into Nebraska, or on to Omaha, where they are butchered in the slaughter houses down there, soon as they get em….we don't need a bill a sale…I get the money in Valentine or Springview. The brands from up here are unknown, get thrown inta big herds down there. I got a friend, he is a true friend, I ain't got no worries bout him."

"What about the price?"

"I ain't set no exact price, but its gonna be about five bucks a head under the going market price. We don't get paid until my friend gets paid, so his drovers gotta get through, and get paid first. I pick up money for the last trip when we go on the next trip."

"Who is this dealer?"

"Olaf, I think its better for you if you don't know. I will not tell him of any in our band, either."

"Our band?"

"We need at least five and maybe six. The less the better. I got Red Shirt, and Frank Waugh now, I could use Billy, but Mary ain't gonna like that, and I don't think he is ready for the long rides. Ollie Dion is game, too. I need you, and I'm thinkin Harry Ham."

"The others are trustful, but Harry I don't know. He ain't never been a rustler, he don't seem the type a guy fer that."

"Trust me, he rustled some cattle. I know. I was Sheriff. Don't need to say no more at this point. I think I can convince him. Also, he needs the money, and that's important. We can 'buy' these beeves pretty cheap," he smiled.

"Harry needs the money moren us. Owes money to his family, always talkin about his brother and dad. He's been wolfin, a good shot in case we need it."

"I don't want to do no shootin. We need fast horses more than fast triggers. Its real trouble if we shoot some lawman or cowboy off the spreads. Those boys hold together. They would hunt us down. No, we wanta stay under the ridgelines. That's why we need out-riders. We gotta share more outta the take.

"Could work."

Harry Ham Considers, With Reservations

'Goddammit,' Harry thought, 'how did I get myself into this? What the hell have I done? I worked hard, I done work I never wanted to do, but had to do it. Choppin' wood bein one of them, ridin in snow and rain chasin wolves when a man oughta be by a cabin fire. Shit, whatever it was, it never made me no real money.' Without saying much Harry had up and left his White Swan farm to his older brother, and unrelenting judge. "Three years, Harry an you ain't done much with the place."'

Harry looked away, out across the black, plowed 40 acres of sod, and thought it was something. Plowing in the spring, the wet gumbo clung relentlessly to his slogging boots, he scraped it off the moldboard twice up every furrow. The plow point dug into the mud, jerking the handles upward, nearly out of his hands. Harry continually regulated the depth til his shoulders gave out. He stopped plowing, then waited out the rain too long; a few long days of summer sun scorched the dirt to concrete, the plow nose jumping out of the furrow to skim across the grass. He reined his horses in, pulled the plowshare back to the furrow. His team worn thin and unmatched to plowing, he borrowed John's oxen to finish. Not like John's farm, with a wife to help, and clapboard house and barn, painted even; but he had a start, a log and sod house, a lean-to barn and a pole corral, not much yet, but a start. The judgment hurt but went unanswered, as all such comments had before. He did not argue with John, nor counter any comments with his own logic, any defense of himself. John, his father's first and favorite son, walked like a titan across Harry's landscape. Three years, one to fix up the cabin and plow, another to raise a fine crop of wheat and corn, then total ruin the third when the rains held off til late August, too late to save the dry, curling leaves of the dying corn; or the wheat, in July too short, thin and wispy to even scythe. With his last money from home, supplemented by timbering, he had bought seven cows and turned them into the wheat stems. By October, the cows were healthy, but the field resembled a stockyard. Cows had tramped mud from the rains that came too late, top soil ran in rivulets to the Missouri, his dream of an Iowa-style farm in Dakota turned to fog and haze, gumbo and water, mud and cow shit. The critters stood head down, dark, mud-streaked noses dripping with cud slime. The suspicion that John brought him along to Dakota only to lord over him crossed his mind again. He respected his brother, might have even loved him, though as rare as they were abrupt and pointed, the innuendo of failure inherent in his criticisms burned a hole in Harry's chest.

"Jack, I'm leavin White Swan in the spring. Coming over west, start again across that cussed river. I'm done with plowin."

"Harry, I got room for a damned sight more than seven old cows, bring em along. Where you thinking to settle? You talk to Olaf Finstad?"

"No, but I could. Maybe somewhere near him, yer thinking? Closer to the bottomland. I like being in the trees, cuts the wind. We had trees in Ioway. Theys water in the creeks there, ain't they?"

Jack welcomed a new neighbor, and he knew Harry, a man whose conversations did not offend, if they did not elucidate, but who lapsed into long spells of what Jack took at first to be periods of quiet cogitation. While logging on Blackbird Island, he would realize that Harry spent those interims in deep contemplation of the bucksaw's mysterious movements, as it turned trees to dust and cordwood. Where John's comments stung, Jack's were accepted as truths, even as helpful, Jack not being his brother, but less accusative in tone. Jack, John Jergins, and Olaf helped Harry build a log cabin, one considerably larger and finer than the inherited woodpile at White Swan, two rooms, and a stone fireplace. Hard work, helping a neighbor, was common currency.

Jack poured himself coffee from the enameled tin pot on the stove, a new addition to Harry's lachrymose cabin. He hooked his leg around a chair, leaning over the backrest, looked Harry in the eye and said, "I need some help with some beeves, wondered if you got some time?" Harry knew what Jack meant, and hesitated, looked at the stove, pulled up the other chair.

"I cain't get involved with rustlin, I gotta a brother whose a sheriff, and a father that's dang near a preacher. It ain't my life. I come too close already, Jack, as you well know. I ain't got the stomach for it, even when I tried."

"Listen, you didn't have a plan, you didn't know where to sell, and like all the waddys gracin' the end of a rope in the Rosebud the last 20 years, you stole from the wrong people."

Harry looked at the floor, and shook his head slowly. "You don't mean to use blackmail on me, cause I rustled the one time?"

"Nah, nobody knows about that but you an me....Also, you ain't got jack shit for years a working the range for mavericks, and I ain't either. I made a good deal in Valentine a while back. I worked some U+ cattle I found west a here. I did it alone, and I cain't take that chance or do that much riding alone. I plum wore out a horse. You can do well, we can do well, if we work together."

Jack rose, walked out the door toward the corral. Harry followed quietly, deep in thought.

He kicked at some dried gumbo clods, mashing them under the toe of his boot. "Those other riders, you know we could trust em? Who are we in this with? Billy's too young. Frank Waugh? Drapeau's or Dion's? You got Olaf in on this too?" Harry knew Jack's friends, how often they worked together. "Ben Diamond"?

"Harry, my plan is to keep this between you an me for now. I will gather the riders, and we will meet out west. No sense in anybody knowin' anything until we commit ourselves. That's the protection we all need. I'll get yeh word on the meeting place. Showin' up commits yeh with the group. Pack enough fer a long week, like yeh was wolfin'. We ain't going near any towns just yet."

"Yah, work together and hang together. I ain't forgot those two boys we saw bendin cottonwoods over on Ponca Creek. Likely never forget that. And I heard more about hangings in Nebraska, vigilantes, people going crazy as 'coons."

"Hands that get caught ain't taken the proper precautions, like I didn't do my first time. I aim to do it right hereafter. Start to roundup in the late winter, no cowboys out but a few line riders. In day time, outriders on the watch, get the cattle herded into the tree lines, coolies, and deep draws, or behind the south buttes, then do only night drovin'. I need some lookouts, and drovers. We do it on shares so's you get fair pay. Take a hundert head, a workable herd, split it five ways, you, me, Olaf, Red Shirt and Billy. Maybe Billy only gets a half share, he ain't but a kid and part of my family. We could get $400 a piece on a good trip. Take it back, buy some legal cows, and you'll be a rancher. An John, you know yourself, nearly ever damned rancher west of the Missouri cuts some corners, and lots more rustlers are getting away with it than not. If that weren't so, the Association wouldn't be so damned worried and bothersome."

"Come out and help me just on the roundup side, the drovin. Leave the sale to and me an Red Shirt. There won't be no chance of getting caught then."

"Jack, truth is I damned well need money." He could not bring himself to seek John Ham's help or even his father's. Time for that had all passed. He was on his own now, cut loose from the family through determination laced with indecision. No alternatives presented themselves to Harry's mind. Rustle or don't.

"I've got it worked all out, Harry. Most a those waddys you see decoratin cottonwoods got caught cause they had no out riders, or they tried to sell to a honyocker or rancher who turned em in. I got an outlet in Nebraska, it's worked before, and I don't need bill a sales, regardless of the brand. And we don't take from our neighbors. What I need is hands I can trust. You, Olaf, Frank, Red Shirt, that's a lotta trust."

Jack rose, sat his cup on the table and looked at Harry. He said nothing, but stared at the floor. Jack flopped his hat on, tapped it down on the top and went out the door. "I'll get back to ya when we set out."

Harry Joins the Gang

April nights still froze the day's melting snow again, making the mornings slippery, the ground unforgiving, horses careful in their track. Winter hair began to slough off, leaving patchy spots on Jack's black gelding. He eased him up out of the Whetstone creek bed, sliding in the shaded areas, gaining purchase on the warming grass now hit by wane sunbeams slithering between the cedars. He could see the black silhouette of Harry Ham across the lower flats, angling across the space from corral to house. Two horses ambled around the pen, noses under the pole corral probing for the few grass blades within reach. Jack's horse crunched through an ice covered pool of water, drawing Harry's bowed-head walk to a halt, turned, startled. Company too often meant inconvenience or even trouble.

Seeing Jack did not erase his scowl. Over the years he had only reluctantly forgiven Jack for the comeuppance he received at his hand for stealing the Nelson cows. Jack had helped him get started west of the river, and he would always be beholdin' to him for that. After the incident with Jack as sheriff, they had worked cattle together again, on occasion, had helped neighbors at roundups, met in Oacoma, attended the same barn dances, where talk of his escapade never emerged. Jack had honored the unspoken code of silence among neighbors

But the debt to his brother remained the most hurtful thing gnawing at Harry. True, John had not raised the issue in their infrequent meetings, their father had never mentioned it, yet it would continue to haunt Harry until he repaid it, proving his west river venture a success.

"So what brings you by, Jack? You serious about what you proposed?"

"I'm thinkin' about an operation further out in the Rosebud, area you know from wolfin'." Jack let the thought gain meaning, not explicit.

Harry turned slowly around, moved on toward the house, a move Jack saw as an acceptance. He had not objected much on any account. "You heard about the new laws?"

- 184 -

"Olaf told me...I don't know what to make of it...I don't see em coming after us much, as you said, there ain't much law anyway."

"Well, ther makin brand books and puttin brand inspectors at all the river crossings. They got the hide law at butchers and slaughter houses, and it ain't long til they get more law. We move now, before any more citizens come west, we still gotta chance to make a few bucks....Harry, be up on the Flats at sun-up tomorrow, we'll go west."

Harry awoke two days later on damp prairie grass to find himself a rustler. His own brother was a deputy sheriff, his father a saintly, strict law abider who had shaped his sons in his own image. No, he did not want to be here, but decisiveness had abandoned him again.

Hat Trick

The band settled the cattle into the Niobrara bottom lands, near the river for water, and over the river south to keep the herd from straying back to their homelands, the natural tendency of cattle, especially these white faces and shorthorns.

Harry unsaddled his horse, and pulled his new rifle from the scabbard. He had retired his old Sharps rifle for a new Army-issue 30-40 Krag saddle-ring carbine, a weapon with better accuracy, quieter, and near smokeless powder. "Jack, I need to sight in this new rifle, and here in the river bed works better, sound won't carry so far."

"You came all the way here and ain't sighted in a new rifle? Must notta expected to use it much."

"It's sighted for 300 yards, and I want to see what 100 yards should be. The sight is adjustable, I can slip it back and forth to change ranges."

"Harry, I heard yer a great shooter, but I bet 5 dollars you cain't hit my hat at fifty yards?"

Harry grinned slyly, thinking something was up here, but bit, and said, "Yer a joker, Jack, but I'm game. Walk off a fifty paces along the river and let's see what this rifle can do."

As Jack walked off fifty long strides, he dipped his John B. Stetson hat into the river, and commenced to roll it around a box elder branch. This hat was one of John B.'s best, which could be shaped when wet, and pop out into its original shape when unrolled and dry. Wrapping the chin string around the rolled-up hat on the branch, it measured about three inches around. "Hit that, Harry, its my hat!"

Knowin he'd been worked for five bucks, Harry smiled, rolled onto his belly, rested the Krag on a log. He adjusted the rear sight down, clicking off two notches, his best guess at proper elevation. Jack was only half way back when the first shot bounced the hat 20 feet along the sand bank. For good measure, he fired again, sending it into the river. Jack ran back, grabbed his hat, and unrolled it to find 3 holes had passed through the brim, and two in the crown. A good hat despoiled, and five dollars, gone too. "Damn, Harry, I thought you didn't have it sighted in at 50 yards yet?"

"Looky there Jack, yeh got some air holes ventilatin yer warbonnet an it only cost ya five bucks!" Sadly surveying the wreckage of a hat he had worn with pride, he asked, "Harry, John Ballard told me in Oelrichs, that you shot seven wolves with seven bullets when you was wolfing. That so?"

"Its true Jack, but only two of em was runnin', the others were just walkin' or sittin' there lookin' at me."

Famine in the Rosebud 1884-88

*Y*et, *there are cycles in the rewards for man's endeavors, as there are cycles in the weather, and in the West, those will likely coincide.*

The mid-to-late 1880's saw weather and climate conspire to take back the bounty and promise of the newly worked prairie.

Weather is fate's tool. The vicissitudes of weather oft altered the coarse of mankind, and it conspired to ruin the promise in man's striving to gain reward from Dakota. The Great Dakota boom began in the up-cycle of good, temperate, even mild, winters and summers. In mid-decade of the 1880's, the cycle broke bad, winters turned harsh. Alaskan gales prevailed. Snow whipped into roof high snow banks around houses, cattle starved and froze, horses even, unable to scrape through hardened crusts, fed on tree bark. Wells and springs froze. Game vanished south with the winds. Grouse and prairie chickens lay frozen under snow mounds for scavenging, bone-thin coyotes. Leaving home for a trip to town, even if only for essential supplies, lay fraught with danger. Storms descended with no warning, disorienting travelers, turning them in circles, freezing them in their blankets, their buffalo robes, leaving their bones for searchers in the spring. The Chinook winds of spring thawed the snows too quickly, the rivers broke up early, the hugest ice blocks ever seen crashed down the tributaries, flooding bottom lands, uprooting grown trees, sweeping all before them into the Missouri, itself rising to record highs. Pierre city flooded out completely. Even settlements up in the breaks sustained irreparable damage.

Some winters brought little snow but much cold. For there were no warm spring rains. Winter wheat that had survived, stunted. Spring thaws barely ran enough to wet the creek bottoms. By the Fourth of July, the few corn stalks able to pierce the heat scorched, plastered gumbo stood ankle high, fields straddled cracks in the earth a foot wide and a yard deep. New spring grass had struggled to rise above the dried brittle remains of the previous summer, but curled into desiccation. Ponds vanished, cracks inches wide in the dried mud the only evidence. The White River stopped flowing; green pools of slime collected tadpoles, minnows, tiny bullheads, which the magpies and crows, never seeming to suffer from drought and pestilence, pecked and devoured. Spring wheat hardly germinated. July wheat stalks grew ankle high, a few unfilled heads labored, and lost. Cattle and horses cleaned up the vestiges of crops, then languished in what shade they could find. Plums and berries shriveled in the dry creek beds. Only predators and scavengers multiplied. Magpies sucked the moisture from the eggs of grouse and prairie chickens, coyotes survived on the weakened birds and on prairie dogs forced to forage farther from their protective holes. Wolves ranged wider, east from their Wyoming homelands, in search of cattle too weak and listless to resist or run.

After the second year of withering crops, a Sahara summer, half of the pioneers packed the family pictures, peering out so stolid and confident in blacks and grays and white, with a new appreciation for the prairie's unforgiving nature now, bartered what remained of their possessions for a train ticket back to Iowa or Illinois. No rain meant no grain.

The remaining hardy or foolhardy pioneers finally were blasted off the promised land by the blizzards of 1888-1889. Snow blew in from Alaska unchecked in November and accumulated exponentially until the following April. The "Die Off", ranchers called it for years after. Upon accounting their positions in the spring, after cowboys rounded up the remains, the cattle bubble of the 1880's burst. Syndicates from the US East, England, and Scotland lost all, only to struggle and to rise again.

A Man's Gotta Do What a .....

He pulled her leg over his own left leg, and covered her softness with his hand. The sweetness afterward. Peace, quiet, pure laziness. He drifted back to sleep, an hour, maybe more. Nothing today. Do nothing. Make up for some lost time here.

"Stay a while, Jack, we need you here. The children need you."

Mary would plead no more, but her eyes spoke well for her. Jack's heart said stay, but he knew that survival now required action. He spun the gray gelding away, avoiding Mary's eyes as tears welled up from her oak brown eyes, called to Billy, and they set off west. Olaf and Harry would follow if they were not already on the trail to Chris Columbe's ranch for meet up, all desperate for some purchase of reward. As Jack said in uniting the band, "desperate times call for desperate measures."

Harry and Olaf came two days later, to Chris Colombe's bunkhouse in the evening. They started early the next day, then turned west picking up Red Shirt at the Lamoreaux ranch on the Keya Paha River near the Nebraska border. They worked northwest from there, cutting out, leaving behind everything with a Rosebud brand. Near Rattlesnake Butte, first of the string of small plateaus that run northwest to the Badlands, they turned their findings south for ten miles, stopped for the night with a hundred head, thirty unbranded calves among them. They spent the next day branding the calves with Bar-S. They buried the branding fire and drug cottonwood branches around their work area. Olaf and Harry stayed with them for a day's droving, then turned back by the same route, taking the running irons, checking for anyone following. When they had reached the branding area, the buried branding fire remained well covered, and a light rain began. They turned east, draping their slickers across their backs, spurring their horses toward cover.

Jack and Red Shirt trailed the herd as far south as the Dismal River. They met up with two of Doc's accomplices at the Freyer Hog Ranch, turned over the herd and parted, Jack to the Whetstone, Red Shirt northwest to Rosebud.

Iterations of this trip, in various forms became a constant with Jack since he had convinced himself of the rightness of going wrong. His buyers were better able to avoid or pay off brand inspectors at the Sioux City and Omaha slaughter houses than ranch reps and agency men scrutinizing the large beef sales to the reservation Indians.

Olaf About the Rustlin

'I guess I never knew anuf to ask a intelligent question ta Jack about why he turned to rustlin, but after he was Sheriff for a while, and then the Yankton stage was robbed, and the horse trading business went bad over easta the river for a while, me and Harry and Jack went out on west a ways, and hired on with Ed Lemmon as plain ole cowboys again. He kept his ranch, but sold his few cows after a bad drought that summer. I was let go over the winter, but Jack hung on to do line ridin. I watched over his horses, he still had around 20, and they stayed together with a big black stud he had, roaming across the flats sometimes, stayed in the trees along the creek mosta the winter. Still had fifteen when he got back. Never asked me a thing. I spose some wandered off, and a couple got stolen, that's certain. Those days, lucky the whole mess didn't get took. Then again, Jack had a reputation, even back then.

'When he come back the next spring, he took to rustlin like he'd been doin it all his life. I had learned quite a bit about that game from the Nelsons, they knew mosta the tricks, best as I could tell. But Jack, he went about it in a big way. He never rustled to build his own herd, he sold em, and bought legit cows and mostly horses. Somehow he had a friend over the Running Water, now it's called the Niobrara, and we took to herdin as many as a hundert head at a time across the river, and then Jack and Red Shirt took em on south. Sometimes theyd hole em up in the Sandhills, but in a few days, Jack came back with money. Shared out equal, but maybe not all with Billy, he was Jack's family. Never told me who he sold those cows to. Said it was best not to know casen we was caught. This I knew to be wise counsel, cause I seen most get caught when they try to sell their booty. Seemed straight to me. Billy knew, I think, and I know Red Shirt did, cause a coupla times he rode on south by hisself ta pick up the cash, and Jack came back with us.

'It wasn't long after Jack came back to the Rosebud to stay that Scotty Philip lost some cows, he thought to rustlers, and in fact it was Jack an me and Red Shirt, took em all the way from near the Bad to south of Valentine. Took, I guess near on a week of night drivin. One of his hands saw me and Jack up to Nowlin store and Post Office at the time. Then, later when his boys nearly caught us southa Oacoma, word started getting out that Jack was a big time rustler. Everyone lost a cow blamed Jack for a while, but then Jack worked at makin' sure his neighbors knew it wasn't him. He helped bring in two waddys known to steal off our ranges, and he watched over reservation cows like they was his own. The Bull Creek Brules paid him for keeping their range clear a Scotty's cows, or any other, including the Nelsons, who was going legit for the most part. Gregory County Protective Agency also paid him for the same work. What helped us most in the early days was the Western Stockgrowers themselves. They had detectives looking west and north, thinkin' we was drivin' to Canada. There was lots a that goin' on, other rustlers drivin' cows to Canada, sellin' em then stealin' em back and selling in Montana. Drivin' a herd from the Rosebud ta Canada don't make no sense. Its near a thousand miles. Drivin ta Nebraska weren't that hard.

'They took him to Presho for trial two, three times. Not that anyone else got time for rustlin if they was taken to Presho. Longest time, it was the only court west river, and the jury was always honyockers and small ranchers, so the big boys lost.

'Jack could take a ribbin from his neighbors on occasion about rustlin. Never seemed to bother him when they at least smiled. What Jack would not tolerate was some stranger talking wrong, specially a cowhand in a bar.

'One time in the Hickey House, Jack and me came in, leaned on the bar, having a drink, when one of the waddys at the other end of the bar, raised his voice, "Seems any kinda cow wrangler can drink in this bar, even some that chases other people's critters." Jack froze, dint say a word. "Reservation cowboys prolly can't read brands anyway," he continued.

'Jack twirled his shot glass in his fingers, staring at it, looking down slowly, and then took a slow step toward the cowboy, a tall fella with black batwing chaps and a white shirt. Big hat, likely a Texan. With his second step Jack whipped out his pistol, before the cowboy could react. With another step he jammed it into the ribs of this guy, took him total by surprise, and I'd say he nearly broke a rib.

'Through gritted teeth, "Now, if you was calling me a rustler, back it up." As he stared with menace straight into the cowboy's eyes, pulled the Texan's pistol, threw it to me. Spun him into the middle of the room, and raised his gun to hit him. The fella ducked, backed away fast, nearly fallin down. Knew he'd been had already. Jack eyed the guy straight on, holstered his gun, unbuckled and handed the belt to me. "Now, call me a rustler again, and make your move."

'He stammered to drawl out, "Ah was jist talkin, mighta mistook ya fer sum otha fella looked lock you."

'He raised both palms to Jack, "we all doun get ta town theyat much, I'd just lock to finish ma da-rink in peace and mosey on." He drawled Texan-like alright, and I was surprised that he put up with this, but Jack surely had the drop on him. Jack pulled damned fast on this guy, and he knew it. I seen John Kincaid practicing at Jack's once, and I think he mighta been faster, but not by much.

'The other boys just stood there, couple had their mouths open and another spilled his glass. I had the fella's gun in my hand, so they weren't likely to do too much.

' "Go on, have a drink." Jack motioned toward the bar. The Texan kept his eyes on Jack, and sidled to the bar, slugged back his drink and turned to Bob Hickey for a refill. These boys were cowhands, not used to gunnin fer anyone. They took Jack for a gunman, and you can bet, were sure by now that he was a rustler. They just were not in position to take no chance on Jack's mood. Now I wouldna handled it that way myself, but Jack supposed these were the same waddys that chased us into the river some time back. He wanted them to know that they were damned lucky not to catch him. He went back to his place at the bar, and finished his drink. Where I woulda held my gun on these folks at one point, and either got the hell out or something, Jack acted purely like it never bothered him no more. His temper could cool as fast as it could rise. He drank very quietly, and so did those cow-pokes. Strange thang, really. Jack told me on the way home, that he did not think Bob Hickey would take kindly to him kickin them outa the bar when they still had money to spend. A course, Jack and I did not stay long after, and made a bee line for home when we left.

'Jack had a way bout himself, that people respected, even when they was bein showed up. His green, soft eyes had gone to black when he turned to see if I was coverin the other crew. Thing is, Jack never wanted no shootin. Told me more than once, he never murdered a man, but he always carried a gun, and acted like usin it was but natural. Take this Texan. He knew that he coulda been dead by even his own old Texas ways. When Jack showed anuf game to take him on with fists, he knew he'd lose that fight too. Better to continue this later, if he intended to, cause he had no advantage now. Jack made it all happen so fast only John Kincaid woulda knowed anuf to react like a gunfighter. I could add Doc Middle-ton, as I learned a few years later. And I never again heard no cowhands joke about rustlin around Jack in Oacoma. Nother thing was, Jack wanted no trouble with Scotty Philip, whose hands these probably was. I dint agree with Scotty on much of anything. He sided with the small ranchers on lotsa issues, but in the end, thought most of us was rustlin. Where they come apart was on joinin up with the Western Stock Growers Association, which used range detectives. Scotty was losing cows, and wanted the Mis-souri River Association to hire a Pinkerton, or ta team with the Western boys. Mosta the Missouri Association members were small ranchers, and wanted no detectives or big rancher interference.

It's the Law and That's That

Politicians drew a line across a Dakota Territory map in Washington, and after years of political maneuvering created two states in 1889, North and South. The pioneers of those new states began with renewed vigor the business of creating viable enterprises. Deadwood's rambunctious infancy over, mining and ranching saw a civilized society becoming more conducive to the economic interests of a lawful majority. Neither the new middle class nor the big economic interests would abide lawlessness in its raw, wild west manifestation. Affecting norms of eastern American society as a matter of pride, more ordinary citizens tolerated increasingly less frontier mentality.

Initial efforts to bring justice to the West River were lead by a Gregory County judge of unusual vigor named Bartine. He had visions of a politically more important future, and to profit politically from convictions favorable to the large cattle interests. This ambition fertilized a sharp mind and keen righteousness of purpose. He set up his adjunct office in Presho, Lyman County being rightfully tagged as the center of rustling gangs, to take on the docketed cases for thievery. Jack's name showed up for multiple cases of cattle rustling, and might have led to actual court appearances if Carl Nelson, clerk of courts at the time, had not pointed out that for any one man to have rustled as charged on these occasions, he would have had to have been in three locations at once, herding over 300 head of cattle in one day.

Having been asked to appear in Lyman County court to answer a charge of rustling Nelson brothers' cattle, Jack stomped his snow-covered boots as he entered the courtroom. Shucking off his buffalo hide coat, he stood near the pot-bellied stove warming his hands, answering questions as to name, occupation, address and whether he was guilty of having rustled 34 head of cattle from the Olof Nelson ranch.

"How do you plead in this case," asked Judge Bartine.

"Not guilty, of course"

Judge Bartine, both judge and prosecutor asked "Can you explain your whereabouts on the day of 12 April 1895?"

"I was returning home from Ft Pierre, where I delivered five horses to the Brule reservation agent."

"And did you cross the land where the Nelsons graze their herd?"

"Of course, it was direct on the way home."

"And did you not, in fact, take on home some 34 cows and heifers belonging to the Nelsons?"

Jack stifled his urge to reply sarcastically, maintained a serious demeanor. "That Judge, I did not do. I saw no cows with the Nelson brand while on my trip home."

"Well, did you see cows with another brand?"

"I did see a few cows with the U+ and the Flying V, several with E Bar."

"Mr. Sully, you were seen chasing about 30 or more cows toward your own ranch on that same day.

"Well, now, I was movin' them back toward the home ranges. Big ranches still takin' advantage of us little guys, and the Brule ranchers. You know that I work for the reservation cattlemen. My job is to rid the area of strays eatin' up grazin land of the tribe. Some of those cows were on tribal lands around Bull Creek, some on Olaf's. I knew that the Nelsons didn't want to have them cows eating up their neighbors' grass, so I helped them out. They sure wasn't Nelson brands."

"Now, Olof Nelson says you ran off his cattle, and has charged you with thievery. He saw you on his land, and the 34 head of cattle were gone when he went to get them the next day."

"Is Olof Nelson missing any of his brand? If he is, I ain't the one that took em. He might want to go searchin' back on the U+ range, and see if he can find those cows again. If he has a bill of sale for 34 cows, branded U+ and Flyin' V, he should have no trouble bringin' it here, and I will vouchsafe for driving some cows of that brand west on that day. Just tryin' to help out a neighbor and do my job."

"Mr. Nelson, you got a bill of sale, or are you sayin' that the accused stole your own branded cows?"

"Judge, I ain't got a bill a sale here with me, but I can bring it back, givin time."

"Case postponed until such time as a bill of sale is presented and new hearing date set."

As nearly all the onlookers had by now figured out, Jack had rustled cows that Olof Nelson had rustled first.

In the street again, mounting his horse along side Jack, Olof Nelson, speaking low, said, "Jack I didn't reckon that you would rustle no cows from a neighbor, and a friend at that."

"Olof, you're still a friend I hope, cause you know those weren't your cows. Like I said, just saving you boys some home grass after this hard winter. Stop in when you're down my way."

"By god, I guess I will, you sure owe me a dinner over this one."

What Olof wanted was not dinner, but to get Jack into a different angle of the rustling business. The Nelson boys had managed their own rustling, having four brothers to do the riding. Recently they had reasoned that the big cow companies were facing more problems, with an economic depression in the East and they had decided to move to more legitimate operations. In 1890, a large portion of the Rosebud, in eastern Gregory County, had been opened to homesteaders. Though the filing process would end up being delayed for considerable time for lack of a properly surveyed state line with Nebraska, the brothers anticipated rumors of more homesteaders coming. They began fencing four or five sections near the mouth of the White River, land best for cattle, not so much for farming. The law was becoming more efficient, and the Stock Growers Association detectives had stepped up pursuit of cow theft to a more dangerous level. Gus Nelson had seen Ed Blakeley in Naper and Springview, Nebraska, and had heard that he was working out of Presho and other towns east of his normal operation area.

Olof Nelson and Jack went back a ways. They had drunk together, played cards, and hustled a few cows. Once he, Olaf Finstad and Jack came off from trailing some beeves to Ft Pierre, and had acquired a prodigious thirst by the time they made Oacoma. They did not hesitate, but rode their horses directly into the Hickey House for one wild afternoon of drinking and hell raising. The two Olafs grabbed a bottle off the bar and took great, gurgling slugs. They then began to shoot holes in the bar ceiling until the bartender shouted that the ceiling of the bar was the floor of the hotel, and guests above surely would be "discombobulated". They rode out with bottle in hand. Back on the street, the Sheriff came running, pulled his gun on Nelson and Finstad, but hesitated to pull the trigger on a couple of drunken cowboys.

"Sheriff," Jack said, his pistol in hand, "those boys are just having fun, and nobody was hurt. Don't you just want to put your gun down? I'll see that they leave town right now."

"Jack, goddammit, I got a job to do here, and those assholes are makin a fool a me."

"Now you know it ain't worth killin a man fer havin fun, and by the way, Olof Nelson has three brothers that would hunt you down like a cornered coyote."

"Ah, well, I know yer right but least you could do is tell 'em I was about to shoot 'em. I won't put up with any more of that shit." Jack holstered up, waved his hat, and spurred after the whiskey bottle.

Olof had more than once encouraged Jack to fence his ranch, but there were complications in determining the legal boundary between South Dakota and Nebraska. As such, section lines starting at the border and laid out northward to the White River were uncertain. Surveying was held up, and claims could not be filed, or were contested and lost. For now at least, his right to use land in the Rosebud was still valid through his marriage to Mary.

Billy, First Trip

W hen he reached ten years the stories from Mary and Jack clari-
fied the reality of his birth and natural father, they had done
nothing to hide this history, but explained it to him, made him aware
of himself through their explanation of his father's life. This began to
affect his approach to Jack. He inclined to model his behavior by his
stepfather, but in truth, he was the son of John Kincaid. So often had
he heard references to him, of his skills, his loyalty, his fun-loving
escapades that he found reason to identify with that image. Not long
after his thirteenth birthday, as reality of his birth crystallized in him, he
began to call Jack "Dad Sully", a not so subtle acknowledgement of his
real fore bearer, a declaration of real identity. Neither Mary or Jack did
any more than raise an eyebrow at first hearing. Jack might well have
wished for another John Kincaid, for he had no friend to equal him in
his life now. Little else changed in Billy's outward demeanor or his own
internal caring for Jack. He still admired him, followed his lead, reacted
to his training and guidance. He was surely a child more of Mary than
John, a good and loyal follower. Still, his smile was John's; his sauntering walk, cocking his head like a bandy rooster to listen to Jack or Mary,
as if no matter the comment, it was of import. He had little interest in
side arms, as John had, but handled a rifle well, and loved a horse race,
that not being a small thing in those days.

Meeting old Narcisse Drapeau, Jack's second father-in-law and an
accomplished fiddler, instigated and improved Billy's natural bent toward
music. The old gentleman taught him the Breton two-steps and four-step
waltzes of his youth. He played fast and loud, and sometimes danced a
mean jig as he sawed away. He set cowboys to slapping their chaps in
rhythm, Métis banging cans Indian style. Jack and family attended more
dances around the country because of Billy than through their own amply
charming personalities. That he was John Kincaid's son became most
apparent in the vivacious nature of his playing and dancing.

Billy and Jack were mucking out the pole barn one cool fall day. The acid reek of dung steaming up from the barn floor kept them from talking much as they pitched straw. Certainly Billy had been thinking as he worked, because as they were spreading new hay bedding, Billy stuck his pitchfork in the ground, and removed his gloves. He broke the long silence, "Is it true my father named me after his best race hoss?"

Jack hesitated. What had he meant, that doing so would denigrate him, or of pride and love of horses as a bond? "He... he told me when you were born that he named you William John Kincaid. If he intended that as compliment I could not say. He did not say that your middle name was for me neither. I hoped it was, actually, yet it seemed impertinent for me to ask. He told me of your birth and name in a serious manner, even reverent. We spoke no more of it."

Billy looked out across the flats from the barn, silently. Jack went on. "And for that matter, Billy Boy was a hell of a hoss. He had a faster red sorrel, and we made money on him in Oklahoma and Kansas, but after we ran into a stretch where no one would race against the sorrel, your Dad raced Billy Boy, and won. He rode him to Texas and back, raced him, roped with him. Helluva hoss. Yeh could do for a worse namesake. Yer father would have intended it as a honor; if you turn out to be as good a man as that hoss was a hoss." Billy threw more hay into the nearest stall, looked at Jack with a slight, knowing smile. He turned to the stable wall and reached for his saddle and blanket, cinched up his blue roan. His good spirits lasted through a hard day in the saddle and into his thoughts that evening.

Not for any lack of skill or energy did Jack first refuse to include Billy in the rustling raids. He deeply felt his obligation to protect the only son of his passed best friend. Billy wrestled calves, helped with branding, roped reasonably well, and worked horses with patience and skill. He saddled and rode horses, never being bucked off because he seldom caused a horse to want to buck this new friend on its back, patting and stroking its neck, murmuring in its ear, listening for fear in the snorting, the flickering ears.

By late spring the land had hardly recovered from the harshest winter on record. Riding west the band counted hundreds of dead, desiccated cattle, flies blackening their hides, maggots whitening the entrails. Horses too. Even deer and antelope. Farther north they might have happened onto the bodies of four Hash Knife cowboys frozen to the wasteland, perished in the worst of the February blizzard. Early recovery teams were scouring the north range, but cattle had drifted so far southeast with the wind many would not to be recovered until spring roundup.

Mary's objections had forestalled Billy's joining the gang; yet, with Frank Waugh now off the team it needed another rider. In the end it was Billy's persistence that finally prevailed. At fifteen he simply saddled up after Jack left, trailed him to the west, and walked into camp the second night. Tired, hungry, but savvy enough to have only stayed close to their first night camp, learned the whistle signal for entering camp safely, and had done so. Jack had little option at that point, instructed him on duties and signs for the northeast lookout, to give the danger signal if required, and to indirectly head back to the ranch if pursued.

This venture began much like many others. Northeast of Brandon Springs, the band found about 20 head of cows and heifers, two or three still with calf, some with young calves crowding to suck at their withering udders. They roped and branded the calves, and went searching for more the next day. They hazed the main herd south, they herded together another 15 head and bunched them back at their temporary holding point just above the headwaters of the Keya Paha. Surely they would find more stragglers from the storms as they progressed. By the third day, heading toward the east Sand Hills they had over 50 head, had branded 20-plus calves. Jack felt safer, being farther from probable early searching sweeps by cowhands from the big ranches. Jack rode halfway up Rattlesnake Butte, looked east and startled his horse when he saw Billy waving furiously a mile to the east. The rifle above his head, back and forth, then four or maybe five vertical pumping moves. Cowboys, four or five, headed their way. Jack raced to the drovers, waved them after him, and headed west, leaving the herd to chance, and his band to safer ground. At Ponca creek, just above the Niobrara, by now hardly more than a dribbling creek, they built a small fire in a copse of cottonwoods.

Seeing Jack's answering hat wave, knowing the plan and his instructions, Billy set out at a gallop to the east, finally miles from the encounter, and in wide, sprawling prairie, no riders in sight. He slowed his mare, watered her in the small pools that remained behind after Dog's Ear Creek had stopped flowing. The late spring shade under the few trees turned cool as evening fell, he trotted up out of the creek bed. At the first rise, still no pursuers in sight, as Dad Sully had expected. So he faced a day and night of steady riding home. Or. Or, why not ride back west? He could not be placed with the rustlers now, he was just a lone cowhand, heading west. Where to? Billy knew of ranches and Bordeaux's Trading Post from Dad Sully. That constituted rationale enough. He reined the mare around, spurred her to a trot, headed west. Hell, he had the camp skillet in his saddle bags. They would need that.

Billy rocked in the saddle, the mare steady in her pace, needing little urging. Her day had been a long one, but her nature precluded any lessening of effort. A little bit of work horse in her, maybe, he surmised. He rode into a warming spring sun dropped under the billowing western clouds onto the horizon. Meadowlarks trilled. He would ride into the evening, no chance of finding the band this day. His thoughts turned to this adventure. They had rounded up some cows, calves, done some roping and branding, bunched them up and headed south. Rustling was just ranch life. The excitement came from the unexpected, but even that they would tamp down with caution and experience.

Dad Sully, often enough, maybe too often, expounded on the evils of big cattlemen, the syndicates. They were not cowmen, they were goddam bankers. They left the work to cowboys, paying just enough to keep them from wandering off to a new adventure. The boss cowman kept them working, kept them tired, looking for a night's sleep, an over-fried slab of beef, a night in town once a month. Somehow they still did it, most loved the work. Even Dad Sully talked benevolently of his friends, his own days in the saddle, breaking broncs, wrangling, roping and the impromptu

RUSTLER ON THE ROSEBUD

rodeos at the base camps. Staying up on the nastiest bronc in the remuda. Palaver around the night fire. Jokes they played on each other. Dudes they had known, belittling anyone not equal to their prowess with rope or ability to sit the saddle on any horse. A life culture all its own. Dad Sully saw it as wasting men's lives, wasting horses and cattle at the expense of volume over husbandry. The range was free, the cows cheap, the cowhands cheap. The more stock loosed onto the plains, the more would survive the winters, the droughts, the rustlers and wolves; a profit in the end, just stay tough, fill the range to overflowing, disregard grass eaten to nubbins, the waterholes dry, and the buffalo wallows crusted to concrete.

Now the third night out, around a healthy campfire, Jack, poked lazily at the cow chips, pushed a branch into the flames, calm and reflective in explaining the operation for the next day. Olaf, Harry and Red Shirt listened carefully, more for Billy's sake, at a plan they already knew well enough. He poked hard at the branch, stood, and began raving at the big ranches. "Cocksuckers just take and take, leave little or nothing for the rest of us, and goddammit we were here first." He stalked into the darkness, spun back, eyes catching firelight, his mouth spitting invective. "Bastards. Gun ya down for a 10-dollar, skinny assed cow." He threw up his hands. "How many Indians you suppose died for butcherin a beef on their own land? One that ate up their grass, pissed in their creeks. I've herded thousands off Indian land, saving their grass, and then go back and find another five hundert coming up from the White River bottoms, forded by self-righteous goddam cowboys. If I could, I'd take a thousand to Nebraska every time." He walked around the fire, kicked at a sandbur stalk. Olaf leaned back on his elbow avoiding Jack's fiery eye, continued whittling a plum branch; Harry, pulled his hat over his face, head on his saddle. Ollie sauntered into the brush to pee.

Jack calmed himself, palmed some .44 shells, rolled them in his hand, reasoned that they were safe from being associated with the seventy or so cattle bunched north of the Niobrara. There would be little doubt that the cattle had been a rustling attempt by someone. The herd had left a trail coming across the Keya Paha clearly not the random wandering of cattle. He slid his Winchester from its scabbard, effortlessly levered in a round, eased the hammer to half-cocked, noting the lever still well oiled and smooth. His .44 pistol, needed no such simple test, it rested close on his hip, drawn and wiped clean every day. Silly, thought Jack, his team had their best horses, and that was always the first escape plan. Ride west, or south, depending, but ride hard. Ride close together for a mile, split off under cover of hills and creeks and ravines. Meet up later, at a designated rendezvous.

Olaf wandered back into the camp site with dead branches and twigs, hunkered down to build a small camp fire, under cover of trees and smoke sifting up through the trees not now visible. Yet, if a band of cowboys were to find them, best to act as normal as possible, just on a trip to Valentine or Springview.

Jack still hoped that the cowhands might leave the herd mostly intact, maybe cut out some of their own brand to take back north. He laid out a plan for Red Shirt to scout out the herd early in the morning, get back to the camp just after sun-up. This was for Red Shirt easy work. Jack moved past him, already rolled in his blanket, sleeping his turn before the early morning reconnoitering, and on up the tree line. No need to take chances, he sat with his back to an old oak, staring east across the darkening, rippled landscape. On look-out for movement. In any case, the cowhands would settle in as well. Then again, if they had a good tracker, maybe they could pick up spoor, however unlikely. Better to take care.

Billy rode well into the night, until he felt lost, disoriented. He stopped at a small cut bank, hobbled the mare and slept until first light. Orienting the half-orb of golden sun at his back, he roamed west and south of Rattlesnake Butte. He crossed the trail of the herd, but saw no sign of change in direction, no scattering of cows. Strange he thought. The herd is moving, on toward the Niobrara. Cowhands would have taken it back north, spread it around the Keya Paha. Dad Sully must be with this herd. He stayed in the tree line at Ponca Creek, saw the remnants of the campfire. Reasoned it was Dad Sully's. At the mouth of the creek, looking across the river, he saw no sign of cattle or trail crossing. He slipped from the mare and drank long in the clear creek water, rising up to see Red Shirt just across, finger to his lips, signing silence. Billy smiled, Red Shirt motioned him to cross and explained the situation. "Probably drifters, headin' south, scared us away and saw a chance to make some money. They got the herd in control, drivin' them south for us…how come you come back here? Your dad will not be happy."

Back from his recon mission Red Shirt and Jack forded the river and settled in for hot coffee.

"Boy, I've told you what to do when this happens, what the hell do you think I'm gonna tell your mother?"

"Dad Sully, I never even actually thought of that, but why tell her anything. I'm safe enough…and I got the skillet."

"How many hands out there was there?"

"I saw four. Could be another one or two, but they never showed. I saw em ride toward the herd, but started east like you told me to do. I changed my mind, and turned back west later. I figured that you would get away, and hell, I ain't got no real food with me. Besides we are more than them."

"Red Shirt scouted them out, says they are drifters, rustlin' and running on south, he thinks. Thought he could recognize the paint hoss of a kid raisin' hell around Rosebud for the past month."

"We'll have some coffee, catch up with Olaf. We'll catch em before the day is out." They drained their cups and stretched their mounts into a long lope.

By late afternoon, a thin dust hovered over the southwest horizon. Jack sent Red Shirt ahead as they walked their horses. Wind died away as dusk settled, as Red Shirt returned with Olaf. "Startin a camp just behind a bluff, edge of the jack pines. We could come from the north, in the night, have em for breakfast."

No fire for themselves, Jack and Red Shirt worked a plan, explained to Olaf and Harry, slept for two hours, and all went south. Billy stayed with the horses as the four worked slowly into the darkness.

The sun had not risen, first light casting a pale gray glow on the makeshift camp when Jack fired into the ambers of a dying fire. Two rangers jumped up quickly, scrambled for their guns. "Don't move and you won't be dead. Yer surrounded. …Boys, show yerselves." Harry and Olaf stepped into view from each side of the camp. Red Shirt went directly to the guns he saw, threw them aside, and kicked a holstered pistol from under a blanket before stripping two rifles from the saddle scabbards. Jack motioned the four jabbering rustlers into a group away from the guns and fire. "Now, sit, and shut up!" Red Shirt and Harry roped the weapons into a blanket and drug it toward the hobbled horses.

"Boys, we ain't the law or you'd soon be hangin from one a these trees, such as they are, but we laid claim to these cows first. The calves got my brand. So, we're takin them on to market, as we planned. You follow the trail of the cows on south, and you'll see your boots in about a mile."

The man, blurted out, "You cain't take ar boots, n our horses, that ain't right. Ya cain't leave no man out on this desert like that." Jack stared at him, continued, "Nother few miles, your hosses. As yer walkin, you think of this as your lucky day, not that ya was done wrong. …And not only that, what kinda rustlers build a fire and don't even have a lookout posted? You don't deserve these cows atall."

Sluggish of thought, in a completely compromised position, the group mumbled to the big man, at a lose for coherent thought. Would they hang? They knew the price for what they had attempted. They did not appear to be cowboys in any way. The big man reached for his slouch hat at his feet, another dark-eyed slightly built man pressed his short brimmed gamblers hat to his brow. All wore shabby clothes, and the weapons were old Spenser rifles and two rust streaked Smith and Wesson pistols. The youngest seemed hardly older than Billy. Riff-raff from Deadwood, maybe laid off miners, or just drifters.

They trailed the herd south until mid day, when Red Shirt skirted the herd from his scouting point to talk to Jack. "There's a small spring and pond up about three miles. Good place to hold the herd for Doc's men, but its not far enough to keep those losers from causin trouble again. I'm thinking, take the hosses back north, make em walk that way, would give us time."

"Yeah, that would work. They ain't got guns right now, but that big one ain't the kind of man to forget us easy. If they go north, they will intend to go to Valentine, its natural. I need to meet Doc there, so I don't wanta meet up with any of em."

"Them boys are trouble, Jack. The little paint pony is a Inyun pony. One a the others is a US brand. I seen that kid at the Agency before, and I think the others rode in there about a month back. They drank and sold whiskey. Chased squaws. They're no-accounts. Ther runnin south for good reason, Army kick em outa Rosebud."

"OK, take the string a hosses, leave the pack hoss and guns with us. Tell those boys they can find their hosses in Springview. Take em three days ta hike that. Its outa the way, but you can cut back to Valentine and meet up there. We'll be on the Running Water, directly outa town."

Cheyenne Club Again

The private dining room of the Cheyenne Club boasted a long linen covered table, fully set with silver and crystal. Sitting alone at the head of this luxurious table Mr. John Clay, cattle baron, turned a glass slowly, assessing and finally admiring the amber tone of an imported whisky. Ranch manager, envoy of world-class financial entrepreneurs, and a man full of confidence, sure of his strongly held positions, he relaxed, confident in his successes, eager to increase them. At this point in his life the efficacy and rectitude of the cattle industry drew his most pointed attention. He was, in a word, a superstar, not just to his employers, to whom he returned without fail the gain of their risks, but to the working cowboy and other cowmen. He lived what he believed, and believed what he lived. He had ridden the ranges winter and summer learning the business; even now, he rode hard, endured hardships in ardent pursuit of outlaws and rustlers; he experimented to improve the breed; he chose to forego offices in Cheyenne, rather favored management on horseback; he could not abide absentee cowmen, particularly those who made quick returns and rushed off to Chicago or St Louis to revel in the largesse of the ranges. He lived the credo of hard-core businessman, close to his work. He was the epitome of the cliché "firm but fair". He protected the investments of his employers, rewarded hard work, and refused to abide any erosion of the power of the cattle industry through poor management, disrespect for the law, or inattentiveness to responsibility. For these qualities he gained high admiration. His faults and his few failures must be attributed to his excessive energy in accomplishing his aims. When he decided to be "firm" he could be very firm, to the point of becoming his own law.

No stranger to the Club, he usually partook of its amenities in the course of his business. Normally at home at the Swan Ranch, north of Cheyenne on the Chugwater, he availed himself when work and business coincided. He waved his hand at the butler and directed him upstairs to request the presence of James Craig, Bill Whitcomb and Ed Lemmon at dinner. The three had arrived the day prior for a meeting to discuss operations on the Dakota ranges, and the mutual problems that they faced with rustling.

"Gentlemen, please be seated, drinks will arrive shortly, and we may continue our discussions over a fine elk steak. I personally acquired a very fine specimen on the ride down from the Chugwater. Its flanks have proven of the finest flavor. Bill, I presume the ride here has been sufferable and will ultimately prove worthy of your efforts."

"We came in last night... buckboards never suited me, but I found Jim's stuffed leather seats more comfortable than most." He smiled.

"A toast, gentlemen, to the fine year we have had."

They raised glasses of fine malt whisky from Scotland, and sipped it, savoring it with the respect it deserved.

Clay began: "It has been as we have noted, a fine year at the markets, but we have not marketed all the beeves that we have nurtured. The grass in Wyoming is excellent, and our tallies have been good. Not so much so in Dakota. The losses to wolves and Indians and other predators has affected us inordinately. The 'other predators' seem to have accounted for far too many losses. Wolvers have a chance to decimate the lingering population, given the rate of kill now experienced. Our increased bounty payout in Dakota should indicate an exceptional lowering of beef losses. Yet, we are losing more than I have expected. Gentlemen, I welcome your comments, especially as pertains to rustling."

The three gazed into their glasses, shifting in their seats; they were well aware of Clay's part in the Johnson County War, or Rustlers War, as he called it. Knowing how he had contributed in some unspoken way to the outright murder of several small ranchers accused of rustling left them a bit restless, but Ed Lemmon spoke up.

"We have the same problem as you had in Wyoming some time back. Small ranchers and rustlers, and the difficulty of tellin' a difference. The Rustlers War settled some problems in Wyoming, as I have heard you explain before. It was a harsh solution; we have, I think, felt some kickback from it. The state legislature remains damned stubborn against any 'extra-legal solutions', as the lawyers say. We have courts and law officers, and they expect us to use them."

Jim Craig continued: "But, as you know, John, those courts don't work. They are packed with homesteaders and small ranchers, even townspeople who are sympathetic to the rustlers. It's a hard road to conviction, even when the evidence proves guilt. In that respect, nothin's changed."

"Problem is," Bill Whitcomb avowed, "we can't tell which ranchers are stealin' and which ain't. We got brand books started, and we publish all brands, but new ones keep springin' up on young calves. We ain't stopped maverickin' to any degree." Bill, who had done much of that business himself, had kept his herd sizes up with help from his "friends" was at heart more small rancher than large. He had mortgaged his substantial herd of cattle from John Clay, but sustained them with close herding and a sharp eye for strays and mavericks. John Clay had long ago overcome any naiveté he may have suffered regarding Old Pap, but he knew he was not a cattle thief, and he offered an insight that Clay valued.

Ed Lemmon's position resonated with Clay's own: "There is talk of a large bandit society acting from Nebraska to Canada. Jack Sully's probably the leader. I know him, he is clever and he is wise, and he has influence in the Rosebud. Friends protect him. He stays on the reservation most of the time, law don't come after him there much, cuz they can't get a conviction in east river courts, no jurisdiction. Presho court still lets em all off, too. If we get Sully, we could stop a lot of the thievery."

"Ed, you think he's movin' herds all the way to Canada?"

"Well, it makes sense. Easy to sell there, no law there either, and our law can't cross over the border after em. Then he rustles Canadian cattle back to the US. Two way deal."

Bill spoke up. "I have known Jack a long time, he worked for me on the Platte, had him as foreman for a herd years ago I sent to the Yankton Agency. He's one hell of a cowboy. On the other hand, I don't see no society of rustlers. That ain't Jack. I ain't gonna say he does not maverick some calves, but he is basically an honest man. Ain't got a whole lotta cattle, mainly horses. John, you met him some years ago in this club."

Ed interrupted, emphatically stating that Jack Sully was very capable of leading a rustler's gang. He recounted his story of Jack's horse shooting to protect an Indian. "Probably part of his gang. And, he works for the Indians in the Rosebud, driving our cattle off the ranges."

"Mr. Sully did little to impress me with his presence in this club, that I may say without fear of contradiction, even from you, Bill...with the reservation opened, how is it legal to deny our rights to graze?" Clay asked.

"Tain't, but thers Indians on reservation trust lands, got some herds, and he protects em. Scotty Philip is up on that, sees what's goin' on there."

"Gentlemen, I think strong action is required. Its not just the Rustlers War that stopped the thieving in Wyoming, we have taken the war to the enemy, so to speak. Its actions to eliminate known rustlers, by whatever means. Some methods may seem harsh, but it is justice, truly deserved." He leaned forward, in a lower tone said, "We shoot wolves that plunder our herds, and rustlers constitute a like threat. Mr. Tom Horn has assisted us in that regard, when courts have failed. I commend his services to you. Speaking for our Scots investors, I can assure you that how we proceed with disposing of rustlers will meet with their approval...if not their signed authorizations," he laughed.

"I doubt that his sort of action will play well in Dakota. Last thing we want is another Rustlers War, what with the government in Washington down on us already, wanting to open the ranges to more homesteaders. We are lookin ta lease large sections of the range to hold off the settlers. Washington is important to us."

"Tom Horn can be very discrete with this work," Clay remarked. "As for the legislature, money talks. Our investors will support an investment there, I'm sure."

"To be downright honest, I ain't ever heard Horn be anything but loud-mouthed about his "accomplishments," Bill answered, in a sarcastic tone.

"The trick is, make silence a part of the deal. Word gets out, no pay. He'll listen and shut up....I have known and worked with Tom for several years. There is no finer detective or tracker in the west. As President of the Wyoming Stock Growers Association, it is of mutual interest to eliminate rustlers, none of whom have respect for boundaries.

"I suggest that we continue to pay Tom for his services, his salary coming from your side of the border, and his work done there as well as Wyoming"

"As you know, John, the Fall River County Protective Association wants me to see about a detective. If you can get Horn over here as a detective, not a shooter, let's give it a try…." He looked to James Craig.

"I'm with that, speaking for the Western South Dakota Stock Growers. Joe Elliot has not reported to us for six months, nor has he collected his pay… no one has seen him. Need someone, and he's gotta be a tough sonofabitch. Ed?"

"Of course." He agreed.

"Then let us now turn to those elk steaks. Butler, another round here, and commence the dinner service, if you please."

The Hats

The new hat sat at an odd angle, not snuggly down on the brown and white two-toned brow that his old hat always covered, exposed only on those rare occasions to tip it to a lady, or to wipe away the sweat that had worked with rain, wind, and hard use to form it. Off-white, the rigid oval leather hat band had not formed to the old cowboy's head and shock of hair. He readjusted it, pushed it down, but it had yet to find its true home. The real Olaf, the old cowboy with the slouch hat, chaps and wool shirt remained back in his cabin. Jack and Olaf had this as the first occasion to wear their new hats, a month before delivered to the General Store in Oacoma from Montgomery Wards, Chicago. Both yet to be fashioned to their individual liking, high undented round crowns, straight, stiff brims, white, clean and imposing.

Early morning, 4th of July. Jack had tied two kitchen chairs in the back of the single bench buckboard, plopped a pillow on each, and there sat Olaf and Edith, rather more comfortably than accustomed, all the way to Oacoma. The two prancing Tennessee Walkers fit the buggy perfectly, the oiled leather of the polished, studded tack glinted in the morning sun, the black lacquer of the sideboards mirrored the yucca and prickly pear as they passed. He enjoyed this pair above all others he had owned, and trained, and sold, but for the horse trader, these too must go their way. His plan: show them to their best effect at the Oacoma patriotic parade, catch someone in the mood and in the money for a perfect pair.

While Jack busied himself with untying the chairs, Mary found Martha Choteau, the mayor's wife, and was directed to the end of the stream of wagons and riders forming for the parade. Jack dutifully, if not happily, reined the Walkers to their assigned position, Olaf and Edith seated in front of the General Store, near the mayor, nearly lost among the well chapeaued crowd. Ladies with ribboned bonnets, flowered boaters, and one or two feathered Parisians; the mayor's wife in a silk, red and black chapeau, a bit too snuggly affixed to her tightly combed hair. Mostly though, the more modest women, those not accustomed to show, wore their best sun bonnet. All wore hats. The men sported Derbys for the most part, but cavalry slouch hats with yellow bands up from Ft Randall, wide-brimmed, high, dented crowns suggested the Texas cowboys, as the short curled brims did of the Dakota kind. A black bound-brimmed Hickock stuck out, and more than one well worn Confederate Army silver slouch hat was in evidence.

Wagons with brightly dressed maidens, one with a fully stuffed buffalo, another with six old, weathered cowboys on wooden benches, and a rather large assortment of red, white and blue bunting decorated horse drawn vehicles which preceded Jack's. Other buggies and buckboards formed up behind, some tried to position themselves toward the front, jockeying for best show-off position. Jack pointed them to the rear with little patience.

As Jack settled Mary in her seat beside him, firecrackers rattled, a staccato of pistol shots pierced the air, shouts rang out, whips cracked, and wagons began to move. It was too much for Jack. He aimed the Tennessee Walkers left out of line, slapped reins and in perfect unison, paced them toward the front of the parade. Nearing the front, he pulled his pearl handled pistol and fired six rounds skyward. If the crowd had not noticed, now they did. He pulled the pair up short, settled them into a prancing strut, and led the parade. The mayor seemed a bit confused, but his wife rose and stomped her foot, shouted something unheard at Jack, but too late. He smiled, waved his Stetson, lifted from his seat, and bowed from the waist. He led the parade, and not being satisfied with the display offered by the rather short main street of Oacoma, circled behind the façaded stores, caught the tail wagons, and proceeded to lead it again.

Twice was enough for the thirsty wagoneers, the formation broke, and after attending to horses, all made for the two crowded, smoky, raucous bars. The mayor's wife planted herself in front of the Hadley House, poked her fringed umbrella in Jack's chest as he approached.

"You, Mr Jack Sully, are an *arrogant* man!" He smiled, too full of the occasion to protest, at a lack for quarrelsome words for a dignified lady, bowed again, and circled the umbrella, through the swinging doors.

Jack glimpsed the black tailored coat and white hat on the small framed Marshall John Petrie. Jack attempted to slide to the opposite end of the bar, but the Marshall turned, just then, smiled directly at Jack. He gripped the Marshall's hand and offered to buy a whisky. The Marshall accepted, then stepped back from the line of hats at the bar.

"Jack, thanks for the whisky, and I shall repay you with a piece of information that may be of value to you, and you should accept as a warning. I was visited by a Mr Ed Blakeley this past week. He asked several questions concerning you, then stated that he knew that you headed the cattle rustling syndicate working western Dakota, and that he would without fail "snap off the head of that snake". He asked my support, and of course, as is my sworn duty, I advised him that when a valid warrant could be obtained, he had that. I also told him that I would not tolerate a hanging or bushwhacking to accomplish his ends. He did not comment, only pulled down his hat brim, gritted his teeth in a way suggesting he cared little for my warning. You seem to be the sole suspect and target of his pursuit to rid Dakota of rustlers."

"Well, he ain't got no proof, as you said. I won't discuss my dealin's with you Marshall, we've got that understandin. There's a fine line between what's right and what's legal …. You got jurisdiction in the Rosebud now, that right?"

"I have had for some time, since the land opened up. Times change, Jack, and I will do my duty. I've been a lawman a long time. Can't, nor won't, change. But you need to change. I don't want to come across the river lookin for ya. You got a good ranch, best horses in Dakota. Stick with that, it's a good livin."

"You know it was never *just* about the money….You like another of this fine 4th of July whisky?"

"That's not advisable in my case." He shook Jack's hand, smiled, turned away from the bar.

And so, the end justified the means. Jack found a table and savored another fine Tennessee whisky, and Mary a ginger beer. The first man to approach Jack was Hugh Prentice, president of the Brule County Bank of

Chamberlain. They sparred a bit, but Jack exacted his price. The black bowlered and proud Mr Prentice strutting the finest cartridge and pair in South Dakota, rattled across the pontoons of the Missouri at end of day.

PART IV

RAISING THE STAKES

RAISING THE STAKES
Ed Blakeley with Tom Horn

E d Blakeley rode east from the Wyoming range wars at the invitation of employ by the Western Stock Grower's Association to do what he had been paid well to do there. He arrived in Rapid City sartorially suited for the high position to which he ascribed himself. Black polished boots, a blue-black pin-striped wool suit, white shirt buttoned at the neck, in the evenings formalized with a dark ribbon tie, all under a pearl white high crowned hat with a single crease. He might have passed for a governor or congressman, and surely considered himself their equal. Yet, the fine suit he wore to Rapid carried nary a dollar in its pockets. The turmoil at end of the association's war in Wyoming saw him lose his last payday, one that should have been highly remunerative.

As lead detective for the Association he would, in fact, have a measure of power equal in circumstance with the gentlemen he sought to emulate. As a Range Detective, his word in the primitive courts of law west of the Missouri was taken *prima facie* sooner than the strongest evidence to the contrary; should he find himself called upon by circumstances to become at once sheriff, judge and hangman, that too would find ultimate acceptance in the back rooms of Rapid City saloons.

John Clay had first recommended Tom Horn, a bushwhacker of note, with whom he had worked in Johnson County, Wyoming, to the Association. Needing a respite from the animosity Horn had accumulated in the Buffalo, Wyoming area, Horn came east to apply his remedy for rustling, only to find it not well accepted in an area with growing desire for more civilized, legal remedies through an infant court system. After several WSDSA members expressed concern with Horn's tactics of summary hangings and shootings, Blakeley was asked to visit Rapid City. Small ranchers who had started as cowhands and had friends on the big ranches had come under pressure from Horn. Most did not deserve it. Questions of unproven guilt were raised, and more instances were being referred to courts in Pierre, Yankton and in the middle of west river cattle country, the young cow town of Presho. The court docket consisted mostly of charges for thievery and rustling in these formulating years when complete lawlessness began its evolution to law and order.

Blakeley's salary was modest enough to avoid suspicion of overly ambitious prosecutions, but secretly, a select committee of the Association advanced him a month's salary and promised him $750 for each rustler apprehended, or dealt with in a way which promised his removal from the passel of trouble from which the Association desired riddance. Ed's talent proven in Wyoming was truly that of detective, of being able to get the goods on any small rancher or homesteader who ever stole a cow or horse. He studied the brands of the territory, where the ranches ranged their stock, where the small ranchers' and homesteaders' grazing overlapped the big ranches.

He was a man always on the job. At his core lay a true and hard honed moral code consistent with the laws held most in esteem by his employers, their property rights as extant in their animals and the range as open and free to all. Few Dakota cowboys who knew him failed to fathom the depths of his cold personality; its severity ran like the Missouri under winter's ice. To them he ranked no higher than a Pinkerton agent, not a well regarded breed, rather than gubernatorial aspirant. He took no criticism lightly and would never allow himself the humility of being the butt of a joke. He made no fast and true friends, only business partners and enemies.

He had scrapped by with odd detective jobs, range work, and missions for John Clay. The Dakota Association's incentive plan fit well into his immediate needs.

His acquaintance with Tom Horn promised an insight into Dakota rustling. The Association secret committee sponsored their renewed acquaintance at the Rapid Creek Restaurant, but left Tom to confab with Ed. Talk over steaks soon turned to the work at hand.

"I want to say first off, Ed, this place ain't like Johnson County. These 'gentlemen' do not approve of my methods for early dispatch of my foes. I have intended to make an example of one or two of these home-steaders, and they won't buy it."

"Tom, the Wyoming thing did not set well with a lot of folks, and the plains are fillin' up with more towns and more courts. The ranchers know what happened, that boy dyin' in Wyoming."

"Well, I am a killer of cow thieves, and that is what I expected them to want done when they hired me. I do not intend to have thievin bastards shootin' at me before I shoot them. Don't matter how a man dies in the end. If he's a cow thief, he can die my way or with a hemp necktie; quicker my way."

"Yeah, well, it ain't gonna be like Wyoming here, or we won't either of us have jobs."

"I don't have a job now. These assholes told me to move on already. You're head detective, and you have your orders, so I was told. I can pass along what little I know, but I was not here long enough to pin down any of them. The elk is better then the beefsteak, by the way. That's why I eat here. Only place that ever has it regular in this town. ...but I will tell you, Ed, you got to make an example or yer never goin' to succeed with tryin to take this scum to court. That's been done, and it ain't worked."

"Who are the main suspects?"

"I talked to old Marshall Petrie in Mitchell about a month ago. He knows the Rosebud fairly well, but to my notion has not done much to stop whatever is happenin' there. He says, Jack Sully, the Nelson boys, and some other small guys are still into rustlin' but never been caught. They stay away from the spreads in the Rosebud, so no complaints from there. Doc Middleton trades horses down in Nebraska, and they say he's gone straight, but I doubt it. Nobody trusts Kid Rich either. I ain't met him, but I heard he is of a wild breed and a wiseass cowboy. Not even his father-in-law likes him. Then again, old Narcelle Narcisse is probably rustlin' too. It's just like Wyoming in that respect, the small ranchers all get their start off the big ones. There's a bunch down south a here, mostly move their rustlin's toward the Wyoming ranges or south toward the Platte to avoid the brand identification, makeup a bill a sale. Nobody checks.

Same up north, some movin' beeves to Montana, some crossin' the Missouri when its low and sellin' east river. Then, I hear the inyuns butcher a beef here and there on the range, when the govment lags on issue beef, which is often."

"This secret committee likely to pay up if I get my hands on a rustler?"

"They got the money, and the committee is hot after cow thieves. Wolves get some, inyuns get some but I surmise that blizzards get the most. Still, I suppose going after rustlers is somethin' they can do, so they're doin' it." He sipped his whisky, washed it with coffee. "Stay close to Ed Lemmon. He's a righteous bastard, can't be turned. The secret committee was set up cause there are no doubt some association members that are rustlers themselves. Don't have nothin' but suspicions, but word about me bein' here got out pretty fast. Ed knows everybody on the north range. Go to Belle Fourche an see him.

He scrapped his chair back, stood up, and reached for Ed's hand. "Good huntin'. If these assholes change their minds, let me know. Leave a letter at the Cheyenne Club. And yes, the secret committee will pay if you discretely rid the range of a rustler, any which way, if you do it smart."

Tom and Jack Palaver ~1900

As he topped a small ridge, a whitetail doe with two yearling spike horns sprinted up the draw. Jack drew his rifle, and as the lagging youngster paused to look back, he sent him to his knees with the first shot. He dismounted, leveled his aim, and brought him down with the second shot. This would be a small consideration for old Bill's hospitality.

Jack walked Jim Longstring, the gutted deer tied behind his saddle, taking care in the scrub pine bluffs to stay below the horizon, skirting the ravines. Still, coming up from a small draw, he heard his name called. He rolled to the left side of Jimmy, and booted him into a run, sprinting for a stand of low scrub pine a hundred yards ahead. He made the pines without hearing a shot, slid his rifle out of the scabbard as he hit the ground and pulled Jimmy in a half circle. He leaned behind a cedar, rifle ready, for a good five minutes, until a rider appeared back on the prairie, heading at a walk toward him. The rider raised his rifle above his head with both hands as he approached.

Tom Horn was a mixed blood, Indian and French, according to John Clay, with whom he had maintained a long association. Or he was of Scots and German stock, from Missouri? Much of his life remains a mystery, much of that of his own making. Tall, well over six feet, lean, slim at the waist, a large sombrero, and always carried his rifle, as others worn a six gun. He fashioned himself a hired killer, and boasted freely of it. His tales told in saloons across Wyoming only served to attract a posse of sycophants seeking drinks to satisfy his need for an audience. His tracking skills were unparalleled, learned in the Apache wars where he served as government scout. After the Apaches were subdued and confrontations among ranchers ignited on the northern ranges, he moved there, making his skills available to the highest bidders. These of course were the ranching syndicates. He sided not only with their money, but also with their view of thieves, robbers and what he considered 'no accounts'. It would have been a rare instance for him to assist an accused rustler. Bad for the detective business if known by his employers. He lived by a strict code of loyalty, in the end taking the working end of a rope before he would betray his cattle baron bosses. Yet, he took the time now to warn an old friend.

"Jack, I coulda shot you a while ago. You getting careless and scared?" He smiled.

"I'd be damned foolish not to be scared a you. I still ain't interested in the detective business, you wasted a trip."

"Let's go over to Bordeaux's, his old lady makes a helluva stew and biscuits. Doc talked to you, eh?"

"Yeah, but it still coulda been a trap."

"Not this time. I will not work for them cocksuckers again. I'm headin' down to Denver, but wanted to let you know that a new detective is already here."

"Why dya care?"

"Maybe someday the small ranches are gonna win out in Wyoming. They already seem to be diggin in ther heels like subborn mules out here. Not until the big boys have their way a while though, Jack, and you better be damned careful 'til they get calmed down. This new guy you might know, Ed Blakeley, he was in Wyoming. He's got a bounty deal as well as a salary, so he's lookin' for someone like you to add to his accumulation and to make an example. And he don't like the small spreads neither. Got too much of politician in him, sees his future in the hands of the big cattlemen."

"That would not make him a likely friend."

"Time to stay at home more. There's places fer small ranchers but they got to know their place. Times er changin', rustlin' is a dangerous business now. The big boys leave justice to me and my friend." He patted his rifle scabbard.

Bill Bordeaux welcomed them off their horses and into the house. Settling in after savoring a fine stew, the three men talked about the range, about the changes. "Jack, a man's gotta make a livin', and I have my ways. I go where the money is. I got no truck with hoss and cattle thieves. I use radical means, Jack, but I have warned each a them in turn... no re-ward is out directly for you that I know of. Wanderin around down in this area, I run onta Doc Middleton. He said you might be up to helping me out in Wyomin'. I reckon you don't carry that pistol fer nothing. Doc said you were damned good with it. You might consider coming out to Laramie, Buffalo for a while, and help me out. They pay me well to take care of thieves.

"Hell, ain't no secret, I need the money, but I gotta family, and Mary's 'spectin' again. Ain't no time fer me to be runnin' off. I don't know what you think, Tom, but I ain't no cow butcherer and I ain't runnin' brands. I don't know what Doc tole ya, but I ain't been caught stealin' beeves. I brand what ain't branded, like any man on reservation land. They don't like it, they can get their damned cattle outa here. What's Doc up to? I ain't seen him in a while."

"Blakeley will try to find somethin'. ... Well, Doc is stickin' to the law's line, 5 years in prison will do that to ya. ....ya got any money? We could play some poker again."

"You mean you'll give me a chance to win back all that loot I lost to you in Wyoming last year?" he laughed.

The Specter of Tom Horn Abides

Putting on the hard and fearless tough-guy act for Tom Horn seemed to have worked, Tom pursued his own case for the syndicates no further. Fundamentally, he liked Jack, knew he had been on both sides of the law. Pursuing rustlers in Dakota promised no compensation for him now. The evening banter and card play went well, no large gains or losses on either side.

Jack's thoughts sank into a funky depression as he turned homeward. Jim Longstring ambled across the landscape, a steady head-bobbing walk, Jack rocked in the saddle, feet loose in the stirrups, in deep contemplation of Tom Horn's news. There seemed no way out of his peculiar predicament. His plan to stay on the land and rustle syndicate cattle had worked to this point, but now he had to confront the downside. By remaining in the Rosebud, with the mounting legal efforts of the Stock Growers Association and the resolve of Ed Blakeley and his like, Jack faced a fight or flight situation. Jack and his crew were not bushwhackers, and the Association would just hire another if they shot a detective. Yet, Blakeley and his lot needed no real evidence to bring him down. Shooting him over a half-branded calf would adequately cover their real intentions, which was, get him, dead or alive. That scenario could be easily arranged if they could but find him on this great expanse.

Jack weighed the consequences of continuing, mulled over how much time he had to accumulate what hard cash he needed to completely get out of the business, what the real possibility that the Association could mount a decided effort directly against him.

The feeling of gloom, impending doom, however, did not subside. He rode at a walk, deep in thought. Tom Horn could have killed him, any number of other ambitious men might also succeed. He jerked up on the reins, his stomach knotted; he surveyed the landscape, a creek line on his right, a small butte to his left, he was riding along, completely vulnerable to a resourceful gunman. Even after a relaxed evening, he awakened to the possibility that their opening discussion could have been tantamount to a warning like any other from Tom Horn, who had made a point of giving prior notice to his targets of his intentions. He tightened the reins, and spurred Jim to the low line of hills to the east, leaning low over the saddle horn.

Fleeing became a more plausible alternative to living in constant danger. Thoughts of leaving his family for an extended period, an indefinite period, only deepened the helplessness he felt. Yet, for all his contemplation, his search for solutions, he remained basically indecisive; he would continue as he had. Money could be made, it could solve a host of problems.

Blakeley's Meeting with Ed Lemmon

Taking to heart the tasking from Tom Horn to have a talk with Ed Lemmon, Ed Blakeley set out the following week for Bell Fourche and the Moreau River country northeastward. The prairie stretched on, rolling forever, so few landmarks, low-lying hills with no names. Ed had not ridden a horse much in the past six months, and today as usual, used a buckboard when he could, such being the fashion of John Clay. After Bell Fourche there were no towns, just forlorn ranches, a house here and there, a dugout at the top of a draw for the new settler, but few of them. A day out of town he caught the headwaters of the Moreau and followed its path down the smooth sandy stretches of river bottom, or up the ridges to round the cut banks when he must. He found the Flying V ranch sloped along the river hills, a ranch house of logs with porch drooping off the front, two pole corrals, a low slung lean-to for horses, and two log bunk houses. Cowhands sat against the side of the nearest, rolling smokes, talking, and throwing new ropes at a snubbing post, working out kinks, loosening them for real work. They looked up at Blakeley, but carried on, hardly acknowledging him. Their boss appeared in the ranch house door, came out to meet the new arrival as he dismounted, and immediately took his horse's reins and headed to the pole barn.

"Some oats here for your animal. I assume you are Mr. Blakeley. The commission told me you would be coming by. Has Horn left the country yet?"

Well, right to business Blakeley thought. "Yes, sir, he went off to Cheyenne or Denver, no business here as he said."

It being clear that the "sir" was perfunctory, not meaningful, Lemmon replied "No 'sirs' on this spread, Ed. Come in, we can talk."

Lemmon sat him at the long table in the dining room, went to the kitchen and returned with two teacups and saucers. No whiskey, as he had hoped and might have gotten on some ranches. Back to the kitchen, Lemmon brought forth a plate with a handful of simple store bought sugar coated cookies. Lemmon began dunking the cookies, and poured hot coffee into a saucer which he blew to cool, then slurped the dark brew.

"Horn told me that you knew where to start with ridding this area of rustlers. Interesting country along the way. Not Wyoming at any rate. Grass is the best I've ever seen. You must have a great amount of stock out here?"

"I've got over 50,000 head from here to the Cheyenne south, and to the Badlands in North Dakota." Lemmon called the Shiedley Cattle Co. stock "his", devoted as he was to the owners, his place as Boss Cowman, and the responsibility for the hands that worked the ranch. "I can tell you what I know of rustlers, but there's new ones all the time. Just about every small rancher is branding anything he can. I have found dead Flying V cows, shot so's the calves can be branded and weaned away. Now that is a mortal sin. We have to rid this country of the likes of these sonsabitches."

"I will do so. I cleaned up the remains of the Johnson County mess, after the big shots tried their power game. It takes some detective work, and some examples to be made."

"Well, you'll earn your money here in Dakota, the way it is now. There are some known thieves, and I can tell you who they are, even if I can't prove it. That's for you to do. We want to abide by the law, difficult as that may be. There were times when our form of law was enough. Now the Association does not want any hangings or shootings, it wants to keep itself above the trouble that kind of thing causes. This is a state now, and the law is coming, if not fast enough. For myself, I want rustlers taken care of. I want them stopped. They are causing losses of great proportion to my bosses, and they make me accountable for all losses, whether winter, wolves, disease, or rustlin'. You do what you have to for my part, and there ain't no one else in this room right now. 'Nuf a that... Right in this area, some are taking cows west and selling them in Wyoming. The Association includes the eastern Wyoming ranches, so brand books are shared. That has helped some, but won't stop all of them. I had two or three hands that I suspected, and let them go. Acourse, they just went to Wyoming and took a bunch of beeves with them. Kid Rich is mixed up with the hard core in this area. He worked for me and was a good hand, some rustlers are, but whenever I sent him out line riding, I seemed ta lose stock. He works both sides, in my mind. He is now over at the Cavanaugh ranch, recently married, and I hope settling down. Married one of Narcelle Narcisse's sisters, lived there a while, then was kicked out, to my notion. Narcelle's got a herd of some size, and need of several hands, ... you should talk to him."

"Down south a the Hills, there is plenty of cattle lost to the Sandhills rustlers. They deal in horses a lot, but will take cattle from the south range and the reservation. Lots of small ranchers down there also, and I don't trust no small rancher. In fact, Shiedley policy now is that no small ranchers will be taken on as hands. Too much temptation for them to know too much. There's talk over east about Jack Sully. I had to let goa him some time back. One of my best hands, but two of my boys were stopped from catching a Inyun cow butcher. He shot the horse out from under one of 'em. Course, again, I couldn't do nothing, it bein' on the reservation. He has a place over on the Missouri. Deals in horses, and is the best horseman I ever met. He slicker-broke five horses in one afternoon for me. I like him, but I can't have even a good hand like him on this spread. He's been took to court, but there are so many rumors and false accusations that none of the honyockers on the jury will believe any of em. Ya need to find one you can stick to him, direct. There's a lot of small ranches building' up over on the Missouri, around the White River and the Niobrara, from Ft Pierre south.

"I will look into this Sully. You know any other names of suspects?"

"That's yer job to find out. As a member of the "select committee" I am authorized to tell you that you can hire three deputies. I recommend Sam Moses first, you know him. He has been a stock detective in Wyoming, was a sheriff down south. He's the foreman for Oelrich south a Rapid City now, but he would take on the job. A. P. Long has been a deputy sheriff, and like Sam, you can trust what side he's on. If you could get Sully to work with us, you could probably have an idee on what's goin' on in the whole state. Some say he runs a gang workin from here to

Canada, I myself, doubt it. Ranchers over on the Missouri have their own Association, but won't join up with us. Scotty Philip is the big rancher in that group. Straight arrow, too. Talk to him soon, west a Ft Pierre, on the Bad River. You bunk here tonight, in the spare room. No need to roust out one of my hands from the bunkhouse. I keep a lot of riders, but it's the best way to save cattle. Costs Shiedley more, but its worth it."

The very demeanor of Blakely set Ed Lemmon's teeth on edge. Did not remove his hat indoors; chin jutting forward, restless in his chair as he listened to Lemmon. He knew of him, that he had started as a cowhand before becoming the sheriff of Fall River County, and had taken his new experience to Wyoming for the Johnson County war. Ed knew he needed lawmen, but had met few he admired. And detectives were worse. Blakeley and A. P. Long typified the men necessary, but too cold-eyed even for a cow boss considered cold-blooded in his own right. Yah, he thought, Sam Moses, likeable old Texan that he was, might mellow this iron backed sonnavabitch. I could tell he didn't think much of the ranch house, and damned if I would give him whiskey. Left his hat on as if this were a hog ranch, but sniffed at the furniture. Lacy sleeved Englishman at heart. Thought occurred to Ed, that he liked the men who he sent Blakeley to apprehend better than the detective himself. Sully, Kid Rich, Buffalo George, Olaf Nelson, they were cowboys...at least wouldn't shoot ya in the back.

Kid Rich in Oelrichs

Jack's first encountered Ed Blakeley in Oelrichs soon after his hiring by the Association. The true beginning of spring, so rudely interrupted by another late winter storm, had burst forth across the barren land. The White River broke up, sending house-sized ice blocks hurdling down its path, inundating its flood plain. Buds ventured onto the bravest trees, and animal life ventured out of its winter hiding to gaze hopefully on spring's provenance and prospects. Broke, not a silver dollar to his name since last fall, he had mounted Dolly, his bay thoroughbred mare, and trailed old Buck. His purpose was to venture out to Bill Bordeaux's store where he played stud poker until he won $20 from Sam Moses, boss cowman of the T Bar. He retired to the old dugout under the Wall, cleaned it a bit, and hunkered in, riding out daily to locate critters beneath the Badlands Wall and across western end of the Rosebud. The long cold month of hazing cows, the forlorn dugout home, and the lingering cold had built a thirst in his soul and an equal one in his body. Return to the Whetstone was imperative, but he had the poker money in his vest. He felt flush, confident; he wanted a drink before all the work and hustling began.

At the dugout, he pushed his plunder into the panniers and saddlebags, diamond hitched it to the cross buck and cinched it on a double hitch to Buck. Oelrichs was a rare town of necessity far enough south of Rapid City to save a rancher or a cowboy a days ride to get a drink or a good meal or if he had no other excuses, to "get the mail", something the post office actually provided on occasion. John Ballard gained rights to the post office and ran it out of the store owned by Harry Oelrich's Anglo-American Cattle Co., and he had been first to start the inevitable saloon just up the boardwalk. Worn, wood plank slaughtering houses leaning northward, pushed by summer winds, perched over cracked concrete floors, evidence of Harry Oelrich's dream to butcher beeves close to the range, to lessen the cost of shipping through the railroad cartels, at the end their greed trumped his entrepreneurship. They shunted aside his trains outside of Chicago and St Louis; rotting carcasses pitched out of the failing ice cars along tracks reeked of doom for the enterprise. Harry consolidated his remaining cattle under the Bar T brand and turned his enterprising nature back to what he knew best, raising cattle.

Jack scraped gumbo from his boots on the planks at the hitching post and noted the newly painted, hand scratched green letters on a whitewash slab above the *Buffalo Saloon*. He blinked his eyes adjusting to the dimness, made out the bar, shadowy, motley crowd of drinkers. Ed Blakeley, a Stock Grower's detective, in a dark suit, small brimmed, single crease white hat, cocked left on his pomaded hair, posed holding his drink in three fingers; Kid Rich, a waddy, suspected rustler, but never caught; Narcisse Narcelle, the old French rancher from up around the Moreau River, brown wool trousers, a shirt that was meant to be white, and ever-present moccasins. Ed stood near Sam Moses, still foreman at the Bar T, wide brimmed, high crowned Texas hat over blue canvas pants, gray shirt and vest; Jack started to move to the end of the bar, next to Harry Ham, a neighbor from north of his own spread on the Missouri, but Kid Rich reached for his hand. John Ballard, bartending, levered a wooden bung on one of the barrels holding up the newly planed pinewood planks that constituted the bar, drained whiskey into a half-pint jar and handed it to Jack.

Looking around, Jack saw the semblance of a typical new western tavern. Shot glasses and pint jars lined another makeshift shelf behind the bar, a large mirror had also been framed to the wall surrounded by John's crude attempt at varnished and lacquered shelves. The bar itself, new, unsanded pine planks, laid across three 50 gallon wooden kegs, snagged his shirt elbows as he propped there. Away from the bar front were two more kegs. John had rolled them in, all full of new whiskey from Kentucky, to secure them, and to double as stand-up tables. In a far corner stood a square wooden table, empty save for dog-eared playing cards, with five new pine backless chairs. The devilish grin on Kid's face told Jack enough; it could only lead to fun or mischief, even trouble.

"How many cowboys you shot lately then, Ed?"

He stated "I don't shoot people, I take 'em to justice like they should be when they thieve a man's property," his back stiffening.

"So, you can buy the drinks, Ed, with all the dough you're getting' from those 'brought to justice', right? I heard tell yer getting $700 a head from the Stock Growers for each a those many criminals."

That's a lie and a damned lie. I get paid by the month, like you.

"Well, I hope it ain't like me, cause I chase cows for a livin', not men. Where'd you come from, I ain't heard tell of any hands around here takin' on the badge lately?"

"Young man, I was sheriff of Fall River County until I went to Wyoming last year."

"So, you were in the Johnson County war, eh? Got your butts kicked dinya?"

Bar room banter never appealed to Ed Blakeley, even given the opportunity as a cowboy when he frequented bars and hog ranches. "I wasn't in the "war", so I didn't get my butt kicked, and whether I did or not is none of your business. The fact is there was a whole lot of rustlin' going on, and I helped to put a stop to it. I wouldn't suppose you could understand that, since yer in here spending money 'stead a out working cows. Or is it how you 'work cows' why you got drinkin' money?"

"Course, I know yer joking there, Ed, cause if you thought otherwise you'd be drawin' on me and taking me in, right?" In a more serious tone, "So, you got no business sayin' that, ... or just draw your little goddam pea shooter and piss away at me."

Which Ed did. Ed Blakeley was not a man to take shit from this little "pecker-head", as he thought of him, and was about to tell him. He drew, and fumbling with cocking the little .38 pistol, discharged a round into the floor near the Kid's feet. The Kid ducked under the bar, behind a whiskey keg and drew his own weapon. His first shot passed Ed's head on the way through the tin roof, frightening Ed into a position behind the far barrel in the middle of the room. The hands at the bar scrambled like cats to beat each other out the front door. Jack, to the left of the Kid when firing commenced, dodged behind the whiskey barrel at the end of the bar.

Kid put two rounds into the barrel Ed had hidden behind, and a series of shots were exchanged, mostly into the barrels, draining away amber streams of whiskey to soak into the gumbo flecked, pine floor boards.

John, seeing what was happening to his new, pricey whiskey, yelled for them to stop or they would pay for the whole two barrels. Ed swore, and fired again. Kid laughed and did likewise. "Come out you coward law dog, I'm only gonna shoot you in the knees so you can't ride down honest folk anymore."

"Ya little peckerhead, I think yer gun has done the talkin' fer ya, and I'll be takin' you in across a pony soon enough. It won't take much riding to do that."

Jack leaned against his fortification and refilled his jar with whiskey draining from his barrel, "High quality stuff ya got here, John."

"It's come all the way from Kentucky, cost two dollars a gallon, an' look, its just *runnin' away*." He stayed behind his barrel near the front door. Jack saw him reach up to the coal oil lamp behind the bar, pull it down and extinguish the flame. Getting the idea, Jack did the same with the lamp at his end of the bar, then leaned around and grabbed the Kid, pulling him behind his own barrel. The Kid used the movement to fire off more rounds, drawing Ed back into the fracas.

Jack whispered to the Kid, "Let's go," pointed to the side door, and pulled him in the darkness toward it. He grabbed tight to the Kid's vest, located the door handle, slammed it open and tumbled out into the evening darkness. They ducked around the side of the bar, across a small open space, into a copse of young cottonwoods.

The firing stopped, John Ballard turned up the wick on the lamp. "By god Ed, yer gonna pay for this whiskey."

Ed dismissively slapped a dollar on the bar and stomped out the front door.

Jack waited in the dying light. "John, I'm coming in alone, Kid's vamoosed." He edged inside where John was relighting the second lamp.

"John, stick some bullets in those holes to stop that good whiskey, help me out." He pulled several bullets from his gun belt and wedged them into the holes still draining away. John pulled jars off the riddled shelf, catching what he could, and helped Jack stopper the remaining holes. "Lookit this, Jack, the damned mirror ain't broke," he said, almost cheerfully.

"What those dudes doin' in here, seems like a strange place out away from civilization for a guy like that shooter?"

"Ed Blakeley's a snooty-nosed sonofabitch now, used to be a regular hand, but took on Sheriff here some years back. Lately, he come outa Rapid to see Sam. I think you know Sam. Heard him tryin' to talk him into becomin' a deputy, working with the Stock Growers. Sam is the foreman here now, but I think was a lawman in Fall River County before."

"He's a Texan fer shur, or some other place south. Sam wears his pistola a little bit low. He say yes or no?"

"I did not hear. Narcisse came in with the Kid, you know he married his daughter not long back. He is living up between the Grand and Moreau, doing line-ridin' for one of Narcisse's neighbors it sounded like. Kid was doin' most of the talkin', and it weren't all that intelligible, as usual."

"Harry is my neighbor, but he left kinda fast, I did not even get a chance to talk. What's he doing way out here?"

"Said he was wolfin'. Come in around mid-afternoon, just when I opened, did not say too much, but he's mighty proud of his new Army rifle. 30-40 Krag, he says, side loader, and got a long barrel. Took seven wolves to Rapid yesterday. Said he got every one of them with one shot, but I don't put too much credence to that."

"Might be, John, I seen him shoot coyotes about a mile away. Well, maybe not that far, but he does have an eye. I cowboyed alongside Kid with the Flyin' V. Ed Lemmon likes him, and that ain't no small account a what we call respect. If Ed can put up with his shenanigans, he ain't all bad. He rode away laughing, and he ain't one to take offense easily. I seen him pull monkeyshines wherever he was at, and he can take it just like he can dish it out. If Ed leaves him alone, not much will come of it, but he's fast as a rattler with his pistol. ...Ya got lids for those jars? I might want to take one with me."

"You earned it, I wouldna thought to put bullets in the holes, so I suppose you saved more than one jar."

Ed Blakeley's Deeds

Much of Ed Blakeley's early life had been spent as a cowboy, in southwest Dakota, and into Wyoming. He had always taken a hard line on rustlers, horse thieves and miscreants of any sort. He had ridden with the posse that tracked down some of the members of Sam Bass's gang when he robbed the Deadwood stage on its route from Cheyenne. Lame Johnny was hung, two others shot dead. He watched Johnny struggle, legs flailing,... "Can't walk on air any better than he could on the ground." Disdain and disgust of Johnny's kind in his heart. A sorry piece of mankind, served him right, and he didn't do the air dance long enough to his liking. When Sam Moses took over county sheriff, Ed worked with him as deputy for nearly a year before being recruited to help the Association in Wyoming, finally part of the posse that gunned down several small ranchers, smoked out some others, and was only stopped by the intrusion of US troops to end the Johnson County war.

The Western Stock Growers Association, when founded, included western Dakota and eastern Wyoming ranchers. It had tried a number of organizational changes, such as hiring brand inspectors, publishing brand books and lists in local papers, had gained influence in the Dakota legislature, and had at last even gotten a "Maverick Law" passed which allotted all mavericks to the Association. Some of the large ranchers from Wyoming had moved into Dakota and with them came the idea to hire range detectives, bless them with authority to arrest, shoot if necessary, but by whatever expeditious measure, rid the range of rustlers. Early problems arose. The Association had several small ranchers as members. Some were genuinely trying to become larger, but others took advantage of the insider knowledge gained through the regular meetings and the trust they gained as members to build up their own herds.

Within the first month, Ed rode down on a cow butchering, a young Lakota brave, off reservation, armed with bow and arrows and his butchering knife. At full gallop, Ed caught him in the back with three slugs before he could reach his nearby mount. He cut the brand from the hide, and the earmarked right ear. This he strung on a rawhide thong, with the young man's braid. He thought about scalping, but knew that would not set well with the committee. The braid was enough; no brave would give that up without a fight. That easy, he earned $700.

North of Belle Fourche Ed began tracking three rustlers as they moved a herd of about 40 white faces toward Wyoming. Ed Lemmon had sent Kid Rich to alert Ed of the rustling, who he deputized, and they set out immediately. Kid Rich went with more than a little reluctance. First, there was the incident at Oelrichs which must still be fresh in Ed's mind, second they were outnumbered, there were at least three rustlers, and since the Kid dabbled in the rustling business, he was not sure who they were or whose side he should be on when they caught up with them. Ed allowed as how he could handle two of them if the Kid kept the other busy. Twenty miles west, Kid picked up fresh tracks. Ed told the Kid to follow the herd, stay out of rifle range, but if he was seen, not to engage the rustlers until he had gotten the drop on them. Kid hung back, walking his gelding. He had to see the rustlers before they saw him.

Ed skirted ahead north at a hard gallop over the Wyoming border. He nestled into an outcropping of rocks and boulders south of Devils Tower where he had an open shot across a small, scalloped valley. The herd of about 40 head trotted directly down the valley, a rider on each flank, and one trailing. Ed took aim at the nearest rider and shot him in the back as he passed the rocks. The far side rider turned immediately away, realizing the ambush and responding, and the trailing rider spurred forward, turning southward. Ed's second shot missed the rider, but broke the front leg of his horse, spilling both into the sagebrush. Ed mounted and raced to the unhorsed rider, rifle ready. Kid rode up, still not sure of who the rustler was. Seeing the wounded and suffering horse, Kid shot him in the head. Ed leveled his rifle at the rustler, "You sonofabitch, I caught ya, and you'll get the hangin' you deserve."

The kid wore work shoes, a floppy hat, farmer's overalls; he protested immediately "I got a billa sale for these cattle, in my saddle bag. You shot an innocent man already. He stuttered, fear in his voice, his eyes wide and wild.

"Git it, then."

As the boy turned to his war bag on the dead horse, Ed shot him in the back.

"Tryin' to escape, as I saw it."

"Ed, you shot him cold. He might be tellin' the truth."

"I'll have a look, but we both know he was rustlin' these cattle. He dismounted and searched the saddlebag, and found only a small, five shot revolver among the clothing.

"Settles that. Round-up that other one's horse and we'll take them an the cows back to Belle. I will make it known that it ain't safe to be rustlin' in these parts." Ed could not discount the look of concern in Kid's face or the tone in his comments.

"You helped with the capture here, Kid, I'll see that you get a hunderd dollars for that. You know Kid, you got to take a side on the rustlin business. If you ain't with us, you're against us. I could use your help, and you could make some extra money with anyone you bring in, or help identify. Just pass me information."

He needed money, and he thought that he could work both sides, with no damage to either. Seeing the treachery Blakeley was capable of, this was no time to disagree. He told him that he would keep in touch, but expected more than $100 for anyone caught.

"Listen, I'll get you $200 for every rustler that you bring in, or for information I can use directly to bring em in. I have a post office box at Belle Fourche. Leave any message there, in a sealed envelope. My orders are to bring these rustlers to justice. The first intent is to bring them to court, to make a show trial, let people see that justice will be done. In the case today, we was outnumbered, and I couldn't take a chance on them getting away. Lets get that rustler tied across his saddle."

On the occasion of Blakely's next visit to Rapid City, he ran into Ed Lemmon, and together they arranged to see James Craig, also a member of the secret committee, at the Rapid City Hotel. Over glasses of imported

Scotch whisky, neat, the discussion quickly turned from pleasantries of the day and weather to the progress of detective work on the range. "Ed, Kid Rich told me about how you took those rustlers up north. We have given you a tough task, and we recognize that. We have now paid you for the killing of four known rustlers, and the apprehension of none. The pay is the same for either, but bringing in the lawbreakers is important to us, and the killing of same is causing trouble. Lawmen in Rapid have complained, they don't get the option of gunnin down thieves. There could be an inquiry. The newspapers an politicians support the small ranchers, they don't have any compassion for the losses by our respective cattle companies. In Pierre, they are very upset with what's happening."

"Mr. Craig, you have known me for some time. We are both members of the Cheyenne Club, and this ain't the first time we drank a whisky together. You know I have not misused my authority in handling these cases. They were known rustlers, and I had little choice."

"Well, Ed, I trust that is true, but what we are asking now is that, since you have already sent a strong message, is that we move to a more acceptable approach to the problem. We have courts, and we have more opinion from the papers, and the locals. The legislature has noticed, and we are a state now, we cannot continue as we have."

"Well, sir, I am not the only one still using rough methods. There were two rustlers hung last month up by Oacoma. Who knows who did that?"

"I have not seen any invoice from you for payment, but you were in Oacoma around that time. You sayin you weren't involved?"

"No, some of the locals must have done it.

"Well, you see, whether it's you or someone else, you, and by association, we, will be wrongly judged. To be expected. But, we need for the detectives to have full credibility, to be totally free from taint. When a detective stands up in court, the jury has got to damned well know that what he says is uncontestable." Arguing the point held no purchase for Ed. He leaned back, sipped his whisky and waited. Ed Lemmon spoke up. "Ed, we have money enough to provide help for you when you need it. Hire a couple of hands when you get close. You and Kid did a fine job with those boys in Wyoming, but with two or three more men you could have brought them back for trial. Not sayin you had time, but its one a those cases where we could have tried three rustlers and won. Belle Fourche can get a good jury. It would make a good example. I know, you got a tougher job in the Rosebud, but this is the way we gotta do it."

"Well, ya'll are the bosses, but Jack Sully is leadin' a pack a rustlers from here to the Canadian border. He's bin to court so much he ought a be a lawyer. With the juries he gets and the alibi's they accept, we ain't gonna stop him with judges and law. I'll do what you say an' bring him in again, but I ain't got much stock in the "law" here in Dakota."

"I've known Jack since he worked for me, just a kid. He ain't all bad. That's why the juries let 'im loose, partly."

"Well, you say bring him in, and I will. We stop him, and the rustling will stop, that's my opinion. I doubt that he will take to prison as an alternative."

"If he's guilty, he'll take his medicine. Let the courts have him. I thank you for the very fine whisky, gentleman, and will be about my business."

The Greatest Roundup - 1902

*T*he winters of 1901 and 1902 were long and cold, blizzards had ravaged the prairie grasses, and great drifts had occurred, sending cattle from as far away as Montana, North Dakota and Wyoming into the Pine Ridge and Rosebud Reservations, which lay along the southern border of South Dakota. Political questions on best use of reservation lands raised contrasting opinions from Indian activists, small ranchers, homesteaders, Black Hills businessmen and of course, the large cattle syndicates. At this juncture, President Teddy Roosevelt applied momentum for this large undertaking, using his bully pulpit to threaten impoundment of illegal cattle on the reservations and to make right other misusages of Indian lands. The Western South Dakota Stock Growers Association thus saw fit to organize the operation, with the primary purpose of reuniting cattle with rightful owners on their home ranges. The ranchers also faced an assessment of a $1.25 fee lawfully required for having grazed on reservation land. Historically, it would constitute the largest roundup ever held in America. Well organized by the WSDSGA members, the plan called for sweeping from the Missouri River to the Black Hills, collecting cattle estimated in the tens of thousands, with over a thousand cowboys, 10,000 cow horses, from all the area ranchers. Henry Hudson of the 73 ranch was overall foreman. At his command were eighteen or more chuck wagons which served as sub-headquarters for representative ranches from the Niobrara to the Little Missouri in Montana. The eastward sweep began in the southern Black Hills, herding through the lands at the headwaters of the White and Little White Rivers to their convergence near Westover. Another sweep began at the Missouri River breaks pressing westward, pooling finally at Westover. Intermediate meet-up points were established, along the Keya Paha River, and at Brandon Springs. Stories told by the cowboys participating provide most interesting anecdotes, but details of the organization, exact numbers of participants, and cattle tallied remain somewhat obscured. Not the least reason being that ranchers actively skirted paying the reservation grazing fee. At the pooling points, calves were branded, herds cut out and sent back to the originating *ranges, market-ready beeves moved to railheads. The roundup augured well for big cattle, for the beef empire, in that it demonstrated their capability for a high level of organization which responsibly addressed the contentious issue of reservation leases and grazing rights…at least on the surface. A roundup of this size would never be duplicated or surpassed in America, the epitome of the open ranges, free grazing, sway of big money, would soon be broken by intruding homesteaders and barbed wire.*

Spring Roundup - 1902

In early May, Jack took his team of Harry Ham, Olaf Finstad, Oliver Dion, and Billy Kincaid, with Red Shirt, to the first meet-up at Brandon Springs, designated intermediate meeting place for the eastern phase of the roundup. His team worked with Chris Colombe's larger contingent, which included a fine chuck wagon, and large remuda. As small ranchers, they were tolerated by the roundup organizers, but were expected to cooperate, to sort out their own stock, and that of other small ranchers, mostly on the Rosebud reservation, then move herds back west, toward the big meet-up. The competitive nature of cowboys insured that some rodeoing would attend, intently anticipated as antidote to the lingering boredom of a winter spent shuttered away in a stuffy bunk house or braving cold between line shacks, or for those less fortunate, living jobless in the towns where they had spent all their pay from the past summer. Cowhands, hired on part time through the winter, would come out from their winter "hole-ups", bartending, storekeeping or wasting away in bars in Rapid City and the Black Hills towns. The toughest would be trailing longhorns or other stock out of Texas and Wyoming, prime stock horses out of Oregon, even sheep from railheads east river. It was the great get-together of the West River. No drinking or gambling allowed, job to forfeit if caught. But, palaver, joking, competitive fun, rodeos, would compensate.

The Sully team had a plan. They would, in the midst of the confusion inherent to commencing a large roundup, sort out a hundred head or so of north range, big ranch brands, and move them west but southerly, under cover of their warrant to move their own cattle, as charged by the roundup boss. North of Valentine they would break off, turn their catch south. Also, they knew that some of the hands would be assigned special tasks to push large contingents of cattle east and north, avoiding the reservation tally officers who were legally obligated to collect a dollar and a quarter per head fee. Roundup teams spent the first day at the main camp, getting instructions, intermediate meet-up points, and reviewing brand lists of what to expect out on the ranges.

Jack and team rode southeast on the third day of the roundup with a larger group of 30 cowhands. Nearly back to the Keya Paha River, Jack broke out his team, and headed south. Further west seven or eight miles, was another three-man team, directed to stay farther north, sweep west toward the main camp. Jack's team also, from further south would sweep northwest toward the main camp; they soon found two to three hundred head, and sorted out a hundred of the best looking cows, which sported a wide selection of brands, even some with Jack's and Harry's. Red Shirt and Olaf drove these south a couple miles, past the headwaters of the Keya Paha, toward the Niobrara, settling them in on good grass and water. They then returned and helped Jack and Harry move the larger herd toward Brandon Springs. Once the larger herd was turned north, away from the Keya Paha, controllable by Jack, Billy and Harry, Red Shirt and Olaf returned to continue moving the stolen steers southward. Pushing them steadily south and east, well into the night, they broke for a few hours sleep, then began again at sunup to get the herd well south of the Niobrara before returning to the main roundup. By this time, picking up animals as they moved, the herd was nearly at 200 head. This was a herd too large for Olaf and Red Shirt to handle without drawing attention.

Jack, Billy and Harry cleaned up the camp site and headed back northwest with the herd at a slow gait. The cattle had settled into a string heading toward Brandon Springs. At the crest of a hill his heart hit his throat. Three cowboys were loping slowly down the next hill, crossing the draw in his direction. He turned his horse at a gallop to stop them. Lead horseman was Sam Moses, tallyman, and foreman of the T Bar, acting as east area foreman for the roundup.

"Jack, what the hell, there's a trail of a herd heading south here?" It was a question, with an edge of suspicion.

"Its not tally cattle, Sam, some Colombe and Lamoreaux and other Rosebud beeves. Somma my own and Harry's also. Red Shirt and Olaf are holding them south for a while, bring em north tomorrow, sort out the locals and push the others to Westover. Harry, Billy and I got the herd, prolly three hundred, moving this way.

"Where's Olaf now?"

Jack was slow to answer, it being a situation that he was not prepared for, searching for the words, he answered calmly. "South a here. Him and Billy and me already done the sweep above the Niobrara." At this, Jack crossed the reins over Jim Longstring's neck, casually swung his left leg across the saddle horn, and leaned back in a relaxed, resting pose. He pushed his hat back, wiped the sweat from his brow on his shirt sleeve and dropped his right hand into his lap, loose along his chaps, near his pearl handled pistol on his left hip. He smiled. "We got this whole area covered, Sam, this is our home range, mostly."

Sam took this posturing half seriously. Jack he knew as a tough guy, but also as a joker, not above joshing. Only one of the hands with Sam wore a gun, and not a shooter with a gun, but a cowhand with a gun, not necessarily adept at using it in a tight situation. Sam glanced back at them, both leaning forward, elbows on their pommels, relaxed in their seats.

This was not the time. Even if the story was weak, the case for prosecution was as much so, and calling a man such as Jack a liar even less prudent under the circumstances. The issue would be pride, not cattle rustling. There was another time for Sam. He had a suspicion to follow up later, through the Association. It was Blakeley's job in any case.

Sam swung his horse back to the west, "Lets go boys, Jack's got this area in hand." And with a lingering look back at Jack, eyes fixed upon him, "See you at the meet-up."

At the bottom of the hill, Jake asked "What was that all about, Sam? Headin' cattle south at this point, don't quite make much sense."

Sam turned back and smiled innocently. "Jack's got this area under control, Jake, you know Henry is handling tally cattle a little different, no problem here." Jack was still at the top of the rise, watching them.

Not so much for Sam, but for Jack, relations with the association had just deteriorated.

Jack returned south to Harry and Billie's herd. As he approached, Harry galloped up, spun his horse to a stop. "Jack, who was that, was that Sam Moses?" His face, slack, his eyes dilated with fear. "Who was with him? Was the range detective with him?"

"Yes, it was Sam, two cowhands with him, not Blakeley, nothing to worry about. One did not even have a gun. What's your worry, they did'n see you."

"I don't like takin' chances now, I got a baby on the way."

"Harry, its always a risk. Sam bought it. Even if he didn't, he ain't gonna catch us."

Harry looked long at Jack and turned back toward the herd. Jack pondered the fear in Harry, since he was with a herd that was pointed toward the main roundup. Why should he be concerned? Harry showed more nerves of late, Jack thought. New baby... did not know that. Maybe it was time to cut Harry loose. It took nerve as well as handling a gun or riding a fast horse. He would talk to Harry.

Sam was tired and saddle sore by the time he got into camp, but at the holding point three days later he sought out Henry Hudson, overall roundup boss and Ed Blakeley, relating the story in some detail, along with his suspicion. Ed was in town clothes, a dark suit, no tie, buttoned white shirt. Ed let loose his frustration. Why had Sam avoided the issue, why not follow the trail, "Prove up the sonsabitching cow thieves!"

"Ed, this is a round-up, and how Jack moves some cows ain't gonna make a case for rustlin, even if its true. He could make a case that his boys were movin them south instead of east to avoid the tally. We gotta catch em in the act, or catch em selling them cows. We need to make a case, and its your job to do that. Right now my job is roundin up cattle and tallying brands." The edge in his voice was enough to back Ed away from any further insinuations. He did not want to imply in any way that Sam was in on a deal.

Red Shirt and Ollie stayed with the west-bound herd while Jack and Olaf hustled back toward Brandon Springs, picked up Harry, Billy and the tally herd still working westward, and continued sweeping west above the Niobrara.

At the Springs, Sam only commented that Jack's Indian wasn't with him. "Went to his cabin for the night, Sam. He'll catch us at Westover." Sam just turned away.

Vengeance in Springview and Bad News in Valentine

Jack had just turned into the north end of the single dusty street separating the seven or eight storefront façades of Springview when he spotted a wagon at the hitching rail of the Mob County Bar. Around it, ten or so men gathered, an unusual number for this little speck on the prairie. He was no stranger to this town, near the Dakota border, and just far enough away from his normal haunts to give him some privacy, some chance to have a drink or two. He had met Doc Middleton here three times, without incident or seeming to draw undue attention.

The nooses were still around the necks of the two cowboys' laid-out bodies in the wagon bed. Their hats were over their faces. One had lost a boot, holey, stockinged foot dangling out the end of the wagon. He shivered at the sight, in spite of the heat. The hanging tree he could envision. A cottonwood in a draw near the Niobrara River. Two begging cowboys, pleading innocence, then for mercy. Vindictive anger in the vigilante leader's voice. Despair and resignation in the followers. Were they pulled up with tied off lassoes, or dropped from their whipped horses? In any case, they strangled to death, no quick neck snap to end their r

rustling days.

He reined in Jimmy beside the wagon. "Anyone we know?" He said to the group.

"Olson here found them this morning in a draw near his place. Didn't hear anything last night, but they ain't been hangin' longer than a day. We know their leader, got him in jail now. One of 'em talked, I guess."

"You guess?" Sarcastically.

"Well, hell, I wasn't there, I just heard," responded the deputy, turning to expose his badge as he addressed Jack. No one else spoke. No further talk from Jack would serve him well. He dismounted, tied the bay gelding to the hitching post and went into the saloon. He had come too close to exposing his disdain for vigilantes.

Jack had dressed in his cattle buyer clothes, black wool four button suit, polished black low-heeled boots, white shirt buttoned at the throat, and a light gray, short brimmed hat, set straight forward on his head. More businessman than cowboy. Less likely to draw suspicion. Still, he displayed his Colt in an open holster at his side. He liked the bar, eight high stools lined the front, and a large mirror encased in hand carved dark mahogany set the atmosphere of quality not seen at hog ranches or lesser saloons. He asked for whiskey, the bartender served that and information intended as fact and warning. Nodding toward the door, he said "They's a vigilante group in this area." His caution apparent, his own disdainful feelings regarding vigilante law easily guessed from his tone. He was not one of them, nor with them in spirit. Jack slugged the first jigger of whiskey, nodding, indicating another glass, quickly poured. The burn in his throat occupied him, kept his thoughts unsaid.

The bartender, Jake Utley, went on. "Sheriff Coble arrested that big mouth Art Maupin yesterday, too. Could be they was workin' with him. He vowed revenge on the vigilantes after he got out of prison last month. Came right here to Springview, and been talkin' ever since about how he was railroaded into prison. Prolly lucky to get sent to prison if last night was any indicator… Coble came up behind, I was told, took his gun right outta his holster while he was eating at the restaurant. Took three helpers to wrestle him down, but they put him in the hoosegow."

Jack's old robber buddy, Art Maupin; still a small timer, rustled some, drank more, and played poker whenever he could get up a game. Not well liked because of his bullying and a nasty temper as an accessory.

Jack too, had rustled this area. He most certainly had appropriated a fair number of the local's cattle. This was an area of smaller ranches, but being outside his locale, he did not suffer the qualms of conscience that rustling from his neighbors on the Missouri would have caused. He and Olaf and Harry had tried their new approach here first. They took only half a herd or less, and waited for the rancher's response. If there was no uproar, or serious complain, they left him alone. If there was strong action taken, if the rancher made a hullaballoo they took the remainder of the herd.

So the vigilantes had gotten their men, thus not likely looking for anyone else. Still, the vision of two cowboys struggling against the rope sickened him, the dangling bootless foot. Could it ever have been him? Would it ever be him? He had not worked this area southwest of the Whetstone for more than six months. Probably safe enough.

Light faded in the bar. Jack left his third drink half finished, and turned to the open door, but stopped short to see a stocky man, dressed nearly as he was, approach the hotel restaurant across the street. "Who's that, Jake?"

"That there is the range detective, Ed Blake, something like that."

"Ed Blakeley. Been in town long?"

"Couple a days. Talkin' to the Committee, no doubt."

Jack backed into the bar, and nonchalantly took up his drink. After sipping it, he went out the back door, skirted the view from the hotel café, and came up from the south main street as Blakeley headed into the bar. He ate supper quickly, kept his eyes on the bar door, and went directly up the hotel stairs. He laid half dozing, effects of the whiskey wearing off. Around midnight gunshots awakened him. More than ten, from the sheriff's office and jail. Eleven men emerged, stood talking in low tones, and then dispersed. He went back to bed, but could not sleep. Maupin with the big mouth, threatening the Sheriff, Ed Blakeley in town, vigilante committee active again.

He had ridden up to a lone rider on his way back from Oacoma only a month ago. He recognized Blakeley more for what he appeared to be than who he was, but obvious by his question that Blakeley did not know him. After small talk, he asked, "You know Jack Sully? Don't he live 'round here?"

"Yes he does, but he ain't home, I saw him in Oacoma when I was there today."

"That's straight north about, from here, eh?"

"Yep, go back north and west from here, cross over the White at the ferry, then east to Oacoma. Can't ford the White now, too high and too fast." Jack knew this would keep him occupied for a good while.

Too late now, he thought, but he had had the chance to save three lives, crooks that they might have been, if he had been the type to end Ed's life right then. Doing it over, he would not have done differently, hell, the Association would only bring in another detective, and grow a real vindictive mood. At least now he knew this one. And would not several people in town have been able to tell Blakeley who he was? And Blakeley was now known as a dangerous element to rustlers, small ranchers, and honyockers, all of whom he bunched into one malicious group. 'So,' Jack thought, 'he has determined to clean up the Rosebud by his own ruthless means.'

Jack would have left early next morning, but now waited and watched Blakeley ride out before he ambled down the hotel steps next morning. He could see Blakeley headed northwest before he turned Jim southward.

Meeting Doc at his home later next day, telling him of the murder in Springview, Jack asked, "What do you know of Art Maupin? What was the reasoning with those assholes?

"Too many cows lost, Jack. These boys think they got the right guys. Hard to say, since Art has been in the pen for two years. Other reason could be that he threatened to get even with those who put him away the first time."

"Yeah, they could have done the same to me and been more right. Too bad about those boys hangin' but they was known thieves. Drank too much and talked too much."

Doc turned to a new subject. "Jack, I am thinkin' of leaving this area, going out to the Black Hills area. I have gained the local sheriff's ire, caused by the ladies of the town resentin' the sale of hooch. They don't invite my wife to coffee and tea no more. And most of my hooch ain't exactly legal. I made good money, and I think movin is in my best interests. South Dakota ain't so particular about where I get my stuff, an I found a nice little bar in Ardmore. I tell you this, because you will need to find a new partner for cattle deals. I won't be able to handle that from up there. Out of the territory, too dangerous these days."

"Doc, this will complicate my operations quite a bit. You sure about this? You been getting a fair cut."

"I know Jack, but Association dicks been here in Valentine, talkin' to ranchers. Allowin' how the north Sandhills is losing beeves and askin' for help and cooperation. Some of the ranchers are listenin', agreein'. Other day, I hear em talkin' and when I ambled over they shout up quick. They don't trust me no more. I can feel it."

"Anyone else here that you trust, that I might get to broker for me?

"That I trust? I don't trust nobody. I'm gonna say again, as a friend, you need to get outa this rustlin business. It wasn't such a risk to speak of back a few years, but now, the law has set in."

They sipped their good whiskey, followed with a fine coffee, talked of the old times, how easy it all seemed back then. The changing times pressed upon them, their lifestyle threatened, *angst* underlay the conversation.

Kid Rich Bushwhacked — Winter, 1903

Jack waited for Olaf Finstad at the bar in Oacoma, late in the afternoon, light fading early on this cool winter day. He stared at the mirror, then down at his glass, not caring for more self-introspection. Tension mounted in his mind, thinking about the coming activity. Timber floor creaked, two cowboys entered, blew out some "ohs, and ahs, coldern hells!" shucked long winter coats, moved to the bar, near Jack, and asked for whiskey. Then a second slug, before they turned to Jack, commented on the weather, the snow still in patches on the range west.

"Came from Belle Fourche, three miserable days, only one night inside, at Presho." They finished their second shot, and the taller man said "You know Kid Rich? …He was bushwhacked. Shot down like a dog."

Jack's attention fully engaged now, he turned to the two and asked, "How is he?"

"He's fully done in. I was at the bar where they brought him in a buckboard. Nearly still frozen, stiff as a log, strange the way he was layin'. Doctor looked at him, pronounced him dead. I heard he was a heller, troublemaker. Didn't know him, myself."

"You sure it was him?"

"I just know what folks in the bar and on the street said, for they seemed pretty sure. Shot in the back he was. Murdered."

"Who brought him in?"

"Feller named Cavanaugh, and the Kid's wife, eh, widow was with him. They found his horse standing over him, him frozen nearly, already. Musta been a day or so. That's about all I heard."

Jack turned away, tipped another shot glass full and downed it. The Kid, he thought, who would want to kill him? Sure, he raised hell, pulled pranks, shot off his mouth, but never in serious antipathy to any man. He did not know of any real enemies he could have had. He thought back over the times they had punched together, both at Ed Lemmon's Flying V for a while. Yeah, he had shot the wrangler there after Jack left. Spent two years in the pen. Ed had disliked that wrangler considerably, he beat more than one horse and several had thought he caused a major stampede one night. Ed wanted rid of him, but did not fire him. Then, the Kid had a running disagreement with the nighthawk, and finally, they had shot it out, the Kid too fast, and too good a shot. Ed took him to court, as was his nature and his concern for correctness and the law, and he was guilty, five years adjudged. He served half that time, always with good behavior and soon on good terms with the warden himself, went straight back to the Flying V upon release. Most thought Ed had intervened with the prison somehow, and took him back on. All had been well since, Jack thought, but now there was a mystery.

What did Ed Lemmon have to do with this? He liked the Kid. Praised his cowboy skills, deservedly. The Kid worked hard and never quit on a job, worked the long days of a puncher without complaint. Did he pull off some fool joke on Ed? Still, for all his hardheaded righteousness, Ed Lemmon would never go so far as to kill or have him killed. What else?

The shootout at Oelrichs. Yeah, Ed Blakeley. He would likely not forget the Kid. But, he would not kill the Kid over that thing. No harm was done except to the whiskey barrels, and John, the barkeep was the only real loser on that one. Nah, even that SOB detective would not kill over something like that. Jack was bothered, he had lost a good friend, a cowpoke he had worked and played and ridden with for years. They were natural friends, Jack always leaned toward the funnest cowboys. He thought back. Who could have done this?

Olaf came in, and they discussed the killing. Olaf had not known the Kid, only through stories from Jack.

"Ain't he the guy who ploughed up the main street of Oelrichs, Jack?"

And Jack remembered that late night, drunk they both were, leading their horses down an empty main street toward the corral, when the Kid noticed a new plough in front of Harry Oelrich's hardware store. It sat on the boardwalk, which ran in front of four façaded stores.

"Jack, you ever plow much, you old honyocker?"

"Never did, shithead, but I bet you did, bein' nothin' but a poor farm boy."

"Nope, never did. Gimme your rope end, tie it on this here plough, lets take 'er for a ride."

The plough was new, painted red, yellow trim, a single moldboard with a tricycle style wheelbase and a steel seat. A single lever raised and lowered the plowshare. Jack was as drunk as the Kid, and no smarter under the circumstances. He mounted, tied off his saddle rope, and threw the end to the Kid. The plough handle was down, and Jack's horse first stutter-stepped at the weight, then like a good cow pony with a steer on the rope end, jerked forward. The plough share point dug well into the boardwalk, ripping up two or three planks, mold boarding them aside, before tipping over into the street. Kid grabbed the handles, righted the plough, and yelled "yea haaah!" Jack kicked the horse forward and they ploughed a neat furrow, though not a straight one, down the middle of the street. Thirty yards up, they turned around and ploughed back. At the store, Kid was laughing hard, and trying to steer the implement back onto the boardwalk. It tipped, throwing him onto the boardwalk. He laughed, and called for Jack. Jack came over and sat down, wiped his brow, and elbowed the Kid. "I knew you were a plowboy, you drunk bastard." No one heard him. The Kid was passed out. Jack leaned back rested his eyes and in a minute also passed out.

They were out of town before Harry Oelrich surveyed the damage, but everyone guessed correctly as to the culprits. Still, the Kid seldom met a person who did not like him before they parted. Ed Blakeley aside? Yeah, but still, the whiskey barrel shoot-out did not warrant a back shooting ambush years later.

Olaf and Jack shared a room above the bar, and left before sunup, pressing their horses along the White River toward the west ranges. They planned to sort out some north range cattle and the Nelson mortgaged herd, move them south as they had done often enough. The moon would be full, and the sky clear, reflecting off the snow patches, lending light for the night drives.   They would pick up Red Shirt to help on the drive south.

At the mouth of Cottonwood Creek they built a fire and slowly chewed their warmed biscuits and sipped hot coffee.

"Olaf, I've thought it out, and I'm going north in the morning to see James Cavanaugh and the Kid's missus. I want to know who did this. I gotta know what happened."

"I can understand Jack, but you'll hear about it over time. What can you do, it's too late? We got moonlight, and this ride will take at least two days. What for me?"

"Olaf, lets get some sleep, and you go back in the morning, tell Mary where I'm going and not to worry, I'll come straight back ta home. I just gotta know what happened to the Kid."

Next morning they mulled over coffee with no small talk. As Jack saddled and swung up, Olaf started to say something, but Jack wheeled Jim Longstring north and galloped off.

Jack tacked against a brisk norther and wrapped his scarf across his face, into his jacket front. Jimmy loped for miles, stopping mid-morning at a water hole where Jack chopped a small trench in the ice large enough for Jim's long drink.

Evening the next day, Jack was at James Cavanaugh's spread. Jack went first to the main house. Windows in the Kid's house to the rear were dark.

Over hot coffee, biscuits and gravy, Jack asked about the circumstances of Kid's death.

"Someone knocked at my door, and when I answered, no one was there. I stepped onto the porch, and a voice around the corner asked to see the Kid. He did not show himself. I did not have a gun on me, and I was a bit taken aback because most folks around here are not unfriendly. I told him Kid was in the hired man's house to the rear. He asked me to get the Kid, send him around back. Kid didn't expect anyone, and was as surprised as me. He threw on a coat and went to the back of the house. I went inside, but could not hear voices through the wall. I did think I heard Kid's door shut about ten minutes later, but I went on to bed. Next morning, Miz Rich came and asked about Kid. Said he left in the night with someone, but all he said was, 'Its business.' Said he'd be back next day, but she wondered who Kid left with. Didn't know, couldn't tell her. That evening she came back, said Kid had not returned. I rode out west a ways, and thought I saw fresh tracks in a patch of snow, followed the trail a ways, and then about six miles out, saw Kid's horse, and he was standing over the body, reins down. I saw he was dead, shot through the back, frozen stiff. He had a throat latch from a bridle in his hand. I got Mrs Rich and the buckboard and we took him to Belle Fourche.

"What I know since, was that the sheriff got the doctor, which was way too late, and he and two Indians rode out to Narcelle's ranch to check for missing throat latches. Came back, said all the bridles were OK. I know Narcelle did not like Kid much, but I can't see him bushwhackin' no one. His fight with Kid was over anyway, his sister left Kid some time ago."

"So Jim, whyd anybody wanna kill Kid? Was he doin' his job for you?"

"He was doin' fine by me. He worked hard, and did everthin' I asked. Now's a slow time, and he rode out by himself over the winter, at least partly to check on my cows for me. He shot two wolves, I know that. He would be gone for some time, but always there when I needed him."

"Any visitors other than the last, unknown sonnavabitch?"

"Nope. He went to Belle Fourche once ta month, could have talked to anyone there. Went to see Ed Lemmon a couple of times too, over on the Moreau. Old friend he said, used to work for Ed." He pondered silently for a while, then seeming a bit unsure, he said, "Ya know, Kid helped Ed Blakeley several months back with bringing in two rustlers. Dead that is."

"I heard a that. So the cowhand with Ed was the Kid?"

"Ya, Ed and I sent Kid out to find Blakeley and tell him about the rustling we suspected. They met in Belle Fourche and Ed made him a special deputy for the short run. Just til they got the thieves. Kid didn't say much when he came back, 'cept he had to shoot a wounded horse. Seemed a bit sad about that. The folks in Belle ain't too happy about what Blakeley done. Seems one a the so-called rustlers was from around there."

Olof Nelson Hires Jack to Rustle Syndicate Cattle

The Nelsons and Olaf shared the burden of too many rat-tailed cattle, mortgaged from Montgomery and Shilling, out of Sioux Falls, and Becker and Deegan, out of Sioux City, Iowa. These cattle were run on the Rosebud Reservation, in the creek lines feeding the White River, and as far south as the Niobrara, along Ponca Creek and the Keya Paha River. These remainder cattle had been sorted out and sent back to the Reservation, avoiding tally reps and the $1 per head fee. The mortgagers were calling in their chips. Blaming the cruel winters, wolves and rustlers, the three saw their way out. Jack would be able to move these cattle with near impunity, sell them as he had through his Nebraska contact. Jack understood the ease with which he could rustle up these beeves but had lost his connection with Doc, of important for a clean sale.

Jack wearily dropped off his wagon, full of kindling wood from the Missouri bottomlands, a task that busied him the full day. His thirst turned him directly to the house before beginning the unloading. At his table, making small talk with Mary, sat Olof Nelson. They shook hands, commented on the wind and heat, but Jack knew why he had come to visit.

"Could we talk, Jack?" Olof asked as he replaced his chair under the table and nodded toward the door.

"You could lend a hand unloadin the wood while we do so, if you don't mind." He finished his dipper of water, wiped his brow again, followed Olof out the door, and they began piling the wood near the side of the house.

"Jack, I have said this before and fully mean it when I say that you need to settle into a different operation. You got land here, plenty of horses, and could make a real go of it. The rustlin business is a lot more dangerous than it was ten years ago, hell even five years ago."

"Who said I was rustlin, Olof."

"Well, who says you ain't? Nobody I know, nobody from this area."

Jack said nothing, continued handing him wood, which he stacked neatly.

"Ed Blakeley came by our place some weeks back. Looking fer ya, no doubt. Asked about yer whereabouts, says he's gonna get ya."

"I got no reason to be arrested, Olof. There's no warrant, no evidence. Nothin he can really do but talk about me."

"Jack, he is not the kind to care much about how he does it. He alluded to how he has 'brought in' three or four rustlers from the "Sully syndicate", and I don't think that he meant brought in to a jail, but to a cottonwood somewhere. ... if he gets you alone, he will take his own measures."

"Olof, I believe he's a goddamed snake, but I won't run scared. I could handle him and two like him, ifn he tries me. I ain't leadin no 'syndicate' but I know what I'm doin."

"Well, I did not think I could make an impression on ya, but let me make a proposition, it seems you are not givin up the trade. As we talked in Presho, Olaf Finstad and I got 500 head a stringy steers runnin over west a Bull Creek, just south a the White. I ain't never gonna make lease on those beeves. I need ta have em get 'lost' and off my tally. If yer persistin in your game, ya could give me a hand."

Jack let turned a slip of a smile. "That's the way of the ranchin you want me ta turn to, eh Olof?"

"Well, there's no grass left Jack, you seen that, an yer cleanin up ranges fer that reason. My boys'll have a hundred head er so on that pond down on Cottonwood Creek. Won't nobody interfere. Easy takins. I don't wanna know what ya do with em, but I want half a the end result fer makin it easy. This is gotta be done before the Association roundup, I can't let them beeves get inta the tally."

The wood stacked, Jack leaned on the wagon wheel, drew his neckerchief across his face again. He understood how he might make this work, even without the help he had so often received from Doc. Maybe need to use a runnin iron, but there came the added risk of finding a buyer. "Listen, I might could do this if ya moved those steers over on Dog Ear Creek, leave em in the trees there in three days."

"Some danger, me moving em offn my range, Jack."

"That's the deal, I ain't gonna take the chances a havin the locals see me movin yer cattle. No towns out there. I'm gonna get the blame fer this in any case, so I'm fer takin fewer chances. What's the brands?"

"Brands all the same, Deegan and Becker, not mine. Gimme three days, they'll be there."

"Where's Blakeley now, he say?"

"He said he's got help here in the area, so's he's headin back ta Rapid City, Belle Fourche er some place west. Association meetin."

"I don't want none a yer boys around the cattle when I get there, Olof."

"Understood." He swung into the saddle, tipped his hat at Mary who stood in the door, and reined north across the flats.

The Spring Take - April, 1903

The old season faded grudgingly in the late April days on the Dakota plains, combining winter and spring on alternating days. Even with a bright sun, the freezing wind kept frost on the grass, mud hardened to granite, ice patches slowed the wary horse. The ground froze over night, but by noon the next day, spring sun melted ice, rivulets sprang toward the creek lines, snow patches wilted, coats were thrown open, gloves off. He could feel summer coming.

Next day, Harry guided his brown gelding slowly through the creeks, dodged snow patches, kept below hill lines as he moved west to meet the band. He brushed at the patches of winter coat still on the gelding's rump and shoulders. Billy, Ollie, and Jack had gone the day before, and he expected to meet Olaf near the line of buttes past the Lamoreaux spread.

His conflicting motives for going troubled him, slowed his pace; he considered turning back, but dolefully rode on. This time was no different from previous trips, he needed money. His survival depended on these forays as much as did Jack's. Still, the objective of his planned deception, his betrayal of Jack, and in all likelihood the whole gang, sat like sour meat in his stomach. He stressed physically when he weighed consequences, possibilities for failure, betrayal captured his thoughts. His wife chided him for grinding his teeth in his sleep, little knowing why.

Harry slacked his feet in the stirrups, leaned back against the cantle and rolled a cigarette. The brown gelding dropped his head and chomped at grass. What had Jack said? "Do you remember John Kincaid? A good cowboy, who died hard." He did remember him, nearly 15 years back. What had the question meant?

Along the base of the near butte, Harry saw a familiar silver gray ghost shape glide through the grass and stop, gazing out of black-hooded yellow eyes, nearly a minute. Harry did not move, for he had not brought the big 30-40 Krag. Why was it they seemed to know, he thought, that you did not have a rifle? He pulled up the gelding's head, and still the wolf stared. Now he loped away, thin, had wintered hard, anticipating spring like mankind. Prairie residents alike. For Harry, money accounted for reconstitution of body and psyche, and Jack's way was fastest and surest. He put aside his dueling skepticisms and reined the big gelding westward.

Springview - 1903

On a fine, breezy early May day, Jack and the crew, Olaf, Harry, Billy and Red Shirt picked up Olof Nelson's stringy cows from Dog Ear Creek, and in the course of moving them south, accumulated another hundred head of assorted brands from the north ranges. Across the Keya Paha River, at the Niobrara, Jack settled the herd into the trees, and proceeded to Valentine seeking Doc's help again to dispose of the herd.

At Doc's bar, Jack learned that he had actually sold out as planned, and at his house saw him loading a wagon, preparing to move to Ardmore in western South Dakota, to establish a new outlet for his home made brew.

"I ain't got a lead for a cattle buyer right now, Jack. I been busy tryin to get this place sold, get my stuff on the road. I have earned the guff from several in town, includin' the mayor. Mayor hisself has opened the place right across the street, and my business has gone there. I know when I'm not wanted."

"That's too bad, fer me an you, then. I got around 200 head outa town, no place to move em."

They ambled back to the empty bar where Doc busied himself polishing a glass for Jack's use. "Listen…there was a young dude in here coupla days ago, came in on the train from down east somewhere. He was willed a ranch near Bassett from his uncle who passed on. Said he needed cattle, and I mighta got yer herd to him if yuda been here sooner. He said he was goin' to the Springview area. You might look im up there. He wears a plaid suit and a bowler, cain't miss im."

Jack leaned on the bar, took the filled glass, and mulled over where he stood now. He threw back the whisky and pushed the glass to Doc. "Just one more, pincha water." He pondered the situation, sipped at the whisky. He and Doc carried on light conversation, and solemn farewells, knowing it would be some time before they shared a drink again.

Two hundred head of cattle, a fair piece of work; a good payoff if he could now rid himself of them. The difficulty here spoke plainly of itself.

He would need bills of sale, tallying the brands, working with an unknown buyer. A known vigilante group worked out of Springview and a sheriff had an office in Bassett.

Two hours east of Valentine, paralleling the Niobrara Jack sought out the natural shower at Smith Falls. He stripped, tip-toed into the pool fed by the waterfall which sprung from the Ogalalla aquifer plunging from 50 feet above. Hidden in aspens and spruce, five minutes of the clear, cold water rinsed the sweat of a summer day's ride and the last vestiges of the whisky from Jack's mind. Out of the water, he tip-toed with his clothes to a boulder out of the tree line, let the sun dry and warm him. Cattle again on his mind, he devised an approach to selling off this herd of mixed quality cattle. He would take only the best of the lot to Springview, show them to the prospective buyer, promising to deliver the remainder, the Becker and Deegan skeletons to his ranch sight unseen. With his inexperience this newcomer might well go for the ploy. In any case, grass down around Bassett surely exceeded the quality of that in Dakota. Those cows would have a chance to fatten. He could give him a good deal, considering the low price of this herd to himself.

Back at the herd, Jack laid out the work. He, Olaf and Red Shirt cut out the best looking cows and a few steers to move to Springfield, 74 head in all, crossing the Niobrara to the east. Harry and Billy stayed with the remainder, to wait for a destination.

Jack pulled three different tablets and two or three pens and pencils from his saddlebag. Using the bottom of the skillet across his lap as a writing table he began to fashion a variety of bills of sale. Passing the skillet, he dictated to Harry and Olaf, offering different handwriting styles.

"We don't know all the boss cowmen fer the bunch of brands we got. Could be this guy will recognize some discrepancies here."

"From what I got in Valentine, this fella is fresh from the East. Don't know the cow business all that well. It's a good chance to take, Harry."

Discussion around the fire that night was quiet, tenseness showing, all aware of the more stressful situation that selling to an unknown buyer presented. Harry was first to bed down, quiet in his natural state of fearfulness, devising plans of his own.

Jack walked Jim Longstring down the empty, dusty trail into Springview. It had grown since his last visit, adding a vague cross street delineated by wagon tracks. Jack turned left onto the north-south main thoroughfare. Across from the lone saloon, the bank, Ellis's Mercantile, and the Dagger Hotel imposed an early morning shadow midway into the wide main street. The width suggested that the platters of this fair berg optimistically expected more traffic than it would ever see. Conveniently, the sheriff's office leaned heavily against the north side of the Mob County Saloon. Across the Valentine access road at the corner sat the Emery Creamery. At the far edge, a small square corral held three or four black and white Holstein milk cows. Cream and milk cans lined a small wooden platform to the right of the open, screened, door of the shop. Old Man Emery sat staring at Jack from a three legged milking stool, cigarette dangling from his pursed lips. He raised a tin dipper to Jack without changing expression. Jack turned Jim slowly, dismounted and dropped the reins.

"Its cool, got a cistern 'round back…two dippers fer a nickel."

Jack sorted through his change, found five pennies, dropped them into the open hand, receiving the dipper with this other.

Jack tasted the milk, the thin scum of cream sweetened the draught. "Well, it is cool. Makes fer a decent breakfast."

"Old Lady's got fresh bread an jam too….Ma! Bring the fixin's, the man is hungry." A heavy set, smiling woman, plain flower sack dress, emerged from the dark creamery with half a loaf of bread, butter pot and a jam jar on a bread board.

"It's the same as you get from the hotel, mister, they buy from us."

Jack chewed slowly, savoring the morning air, the aroma of fresh, warm bread. The simplest of things made life a charming adventure. Business could wait a spell.

"You seen a young, whippersnapper here in Springview lately?" he presently asked.

"He has completed his stroll of the town near after the sun come up. Smartly dressed is he. Takin' his breakfast at the hotel, I 'spect. Offered him cool milk."

Jack and Emery exchanged views on the weather and the crops, the growth of the town, interrupted when a wagon pulled up, the farmer aboard stepped over the seat and handed down his milk can, full by the heft of it, and took a receipt from Emery. At this, Jack took Jim's reins in hand, and walked toward the hotel.

Inside, the Easterner sat alone, sipping the last dregs of the coffee cup in hand. Jack introduced himself as John Ridley, but otherwise plied no deception, stating that he had word in Valentine of the possibility that the young man sought cattle for sale.

"I am Peter Mansell, of Cleveland, Ohio. My uncle by marriage is Captain Bassett, and I have been awarded land adjacent to his holdings from the passing of my father. I have been advised that the best use of that land, that prairie, is the raising of good quality beef, hence the reason you see me here. Valentine offered no immediate prospects."

"As fortune would have it, I have a herd of good cattle which would have been available in Valentine had I gotten there a couple of days earlier. Doc Middleton said to follow you here, see what you thought of my herd. We could ride out, take a look before noon. I got two small herds, all right good beeves."

"I suppose then, that I am in luck. I'll have my horse brought 'round. Let us have another cup of coffee."

The two passed time in conversation, Jack explaining the need to move his cattle, the poor state of prairie grass north of the Keya Paha, low level of the river water. Presently, the hotel's clerk brought a spotted cow pony to the hitching rail outside.

Jack pointed out the best of the herd, mostly Herefords, cows with good heft, good potential for calving. The Easterner nodded, as if he knew a good heifer when he saw one.

"You can see the potential in these cows, and the heifers, good stock, come from a purebred white-face bull."

Jack offered a reasonable price, expecting, and getting hesitation. The young man understood the fine art of bargaining well enough. Jack waited, said nothing.

"Uncle Andrew said nothing more than $20 per head, of the best cattle. I could pay no more than that."

Jack expounded upon the bad conditions in the Rosebud, the exploitation of the area by cattle barons, and allowed as how he was in a weak position. He would accept the price of $19 per head if Mr Mansell would buy the full lot of 194 head. Bassett being no more than 20 miles away, Jack promised to deliver the full contingent upon completion of the sale.

"This constitutes a fair price, and a substantial start to my enterprise. Let's get back to Springview. We can settle this over more coffee."

At the hotel, Jack explained the bills of sale, and accepted payment for the first 74 head, promising to deliver the remainder to the Mansell ranges north of Bassett, and receive the additional payment at that time. The two shook hands, and Jack turned to the door. Through the large front window, a sight he feared caught him short. He stepped back, engaged Mansell in further pleasantries, asking if he were interested in some good horses, and assessed his predicament. Four lathered horses stood at the rail in front of the saloon. The big black gelding he had seen before, he was sure. It or one just like it belonged to Ed Blakeley. The other three, two bays and a brown, were also fine stock, not the horse fare of most local farmers.

"I'll just attend to some personal business in the outhouse. Coffee kinda does that."

Jack slipped out the back of the hotel, into the outhouse, then passed the rear of Ellis Mercantile, the Keya Paha County Bank, and crossed quickly toward the creamery. Inside, he asked the kindly Mrs Emery for a further sampling of her fine bread and plum jam. He sat facing the door, observing the saloon, hoping to see the departing horsemen. Jim Longstring stood still, head down, at the hotel hitching post, rear hoof toeing the loose gravel. Ol' Jim was a fine horse, but he did not stand out any more than another random bay gelding. No real concern in that regard.

Jack waited. Mrs Emery busied herself with the butter churn. "I'll turn that butter paddle fer ya, Ma'am, fer another dipper a that cool milk," he queried.

"Well, I got cows to attend to, have at it, and mind ya, have a couple of dippers, we got more milk then we can sell, fer sure."

Jack churned, watched out the door, as within the hour, four men left the saloon and stepped next door to the Sheriff's office. They stayed inside for another half hour, then mounted their horses and loped out of town, west, as Jack feared. Astride the big black, in his black business suit and white Stetson rode Ed Blakeley, speaking to A. P. Long on his right.

A clear and present danger. By good luck, they had positioned the herd to the southwest of the town, about four miles. Jack left the butter unchurned, hit out full stride for Jim, and galloped south. He hoped to get to Olaf and Red Shirt before the detectives picked up the trail of the herd west of Springview, as they surely, easily, would. He slapped reins to Jim's rump, stretched him out, raced to warn his team. Only a low slope in the flat Sandhills terrain hid him from the posse, and he veered east for half a mile to maintain his cover. It lengthened his approach to the herd. Reining back west after three miles, he waved to Red Shirt, his rifle raised, a warning sign. He saw Red Shirt wave, and then Olaf rode around the herd and headed toward them. Jack turned Jim, headed back north, while the two caught up to him.

"Detectives!" Jack shouted. They rode hard, headed back toward Springview, skirted the town east, splashed across the Niobrara, and raced to the Keya Paha. They forded, dismounted and watered their tired mounts.

Jack pulled Jim away, "Don't founder, you beggar…It was Ed Blakeley and A. P. Long. I could not tell who the other two was, but they had some idea, I think, where the cattle would be. They headed outta town west, and they'll find the trail soon enough."

Jack checked the cinch, remounted and walked Jim north. They were safe for now.

"I sold the 74 head, got the money. We didn't lose it all. Red Shirt, you need to head on west toward Valentine and send Billy and Harry back home. Stretch yer pony out. We cain't be sure what Blakeley and Long might have up their sleeve. They musta come inta Springview from the north, not by waya Valentine, er they woulda caught the herd's trail sooner. Sheriff musta told em no herd come near the town. Cain't take no chance. Get a move on, an jist go on west ta home."

Red Shirt needed no pushing, he understood and moved off at a slow lope, set for a long ride.

His luck could run out; he feared that. It was strange though, that detectives and deputies had arrived so soon in Springview. Four of them, on fresh horses, and they stayed in Springview hardly an hour before heading west to the herd, Blakeley in the lead. They were getting better, and they had him in their sights, for sure.

Only the second day upon return did Billy mention that he wanted to go into Valentine with Harry, but he stayed with the herd. "I ain't been ta town fer moren a month, Dad" he complained. Jack said nothing. Yet, that, with Harry's touchiness, might explain the expeditious arrival of Blakeley in Springview. Harry would bear watching; yet he had as much to lose as Jack.

John Petrie Comes Calling

The bed creaked as Jack rolled again on his side. Mary tossed about and resumed her low snoring, an occasional burbled snort the only interruption. This did not keep Jack awake; he might have slept through a thunderstorm on any other night. Now the sparrows in the attic distracted his sleep; the rustling and snorting sounds of horses in the corral muffled their way through the thin walls. He had gotten up to pee, and rather than the chamber pot, had gone outside, cool damp grass on his feet brought him fully awake. Still, he could only lay back and let the dark envelop the room and his thoughts.

Olaf's short sermon had come back to him on nights like this. Now, he could only wonder when he awoke with night-dread if he were too late. The Homestead Act deprived him of the refuge that the reservation had provided for so long. The Rosebud Reservation now encompassed all of Todd County, freeing up land in Gregory and Tripp Counties for farming. Lawmen now had jurisdiction even on the reservation trust lands scattered across the two counties. Their efforts at apprehension would not go unrewarded now. He was a wanted man, he could be arrested, and another stint in jail would be much longer. Third time's a charm, he thought; they would not be so incautious as to leave him unchained until he was in the State pen at Sioux Falls.

Nor could he beat this one in a court. Carl Nelson's sway in the Presho court was gone; Carl had gone on now to other business, in a bank, somewhere in Nebraska. He could be placed at the scene of the thievery by not only Harry, Olaf, Red Shirt, Billy, but probably by several in Springview who saw him come into town, including Will Hollbraugh's widow, that one being vindictive and dangerous...hell, she might even shoot him in the back. He should have gone on, even after daylight, found refuge farther from the town. Without Doc's intersession, finding a buyer, dangerous as that could be, Jack had assumed the risk, against his gut feeling. He and the others were bone weary; going on did not seem possible. Had he lost the edge? Even two years ago he would have pushed on past Springview, gotten completely disconnected from identification with this herd. Better to endure a while longer in a safe haven than live with fear like this.

The sun had fully cleared the trees east of the house when Jack shook himself out of his late morning sleep. Drowsy, he sought out the meaning of what he heard... something, a wagon, a buckboard approaching. Now a muffled, "Whoa, Whoa up." He drew his gun from the holster on the chair and eased to the front window. Below Marshall John Petrie alighted from his buckboard, stretched, and ambled toward the house. Mary met him at the door, invited him in, and offered coffee.

"Out early, Marshall. Must be important business." Mary said as she poured coffee.

"Mary, it is. Jack is home?"

Jack had pulled on his trousers, re-holstered his pistol. It was clear that the Marshall had come in peace, no waving of arrest warrants yet. Taking his boots in hand, he walked softly down the stairs and answered, "I am, John, what brings you here so early on a bright summer day?"

"Let me get right to it. Ed Blakeley was in my office yesterday, pushing me to form a posse and come take you back to Mitchell. He accuses you of cattle thievery, and has recounted the details. I put him off, cause I did not have a warrant. He went right to Judge Lodge, and will have one soon enough."

"Well, what are the details? This is a serious accusation."

"Blakeley has a witness, and 74 head of cattle he says got fresh brands, runnin' iron job. He found em south of Springview, and they are all Dakota cattle. This fellow says he bought them from you, and has the bill a sales. Blakeley says ther all fake."

"That pack a lies don't make no warrant, John."

"Folks in Springview says its you was there, Jack. You been known in those parts. Ol' Lady Hollbraugh fer one, and you know her history. Blakeley's got enuf to get a warrant, and bring ya to trial. You can argue yer case at that point." He paused, poured coffee into his saucer and blew lightly on it. He sipped at the luke warm coffee.

Jack sat, accepted a coffee cup from Mary, and pulled at each boot slowly. "You came all the way here without a warrant. What's yer interest?"

"I want you to come in with me, it will set well with the court. I don't want a posse, and I don't want Blakeley and the Association pushin' me to do my job."

"Well, John, I ain't goin' in just now. What evidence have they? Whose gonna say I stole their cattle? Whose cattle were they anyway, does he really know?"

"Don't do no good to have the court here in yer livin' room. I just know that Blakeley brought those cattle back across the Keya Paha, found some boss cowman to say he never sold those cows. The man who lost those cattle is fit ta be tied according to A. P. Long. Its enuf fer a warrant, surely."

"I suppose, if that was all true." But Jack knew it was. That goddam Ol Lady Hollbrough! She'd know me anywhere and hate the sight a me. The easterner would identify and rail away in the courtroom. Even ole man Emery would have to be forthcoming. It wasn't a hanging offense now, but it meant years in the pen at Sioux Falls. "I'll come in when I have to, I don't mean to trouble you. You been reasonable, and we been friends. If they get to settin' a court date, let me know. I cannot sit in jail playin' checkers and takin' yer pennies til then. I got a horse ranch to run."

"If I know the Association, they'll have a court date real soon. You won't need to wait."

"Maybe not, but 'til then, its settled. I got things to do. I do appreciate yer comin out here. We can have an early dinner, you stay. I'd say ya didn't even have breakfast."

"Least I could do is have dinner at Mary Sully's table. No man ought deny that invitation. I'll leave it be fer now, Jack, the kids an all, but think hard on how its gonna look to the judge if you come in peaceful."

At dinner Jack brought up the possibility of a pardon, he had drafted a letter to the Governor. John Petrie allowed as how he would support Jack's effort.

Jack knew that Mary would hold out, she would have the strength to wait, even years. The children? He could maybe get Billie back home to help out. Least for a while. The girls? They would grow away from him, would outgrow him, go on to new work, new lives, marry; he would not see this. The fear of losing them all become real.

On the Lone Prairie

Olaf Finstad took the half-mile walk to John Kincaid's old cabin in the trees near the Whetstone. The day's end turned red-orange before blue-gray evening descended. Jack sat cross-legged near the cabin repairing the worn latigo on a cinch strap. A light cool breeze began to take the edge off the searing mid-afternoon heat. Olaf pushed back his hat and squatted on his boot heels.

"Ever get tired a sleepin down here, Jack?"

"Of course, but nobody's come by this place yet, so 'better safe than sorry', I say. Trouble is, it reminds me of Ol' John, every time I come down here."

Olaf said nothing, half understanding John's passing, not wanting to ask more.

"What's your plan now, Jack, which way we going? I own as how its time we laid back, got our ranches in order, settle in for quieter times."

"Olaf, could be Blakeley ain't got anuf to pin the Springview job on me when that greenhorn leaves the country, which he will... I ain't ready to be a honyocker yet and I ain't goin to Sioux Falls. I had jail enough in Mitchell. I need money to go to Canada, start over, bring the family up there." He looked down the creek line, darkness, dropping quickly, had settled already around the tree trunks. "I ain't got a good answer, but I don't think the charges will stick in a few years, if I can avoid Marshall John Petrie. He ain't got it in for me like the Association, so Canada could be the answer for a while. Still, with the land startin to open up to so many new people, if Mary leaves we could lose the whole place. I guess she will need to stay, hold on til I can get back. Olaf, I don't know for sure, I really don't. What's the dumb Swede ideas on this?"

Jack looked at Olaf, the essence of a Dakota cowboy. No old country left in him, hardly a trace of his Norwegian singsong accent. His grey Stetson, sweat stains seeping around the headband, brim rolled and down-turned at the front, signaled the statement of his life. He wore a white shirt year round, buttoned at the collar, a dark brown, now nearly black vest, makin's in the left pocket, a worn old pocket watch in the right, gold chain anchored to a button hole. Probably didn't keep good time at all, for he never seemed to consult it. He wore an old .44 pistol, and never seemed to need that either. His boots were worn all round the soles, but well oiled, and supple looking. A true cowboy, he seldom walked, but had done so in deference to the hideaway, Jack noted. Face and hands, wind and sun burned, fair complexion vulnerable to the constant predominant elements of their life.

"Bein what *you* might call a "dumb Swede", I would get the hell out. Stay outa jail and let things simmer down. Association ain't gonna keep detectives on the payroll if there ain't no rustlin. Look out on the prairie now, Jack, the honyockers are coming in passels. Fences are coming, even up on the Cheyenne and north. You know, we gotta go over the White now to get a good herd for drovin. The big boys got their ranges cut back. They're bringin in quality cattle, most all are Herefords, Shorthorns. Makin hay for winter. Winter drift is way down. Brand books and brand inspectors makin sales hard. You got a possible rustlin charge, but I see that as goin away if they don't get you pretty soon and you petition the govner. You just need to avoid Blakeley and his like, don't tempt the Marshall anymore. Canada may be the answer. You got friends Jack, Harry and I, Billy's a grown man, your own older boys can all ride and work. We'll look out for Mary."

"What about Harry? I got a suspicious feeling in me. Things were too close in Springview."

"I can't think he would get us in trouble. We got plenty on him, too."

"If he made a deal, then what?"

"Harry said to me, some time ago, that crossin you would be a fatal mistake. He recalled how you have said you never murdered anybody, but said, 'ya know Olaf, he never said he didn't kill anybody'. I took that he harbored some fear there, Jack."

Jack leaned back against the cabin side, changed the subject. "Roosevelt's orders, 'the fences will come down' held for a while. Well, Ed

Lemmon went to Washington, kissed Teddy's ass, and got a lease of a hunert miles square on the north range from him. Nothing ever really changes for those sonsabitches." Darkness hid Olaf's eyes, but Jack felt the care and worry in his voice. A coyote yap, yap, yapped, followed by the plaintive howl careening off a far hill, and another farther south; then another, north, nature's chorale society ringing the river hills; mournfulness settled into their souls with each echoing refrain of the prairie wolves. They listened in silence and awe.

Olaf whispered. "Remember when they was not coyotees but was prairie wolves, Jack? Texans brought that Mex word with em."

"They brought rustlin with em too."

"No, Jack, rustlin's old as cows and horses. Sioux was stealin Crow horses before you and me was born, before white men ever came here."

"Texans brought their own tricks."

"Jack, I would say that you and me and Harry are the best rustlers in Dakota, and that's sayin somethin. An, the only thing that will make it right is ifn we don't get caught. Which we ain't yet. There's a lotta old cowboys quit rustlin, gone legit, making out OK. Look at the Nelson boys, the Drapeau boys, about every other rancher here in the Rosebud."

"Yer always talking about quitin' Olaf, but you never do. Why don't you follow your own advice?"

"Same as you, Jack, I need the money," contradiction in his voice.

"I rode many a night under a moon like this."

Olaf sought a bit of relief: "Gotta bottle back in there?'

"Nope, never keep it on the place, I cain't be trusted with myself on that, even down here."

They listened to the coyotes for minutes, then Olaf rose, slapped his gloves on his leg, bid a hand-wave goodbye, and wandered slowly, scraping his feet through the grass, back to his horse. Even in the dark, Jack saw Olaf, the loyal old cowboy, his head down, legs bowed, ankles turning in his high heeled boots, seeking a saddle for redemption.

Going To Bordeaux's - Fall 1903

Red sumac crept up the draw sides toward the hilltops, yellow leaves graced the young oak and ash in the creek beds, interlacing the dark green of cedars, and pale yellow-green of cottonwoods. Summer air warm in an essence now tinged with coolness lingering later into each morning. The turn of season, always a melancholy foreboding of the harshness of winter. He seldom measured time by years, surely not at century marks; he rose to the occasion of the season, the hustle of new life, new opportunity in spring, to the unrelenting work of summer in the face of heat and dust and sweat, and to the finishing and laying aside for the cruelty of winter that had been the bane of his existence and métier of his driven life. He was aware today that this autumn portended more than the endurance of a harsh winter. What had Olaf said?

"Jack, the century has turned, it's the 1900's. It's a new time. There's a train in Bonesteel now. Hard to believe.

"Olaf, what's a railroad got to do with it?"

"Well, we also got a lot more neighbors than we had when it was just you and me an John on the Whetstone. There is law now, and with more people there will sure as hell be <u>more</u> law. Some people just don't take to honest labor for a livin', they get a position with some county or state and get their satisfaction, such as you may call it, from the power of office."

"You know, we can still ride for a day and not see another person. It still takes a day to get to the nearest town. This land still belongs to the Inyuns, and we're just here cause they let us. The government can't take any more of this land from old Red Cloud or Spotted Tail. They have taken all they can." He paused and thought, 'not only that, more people coming in shows a need for more horses.'

"We been a state now for moren 10 years. We got a genuine legislature and a governor. And worse, we got sheriffs in about every town. I don't think no good is gonna come to us from this. How many times we had to cut fence to get to the Niobrara lately? You think Ed Blakeley is gonna forget us?"

"Things change a lot slower than you might think, Olaf. We ain't seen the last of good herdin' yet. There are so many Flying V, U+, and other syndicate cattle on the Rosebud, the small ranchers are just about beggin' us to take em away. That's for sure."

It ain't gonna always be that way, Jack. Look at the Nelson boys. They are deedin' up. They are fencing half the White River area."

Part of strangeness of the conversation was the thought that Olaf could go a whole day on the range without saying a word. Jack would say: 'We got enough for now, lets move these critters south."

"Yeah, OK." Then he was off to Nebraska, gone for days, and only "Thanks for the coffee," or "The water's high in the Niobrara." Rein his horse around, and back to herding. He was not unfriendly, just quiet. Stoic.

Now, alone, with only thoughts for company, a day's ride ahead, Olaf's low monotone crept back. Was something different now? August Nelson had said about the same thing, a year ago. "Start fencing, Jack, this land is not gonna stay open. You want some of it, stake it out. You got the trust of your neighbors now, but with land, even that don't go far. Land is all we can count on."

"I trued up, Jack, just like a damned homesteader. What land I can truly claim ain't enough, but its legal, and I can add to it with countin squatters rights and some leases, and some releasements I can see comin. I been here since anyone else but you and soldiers lived west of the Mo. Gotta count for somethin."

Jack lay back on a patch of buffalo grass, feeling the curls scrunch under his back. Could he be a rancher, stay at home, tend to his own stock? Rumor had come through Chamberlain and Oacoma. If you see Jack Sully, notify your sheriff. Ed Blakeley has been snooping around in Bonesteel, Springview and Oacoma, working at connecting him to the herd at Springview. The pressure was comin from Blakeley and the western side of the state.

Who all might have seen him in Springview? He had declined a drink, other than cool milk. Few were on the main street, but it surely had been Will Hollbrough's old lady loading a wagon at the general store. Rough looking, raw-boned, no bonnet, hair pulled into rough braids, walked with the long strides of a homesteader's hard working wife. She had not seemed to have looked at him, and he had not been close to her. No, he remembered now, she had stood with her hands on hips, and looked right at him as he came out of the hotel.

He harkened to years back, when rustling was the main occupation of the drifting populace of the west river, her husband Will ran a hog ranch, north of Springview. He also ran some horses and cattle when he was not selling whiskey. Jack had stopped there two or three times on trips to see Doc. The last time, he met a young cowhand, who had hired on with Will to do his herding so Will could tend bar. This young man had also been active in a rustling gang for over a year, one that worked both sides of the river, and along the Niobrara. Will lost some cattle and horses one night, among the suspects being Jack himself, though he was sheriff at the time. Will had complained to the Army at Ft Randall about the local rustling problem, and received little satisfaction or support from the military leadership. After the recent theft, the irate Will screamed at the commandant at Ft Randall, and raised general hell about the loss. He accosted everyone he knew about it, which may have included some guests at the hog ranch who feared that the soldiers would respond. The Army was at that time the only form of authority in the area, but their mission was not rustling, unless it could be traced to Red Cloud or Spotted Tail's bands. They were not lawmen, and avoided the trouble chasing rustlers would have entailed. They herded Indians, and had little interest in the cattle industry. One cool fall morning, Will and the cowboy went to the north range to bring in his horses, and did not return by noon. Mrs. Hollbrough found them both hanging from a cottonwood along Spring Creek.

She had openly vowed to avenge her husbands death, and kept the hog ranch working for several years, eking out an existence and hoping to glean information about the hanging from the bar talk of wayfarers.

When the establishment fell on hard times, her money gone, she moved to Naper, bought into an old established ranch on the road to Springview. Nothing much had come of her persistence, and Jack had dismissed the old rumor from his mind by the time he drove the herd to Springview. Now it came back to him, and his gut knotted. He had to believe she saw him, and would connect him to the herd. She would not forget Will's failed candidacy for Charles Mix County sheriff, which they rightly thought a result predetermined by the Lamont organization. She had reason for revenge.

Now, having realized the extent to which he may be exposing himself, Oacoma was not a good idea. He needed supplies, but Harry or Ole could do that for Mary. He remounted, and turned back to the Flats. Talk with Mary, get her staked with the spread. She had Indian rights. Stay away from the local talk and towns with sheriffs. Find a lawyer with the grit of that mean sonnavabitch Bartine. Go the legal route. Don't push your luck, even if it has run good for so long, life is not fair, and luck does not last forever. His past stint as sheriff had taught, yah can't jail em if they do not have a charge written. He could build an excuse for being in Springview.

Mary listened, and though silent, he knew he had gained her approval. Being apart had been the mode of their life. Staking out a claim was a good thing. It would mean a change, an acceptance of what must be. She looked at him, and he looked up, directly into her eyes, with neither the usual jaunty remark nor sly smile; for all his youthful looks at his age, he was at last growing old. He had accepted that he was over fifty, so it must be, even if he did not know his birth date. She could hope for change in him, if only it was in time to fulfill her own ambitious but very real dreams of a peaceful home.

The red sumac stood out so strangely on the prairie. Color against the khaki tan grass. It was Olaf's talkin, as he seldom did, a small red patch of warning in the ocean of baize stoic silence. It amused him for the moment, but he did not believe in omens any more than he believed in god or predestination, or old Lone Bear the medicine man. He spurred the big bay to action. The big rowels jingled, and higher spirits jangled away his natural Gaulic pessimism.

He ruminated silently on the fickle nature of active men. Returning from a run to the west, he longed only for the peaceful home she made for him, but after days of quiet work and activity around the ranch, being at ease, the need for change nagged at him, he longed for the stress and strife, for the adventurous hunt. For the range life again, rocking in the saddle, totally free. Man never satisfied, wishing for the other condition, bored or tired of the present one, whichever it might be.

He wrapped his war bag again in his bedroll, and that in his slicker. He filled his saddlebags with biscuits and pemmican to last three days. He sent the kids out, went upstairs with Mary, and loved with the fervor of a man departing. He relished the sex, but it was more the need for attachment. He lay with his hand on her belly, peace now, surely, but fear like a sliver under a nail, crept in; a sandbur removed, but a spine stuck. He could not sleep as he usually did afterward. Not this time. He sat up, and told her of the oak tree at the top of the Whetstone, straight west of the house, just where the Flats drop into the creek. He placed her back to the east wall; looking straight out the west bedroom window, it was the first tree. On the east side of this big cottonwood, two feet deep were two tobacco cans containing nearly $10,000 dollars. Only they now knew. There were two other cans buried by trees, and he would show her how to locate them exactly when he returned. He had laid out the locations on angles from the first oak, but directions were not simple to explain. She should never dig in daylight, and only use the money if needed for the filing, obtaining lawyer help to gain the land to which she was entitled. She reached across his chest to pull him closer, and did not speak.

Darkness settled in to cloak his departure. Still, he rode west into the creek line before turning north to follow the trees onto the western Flats. He thought of Bad Nation, west along the White River, and expected there was whiskey there, surely a bottle or two. It had been awhile; he would take some time to blot out the pessimism, restore thoughts, think things through, make a new plan.

Harry Follows

'Yep,' Harry thought, 'he had stayed all these years. Now he was a rustler, and getting out was not gonna to be easy. He had seen Jack face jail time, and had not given up any in the band, but he could not imagine himself in such a situation. He still had time. His own brother would hunt him down like a coyote. The disgrace would ruin his father. Blakeley had offered the only chance, but that could go south fast, Blakeley bein such a sonnavabitch. I could trust Jack who's the crook, before him, who's the law, for sure. Then again, if the law offered Jack an out if he gave up the gang, then what? He thought of the Nelson boys, and how in the hell did they know when to quit, and how to make a go when everybody knew they was the biggest rustlers in the county for a long while. Shit, Jack just never knew when to quit.'

When Harry Ham came by the next day, Mary asked him to bring supplies from Oacoma, that Jack had left for she knew not where. Harry knew well enough that she surely did not know, for Jack would not burden her with that knowledge should she come under tough scrutiny. He knew Jack. He knew his habits and his foibles. He had time.

Harry and his brother John came to Dakota with the best intentions, to start their own homesteads and work hard. They had persevered through the depression of the late 1870s and the horrendous blizzard of 1880-1881, which decimated the plains, killing cattle by the thousands and horses by the hundreds. Deep snows accumulated in Nov and Dec, the cold settled a hermetic seal over the land. Settlers froze in their homes, men foolish enough to venture forth to care for cattle, not to be found until summer, curled into fetal shaped racks of bones or scattered by coyotes like so much kindling. "Cold as Hell", a phrase born of this winter, redefined man's concept of eternal damnation. Jack's horse herd vanished into the wind, seeking whatever tree bark and blades of grass in the crusted snow. Harry's cattle froze in place or starved, unable to reach the grass in the snow beneath their feet. It was the winter that taught ranchers the lesson of haying. Store up grass for such disasters. Some of the Scottish and English cattle ventures bellied up completely, losing equity and profit, with no reconstituting capability. Those who could rebuild looked to Texas again, driving longhorns north in summer. The difficulty of rebuilding herds exacerbated by the low supply of cattle raised prices that small ranchers could not meet. They turned to rustling of necessity. Harry's spread was near those of Jack and Olaf, and they helped each other through the exhausting winter. Being near the Breaks, they scrabbled for wood, chopping and sawing together, shared lean stores of flour, beans, sugar, trekked to Oacoma in supportive teams, avoiding seep holes in the White River ice, once even huddled in the wagon bed when an overnight storm blinded their homeward course. As shared strife will bond men, this terrible winter made brothers of these three. When spring finally found its footing on the windswept barrenness, they sought out their depleted herds, searched the breaks for survivors, and finally, rounded up cattle, regardless of brand, from the widest reaches. They nurtured their nascent herds, and branded maverick calves the following spring.

Fearful nature bonded them, but fearful man would split them asunder.

Harry returned from his resupply trip two days later, assured that Jack had not gone through Oacoma for supplies or drink, nor likely to Chamberlain. No one had seen him. He must have gone west. If he had realized the danger he was in, he might have gone north to Canada, but from their last discussion, Jack had not given the sense that he suspected the law has near, or even vaguely shown awareness that it was closing in. If Harry was wrong, Jack was well on his way to Canada and out of any scheme or plan that Harry had arranged with Blakeley. Trailing outlaws around the Great Plains was a job for Sam Moses or his like, not for a man with a family and ranch needing his attention. Harry cleared the wagon for Mary, and headed back east. It was three miles over the Flats before he could cut south, unobserved. He was nearly at the mouth of the Whetstone before he hooked back northwest into the trees lining the trickle that was left from summer.   Harry tracked wolves.   The trail of a man on horseback was comparatively easy to ascertain.   He saw the hoof prints in the damp creek bed, and a trampled grass trail leading west out of the trees and over the rise. It looked to be a route used regularly.   From there he could only guess, but since the only two alternatives for Jack would have been straight west or a long angle southwest, he decided to stay on the more northerly course, follow the White River, as he suspected Jack would. It would take him to the first settlement, Bad Nation.

Bad Nation

B ad Nation was well and rightfully named. Whirlwind Soldier would not
live like his kind, could not find in his nature the complacency of the
around-the-fort Indians. He had fought at the Battle of the Greasy Grass, had
taken scalps. He had tasted blood and hated the white man, if not individual
white people. His face a brown wrinkled oilskin, unsmiling, but a deceptive
plainness in his round face that hid the toughness. Living at Pine Ridge under
Red Cloud agitated him to first leave the reservation. Cavalry tracked him
across the White River and brought back him with his band. Some months
later, he petitioned the Indian Bureau for a tract of land south of the White
River. This was a compromise good for both sides, removing a thorn at Pine
Ridge, but keeping the band on the reservation. This was a band of angry
braves, and not of the nature to settle easily wherever their squaws might pitch
their lodges. After two years the village itself boasted three log cabins, eleven
teepees and 8 Army issue Sibley tents, turned dusty gray. Two new slab side
houses were being built, slowly, for lack of money and lack of ambition. The
band had brought 200 cattle and an ever-changing number of horses, depending on the adventures of the young braves. The cattle were closely herded, and
few were lost during the first year, though it diminished when more than 20
were slaughtered for food during the winter. Tough times were certain for the
short run of this band. A strong leader, Whirlwind Soldier controlled whiskey
in the village, knowing too well its affect on his tribe.

Jack put aside his weariness as he dismounted and slowly ambled to
the largest log cabin. Whirlwind Soldier met him, "*How kola*, horse thief,
you come to take my last ponies?"

"No smart man steals your horses, friend, they all run back home to
Wyoming and Nebraska where you stole them from."

"We eat now, you come to my cabin, stay tonight. A friend of Red Shirt
is my friend. You can keep your horse and saddle for now," with a sliver of
smile . "He did not come with us, but we would have him." Jack let this comment pass. He knew there was no part of a renegade in Red Shirt.

Jack pulled smokes from his saddle bag and offered a sack of Bull Durham to Whirlwind Soldier. "We smoke the peace pipe for now, eh?"

"Yes, for now, you old crook." He was not only bantering in the tongue-in-cheek Lakota style, but setting a tone, knowing Jack had no doubt stolen more than one of his horses, but having come into the camp, would respect the hospitality of the plains. It was likely that his braves had run off a horse or two from Jack as well.

Whirlwind Soldier's squaw fried bread, and poured a flour and water gravy over the antelope steaks. A hot meal, even tough, stringy antelope, refreshed after three days of cold pemmican and water, the biscuits all gone. Jack drew on a pipe with chief of the band, and asked about the camp, the cattle, and how they had fared over the summer.

"You have whiskey here now?"

"I can sell you some, but you take it away with you, not to drink here. No drinkin here, only once each month. Those who work have a drink together then. You know this."

"I am leaving in the morning, and will keep it all for myself. Two bottles are enough, if you have them."

"Its OK. You have them from me." Jack gave him money, knowing he would have the whiskey in the morning.

Two days later, Harry Ham was at the cabin. "Ya, I see Jack. He go south, not hurry." Whirlwind Soldier, knowing that Harry was Jack's neighbor, shared information he might otherwise have remained vague about. Laconic to a fault, the Lakota remained wary of sharing other men's doings. Asked for a bottle, he replied, "No, Jack buy two bottles, I have not so much. You drink with Jack."

Harry now sensed that Jack would repeat his old habit of drinking away from bars. He turned his horse back east, strange to the old Indian's eyes. Harry knew now he would have time from now til the whiskey ran out at Bill Bordeaux's. Not much time to lose with just two bottles. Maybe Bill had some on hand, enough to keep Jack occupied until the Marshall could get there.

Coming Down from Rosebud

John Petrie came alongside, pulled Jack straight in the saddle, looked, saw he was awake. He sagged forward, "Fer chrissakes, what is this, where the hell am I?" He heard voices, a blur of words, an ache in his chest and a most powerful headache. He leaned across the saddle horn, his weight on his ribs, rocking with the horse. He pushed off the horn, trying to see, where was he, the ache in his back, his legs, and ever throbbing pressure in his head. He tried to talk, his mouth and throat "On the way to Mitchell, Jack, you'll get plenty of rest there..." His hands were roped to the pommel, twice around his waist, and on to his feet, secured in the stirrups. "Oh shit. Yer takin' me to jail..." He recalled opening the second jug of whiskey with Bill Bordeaux at his Rosebud cabin, they talked, but then nothing. Out cold when they found him, three men hoisted him to the saddle and trussed him tight. The Marshall mercifully held his canteen to Jack's lips. "Get me out of these ropes, I'll go peaceable." "Not this time, Marshall," someone said. It was Ed Blakeley. So he had found him. How did he know where to find him? Jack's mind turned to escape, but just now it was impossible, he would need bide his time. "Where is Bill, he not with us?" "Got no reason to hold him, lessen you talk, mister. So, you are Jack Sully. You are the rider that told me Jack Sully was in Oacoma when I met you on the prairie last year, you sonnavabitch. I could have had you right then. "Well, I did see him in the big mirror at the Hasty House, but I guess he was not there when you was." With just the slightest bit of smile he could muster. Blakeley was a sour bastard. Jokes on him didn't set well. It turned out the longest, most painful ride of his life, hundred miles, every bone and muscle straining with each step, they galloped some, but it was torture after a half mile. The ride had been cold, now the wind continued to whip into gusts around the buildings in the empty streets of Mitchell. Two deputies half carried him into the cell before the ropes were removed. Blakeley watched everything attentively, searched the cell, yanked on the window bars before leaving, watched the key removed, and tested the cell door. He smirked, "Don't let him out for any reason, and I mean, he can pee and crap in a pail. Have his food brought in and hand it through the bars." With venom, "Yer going to trial, and yer going to the Sioux Falls pen for a long time." Even a worn straw mattress on the hardwood bed felt good. He slept for nearly a day, fitfully dreaming, awakening, the reality of the cell shattering his rest, to roll on his side, sleeping more, blank out reality. Think about home. Mary. Anything but his current dire straits.

In the Jailhouse Now

When he could sleep no more, avoid the despair of the situation no more, he sat up and surveyed the cell. A structure of red brick, new cement, metal bars and door separated his cell from the sheriff's office and desk, gun and coat racks, just across from his cell. Four or five more cells were aligned along his wall, each opening to the hallway. Prisoners could neither observe nor visit openly between cells, which had divider walls of brick. The bed was hardwood latticed, with a thinly stuffed straw mattress. A wooden shutter to stem the cold wind inside the cell covered a three-foot square window. Behind it Jack found the opening fortified with four vertical iron bars set solidly into concrete. All in all, a fine monument to Mitchell's growing populace.

Finally, Marshall John Petrie came to the cell door. He wore his straight brimmed hat, as always, his white shirt buttoned at the neck, and his black vest buttoned across his slim frame.

"John, you can't hold me here forever, I need a lawyer, and by the way, what are the charges?"

"Jack, I got orders to hold you til the trial, if it takes a year. Its like I told you last month, you been linked to 74 head of stolen cows in Springview. Blakeley's got the bit in his teeth, cowmen on his side, and he is callin' the shots right now. We can play some checkers when youva mind to."

"Not a pass to go out and eat and while the time like before, eh, John?"

"No chance."

"Who knows I'm here? I need to talk to my family, Mary and Billy. I still got a ranch to run. I don't know that they got any proof on me anyway. I been before the courts before."

"Jack, I just don' think it's the same now as back when I took you in for stealin wood. The courts been tightened up. They could get a jury that you would not like here in Mitchell. It ain't West River courts no more."

But Jack knew. The Marshall's jurisdiction now extended west of the river; the old reservation lands whittled down by the Dawes Act. This was serious, and Blakeley had the power now. Lawyers were more careful of how they handled cases, many wanting to advance their political careers, knowing where the influence obtained. Bring in a big time outlaw, make a name; support from cattle barons who now influence the legislature, lawmen and courts. 'Ain't no Carl Nelson here in Mitchell to "assist" with records. No fires in the court house, and no croton oil in the jury's food.' The indignity of having Ed Blakeley and the WSGA stand him up in court, upbraid him, and then send him to the Sioux Falls pen for years flushed over him. His mind still calculated escape. Had to be a way out.

Within a few days Jack extracted from the Marshall that his trial might be two months in coming. Blakeley spread word of his capture wherever he traveled, and determined to make the point that no rustler could evade him and the Association detectives.

"John, I know you cain't let me out, but how about a small tipple of sauce with my meal tonight? Cain't cause no harm, I have no place to go."

"Well, we been friends a while, doubt if there's much you can do but if ya get loud and feisty, I'll not do it again."

"Look here John, pour me a cup, and when I get outa hand, don't give me no more. I'm gonna keep calm. "

Out of the bottom drawer of his desk, Marshall Petrie brought forth a plain bottle with a fine amber hue, poured half a cup for Jack. He unbuckled his gun and holster, placed them and his keys on his desk, and passed the cup to Jack.

"So ya don't really trust me then, John?" Jack said as he settled back on his bunk with the tin cup.

"Biggest part of bein a Marshall is doing the right thing. I stuck to my duties for all these years, and I still got a job. We been friends, and we can stay that way as long so you cause no trouble. No doubt in my mind that givin the chance, you would make your way out of this jail any way you could, cause ain't no friendship'l stand in yer way from getting sent ta the Sioux Falls pen."

Jack looked straight at John, then smiled, "Spose yer right, at that…I expect if I could get away, I would, yer duties notwithstanding. Then again, I don't see that a judge is gonna be able ta convict me a rustlin. I gotta bill a sale, an sold em fair n square to that young buyer in Springview".

"Jack, I been told that yer bill a sales ain't gonna hold up. Ed Blakeley spent some time and riled that young man til he is lookin fer blood. Ed is gonna have ya, Jack, he's staked his reputation on that. Thinks you run a gang of 300 west of the Missoura. That so?"

"Hell, John you know its not. There ain't many men that would agree to share the fruits of their rustlin, and how the damned hell could I control that many men runnin around the west prairie,

Jack looked into the cup without comment. He slid forward offering the cup for a refill.

"When ya get outa Sue Foo, it'll be plain what ya gotta do. Like ya said, ya got friends. You kin make a new start. Ya never was scareda work…did ya hear, they hung Tom Horn in Cheyenne. Even he could not duck the law."

"Well, Tom done me right. I got no use fer anyone that works for the cattlemen's associations, but Tom was a stand-up guy."

Jack sipped quietly, then changed subject. "I need ta see my wife, John, I need ta know how the kids are doin. You could aid me in that regard."

"We'll see about doin that Jack," and pushed back his chair, the conversation ended.

After Olaf Finstad heard of Jack's jailing he went directly to Mitchell. "Get Mary to come over here, Olaf, I need a pillow, no two pillows, and one of her duck down quilts. Its cold in here. And some hacksaw blades, he whispered, and get me set up with a horse and new clothes someplace west of here, find someone you can trust. Come back and tell me how much money it will take. I'm gonna get out of here some way."

Jailhouse Ruminations - 1903

J ack and the Marshall set into a routine of checkers in the morning, and cards in the afternoon. He took two meals a day, brought in from a nearby restaurant. Always baking powder biscuits or cornbread, decent fare. A deputy sat up in the office each night for the first week, but finally, since Jack slept through each night and caused no problems, he began sleeping in the Sheriff's chair until, in two days, allowed as how he could "sleep to home at night". On Saturday night, the first week, two drunks were brought in, and loud objections notwithstanding, slept off the effects of bad whiskey and were released in a noticeably more sublime mood on Sunday. Still, Jack had plenty of time for undisturbed reflection.

He mused on his first meeting with "Doc Middleton". He had heard the name in a hog ranch discussion with a cowboy from the Dismal River area, who had been in the horse business. The cowboy had been with Doc in the Sand Hills, chasing wild horses, bucking out whole strings, selling, trading, and "what have you", as he said. Jack calculated that it could might as well mean cattle. He had ventured down to Valentine looking for this gent Middleton. The barkeep at the Heart Saloon in Valentine pointed to a back door where this Middleton fellow was apparently in a poker game. The room, blue with smoke, boasted two dim wick kerosene lamps, over green felt covered tables each of six players, kibitzers straddling chairs, arms across the backs, a rustling and low murmur of voices, a sharp curse, scraping boots, glasses popped down, and cards snapping at lay downs. As his eyes adjusted, Jack could make out none of the players, until one rose and started toward him, grabbed his elbow and with a smile, shook his hand. He guided him out the door, and to an open table at the far end of the joint.

"My god, Jim Riley! Great to see ya, gunslinger!"

"Jack, I don't use the name Jim Riley much anymore, and though I suppose its no big secret, I go by Doc Middleton in these parts. Don't wear a gun neither. Too tempted some times to use it on idiots." To which Jack laughed hardily, knowing how true the statement.

"Just the two men I seek," he laughed, "let's talk." Over a bottle of whiskey, some poker, they caught up on old times, until later that night they talked business. Doc had stayed in the north Sandhills, in Chadron, Valentine, and Naper rather than face more than a few Texans who had grown "adversities to Jim Riley's shooting style", as he put it. He had made good in the horse business, finally too good for the local sheriff and a vigilante group. They ran him down, killed some of his gang, and sent him to prison for five "rather unproductive years".

"I still am in the horse business and the bar business, but it's totally on the up and up, Jack. I do mostly buyin' sellin' and tradin'. I could use some more horses when you can bring them in. West Sand Hills have been worked out, not so many ponies out there."

Jack told the story of John's death, at least most of it. He asked about Big Red, the sorrel thoroughbred. "Jack, I kept him for some time, and had several fine foals out of him. Lost him in a horse race a year ago. He was the greatest horse I ever had, and I owe John a debt. Take a look at a couple of the colts I have from him, and take one with you. I wouldn't feel right if you didn't."

Feeling Doc's reluctance to involve himself in the rustling business again, Jack took his time. Over the next day and evening, never averse to a deal, they worked out an arrangement where Doc passed the information about cattle that Jack brought to Nebraska on to a contact with somewhat legitimate dealings with Omaha slaughterhouses, and ranchers on the Loups and Platte Rivers. They agreed not to share names, and not to have Doc do any riding, only to act as intermediary, passing information about places where Jack held cattle, pick-up times, prices, and to pass money between the two dealers. Doc insisted on secrecy and keeping segments of the operation separated. In this case, Jack had decided to only rely on Red Shirt or himself to make exchanges. They never talked to the pickup cowboys; they stood off, a hill away, and accepted an arranged hat wave to pass the herds.

This time it went wrong. Blakeley and his posse had found the critters before he could continue on south to Bassett.

He thought again about that long-barreled bay colt Doc had given him. Doc had haltered him to graze on a full-length lariat in the pasture near Valentine. "How about naming him Jim on a long string, Jim Longstring?"

"Works for me, Jack. He hasn't been ridden yet, but he sure is halter broke by now." Over time, Jack worked him into the best horse he ever had. Part "hot blood", he could outrun and outdistance nearly any horse on the prairie, the quintessential tool of the successful rustler.

The colt from Big Red, something from John Kincaid. The vision of John in the lantern light, at the bottom of Whetstone Creek, so many years ago haunted him again. He felt the cold bones of John's gnarled hand as he placed his own over the pistol. "I'll cock it for you , but you have to pull it John, I'll help but you have to pull it." He tried, and Jack helped, and John's pain ended. In death, his eyes looked the same, staring vacantly at the bright evening star.

Lightin' Out, Christmas - 1903

Mary came, and in addition to the blankets, brought three hacksaw blades, slipped them into his back pocket from her sleeve when she hugged him through the bars. As the blankets and pillows were searched, and Mary's food basket, Jack backed to the bed and sat down, slipping the blades casually next to the wall, beside his mattress.

The bars on the window were iron, not steel, and cemented fast. Working late at night Jack first hung the comforter across the window, then, holding a pillow around the bar to dampen the sound of the blade, he sawed relentlessly at the metal. He secreted a tablespoon of potato from his evening meal, mixed the filings with cold potato, and plastered them back into the saw marks before closing the shutter. He could not bend the bar as he had hoped after filing through at the window base. He had to cut through the bar at the top as well. With one bar cut out, he dropped his boots and shirt out the window, wedged himself into the opening and worked his body through. He dropped head first onto the ground, tucked and rolled, brushed himself off, and pulled on his boots and shirt. Cold northwest wind pierced to the bone. He went to the front of the jail, tested the door and eased it open. He grabbed a mackinaw off the wall rack, and went back out, walking the back streets until the barbershop opened. While hot towels swathed his face the County Sheriff came in, deputized two waiting men, and told Jack to "Get up, mister, we need every man, Jack Sully's escaped and makin' a run fer it."

"Excuse me, Sheriff, but I must advise you that I am suffering a disabilitating case of gout, and have not the constitution to ride. And sir, I doubt that I may be legally deputized, for I am not a resident of this county, ...Davison County, is it not? I am just passing through on my way to Sioux Falls." This Jack related in the most roundly affected tone that he could imagine might hopefully be mistaken for East Coast, maybe even English.

The sheriff hastily glanced around the room, pointed at two men waiting for service, beckoned them to follow, then turned and walked out.

Jack finished his shave while the posse thundered down the main street, heading west. He found an old wagon horse in a corral on the edge of town, and rode bareback southwest to the arranged meeting with Olaf, who had brought new clothes, a big buffalo coat across the saddle of Jim Longstring. Knowing that the posse would soon get to Sully Flats, Mary would know that he escaped. He headed south, stayed east of the river past the mouth of the Whetstone on the west bank, and found the Ellis homestead just up from the river breaks at White Swan. He and Joe Ellis had cut wood together, and had been neighbors for twenty years. If he could trust anyone, it was Joe. Jack hunkered in, braving the cold only to help Joe with scavenging for fire wood, and tending his stock.

Two heavy snows in late fall half melted into crusted banks, patched with a fine piebald gumbo dust, which the wind whipped up from dry, plowed ground. Joe's fall plowing had upturned nearly twenty acres on the small flat north of his house, and now the wind forced it sifting through cracks in the caulking. Jack picked his way over the broken ground, avoiding the hardened snow banks that could bloody the horse's cannons. Down the gully to the river, he led the horse slowly across, avoiding the snowed over spots which could hide air holes the river carved from the underside of the thick ice, even in this aching cold. As the early evening light faded, he worked his way cautiously up the creek line from the abandoned Whetstone Landing. The bare, winter trees could hardly hide a lookout, if the Sheriff had posted one. Not likely; no man could weather this cold for nearly two months since his escape. He used the cover of scrub pine outgrowths, stopping to listen, surveying all the landscape. In the descending darkness, he tied the horse in the trees and tromped through the brittle grass across the open space from the spring at the top of the creek, following the stone boat tracks one of the boys had plowed in bringing fresh water to the house. He looked through each frosted window where the children had pressed their fingers to draw stick men and horses, but saw no strangers. Finally, seeing George in the lantern light, he tapped on the window and motioned him outside. They embraced,

Jack patting his shoulder, and whispered. Yes, Mom was upstairs, and all were well, runny noses and minor coughs aside.

"Eva is out of bed now, but weak, coughs all the time. Take some time with her, Dad." George went for Jack's horse in the creek line.

The family was together, and on that wintry night, floors drafty, windows caked with frost, they feasted on baking powder biscuits and jam, grouse and gravy. The cold permeated, and even with the pot belly stove and kitchen stove stoked high, the house was very cool, though not enough to dampen the warmth of having the father again at the head of the table. The milk cow was still wet, though the output was down to a half galleon; yes, they had visitors for two weeks, shadowy horsemen lurked in the tree line, but none in the past month. Talk of his situation and peril could not be avoided. Two days was all that he could stay, even that at some risk. No, he assured them that he would not be sent to prison, he had done no more than others, and no, he would not get caught, "Jim Longstring is too fast for any of the sheriff's plow horses." Little Claudie seconded that thought with spirit, for he loved that horse. A warm scene for the patriarch. For the man who spent weeks away, who loved his family, without doubt, but also a role, a reinforcement of influence. To the daughters he was "father"; to the boys, even Billy, he was affectionately "the old man". Billy brought out his fiddle, went through Turkey in the Hay, a Basque dance tune that he only knew from old Narcisse, and finished with "Drink To Me Only With Thine Eyes". Tears welled in his eyes, and he strode to the bedroom.

The third day, wind-whipped snow flurries in the morning lessening the danger of visitors, so Jack stayed the day. With the gusting winds in the afternoon dropping to total stillness as evening light faded, he made his way back down the creek valley and across the Missouri ice to Joe's place.

The winter warriored on, slashing its sword edge of cold across the prairie, pausing only to gain new lungs, to breath deep of Alaskan snow and frost and ice, huffing and puffing its breath unrestrained across the vacant range. He whittled horses and dolls, even a wooden Peacemaker pistol. He chopped kindling wood and split logs for Joe and Liz Ellis, sharing the winter work. He hunted deer in the breaks, and once rode to Chris Colombe's to stay a night and bring back a deer for the Ellis's. He did not drink in their home; it was humble, but deserving of respect.

He reprised his trips across the river to sit with Olaf and Harry, to plan for something early in the spring.

"The law has been to every one of your neighbors, Jack, they are looking hard. Ed Blakeley's been holed up in Bonesteel, and it seems he has you as his main target. You are going to be pressured in this area. There is money out for your arrest."

"Olaf, I am feeling the same thing. This Blakeley is a stubborn asshole. I ain't the main cause of his problems, hell, I been accused of stealing beeves all the way from here to Canada."

Harry languished at the door. Olaf hovered in the warmth over the cook stove, laid his mittens atop the pie warmer, finally said, "Jack, its not the truth that counts here. He believes that if he gets you, runs you through a trial and into the pen, he'll stop all the rustlin'. He has convinced his lacey-sleeved bosses that you run a syndicate, and the price on your head he has got raised. Its money he's after, but its also stubborn pride. He's been around here now over two years, and he ain't got you."

"They got a warrant out now. The law is sidin' with the Association. The newspaper in Chamberlain has called you a "villain", and "outlaw". You ain't Robin Hood any more."

"I don't think I ever was, Olaf. I never gave my money away, don't think you did either. I helped my neighbors, and my neighbors helped me. We all done it. There ain't no kinder hearted man around than you, yourself."

"Well, they wrote about you givin' a cow to a poor lady, about bringin' the little red pony back to the honyocker. About you buyin' drinks at Oacoma."

"Its no more than other men did for their neighbors."

"Well, some of it, but I never knew a man to give his lone milk cow away."

"Olaf, I mighta been drunk, who knows?", he smiled.

PART V

A MAN
IN A BUGGY

A MAN IN A BUGGY

Harry's Dilemma

H arry left confused, riding quietly with Olaf til the trail turned south to his spread. "I just think Jack is takin' on too much right now. He should oughta head out fer Canada, let the local law cool their heels."

"So what about going west and getting' another herd, you for that?"

"It ain't no different out there from what it ever was, Harry, late winter's the best time to latch onta the biggest herd, get some cash. We surely need it, with this winter's losses. It's been a hard time for me and the Missus."

"That's true fer me too." If he knew where Jack holed up now, he could talk to Ed Blakeley. Ed already owed him money, yet with Jack loose again, would he pay up? Would Jack even come back to his spread? The risk was getting higher. He was a connivin' man. If he went west with him, might be able to keep track of him, make some money, and deal with Ed again.

"I'll wait til we hear from Jack again. Mite cold to be travelin' now."

They parted, in freezing cold, each with thoughts of a warm hearth. Next day, Harry set out for Bonesteel, a day's ride south. He took care to skirt the local spreads, even the honyockers. His heart seemed to freeze up with the weather. He had always admired Jack, but it remained a feeling mixed with envy at his easy way with people, regardless of the general feeling that he rustled for a living, and was suspect for any number of losses, local folks seemed to forgive him. Had he been proven in any case, maybe they would not have felt that way, but when Jack put his arm around a man's shoulders, whatever enmity between them seemed to wither.

Jack, as leader, confined their rustling in the local area to mortgaged cows, such as the ones he and Olaf had from Becker and Deegan and done so poorly by. The real problem: the law would connect Harry and Olaf and Red Shirt and Billy. They would all go to prison if they weren't careful.

He warmed in one of the makeshift bars in Bonesteel, and toward evening located Ed at the only restaurant in town. Recounting the news of Jack's escape threw him into a lengthy swearing, hat throwing tantrum. He brushed the sawdust off the brim, and composed himself. "Its been a while, where is he now?" Harry pieced together the story, side-stepping his own knowledge of Olaf's help and that he had seen him.

"No one has seen him or knows where he is now. Its coldern a well digger's ass, nobody travelin' much in this cold. I been caring for my own herd most of the time. I came to see about my money, and to see what you want to do now."

"What money you talkin' about?" Ed snarled. "I gave you the location of Jack at Bordeaux's, I directly aided in his capture. Tain't my fault he got away."

"No, Mr. Ham, I said capture and conviction of outlaws, not just capture. You'll get your money when I, with your help, get him inta Sioux Falls."

"I don't remember no "conviction" being said. I did my part and want my pay."

Ed needed Harry, and could see his neck bristling, he might lose him over this, but he himself would get no pay until Jack was convicted...or dead. "Here's a hundert dollars. I'll keep the same deal with you, and pay another two hundert in addition to the seven hundert you almost earned. I ain't got no further money, I ain't been paid myself. This'll get you through the winter, and we get Sully this spring, if he ain't in Canada."

Harry leveled his eyes directly at Ed, contempt, distrust, and disdain in them. Ed turned away, let it pass. Harry would go for the money if he did not agitate too much. Ed attributed a weaker sense of character in Harry, but a useful weakness when fortified by the prospect of money or personal gain.

They finished a bland dinner of fatty hogs knuckles, but the biscuits were first rate. All the time, Ed talked of Sully and the harm he had caused. He charged every new rustling escapade to him, talked of a syndicate that included gangs in Wyoming, Montana and even Canada.

Harry kept his counsel and thoughts to himself. He had no incentive to dissuade Ed of his grandiose illusions. He could make some money off the cattle they got in spring, and he could still work with Ed when Jack and the band came back to the Whetstone. Maybe he could get a line on the Nebraska connection. Too many reasons to keep doin what he was doing. Harry drifted out of the restaurant, toward the line of bars down the street. Ed watched him go, and shook his head. For him his first day here provided all the excitement he needed in this wild, wide-open, ramshackle town.

Spa on the Whetstone

The good Doctor Buchanan stopped at a rocky outbreak on the edge of the Whetstone riparian, wiped his brow again, the mid-day April sun already foretelling a hot summer. He adjusted his trousers in his calf-high lace boots. He had dressed too well for this walk in the wood, thought he. On the map, such as it was, the creek looked shorter; should have been at the headwaters by now. Yet, he persisted: the water tasted of iron to him. It could hold the ingredients of a spa spring, redemptive waters. He pushed up out of the tangled grape vines, onto the grassy hill-side, and proceeding, another hour traipsing through the tall prairie grasses, he glimpsed the roof-line of Jack Sully's home, near what should be the headwaters of this marvelous little spring. The water so cool, clear, and even now, in the heat of summer it splashed merrily around curving rocks and little waterfall drop-offs in more than adequate flow to meet his purpose. Searching for the source, he dropped back into the tangle of wild grape vines, bushes and honey locust trees, quickly finding the frothing surge from the hillside, and Jack's make-shift retainer dam.

Mary surveyed the approaching shadow, discerning quickly that he was no ordinary cowboy stopping by for a meal or fresh water. With such attire, he would surely be either a dangerous Pinkerton or an innocent nat-uralist. In any case, he wore no gun, and as he approached, smiled and touched the brim of his wide slouch hat. His coat open, sweat standing out on his forehead, he presented no immediate danger.

"Madam, a lovely day for the laundry", he said noting the clothes pins at Mary's waist and fluttering shirts and trousers on the line beside the house.

"Yes, and welcome to our home, do you care for fresh water? You seem to have come a ways on foot. Have you lost your ride?"

"Walking is my natural mode of travel aside from carriages and trains. It tones the body, and whets the appetite I have found. But, yes a fresh drink would be most appreciated. I note your fine spring below, but hesitated to dip my canteen in such pristine water as in the holding dam. I am Dr Buchanan, from Ohio," as he offered his hand.

"What might your business be so far from Ohio, doctor?"

"I have committed my doctoring skills to natural healing methods for respiratory ailments, gout, and general malaise. I have had success in this vain, but wish to expand my studies and practice westward, to use to advantage the wonderful clean air abounding here, and the soothing balm of spa waters, healing waters. I must say that I find this brook nearly at your doorstep has great potential for my purposes."

"We have little illness among us. We have benefitted in that regard, surely, but had not attributed it to the water nor air, but to good fortune, mostly. Sir, my husband is not presently expected, should you wish to speak with him."

"I will say that I am prepared to make a generous offer to cooperate in use of the spring, and provide more than adequate recompense for rental of sufficient land for a hotel with spa. I am backed by my family's resources, and a highly respected bank in Ohio."

"I will advise my husband of your intentions…where might he meet with you upon his return?"

"This is but one potential site for a spa, I intend to survey further up river. Should this brook, with its fine prospects prove the ideal location, I will return and discuss any matters relating to further development of the project."

"Some company here would be most interesting for the children, and myself. It is a lonely place at times."

"Madam, I take my leave, to meet the boat at the Missouri end of this brook by evening. Your name is…?

"Mary Sully, and my husband is Jack. We have lived here for many years."

He took well-advised her loosely veiled claim of possession.

Jack saw this as the threat that it was. What he had not done, what he knew he should have done but now could not do. Legal claim to the land lay with Mary, her Cheyenne and Lakota heritage, her right to reservation land. He had discussed necessary actions with her, but now pressed upon her the importance of laying legal claim. A lawyer, use the money he had buried, get this done. Taking first tenancy of the land, living on it, working it, did not suffice as grounds for possession now, in a changed world where only the law mattered. He knew John Petrie to be right, as they had chatted over checkers, he could not beat back changes forever.

Leaving the Rosebud – April, 1904

Summer lay close by. Across the spring-source of the Whetstone, among the deeper ungrazed grasses, the first flowers of spring dappled the hillside. Prairie Smoke already spread its pastels among the puccoon, bluebells, even some milk vetch added its reddish hue to nature's impressionist artistry. Mary stood admiring, and needing to say nothing, she handed Jack a basket with a blanket, two oranges, chunks of newly baked bread, a cup of butter, and a small bottle of wine.

Eva watched, familiar with the intimacy of their private ritual. She coughed, unnoticed by the two, suppressed as best she could another bout of rasping expectoration. Her persistent ailment had worn at Mary through the winter. Eva's condition had improved, then deteriorated again in March, now slowly improving with the warm spring air. Along with some mysterious elixir, the Chamberlin doctor prescribed walks, fresh air, and a healthy diet. Mostly this regimen proved helpful, but there were still days when she would not rise from her bed. Today she had walked by the spring, freshened in the spring water, walked barefoot across the rocks and creek bed. Ever optimistic, aside from the coughing, she thought herself much improved. She could smile as mother and father strolled toward the spring.

Light faded as the two finished the meal that served as pretext for the lovemaking that darkness allowed. Jack moved the nosegay picked from the painted hillside from the basket and spread the blanket across the cushioning grasses. The intensity of the lovemaking betrayed the quietude of the hillside, made urgent by the departure they knew must come with sunrise. What Jack might have earlier dismissed as rumor or fear mongering he now found credible. A. P. Long had spent several days in Presho, and Ed Blakeley wandered forth from Bonesteel, had even stopped at the house on the Flats, inquiring of Jack's whereabouts. Mary had staved off further inquiry, advising Blakeley that Jack had gone west. Which he now intended. Olaf reported word in Presho that A. P. Long carried a warrant for Jack's arrest, based on the bungled sale of the 74 head of cattle in Springview. Fight or flee, and flight seemed most appropriate to both Jack and Mary. They both acknowledged between themselves that the separation would be extended. Now the heat was on, the old evasions ineffective, vain in the circumstances. Jim Longstring fed on oats for the past week, the pack mare as well. He had diamond hitched his pack, stored in the pole barn. He would not bid farewells, Mary understood his need to depart quickly, leaving the children with no knowledge of his destination.

With a faint gathering of light in the east, Jack led the mare out of the corral, mounted Ol' Jim, and cantered down the slope, through the winding path in the trees of Whetstone Creek, and loped up the hill, glancing quickly at the love nest on the hillside before intertwining himself with the hills and draws west of the flats, on to the White River breaks.

Gone to Canada

He mused on the strangeness of Texas and Oklahoma when he was there. The robust rogues in the bars, the callousness, the mean streak that passed for toughness which ran through so many. The cold business manner of even the storekeepers' wives. The ruthlessness of the boss cowmen. Not only toward their own cowhands, but toward the other trail herds and herders, toward the Indians, toward coyotes and wolves and buffalo and mustangs in their path. Why would Canada be so different? With the trail herds, your life could depend on the camaraderie of your fellow cowboy, his loyalty, knowing his own safety resided with you as yours did with him. Who did he know in Canada? Put aside your fear he told himself, you have always made new friends quickly. But his own arguments proved weak against these sentiments.

The sun warmed the spring air as he traversed the northern plain over the Moreau River, and with it his spirits, brooding festered in darkness. He had at first ridden during the moonlit nights, skirting the homesteads blossoming in the newly opened ranges, but now felt secure with daytime travel, away from familiar faces. Jack slapped Jim on the flanks with the reins, and took up an easy lope north. Thoughts of what he left behind plagued him. Who were his real friends? How fared his family? Eva's illness; what if his daughter' health worsened? Indecisiveness haunted his thoughts. He rode on north, but his concern for family gripped him. He remembered Doc reciting his own attempt at avoiding jail. Before his capture, trial and sentencing, he had had a letter in his possession, a deal with the Governor of Nebraska to expunge his outlaw past from the record and redeem his future, to avoid jail time. Doc was betrayed by the bounty hunter. Jack pondered such an arrangement, possibly through John Petrie? But, as with Doc, once captured, the prospects for a reprieve were moot.

As he worked his way up a creek branching off the Moreau, he happened upon an unusual sight. Two wagons, one with wooden posts, another with barbed wire rolls worked their way north. Four hands dug post holes, four set them straight and tamped them solid. He recognized none of them, and ventured up the draw to enquire about this enterprise.

"Ed Lemmon has leased the whole north range, got Teddy's OK. He aims to fence the whole 850 thousand acres. Long term."

"I thought Teddy ordered the fences down. The range open to all again."

"Well, Ed says Teddy understands the rights of good cattlemen to use the ranges properly. Seems he and Ed are old friends. He set this range aside fer Ed, who is, by god, a good cattleman."

"I once worked for Ed, I would not discount that assessment. I just had heard that Teddy supported open ranges. Times are changin'." Caution forbade him to say more, and he swung Jimmy northward, reminding himself of the power of the syndicates. They had guns on the ranges, an open door to the President himself. His stomach stirred with resentment. "God dammit!", he swore in frustration.

A sarcastic grin crossed his countenance as he walked Jim into the new town of Lemmon. Ed Lemmon, big shot now, what next? Platted out a grid, sold the lots, took up an office, and named the place after himself. Best to avoid Ed, that was a cinch, though he was unlikely to be in the town proper. The ranch obsessed him.

Bitter Lemmon

Over two hundred miles from the Rosebud, Jack expected to find no one who would recognize him. Even so, evidence that his intentions were toward Canada would be to his advantage. Shaking off the trail dust, slapping his hat on his trousers, he made for the only bar in town. As his eyes widened, becoming accustomed to the darkness, two waddies conversing at the bar, and rattle and murmur of a card game sounded from the back. Jack ordered whiskey, leaned his elbows across the bar, and let the sour mash sting away his weariness. Jack tapped his glass on the bar, indicating another. The two cowboys turned toward him, looked hard, and came toward him. He waited quietly for his refill, ignoring their approach.

"Jack, remember me, Moss Hardabee, from the old Flyin' V. What you doing up this way? This here is "Bone" Macklin, we come up from Ft Pierre just yestaday, they said ya was ranchin on the Missouri, some Frenchie was lookin fer ya. Someone is sick in yer family. A girl?"

"I do remember, ya ran the remuda for Ed Lemmon then. You work fer Ed still?"

"Nah, went to Texas fer awhile, came back with a herd coupla years ago, been around Ft Pierre til now.

Jack felt something more than circumstantial about this meeting. He poker-faced the word about Eva. "I'm up here ta pick up a stud horse in North Dakota, part thoroughbred. I'm runnin a large herd now, need some real good studs. Where you headed for?" But true, Eva had been recovering, yet not fully recovered from one of her bouts of anemia.

"Headin to Montana. Bar 8 spread over by Miles City."

While otherwise he might have stayed the night in the hotel, freshened up, he resupplied his dwindling provisions, and pressed on north seeking cover both legal and physical. The state line might not stop the Association detectives, but it would slow the legal process, if caught.

Further north, as he entered the North Dakota Badlands, he took to the ravines and gulches, never silhouetting himself on the sky line. On the grassland just a half hour back he had seen the leavings of a fresh kill, the heifer pulled down recently, gutted, buzzards about. He noted it, but proceeded on. He rounded a stone spire, came face to face with a large gray wolf. Surprised and cornered, he bared his teeth, looking for a way out, prepared to fight. Jim Longstring, surprised, sun-fished to the left, nearly unseating Jack. The wolf, tarried, snarled as Jack reined in Jim, then loped off around the bend.

It could not have been, but it looked exactly like the wolf in the blizzard, long ago. Dark linings around the yellow eyes; not calm now, cornered, prepared to fight. Jack pulled his Winchester from the scabbard as he dismounted, but the wolf was gone. Harry had told him that wolves never attack humans, but here the threat seemed real. He waited, but the wolf had weaved through the badland sandstone maze, only the dark visage remained in Jack's thoughts. What did it mean? Nothing? No, it was an omen; good or bad? The calm wolf of years ago had meant he would survive. This one, warned against continuing?

Jack remounted, pressed his hands on the saddle horn. Being neither a religious man nor one accustomed to living his life tailored around dreams and visions, he first dismissed his thought about the wolf's implications. Lakota dreams, sweat lodge philosophy he had dismissed years ago.

Jack nudged Jim forward, kept his rifle in hand, and progressed slowly up the ravine. He would kill that wolf if he had lingered to partake more of the heifer on the plain. At the top of the ravine Jack dismounted and sat on the buffalo grass carpet. Plainly, the wolf had vanished, as wolves can. Had he left his home too soon? There was unfinished business that he had marginalized in his mind, flight seeming the only longterm solution. Now, he began to reconsider. The prospect of a pardon by the governor remained a possibility. Doc had nearly succeeded in that regard, and he had heard of others gaining reprieves. Reputation aside, he had at present only one outstanding warrant, a deal to stop rustling in return should appeal to the Stock Grower's Association. Failure to complete registration of land for Mary left the entire ranch in jeopardy. This

Doctor Buchanan presented a clear and present danger, maybe an immediate peril to his holdings on the Flats. Fear that Eva's condition had worsened bored into his thoughts, he could not dispel the concern. She had relapsed before, nearly dying. He had left unfinished business on the Flats. A heavy sense of guilt at having run away flooded over him. He was leaving his problems for others to fix, the burden upon his family, on Mary. Olaf, Harry, Billy, they too needed their exoneration through Jack's reprieve.

'It ain't the wolf,' Jack thought. He mounted, pressed the right rein along Jimmy's neck until he had made a wavering, long loop, headed back down the ravine. He could not have explained it, the longing for home had set in after just four days. The wolf omen seemed to confirm what his heart was demanding. He would find a way, he could not leave Mary with the burden of the death of a child. John Petrie would help with a letter to the governor if he approached him correctly, appealed to his good nature and their long-standing friendship.

Another Homecoming

Jack mounted the last hill west of the Whetstone, reined in Jim Longstring, stretched in the saddle. Across the valley stood his house, whitewash fading already, but glowing orange in the late afternoon sun, a lone ship on the plain. Great clouds, white as new snow cotton-balled up in the west, gray undersides growing black on the western horizon. Dark thunderheads formed, a rain trail already nearing the ground, moving east, promising relief for man and beast from the persistent heat of the early summer sun. By sunset, maybe some rain, some much needed rain. He poured hot canteen water over his hair, wiping his face of the dust.

The door of the house swung wide, a small, skirted figure rushed out, waving her hands, followed by a larger, similar form, though clearly Eva. A wrenching gut feeling of betrayal quickly followed the flush of relief. They had not seen the silhouetted rider yet, these girls at play, but would have rushed down the hill had they. Papa, coming home. Brooding clouds out west behind him, the sunny, welcoming home before him. He waved his hat, still unseen, slacked the reins for Jim, who needed no persuasion to proceed to the pole barn. He was home again. He would deal with it.

The girls were growing, becoming young ladies, already good cooks. The boys missed him more each time. Billy often went with him, but Frank and John were more sullen when he returned, resenting his absence, but also the jealous return, with the girls gushing enthusiasm, the father's fawning attention to them, and Jack's evasive, incomplete answers to their own often intrusive questions. "Papa, where were you this time?" "Where is the new horse?" "Where's Olaf, and Harry?" "Can I go with you next time?" Time leavened all, and next day a calm settled in as he surveyed the work before him, the focus on horses, assessing the value in the new colts, halter breaking yearlings for sale, a brace of mares for harness, and for Jack, working out a four-horse team for Joe Blackbird's timber hauling operation on the island.   Back home felt good, felt right, yet his sense of caution and his faith in his knack of escaping incarceration concealed his denial of the magnitude of his immediate danger, of the intensity and passion of his pursuers.

Hearth and Home

M ary slept quietly. The last of the half-moon sunk near the horizon, the room nearly totally dark, but he seemed to envision the top of the oak, west on the ridge near the creek line. Is that why he had come back? It now occurred to him. He had not thought so, until now. But it was not, it had never been for money alone. Money for the spread, which was what counted. Mary would need it all. Why then?

He remembered the ache in his bones as he approached the North Dakota border, an ache he seldom felt on his other long rides. He sensed his aging; naturally his body would protest, but did his bones foretell trouble, even danger? What could he do in Canada, to lay low, and for how long? He was a cowboy, but even there the winters were longer, colder, tougher to weather out. The summers were as hot and dry. How long an exile? How stubborn was Ed Blakeley? How long was the Association's memory? He had alienated the powerful, among whom he might have found a sponsor to request a pardon from the Governor. Not Scotty Philip, Ed Lemmon, or the like. Maybe Marshall John, or even the Nelsons, who were now well respected businessmen. Still, John Petrie remained a friend, and harbored a sympathetic sentiment akin to Jack's loathing of the wicked syndicates, contrary as that was to the law to which he had committed his life. 'I've been thinking too much, worryin, ...just do something. I ain't gonna live forever anyway.' He had problems to solve, threats to Mary's rights to the land, a reprieve to seek. Clearly, flight had failed as the resolution.

Now, as he lay thinking, a new thought dredged back the dread, as he remembered. He had skirted Scotty Philip's ranch, well to the west as he returned south. Near the Cheyenne River as he was breaking camp in the late afternoon two hands came along the river bottom following some Flying V cows northward; he could not avoid them. He had not known them, but one asked if he were not Jack Sully, whom he had met once in Ft Pierre. Jack had smiled, shook his head, and casually nodded to the north, explaining that he had seen Jack Sully in Lemmon, headed to North Dakota to pick up a thoroughbred stallion for breeding. They finished rolling their Bull Durham with little comment, and moved on. At Midland, before he crossed back over the Bad River, Jack had stopped at the post office for water. There were no cow ponies there, only a buckboard, and he had not seen anyone other than the postmaster. Had he known him? Had he known which direction he took from there?

Yes, he was back, and reality with its fear of capture was back, …impending doom sunk into his stomach. He rolled on his side, tried to sleep, block his thoughts. Did the law and range dicks know his movements? For three days the flats had been empty, no forbidding forms loomed into sight, as he kept watch from the second story windows. Shorty had brought some mail, plodding slowly up the hill from the south creek line, as if he were wearing snowshoes. He had been only mildly surprised to see Jack. He left with butter and cheese, a letter to the Jandreaus.

Mary turned over on her back, snuffled, almost words, and sighed. Being beside her again warmed him. Yet, he could not remember the last time he had said, "I love you". It was never necessary. The sentiment never sought. But it occurred just then that maybe it was, maybe he did need to tell her. Not necessary for Mary's love, but what he needed to do, to reassure himself. He remembered now when last she had told him. He had just promised her a piano. One better than her father's, that she had played when she was a girl, a part of life that she left behind, first for a storekeeper, and now Jack and his barren prairie life. Had she been asking for just that little bit more when she pulled him close, saying, "I love you"? For him to say it, too? He had come back, he knew she understood what that meant, what that said in its silent commitment about love for her, but tomorrow he would tell her.

Late that day, a buckboard pulled into Scotty Philip's ranch, and his sister-in-law related as how she had seen Jack Sully in Midland, or surely thought it was him. Next day, Ike and Sage, his two northern line riders came in, saying that they had seen Jack Sully on his way to Canada two days before. This did not rhyme. The following day Scotty took time out from preparations for the spring roundup to send his sister-in-law by her buckboard to Presho to advise the Sheriff that Jack had not gone on to Canada, but had returned to the Rosebud. The Sheriff offered his hand for her to alight the seat, but she handed the note to him and with only a fleeting frown, slapped the reins on the two mares and followed north in the dust.

'Breed squaw, he thought, not that I care.' He tore open the envelope and snorted as he read it. 'Hell, what does the man think of me anyway?' He had been Sheriff two terms now, and knew his duty. He liked Scotty, but this was down right insulting. While his sympathies remained with the small ranchers, the law had come and the courts changed; he would do his duty without advice from Mr. Philip or the Association. He went back to the courthouse, sighed as he slouched onto his chair. He'd have a drink later. He took pen in hand, a clean sheet of paper, and wrote a note to Marshall Petrie. "Take this to Mitchell tomorrow morning, Arlo," he told his deputy.

Word Travels

A message from the Rapid City telegraph office prompted Ed Blakeley's trip by rail to Valentine, and buckboard to Bonesteel. A. P. Long was already on his way to meet Ed from Mitchell, a meeting with John Petrie had set in motion the forming of a posse, and meet up point on the South Whetstone. A. P. had convinced John of the importance, the imperative, that justice must finally be exacted in the case of Jack Sully. There were political pressures, Western South Dakota Stock Grower's Association authority, Scotty Philip's influence within the Missouri River Stock Grower's Association brought to bear, and not least, a series of newspaper articles more malicious and sensationalist than plausible, about the outlaw Jack Sully. Within three days John Petrie had positioned an operation to capture Jack. His orders to the posse were to capture, to see justice done through the courts. His instructions made clear that the warrant for Jack Sully's capture sited rustling, not now a capital offense, that the days of hanging thieves had been abandoned.

In his own separate instructions to Harry Ham and A. P. Long, Ed Blakeley contrarily, made it clear that escape should be prevented by any means. Details of how they would preclude a recurrence of another Jack Sully escape were laid bare, plain to both. Harry cleaned and oiled his wolfing rifle. A. P.'s scabbard held a new Winchester. They rode two of the fastest horses Ed could appropriate. He, in deference to having the Association too closely linked to whatever outcome might obtain, planned to stay in Bonesteel. If the Marshall insisted upon the legal system prevailing, so be it. The Association's intentions would be well served.

"We still got the agreement on how ta handle this, Ed, I ain't talking about anyone else associated with Jack Sully. If I do, they will have me out as well. You get Jack, and this thing will be done."

"I have agreed, Harry, and I am a man a my word. And I mean to have Jack Sully, *now*. Anything less and this agreement is gonna be called into review by me an you. Ifn you gotta shoot his horse, don't back down. If ya gotta wound him, that's up ta you. This is the best chance we have had, and ya better make it work."

A Bright, Sunshiny Day

Marshall Petrie came in a buckboard, trailing ten men from Mitchell, including some Association men, and two local neighbors. They all were sworn to apprehend Jack Sully, according to the warrant the Marshall had in hand. Of the two neighbors, the Marshall called Ben Diamond aside, spoke in lowered tones. "Go on ahead, Ben, talk to Jack, get him to lay down his gun and come peaceful. We are gonna surround him, he won't get away. I don't want no blood shed, but Jack is gonna have ta come in this time."

Ben Diamond had listened carefully to the Marshall. His own loyalty to Jack extended to that of all of his neighbors. They liked, admired, had benefited from Jack's neighborliness. Yet, the law must be respected. He knew now that Jack had returned, questioned his reasoning, but ultimately could not betray years of friendship. He would reason with Jack.

The sun was high, a light breeze blew from the south, a few scattered wooly white clouds trailed off to the west to build for an evening rain. Ben entered the house to find Jack at the stove, Mary no where in sight. The children looked up, forks in hand as Jack flipped pancakes.

"Jack, a good morning, and I need a few minutes. Where is Mary?"

"Crossed the river last evening to see the Jandreaus. She needed some time away, took Frank and John with her."

Ben followed Jack into the pole barn. "What brings you out this way taday, Ben?"

"I come with word from Marshall John Petrie. He is askin that you take off yer pistol, and come peaceful. He has ten men or so, he has come from Mitchell to surround yer place. Jack, its serious, and there are Stockmen's Association men with him."

Jim Longstring munched on oats in his stall, already saddled. Jack lifted up on the latigo, tightening the cinch and finished it off with a half-hitch. "With fair play, I am equal to any three of the best of em." He pulled his pistol, rolled the cylinders, replaced it in his holster and mounted.

"Jack, they're here now, take ta the Flats, head north, they ain't up that way yet." Urgency plain in his voice. Jack unlooped the pack mare's lead rope, reined Jim Longstring around the edge of the barn, spurred to a high gallop directly toward the west and the creek line. "Jack, no!" Ben yelled.

Nearing trees at the creek's edge, he heard the first shots, shots overhead. He took his old path across the creek, but clearly shots were coming directly from it. They had cut him off. He whipped the reins against Jimmy's neck turning him away, and could feel him flinch and take a half-step; Jim was hit. Pistol shots. Ten, twelve. As old Jim leapt over the narrow creek just below the spring, crashed through the chokecherry and plum trees, Jack loosed his left leg from the stirrup, hooked the cantle and laid across Jimmy's right side, Indian style. More pistol shots, but now Jim Longstring proved his thoroughbred heritage and out-raced their range. As he neared the hill crest, Jack raised up, his boot toe sought the left stirrup. Old Jim Longstring had done his part.

The rifle bullet splintered the left rib cage, passed through a kidney, exited through the right lung. Bullet force blasted him from the saddle, bounced him into the salt grass and flowers. Within the minute, he regained consciousness to great, pulsating pain in his abdomen filling fast with blood. Movement sent excruciating shock throughout his body. Each attempted breath tore his lungs, sent a wave of pain again through him. Jimmy turned back, nuzzled his face, sniffing, then jerked away, snorting, as he smelled the blood in Jack's mouth.

Marshall Petrie in his buckboard had arrived at the house as Jack had entered the Whetstone Creek tree line. He knew he had men covering that escape route, heard the pistol shots, and made directly to circumvent the spring, coming up the hill from the north. Just as he navigated the team around the spring head, he heard a rifle shot, saw Jack thrown from his horse. Among the first to arrive at Jack's side, blood foretold the outcome. Jack seemed to move his lips, his eyes squeezed shut against the pain and the brilliant May sun. "John, I'm bad hit, I need to go home", in a rasping whisper. He, Ben Diamond, two others lowered Jack carefully into the back of the buckboard. Jack failed to stifle groans of pain on the rough trek to the house, finally passing out again.

At the house, Eva and the other children ran to meet the wagon, trailing along, looking aghast inside, until it stopped at the doorstep. Lifted gently from the wagon, Jack whispered, "No, not inside... here". Eva, tears streaming, cradled his head as he lay in the dust of the yard, his lung sucking faintly for soft summer air. "Love you", as he looked into her eyes.

Jack, Why did you run, you needn't have."

"I'm 59 years old John, I could not stand a long stay in prison... Eva,...Love...to...Mother."

He struggled to breath, but against terrible odds, his eyes filled with the cloudless blue sky to see no more.

May 16th, 1904, Jack Sully expired; on the Rosebud prairie he loved, with his boots on.

EPILOGUE

Harry Ham and A.P. Long ambled slowly up from the Whetstone, saw the Marshall kneeling over Jack, others making their way quickly to his side. Captured at least. "I could not get a shot at the horse, nothing but his butt…when he raised up it was right then, or he woulda made it over the rise."

"True enough. I wonder if he's talkin," said the other as they turned back to the trees, mounted and worked their way down the stoney creek bed from whence they came.

Mary arrived home from neighbor Jandreau too late. The shock of Jack's death consumed her, left her prostrate over him, yet how this had transpired replicated a vision which she had over and over foreseen. A vision she had fought from her mind, only to have it recur in the half-slumbers of early mornings, and now the reality lay before her. The foreboding extant. She rose up from Jack's breast. She wiped her cheeks, and did not cry again. She surveyed the distraught family about her, and went on with the duties of widow and mother.

The second day after Jack's death, Mr. Fred Lee, a photographer, arrived uninvited at the home on the prairie and proceeded to record on film the only known photo of Jack, at peace, in his coffin. The black hair groomed back, a black frock coat, white shirt neatly adorned him.

Another day hence, 20th of May, the neighbor's wagons and horses began forming a long line behind the open wagon carrying Jack's coffin. Quiet murmurs of discussion, sorrowful greetings to Mary and the children could be heard above the dueling trills of two meadowlarks, under the watchful surveillance of two circling red-tailed hawks.

Frank Waugh searched for Red Shirt, but failed to locate him before he must, with Louisa, leave for the Whetstone. Old Bill Bordeaux arrived from Rosebud just as the funeral procession made a sweeping circle of Sully Flats, back to the small knoll south of the house. There Jack was laid to rest.

Harry Ham and Olaf Finstad visited Mary the day after the funeral, as the rumors flew about, creating the enduring mystery concerning who shot Jack Sully. From this meeting, Mary insisted that no further inquiries be conducted, no vengeance sought. She meant to carry out Jack's oft repeated wish that no harm ever come to those working with him.

Yes, she knew this man so well that his failings and faults, so easily accepted within her deep love, were but smudges on a crystal, a small fissure in the face of a great mountain, a glint in a diamond's refraction. He could leave his family for days, sometimes weeks on end, return as if he had not tarried so long; and die because he returned that one time too often.

As Joe Ellis told her at the funeral, "There were worse men than Jack...he was blamed for more than he ever did, but he was a good neighbor. He always gave more than he got........."

Two headstones now at the burial site continue to cloud the reality of Jack Sully, adding, if anything, more fodder to the myths grown up around his most colorful life.

The first headstone reads:

SULLY CEMETERY...SULLY, JOHN (JACK) 1839-1904.

By Burke-Lucas-Herrick Historical Chapter 1987.

Ten yards north, a newer headstone reads:

JOHN SULLY

PVT CO K

1 MINN INF

1850

1904

The older gravestone in Sully Cemetery on Sully Flats, near Lucas, SD

New gravestone

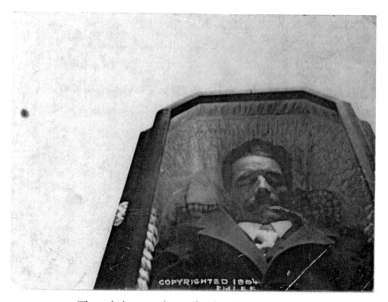

The only known photo of Jack Sully. Taken in his casket,
on the day of his funeral

Young Claude Sully with "Old Jim Longstring" on the day of Jack's death.
Note the small x marks where the horse was hit by pistol shots during the
escape attempt.

BIBLIOGRAPHY

Roundup Years, Old Muddy to Black Hills, Bert L. Hall; Centennial Edition, State Publishing, Co. Pierre, SD, 1956 edition.

West River 1850-1910, John Simpson, Pine Hill Press, Sioux Falls, SD, 2000.

Boss Cowman, The Recollections of Ed Lemmon 1857-1946, edited by Nellie S. Yost; University of Nebraska Press, Lincoln NE 1968.

My Life On the Range, John Clay, University of Oklahoma Press, Norman, OK, 1962.

Last Grass Frontier, Bob Lee and Dick Williams, Black Hills Publishers, Sturgis, SD, 1964.

The Cattlemen, Mari Sandoz, University of Nebraska Press, Lincoln NE, 1958.

The Luckiest Outlaw, The Life and Legends of Doc Middleton, Harold Hutton, Swallow Press, Chicago, 1974.

Voyageurs, A Novel, Margaret Elphinstone, Canongate Books Limited, Edinburgh, 2003.

Fort Randall on the Missouri, 1856-1892, Jerome A. Greene, South Dakota State Historical Society, Pierre, 2005.

The White River Badlands, Dr Cleophas C. O'Harra, SD School of Mines, Dept of Geology, 1920.

Tripp County South Dakota – 1909-1984, Diamond Jubilee, Committee for the Diamond Jubilee, Winner, 1984.

Tripp County 50th Anniversary – 1909-1959 September 6&7. Executive Committee of the 50th Anniversary, Winner, 1959.

CPSIA information can be obtained
at www.ICGtesting.com
Printed in the USA
FSOW02n0722280716
23192FS

9 781457 546969